THE SHADOW CYCLES

THE SHADOW CYCLES

Philip Emery

IMMANION
PRESS
Stafford, England

The Shadow Cycles
Philip Emery
© 2011

Cover Art and Design: Peter Hollinghurst
Editor: Sharon Sant
Interior Design and Layout: Storm Constantine

Set in Palatino Linotype

IP0103

An Immanion Press Edition
http://www.immanion-press.com
info@immanion-press.com

ISBN: 978-1-907737-10-7

Immanion Press
8 Rowley Grove
Stafford ST17 9BJ
UK

THE SHADOW CYCLES

"Blood, and darkness, and fear."

Chapter One

This night, after the day's battle, the swordsman sits in a tavern and broods over the blood.

Presently a second swordsman, rangy and assassin-faced, comes over and stands over the table of the first. The muzzy conversations about the room all still.

"Are you Gemmored, of the ice-wastes of Karnath to the north?" asks the second swordsman. He wears a long cloak that splays down to show sleekly fashioned armour hauberking his chest.

Gemmored takes another solemn draw of his ale and looks nowhere.

"You have a name for skill," the second swordsman smiles. From his side he pulls free a warsword. The stillness in the tavern begins to fidget.

"Tomorrow the siege of this city will begin again," murmurs Gemmored. "Have you not had death enough until then?"

The second swordsman smiles again, this time with only half his mouth, and with the tip of his warsword taps the pale leathern scabbard laid across Gemmored's thighs. "Some say it's the sword that possesses the skill."

Gemmored looks down and lifts the weapon onto the table. He strokes the blade free and lays it beside the scabbard, but doesn't take his hand away.

The blade is massive. Longer and broader in the steel than it's natural for a sword to be. There is not so much as a single scratch or nick marring the fluid chevroned watering of its sleek grey flats. The hilt is carved antler bone. At the end of the hilt is a smooth, perfectly round ruby. Gemmored stares at the sword. His eyes are the same colour as the steel.

"There is some truth to that," he says.

At the centre of the gem is a flaw, a particle of blackness. It gives a flicker. Something in the other swordsman's face tightens and he blinks.

While he sheathes his own weapon and leaves without another word, while the not quite so muzzy talk gradually starts up again through the tavern, Gemmored continues to stare at the sword.

Finally he stands. He too is massive. Brutal with muscle. Tall enough for a dark mane to brush the roofbeams. He pulls around his shoulders a cloak of the white pelt of the northern bear and with a mournful slowness resheathes the sword.

Someone shrieks somewhere as he steps outside. Perhaps an injured soldier losing a limb to the crude skills of a physician.

The city is flared with restless lanterns, people making the most of one more night free, one more night alive. Forges are pounding and glowing, repairing weapons. Beyond the walls the dark plain is riddled with campfires as the besieging forces do the same. Countless fires. They char the air. As Gemmored has said, there'll be death enough tomorrow.

He looks up to judge how far away the sky might be from daybreak and sees a crack of flaming brilliance rifting between stars and void.

For a moment he thinks it a fireball catapulted over the walls. But this fire does not rush through the night - it hovers - above him. Nor does it shed light beyond itself. It has a shape which flickers and flurries restlessly and Gemmored feels a kind of fear that is always different and yet the same each time he feels it.

Then the *rift* plummets and the swordsman is engulfed in a burning which is not pain or anything else he has words for.

Chapter Two

They pull through the darkness. Smoothly straining on the oars... glistening, sinewy men and women... hauling stroke after stroke of dark ocean behind the triremes...

Pull. Backs curling over... pushing the oarhafts down and

forward... lifting the oarhafts... plunging the blades into the sea...

Pull. Each long, disciplined breath as one... each bank of straining arms... each spine bending, hunching, arching... another oarstroke further... another oarstroke nearer...

Pull. Each dragonreme... under the guiding stars... under the darkness... over the darkness... through the darkness...The time has come. The Phoenix is choosing her prey. Soon they will arrive and the galleys must be there to meet them.

A navigator stands on the bowsprit of each dragonreme, each with the sole duty to look into the sky. Their shouts go up almost in unison.

Almost as one the banks of oarcrew pause. Their arms drop out of the cadence of urgent strain.

Many twist on their benches, turn and lift their heads to see. At last. Some sit stiffly, staring over the sterns across the dark vastness behind the ships.

When the Phoenix chooses its prey. The words have come to mean 'perhaps never' over the generations. Or perhaps 'in my children's time, or my children's children's'. But now...

They're afraid.

They're all afraid; the oarcrew; the Sword-Mariners, men and women in jerkins and breeks of tight otherworldly mail; the oarsmasters, one to each ship; the helm, one to each ship's rudder-vanes; even the navigators. But the fear of the first ones who turn and look up is different from the fear of the others. It beckons their eyes. Then the first cries and mutters of astonishment and awe go out and all the rest of them, every last one on every ship, looks up.

A flame flickers down between the stars, arcing and falling, a blue coma waked by red and white and yellow flurry.

The first choice of the Phoenix.

Some of the Sword-Mariners of the first dragonreme to reach him send down a rope and haul him up out of the sea. It takes seven, nine to pull him aboard. A cuirassed giant. Dark-maned. Taller and wider than any Mariner. And the scabbard at his side holds a sword twice the length of their own, even if it had not been straight but arced like theirs. Its pommel is a smooth, perfectly round ruby.

He rests on hands and knees on the deck for a moment, breathing deep. He pulls the great white pelt on his back more firmly across his shoulders and stands.

The first of the five to plunge out of the sky.

The first choice of the Phoenix.

Chapter Three

Sstheness ceases undulating on the stone floor. In the hunched hollow centre of Leviathan's petrified heart only the dimmest echoes of teeth snapping together can be heard, yet she raises her head. She twists out of the foetal and flings her naked body against the wall, clinging, listening.

Her quickening breath comes through parted lips. She drives herself harder against the wall, thighs and belly and breasts and cheek. Listening.

Then she feels it. The vibration. Leviathan's sullen ghost of a heartbeat kneading her own.

Her fingerstalls - long, wicked, part-claws part-sigils - twitch. A breath darts in and she digs them into the stone and draws them down, a stairway of gasps jerking from her throat.

She slips back from the concave chill of the wall and watches, trembling. Something swells from the scores and oozes down to pool on the floor.

She eases down in front of it, crosses her legs. She wraps her arms around herself in defence against something other than the cold. Her sigil-thorns begin to twitch again, this time cutting into the flesh of her shoulders.

Bleeding. Sstheness loves the bleeding. The sweet familiar bleeding. Every part of her is covered with scars, remembrances of pain. But even they can't comfort her now.

The pool of discharge from the inner wall of Leviathan's heart congeals quickly into a wafer of slick.

Sstheness sniffs and from the quality of foetor knows it to be ready.

One hand unwillingly leaves her crimsoned shoulders and slides its sculpted appendants beneath the wafer. It makes a gently tearing suck of a sound as Sstheness levers it up.

And over.

A stigmata gradually resolves on the exposed glistening underside. A pictogram.

A sword.

Chapter Four

The desert is littered with bloody stains. Flies already swarm over the battlefield, seeking the open wounds of the slain before the suns can burn them dry.

Only two figures rise above the charnel layer of hoods and blades and jehad swaddlings to throw shadows.

One of these is a squat, capering, mewling form. The followers of Geemass, lord of ghosts, always bring such a mind-shattered token into their battles. He scampers over the sand, twirling and slobbering. His sandaled toes stab and stagger between bloodstains in a dance that insanely veers, step to step, from delight to terror.

Only two figures rise above the charnel layer of hoods and blades and jehad swaddlings to throw shadows.

One is a squat, capering, mewling form.

The other…

Gel stands on a dune of sand and blood and corpse. Tall. Unhooded. The yawning hollows of his cheeks. The cruel jut of the bones. His hair is lank and copious and ethereally fine, so fine that the dome of his skull would be plainly visible beneath even a single sun.

He stands with his hands grasping his labrys just below the twin steaming heads. The end of the haft rests on the mound. It's as tall as he. The sweeping crescents of blade are red. Not streaked or splashed - the colour flushes the metal as if from within. No fly comes near it.

For Gel killing is a sensual pleasure, but aftertasted with guilt and self-pity. His eyes are closed, the trembling lids shutting all three in.

The mewling talisman of the lord of ghosts continues to dance.

The labrys to flush.

9

Gel's eyes remain shut, blind to a new sun that appears in the sky, burning differently than the others, more frantically...

Chapter Five

Another shout comes from a navigator on another dragonreme.

Another flame spears down through the stars. The second choice of the Phoenix.

Then another shout, but this one different. Eyes drag away from the sky and look across the sea.

More ships are coming. Sitting lower, rising a bank of oars higher than the dragonremes. Quinqueremes. Catapults and spiked boarding planks crane out of their decks. Cold, anxious murmurs break out.

Below the decks of the dragonremes the wolves have begun to howl.

Chapter Six

The Phoenix does not burn Gel. The yawning hollows of his cheeks. The cruel jut of the bones. Hair lank and copious and ethereally fine. The Phoenix holds him fast. Its flame is all around him, blinding him. It rushes and buffets and he senses speed and distance beyond imagining, but he does not burn.

Then he's falling, still blind, still penumbraed in fire. But this is a different kind of flame. Smoother. Not alive in the same way.

Then there's no fire of any kind about him, and he starts to burn. He has plunged into blackness and the cold of it sears. He gasps with the sharp shock, but his mouth takes in nothing. This is not air or water around him. There are no seas in Gel's home realm, the realm called Gnomon, but he recognizes a similar kind of shifting oceanic quality to the presence about him. Subtle turgid continents of icy flux. Currents of immensity pressing against him. Also, he feels himself being lifted, floated. He kicks in that direction. The burning chill on his skin makes it hard to be certain, but he senses his chest beginning to pain for breath.

His head breaks the surface of the blackness and sees sky, a crisper, star-flecked darkness far above his head.

Looking down he sees that the blackness he was swimming in stretches away in all directions like a horizontal abyss. Ships move across it.

The dragonreme nearest Gel rows closer. Two of the other kind of galley, the bigger quinqueremes, also approach. One follows the dragonreme, one comes from another direction. The prow of the dragonreme comes almost above Gel's head. A voice yells out and the banks of oars on either side pause and lift and the prow shifts.

Gel understands the words even though they're not spoken in his own tongue. A rope spirals urgently down. Gel grasps it with his one free hand. The hand not still clasping his labrys.

He's neither forgotten nor remembered that he holds it, part of him as it is, part of it as he is.

He twists his arm around the rope and the strength of many arms haul him up. He skips his feet against the pale plates of the galley's hull, in time to the hauling. Even before he reaches the deck another shout goes up and a flute urges a brisk tune. The oars drop back into the flat black sea and pick up the same forceful rhythm.

The quinquereme rowing behind is almost within a ship's length. The other pursuer surges down on the dragonreme from the side, plainly intending to ram. But within a few oarstrokes Gel's craft starts to pull away. Orders are yelled on the ramming ship. It begins slowing and turning across the black surface, almost slewing into the other quinquereme as it frantically tries to alter direction.

Gel is on deck now. Around him are men and women in jerkins and breeks of tight, scaled, otherworldly mail which is neither metal nor leather, finned morions on their heads and short arc-bladed swords in their belts. One of them bows, says something to him. He again understands the words, but not their meaning. A greeting of some sort?

He unwinds his jehad swaddlings from his gaunt body but thrusts away the blanket offered.

Rillings of the oceanic darkness still cling to his skin in burning-cold gulleys, no matter how hard he rubs himself. They disappear under the chaffing then reappear when his palm moves on.

He wonders, is the cold dark or the dark cold?

The dragonreme pulls away further from the towering prow of the remaining pursuer and Gel turns to look forward. Ahead are many more ships. A circle of galleys similar to the one he stands upon are hemmed about by the bigger quinqueremes.

He turns back. Both kinds of ship slide over the blackness in a wafting velvet motion. Their hulls do not dent the skin of the dark, nor push through it. Their keels cleave it without wake. And no shimmer of it clings to the oar blades as they lift up. The bigger craft has a certain surging power, but the smaller has a grace and swiftness that makes the bigger seem ponderous in comparison.

So far back is the pursuing galley that the shouted command barely carries to the dragonreme. In response a trembling hazy gobbet of dark, like a bolus of the oceanic dark that the ships race across, catapults from the quinquereme's prow across the stars. It curves down just short of Gel's craft. On the narrow deck, the Sword-Mariners in their otherworldly mail grind out low tense murmurs amongst themselves. The helm at the dragonreme's stern tightens his grip on his craft's twin vanes and calls for yet more speed. The oarmistress beside him picks up the rhythm of her flute to even greater pace.

Gel notes that no flute sounds from the larger ships. The quinqueremes are paced with drums.

The dragonreme rowers respond. There's no wind, but Gel's long ghostmist of a mane streams in the draught of the speed.

The catapult arm on the pursuing ship snaps again, and another gobbet of dark flies for the dragonreme. This time the trajectory is higher.

Gel watches the wearers of otherworldly mail and blade edge about.

They scatter as the gobbet lands on the narrow deck. It lands silently, amid their yells, splintering no planks. Its hazy sphere flattens and scutters about crazily in tentacles of fluid dark.

More dark. Gel snarls. This realm is full of darknesses.

At the sides of the deck the rowers wince and sway their torsos and scowl in alarm, but none of them leaves their oar. Sword-Mariners stamp at the tentacles, curse at them. The helm shouts again, and again the oarsmistress' flute ups its frenzy.

Another gobbet spits from the pursuing ship.

Gel hears it named in the shouts around him.

"Shadowfire!"

And Gel realizes what the sea is at last, what the ships are sailing through like dreams across obsidian.

The sea is shadow.

Chapter Seven

In the heart of Leviathan, Sstheness again presses her body against the wall. She listens again to the ghostly monstrous pulse, feels it lumber through the twisting tendrils of passages, feels it shiver the icy harshness of the wall.

One of her sigil-thorns smoothes a damp curl of hair from her eyes, carefully incising her brow in the same delicate act, before it joins the other fingerstalls sinking into the wall and again sliding down the stone.

Her gasps are louder this time.

While she waits for the discharge to pool on the floor, a pearl of blood trickles from her brow and past her temple and cheekbone. Her tongue tip curls out and pricks it. But Sstheness quickly tires of the aching effort of delicacy. Again her claws cross and reach and saw at her naked shoulders until the wafer is ready.

This time the stigmata on the underside of the congealant forms into a pictogram of an ax.

Chapter Eight

Ruddy ravines of dawn still linger in the sky and the seamews wheel and moan.

13

Zantalliz stands on the reef beyond the isle, head bowed and dreamlost. His raywing cape is still damp from his swim and clings to his back. The storm in the night has left some of its rage behind. Foaming waves worry at his feet and winds spit salt into his hair and exquisitely boned face.

Finally he raises his long slender brows and strange eyes to watch the war-ships approaching.

They surge their high broad prows over the nameless sea. Zantalliz knows that no sooner will they anchor off the reef than boats will be dropped and heaved over the coral, then rowed fiercely across the clear green lagoon. Then the first of the warriors will leap down and stride ashore. They will be helmed and mailed, grim jawed or shouting, malicious grins ripping their faces, teeth the colour of scar-tissue, sword or halberd or bow or death of some other shape in hand. Zantalliz imagines them stamping onto the coral. Imagines them coming toward him. Wonders what the pierce of iron feels like. His stomach hardens but some kinds of fear are acceptable. Some kinds of fear are not tainted.

He walks forward. Polyps and sponges and anemones swell above the water to meet his steps. Bright shimmering little shoals dart around his feet. He stops at the edge of the reef.

Zantalliz raises his arms from beneath his cape and in them rest a large scallop. He breathes on a lockless nacin clasp and before the bloom of moisture can shrink away the clasp looses itself. The two halves of the shell spread out over his forearms and hands. Fastened at the hinge are translucently fine pages covered in symbols and shapes. His thumbs stroke the furrowed backs of the shell as though soothing it. The diaphanous pages rush over as if struggling to escape their binding. Then, although the wind is as gusting as ever, they stop.

Zantalliz brings his eyes down again and begins to read. His lips move slowly at first, then more quickly, tracing the symbols on the page with murmurs. The symbols stir. By the time he moves onto the opposite page the sky has become overcast.

The symbols on the second also stir, sluggishly at first, stretching, contracting, pulling apart, weaving into new patterns, changing from curving rolling shapes to sharp daggerish slashes.

By the time Zantalliz nears the end of the page the clouds have clustered out the new day. As he reaches the end the page whips over and he glances up.

Still the ships come. Their sails now wrestle with the strengthening wind, but still they come. The sea is no longer ocean but sail. Even calling back the storm will be useless. He will die. All his race, waiting on the isle will be slain. All their books bound in scollop shell or driftwood, shelved within caverns and honeycombs and grottos of reef coral, browsed by rays and sharks, wandered by sea stars and crabs, every precious one of them will be dredged up from the sea. Will be rent and spat upon and burned. Zantalliz feels something rear in him which is unacceptable, and returns to the book.

The symbols on this page feverishly rill about as he speaks. Darting and rippling like the shoals at his feet. The wind shrieks and tears at his cape. The first lightning cracks across the sky like jagged spite.

And now there is the deep fear which always comes in the performance of such a task as this, the fear that beckons to the heart and can always be recognized but never known. Zantalliz feels laughter bubbling up like maniacal vomit as he shrieks back into the wind.

At first it looks like another rip of lightning. But it crackles crimson, and has a flickering horizontal span edged with blue. And it streaks down at Zantalliz not in a blind crooked path, but straight, as after prey.

Chapter Nine

Zantalliz still holds his book.

He has kept it clasped to him since the Phoenix snatched him from the reef of his doomed isle. He wrapped his arms around it on the burning journey from his own sea-swathed realm of Voyage to this. He crushes it to his chest as he plunges into another, very different sea, and is pulled from drowning in darkness onto a dragonreme's deck. He clutches it even as the dragonreme crew carefully remove his

Shadow-soiled clothes and drape blankets over his slender shoulders.

Chapter Ten

Leviathan's heart is clammy with sweat and blood and Sstheness' teetering breaths.

She barely glances at the stigmata of the book forming on the underpeal of the next slick wafer.

She staggers up and again claws at Leviathan's heartwall. This time, from the new wound, not one but two rivulets begin to flow.

Chapter Eleven

The spider pauses one final moment on the palpitating chest of the prince stretched taut across the wheel. It creeps along the snapped body and over the eyes that glare like mad cinders at the ceiling of the torture vault. It drops to the floor among the gloomy shapes of braziers and chains and racks. It scuttles for the steps.

The iguana squirms its way swiftly up the steps. The cries from the city above grow louder in its ears as it climbs.

They're louder still as the raven flutters from the palace balcony into the vermillion sky.

The city is turmoiled with screaming. The raven knows that the streets below are surging whorls of panic, but doesn't look down. It glides with cold satisfaction on the updraught of the horror above sacrificial teocallis and between agate spires that elbow their angles into the twilight.

From time to time an arrow hisses up past the raven's wings, but never near enough. A curse comes with it. And sometimes a name. Both falling away like the arrows.

The raven alights on the dizzying gatearch set into the city walls. It looks over the pampas. Behind it the city still howls. Men. Women. Children.

But it doesn't look back.

The realm called Aftermath knows only twilight, but twilight is enough to see what it leaves behind, what is turning the entire city into a torture vault. It's the sight which is turning them mad.

The raven flutters down toward the skittish mare waiting at the base of the wall.

The old tatterdemalion of a rider urges the mare away from the city of angled agate spires. The battered feathers of his ragged manta riffle behind him like wings.

The tatterdemalion's name is Harnak. He rides from the gate on one of the five roads that stretch their paving towards mesas reduced to rubble by distance. It was along another of these roads that he had led the madness to the city.

Perhaps another yet would take him away from the seething red and yellow and blue light appearing in the sky? The light whose shape is as undulating as his own. The light which travels as straight as any road. The light whose speed is faster than any horse.

Harnak pauses.

Even if there is no escape he could at least spur back to the city and witness its final throes? Return to the palace for a last glimpse at the broken corpse of the prince?

But it's too late even for that.

Chapter Twelve

Sstheness trembles as she peals away the next rivulet to congeal. The shape darkening on the underside of the wafer is a spider... no, a lizard... no, a bird... no, a man... no...

Chapter Thirteen

The dragonreme carrying Harnak arrows through the outer rim of quinqueremes, severing a boarding plank that bridges one quinquereme and a dragonreme. The impact sends the dragonreme askew and its prow glances a gouge in another quinquereme's side before slipping into the protective inner circle of dragonremes.

Many of the quinqueremes have dropped their hinged boarding planks onto the decks of dragonremes, the end spikes digging deep into the decks and locking the ships together.

Corsairs swarm over the bridges, catcalling and laughing. In contrast to their quinqueremes they're outfitted lithely, in leathern breeches and boots and jerkins, all blood red. Their blades are narrower and straighter than those of the dragonreme Sword-Mariners, and they swing them with an abandon that contrasts with the disciplined swordplay of their counterparts.

All of the Phoenix Prey, Gemmored, Zantalliz, Harnak, and Gel all stand on different dragonremes.

Gemmored, the swordsman, of the ice-wastes of the realm called Darkling, fights by the side of the Sword-Mariners of his ship. A supple cuirassed bear-pelted jokul. He arcs and thrusts and angles his huge warsword, sometimes two-handed, sometimes one, moving to the great weapon's weight, guiding it. The Corsairs besiege him but fall back time and again in splashes of shrieks and blood.

He swirls and stabs and slices open torsos and sweeps away heads from necks. Sometimes he fulcrums his swordstrokes against his wrist with the unfaceted ruby pommelling the bone hilt. The dark core to the gemstone flickers.

And as it flickers the grim pride in Gemmored's eyes, eyes the grey of frosted steel, dims. Twists.

And as it flickers the blade becomes lighter in his hands and heavier inside him.

Zantalliz of Voyage still holds his book.

All around him the Sword-Mariners fight. Protect him from the blades of the Corsairs who strive to reach him. But the sharp, stretched rasp of swordmetal against swordmetal is a distant sound in his thoughts where waves purr on faraway coral.

He has opened the scallop and the pages turn over without touch, one after the next. He stares down at them, strange eyes hardly blinking, even as a Corsair blade almost cleaves his head.

Every book in the caverns of his people's isle held every moment of their history, beliefs, arts - the grammar of their being. The properly fashioned wish would lay open the appropriate page. The correctly spoken bidding would shape the words and grammalogues into knowledge or fluent rituals of shape and symbol.

But now.

Each page slowly curls, one after the next, each a pale, blank leaf...

Gel eases thoughtfully through the melee on his galley.

Now and again his labrys flashes out, a shrug of skim or sweep, and a Corsair or Corsairs die, and he snorts.

Harnak stands on the deck of another dragonreme, still in the feathered rags and the old-man shape in which the Phoenix took him. The rags have lost some of their stench in the fire or the journey. Harnak does not like this.

The battle is different on this galley. Harnak's form is smaller than Gemmored's, not such a beacon for the Corsairs. The fighting is wider-spread, as with Zantalliz' ship. But Harnak is not dream-stranded as Zantalliz who stands oblivious and ringed by defenders. He has taken a sword and has quickly decided ally from enemy.

This realm is different from Aftermath, his own. Both the Sword-Mariners and the Corsairs are different in clothing and face than any he's known before. Their words are different, though he can understand them. This night is different and covers the sea as well as the sky. And somewhere wolves are howling. But at least...

He parries a Corsair's attack and skilfully slips his own sword through the man's throat.

But at least there is blood.

Soon the force of the Corsair boardings fade and slowly the Sword-Mariners begin forcing them back toward their own ships. A few of them turn their blades to the oarsmen and women. But these are dragonreme crew, not chained slaves. They have their own blades which they pull from beneath their benches.

Back the Corsairs go, curse by curse, backstep by backstep across the dragonreme decks and edging along the boarding planks. But as they go they start to flick glances skyward and their shouts become taunts.

The dragonremers follow the glances and they too see the movement below the stars. The first warning shout comes from a Sword-Mariner.

"Pitspoor!"

They come down onto the dragonremes like taloned rain, their pads thudding onto the decks, eyes lambent with malevolence.

Again the Sword-Mariners set to. More blood splashes the decks. A bitter smell wafts. Shouts. Cries. Hissing. Gnars. Shrieks.

One Sword-Mariner slips, his blade sailing from his hand and spinning into the sea. The Mariner yells in horror, jumps to his feet and charges for the galley's rail. Ignoring the Pitspoor he's been facing, ignoring the gouge it rips from his arm as he runs, he dives overboard.

The sword has vanished into the Shadow. The Sword-Mariner plunges into the blackness at almost exactly the same place. A few other Mariners and oarcrew glance after him, but are too engaged in the battle to watch.

Shouts. Cries. Hissing. Gnars.

The Sword-Mariner slides to the surface again, his morion gone, his mouth open and spouting blackness. His otherworldly mail gives a kind of strange buoyancy but he struggles to keep afloat. One arm, the wounded arm, is aloft, and it holds the blade.

No one throws a rope. No one has the moment.

The Mariner struggles a moment longer, gasping, fiercely scanning his dragonreme for hope. Finding none he swings the blade around his head. His mouth drops into the Shadow again, comes up sputtering dark. He scans the dragonreme again.

Shouts. Cries. Hissing. Gnars. Shouts.

He swings the blade with a yell of defiance and despair, sends it spinning and clattering onto the dragonreme's deck as he slips down into the Shadow.

The Sword-Mariners' mail, which has armoured them well against the Corsair's steel, gives little protection against the Pitspoor.

The deck of every dragonreme is slick with blood. Whatever comes from the Pitspoor's veins joins it after spattering and jumping along the Mariners' blades. But mostly, there is blood. The Pitspoor are overwhelming the dragonremers, clustering mostly on the ships carrying the Phoenix Prey.

Then the wolves are loosed.

They're brought up on decks by a new kind of dragonreme crew. They wear neither the vestments of Sword-Mariners nor oarcrew. They wear simple breeks and jerkin, a leather gorget around the throat, a gauntlet on the hand that holds a wolf's leash. Their eyes hold something of their wolf's eyes - something not lost but missing, something more, an indifferent intensity, a glimmer of ice.

Gemmored recognizes the glimmer. He looks up by instinct. In the ice-wastes of his birth, carrion birds follow wolves. He looks up for ravens.

Though these wolves are different to those he knows, Harnak smiles.

Gel has never seen a wolf. But he also smiles.

Zantalliz stares into his book.

The wolves on the dragonremes are mostly black. Sleek. Their movements are fluid and dangerous without suddenness. As soon as they set eyes on the Pitspoor they stop howling.

The handlers hunker down beside them, faces close to muzzles, and slip the leashes off.

They move forward slowly at first, as if their bodies are stalking their snouts. Then their muzzles curl, unsheathing their teeth. They move with a speed similar to the Pitspoor, blurred in a way that has nothing to do with velocity, or time, as if they obey slightly different laws of being. Snarling, they weave easily between Sword-Mariners and Pitspoor. Their jaws flash.

And soon the battle turns again, judders without clear advantage to either side, like two struggling tides meeting.

Then, above the shouts and cries and hissing and gnars and shrieks, a wail.

In the sky the Phoenix flares again, and again a pennon of flame arcs down toward the sea.

Both dragonremes and quinqueremes erupt in a wild new urgency. Savage, desperate orders roar out. Oars plunge down and rake through the Shadow below. The Pitspoor take to the air, some hauling wolves fastened on them, and vanish in echoes. Those ships locked together strain to break free. The decks of dragonremes are torn by the wrenching away of boarding spikes.

Every galley struggles to make for the place in the sea where the flame trail has ended. Some of the dragonremes already point toward it and already one or two have disentangled themselves from the carnage and are picking up speed. These pull ahead with lunges of rowing, arrowing wakeless across the obsidian.

Then a last cry - from the fastest dragonreme - a cry of realization that not all the Corsairs' galleys have laid siege to the circled dragonremes. Quinqueremes loom everywhere, all over the Shadow. One has almost reached the point where the flame has fallen. Breath slumps from the dragonreme oarcrew as the quinquereme lets down a rope.

Chapter Fourteen

The last rill from Leviathan's heartwall, the last squirming, liquid, medusa-lock has slid to the floor and pooled and congealed into a last wafer.

Nausea-weary, Sstheness has judged the foetor and peeled the scale of slick and watches the stigmata darken into a scar.

A scar.

Then amid the echoey hollow of Leviathan's heart she hears a vast new gossamer tremble. She crushes the last wafer against her breasts and belly, scrapes its crumbling shreds against her skin. She rolls back and undulates her raked shoulder blades and spine and buttocks and legs against the dank floor.

And laughs.

Chapter Fifteen

After the final member of the Phoenix Prey has been taken by the

Corsairs a stillness settles across all the ships. The quinqueremes turn away. The dragonremes follow them, rowing with dejected steadiness, falling further and further behind. Though they have taken only one of the five, yaps of Corsair laughter drift over the Shadow while the dragonremers lapse into solemn silence.

Gel finally snatches at one of the blankets proffered him and slings it over his back. "We could easily catch them," he barks at a Sword-Mariner standing near him. Gel grips his labrys fiercely. Its two sweeping bladeheads are dry but they flush - almost pulse - deep colours. The colours of Corsair and Pitspoor woundspillings. His skin before the battle had been wan. Now it's deep with colour.

The Sword-Mariner looks at Gel with a wariness that's both more and other than respect, and shakes his head. "You are Phoenix Prey, and too precious to risk."

On another galley Harnak finally sloughs off his tattered manta and wipes his sword on the rag. "Was the Phoenix the fire that brought me here?" he asks a Wolf-ward kneeling on the deck leashing his charge.

On a third galley Zantalliz asks nothing. He still holds the book open. The pages still turn over without touch. He blinks at each one, each still a blank translucent leaf, some newly flecked with blood.

"And where has the Phoenix gone now?" intones Gemmored, his great bare blade still dripping on the deck of his galley. "To where we go," someone calls from the bank of oars just below the swordsman.

The rower's back curls over... skin stretching over the knots of the spine... pushing the oarhaft down and forward... lifting the oarhaft... wearily pulling another stroke... another stroke...

The navigators, all silent throughout the battle, murmur to the helms at their sides.

Eventually, long after the quinqueremes have vanished over it, part of the horizon rises - a mass growing steadily larger like a pupil in the dark.

"Land?" murmurs Gel to the Sword-Mariner who has remained by his side. But the Sword-Mariner says nothing.

The galleys close the distance. The mass is broader at the top, tapering slightly as it descends to Shadow level.

But Harnak soon notices as his galley pulls nearer that it tapers not with the smoothness of something built or crafted, nor with the natural unevenness of rock.

Just before the mass touches the Shadow there is a wide glittering line of jagged light.

"There," urges another galley's helm to Zantalliz who still stares at turning empty pages. The helm points to the light. "There! The Beckoning Gate!"

Finally, when the mass looms like a mountain before the flowing galleys, Gemmored can make out on the very top twin colossal stelae, and below them the two hollow orbits like vertical amphitheatres, and below them, at the end of the snout, the flickering crimson-yellow flames between the bared teeth the size of spires. A face set in its own death-mask. What had once been bone, the horns and the teeth, are now chalcedony. And the skin, with scales almost the width of galleys, is no longer green flesh but solid jade.

"This is where the Phoenix went," murmurs Gemmored, staring at the Beckoning Gate, the eternal snarl of chalcedony and fire.

"The Phoenix is part of the dragon's breath," calls another of his ship's rowers.

"Dragons were before land," sings the rest of the oarcrew.

"Dragons were before land," chants the ship's navigator, who still looks only at the stars. The ship's helm, Sword-Mariners, even the wounded and the dying join them.

"Dragons were before land," the song is taken up by the other galleys, one by one.

"Dragons were before land, when the world was only sea and sky."

And the pages of his book stop turning and Zantalliz looks up.

As the galleys approach the Beckoning Gate each of the Phoenix Prey expects the jaws to open. What then? Death by the dragon's fire? Return by that same fire to their own realms? There seems no reason for either outcome, but as the chalcedony teeth tower over them and the flames behind those spires roar out in heat and sound, the expectation rears into spate and drowns reason.

Then the first galley swings to the left of the jaws.

Then the second to the right.

And so they go, to left and right, one or more at a time.

The Gate beckons, but does not admit.

The galleys row across the face of the dragon, as wide as an isle. Then they turn down the sides, raise oars and drift on the Shadow. For the first time the Phoenix Prey realize that not only have they moved toward the dragon but the dragon has moved towards them. Its scaled length, seemingly worming back to the horizon, is clearly sliding past the ships.

Eventually the galleys on both flanks come to an immense pucker running along the jade just above sea-level. Stone ripples and wrinkles fall into the dragon's sides. Each pucker yawns up above the height of a dragonreme and down into the Shadow, and the Phoenix Prey know they have come to the real gates.

The helms on the ships ply their rudder-vanes and each galley veers into the yawn. All the ships carrying one of the Phoenix Prey have turned to the same side of the dragon and entered the same gate. The Shadow sea is there already. Once inside, each ship lowers oars and gently strokes the Shadow. All are silent except for the moans of the wounded, and even these are muted.

Above is a vaulted cavern, ahead a dock. Each galley manoeuvres into a lock, formed of rhyolite groynes jutting from the quay into the Shadow. A silent staring throng has gathered on the quayside.

Dockers clamber up derricks affixed to the locks and swing booms over the galleys. From these hang hooks at the ends of chains which oarcrew catch and slip through iron hoops fastened to the bulwarks.

Once a galley is secured by these, other dockers haul closed its lock's gate.

As soon as this is done the trapped Shadow vanishes - not draining like water but swiftly fading like cast shadow which loses its sun - leaving the galley swaying in mid-air by its chains.

A young woman, sleek, tuniced, with long auburn hair, strides from the crowd which seems to part with special respect. She stands on the edge of the quay. Her thumbs loiter in her belt.

The galleys carrying the four Phoenix Prey are the first to extend gangways to the dock. Each of the four is invited to be first to disembark and each is brought together with the other three. A blanket is reverently placed around the naked shoulders of Harnak, similar to the blankets now draped around Gel and Zantalliz. They look at each other, plainly none of them belonging where they find themselves. They look out over the throng. These are mostly in light chitons and himatia, the young in tunica - all in sandals. All those close enough stare at the dark-maned giant mantled with the great white pelt who still holds his huge sword bloody and unsheathed. They stare at the almost equally tall but gaunt figure with hair like mist, propping a two-headed poleax on the dock.

Already one or two voices murmur, "When the Phoenix chooses..." And others take it up.

The throng stare at the blood-stained tatterdemalion whose gouged old face is the least haunted of all four of the Phoenix Prey, whose lips even possess a subtle kink of amusement. Stare at the smallest, most exquisitely slender-boned of the four, who clasps a large scallop shell to his chest, and whose strange eyes look without seeing, like a child in darkness.

The young, sleek, tuniced woman with auburn hair watches. Face still. Almost cold.

The captured and wounded and dead are disembarked. The captured Corsairs jerk and mock and spit as they're led away. The dead and severely wounded are gently laid on quayside pallets. Names are called. Cries of concern or anguish go up. Eddies of movement disturb the crowd as people struggle to reach the pallets.

Almost suddenly the scene slides into turmoil. The chanting goes on, "When the Phoenix chooses..." but individual jeers are also shouted - the four Phoenix Prey glance from each other to the crowd to each other. The last of some of the galley crews, the oarcrews, disembark. The last dragonreme is enclosed in its lock. The Shadow evaporates beneath it and it swings on its chains. "When the Phoenix chooses..." The Shadow beyond the locks remains – still and flat and pendent and stretching back to the puckered portal in the dragon's side.

The sleek, tuniced young woman with auburn hair now kneels by one of the wounded laid on the quayside and speaks intently to the

Sword-Mariner who tends him. "When the Phoenix chooses," she says. Then she slips a wavered-bladed knife, a kris, from her belt. She glances over to the Phoenix Prey, a look too full of emotions to fix a clear expression. The crowd again parts. A small body of swordsmen and women come forward, hawk-helmed with faces between wide beak-jaws. Each wears a sleek gambeson with a dragon design across the chest. Each has an empty sword scabbard hanging from a belt. The woman makes an impatient gesture and they move to the Phoenix Prey, bow deeply and lead them back toward the crowd.

It parts with as much readiness and deference as for the woman. The corridor of stares and caught breath stretches into the distance, allowing Harnak and Zantalliz to see what the far taller Gel and Gemmored have already glimpsed over the heads of the multitude. A city.

The crowd turns and follows as the Phoenix Prey are escorted away. They're taken along a wide dolerite-paved avenue, sometimes edged with colonnades, regularly passing under great crescents of petroglyphed arches, past regular wynds, up or down gently sloping ramps or flights of steps. They go past or glimpse buildings of various shapes. Some tall, some wide, some angular – houses, cisterns, bathhouses, gymnasia. Roofs are either flat or unaccountably sloped.

All is stone.

When high on the tells, courtyards can be seen. And trees. And gardens and plazas. There are cropfields beyond the city at the very sides of the dragon. This is a realm within itself.

The buildings are dolomite or granite or rhyolite. And not of brick, no more than the roads are flagged. There is a *smoothness* to all – as though hands have cupped it, stroked, moulded, sculpted it.

The march goes on. Zantalliz stares unseeing into the backs of the escorts' gambesons. Gel casts about left and right, taking everything in. Harnak does the same, but only with his eyes. Gemmored still holds his sword unsheathed. And the crowd, the citizens follow, like a spellbound tide returning, still murmuring "When the Phoenix chooses..."

Through arch after arch they go. And all the way is lit by great copper braziers.

And the vaulted roof-sky is porphyry. Purple porphyry ribbed with rainbows. Emerald, garnet, spinel, sapphire, ruby, opal, chrysoberyl, topaz, amethyst, jasper, a hundred other precious crystals.

Finally the escort passes under a last high-finned arch, crosses a vast esplanade, climbs up a final approach of steps, and enters a majestic porticoed building, by far the tallest in the city, a spire of bluestone.

The four are led into a vaulted atrium, layered above with traceried cloisters honeycombed with arched entries into darkened passageways. They walk up basalt stairs and over tegular floors of turquoise and amber. Between the third and fourth levels of cloister the escorts show them to a table and chairs positioned on a mezzanine jutting out over the atrium well.

Gel is impressed despite himself. The table is onyx. Onyx is a precious stone on Gnomon. Something only for the walls of palaces.

Harnak notices too. It reminds him of his own realm, though the pattern of onyx is more regular than the bands through the agate spires of his own city.

Here the escort leaves them, and here they sit silently. Zantalliz lays his book on the table but takes neither hands nor eyes from it; Gel slides his labrys onto the table and restlessly alternates between impatience and amusement; Harnak sits back and folds his arms impassively; Gemmored stands, staring out over the well, his hand still fused on his antlerbone swordhandle, until a sleek figure enters the atrium and strides to the stairs.

None of the four recognize the woman as the sleek young woman from the dock until she nears the table. Her long auburn hair has been unskilfully cropped close to her head. It changes her face, sharpening her bones. Her face seems paler.

She takes a chair and sits, resting for a moment, then swings a foot onto the chair and hooks her arms around her knee. She appraises the Phoenix Prey with a look different from any the crowd gave them. Cool. Quizzical.

"What is this place?" asks Gel.

"I'm Phariane," she says, "and this is Dragonkeep."

"And you are its queen?" asks Harnak.

She smiles. "Dragonkeep has no queen."

"So this is not your palace?" asks Gemmored.

She huffs. "This is no palace. This is an archive."

"A warehouse of stories," says Gel, running a fingernail impatiently along the haft of his labrys.

"Of documents, of manuscripts," replies Phariane. "Chronicles, annals, pandects, scytales…"

For the first time since the Phoenix dropped him into the Shadowsea, the haunting recedes from Zantalliz' strange eyes. He looks up from his book.

"And is the story of Dragonkeep here?" asks Harnak.

"Of course," says Phariane. "And you may hear it later. There's time. Though perhaps not much, now that you have arrived."

Now Gemmored turns from the atrium well. His great white pelt mantling his shoulders is still matted with Shadow. His face is fierce and weary, helpless and malevolent, immanent with pain. He has carried the sword since the battle on the dragonreme. It has no weight in it now to weary his arm. With every slaying it made on the ship it grew lighter. With every slaying his arm grew wiser. With every slaying a familiar burning flowed into his body. The killing of a Corsair was bad enough, the killing of a Pitspoor a hundred times worse. With each the dark core of the gemstone pommel would flicker ever more wildly.

Now it dances like a flurry of madness. Stains, both red and otherwise, neither wet nor dry, rivulet the blade flats like cracks.

Gemmored's voice is an ominous purl.

"I am Gemmored of Darkling," he says to Phariane. "I ask your permission to sheath my sword."

"You may have sheathed it at will," says Phariane.

"It is something better done privately," he replies.

Harnak glances at Phariane.

She pauses, then says: "Each of you has been chosen by the Phoenix. You are one."

Gemmored stares, decides, and lifts his sword as if forcing it through the air, finally dragging the tip to the lips of the pale scabbard at his side.

"My ax is called Bloodbane," Gel says to him. "Is your weapon named?"

Gemmored nods without looking up. "Doom."

He slides it quickly into the scabbard. As he does so a throatless scream breaks and crescendoes, echoing through the atrium well and dying as the sword sinks to the tang.

Chapter Sixteen

There are echoes.

From darkness the fifth Phoenix Prey has been torn by fire, and plunged into more darkness - a sea of Shadow, only to be torn from this also, by a laughing taunting galley crew in blood-red leather.

Only to row again into darkness.

Now Rorn of Nightwake, the Waste-Ranger, walks dim passages lit by puttering tallowy warts and quivering with echoes. Hard echoes and softer. Bone echoes and meat echoes. And there are other echoes.

Rorn remembers, not so long ago, walking slowly across a silica viewing floor, his steel-studded boots echoing through a cavernous hall unchallenged. Then, a mordant smile had kinked his lips as he looked down into one gigantic crucible after another.

So, he had thought. It was true.

He's visited such exalted rooms before, and always, as now, without permission. But those few who sometimes walk outside the Beckoning Mansions are forbidden no way or chamber within them.

The kind who walk outside, Rorn's kind, usually feign respect for petty laws and lawmakers. They observe tiresome edicts they could break at will without punishment. Rorn, though, prefers honest disobedience, relishes the looks of affront and reproach.

"Waste-Ranger!" someone calls. "What brings you to the prophecy vats?"

"To see for myself," says Rorn, turning. "Or rather not."

It's a young man, a scrier, so young that he can be hardly more than an apprentice. The affront is there, and the reproach too, on the smooth intent face. But at Rorn's words the scrier's expression collapses into uncertainty, blinking like a child trying to understand dread.

Rorn turns his back, hooks his thumbs into his belt, wanders across the floor looking down at one vat then another.

"So it's true."

On his last visit, the vats were lambent - winding umber and magenta and cyan and ochre and celadon, entwining the spectra of possibility.

"Come here."

The young scrier uncertainly walks over and stands next to Rorn. He looks ahead, at the great quartz wall of the hall, rather than down. Rorn keeps staring through the transparent floor into the vats. The magma of prediction is stilled and black.

"It's as the rumours say. The future's at an end."

"Is word spreading?" asks the scrier.

"All over the mansion."

"What of the other vats in the other mansions?"

Rorn's lips sour. "Questions must feel odd in a scrier's mouth."

"This is not the fault of the scriers. Some will no doubt blame us but –"

Rorn swings about, his shoulder roughly jolting the scrier, and stalks away. He comes to a window in the quartz wall and looks out across the realm of Nightwake.

The scrier steadies himself and reluctantly peers down. "It may not be so." His voice is strained. "It may be that the prophecy vats still show us what's to come."

"You mean darkness?" Rorn laughs like a slap. "Darker than this?"

He looks across a wreckage of utter unending night, unsullied by moons or stars, prowled by things suited to blindness and ruin. A realm where man clings to survival in impregnable noctilucent mansions. Only a few can and do step outside these to take messages of possibility and comfort across the dark.

"Waste-Ranger!"
Rorn spins and runs as the scrier shouts.
"The vat!"

Rorn had run, skidded, almost fallen coming to a halt. There had been a stirring of light in the magma of the vat directly below. But this was a different light. Not glowing but flickering. Not swirling but growing. As if something on fire, or perhaps *of* fire, was swimming up through the blackness, about to burst out.

Chapter Seventeen

Now Rorn does not run. He walks, and only with aid, dim passages lit by puttering tallowy warts. Since disembarking the quinquereme, two muscular Corsairs have held his arms. The act is part support, part restraint. Rorn is now a vague creature in thought and body, aware only of the echoes, and of the rills of the Shadow still chilling his skin like slashes of ice. So, since restraint is unnecessary, the harshness of the Corsairs' grips can only be malice or mockery. Something about the Corsairs reminds him of himself - perhaps that?

Now two others appear before them. They are longer, sleeker figures than the Corsairs, with blades like sickles. Unlike the Corsairs they wear casques. These casques enclose their entire heads. These casques are shaped like skulls. And seeing them, Rorn realizes what some of the echoes are.

Skulls.

Rorn droops his head, looks back.

Skulls.

The floor is strewn, carpeted by skulls whose jaws gape and snap, gape and snap...

In his fogged awareness something spins. Something closes around his breath.

The two skull-casques take Rorn's arms from the Corsairs and yank him onward. The exchange is made in silence, with hostility between the two pairs bristling in the wordlessness.

They take him deeper into the labyrinth. They move through

scabrous twisting passages with bowed stillbirth walls. Weeping umbilicals stalactite down, some of the longest sliding across Rorn's face.

There are more echoes. Some, he realizes, are laughter – he's taken so long to recognize the sound because of how hard it is to believe in such a sound in such a place.

Through yet more passages they take him, branching, snaking, gloomy passages.

Rorn's stomach is too weak to turn at the stench.

Sometimes others pass by singly or in groups. Sometimes they spit on him. The skull-casques take no notice. Their grips on his arms are as powerful as the Corsairs' holds had been, but less harsh.

There is something about the cool, steady skull-casque grips that makes Rorn miss the harshness.

He is almost thankful when they pull him to a stop.

Before him is a glistening black barrier. Some kind of growth? Some kind of goitre? A knot in the depths of the scabrous labyrinth. And now he knows what the other echo has been. The one neither hard nor soft, the one haunting all the others. Unlike the skulls, or the voices, this is not so much a sound as a pulse.

The knot distends. Two lips appear top to bottom and spread - like a splaying gateway. The skull-casques throw him forward and he slips through the opening into yet more darkness.

He lands hard on elbows and knees and sprawls on cold, slick stone. The opening closes behind him and seals in the new darkness. It's somehow transpicuous. There's no light in the cell, not even the pathetic tallowy gutterings of flame of the labyrinth. Yet he can see clearly, with a livid vision that doesn't penetrate but rather feeds on the dark.

Someone moves, leaps beside him and he turns his head to see. Young. Naked. Seethingly feral. With long straggly auburn hair and bared teeth. And talons longer than her fingers. And scars, some still bleeding, across her shoulders and breasts and arms and belly and legs. She lies beside him. Her face is a breath's width to his face. She stares into him and he recoils sluggishly, groping for desperation or anger or humiliation – for anything to sting his mind and body into quickening, to wrench it from this sucking, shambling morass of a state.

He rolls away, until he reaches the convex wall of the cell.

He struggles against it, forcing himself against it to climb to his feet. And then she's behind him again, pushing her body into him. It's bony with power. Fierce ribs and knees and hips pinch him against the wall. Her taloned hands somehow grasp his wrists. Her jaw digs into his neck. Words seethe in his ear.

"Welcome, Rorn of Nightwake, Phoenix Prey, to Leviathan."

She spins him round and pitches him back against the wall. He leans on it, gasping, watching her.

She watches him in turn. She reaches out a palm and lays it softly on the side of his face.

Rorn's eyes strain sideways.

The talons are fingerstalls sculpted into half-sigil half-claw.

She slightly lowers her hand and touches the tip of one fingerstall against his cheek. It sinks a delicate fraction into the skin and draws a slow shallow of indent. As the talon passes, a needle of crimson swells into the channel.

Rorn stays rigid, arms free but still stretched out against the wall as if pinioned. Rills of Shadow begin to stir. He can feel them - gelid slithers slowly inching up his body. Over his chest. His neck. They cluster there, melding into one icy burn, then flow up onto Rorn's face and into the newly opened wound. The glistening slit quivers as the Shadow enters, as if swallowing.

Chapter Eighteen

"This is the throat of Dragonkeep," calls Phariane to the Phoenix Prey. She's only a few steps ahead of the four of them, but the roar of the fire is growing louder.

She has led them out of the archive and across the city again. Again with the throng following them, again murmuring.

"When the Phoenix chooses..."

She has led them along another wide and straight avenue,

perpendicular to the one they had taken from the dock.

More vaulted arches to pass through - these again petroglyphed with sinuous and angular stories, unknown but familiar. More braziers cupping bright yellow flames. Now and again one of the Phoenix Prey glanced to the roof of Dragonkeep... glittering streaks of green and blues and dashes of white or yellow or blue or red or green or violet among the porphyry.

Gemmored's sword was sheathed at his side. His walk was lighter, but his expression still clouded.

Eventually the avenue had come to a long shallow stairway, each tread several strides, finally entering a cavernous entrance in the cliff that ended the city.

The throng had waited at the foot of the stairs. Gradually their chant mixed with, and then was lost in, the roar growing from ahead. A roar like molten havoc. A roar like volcanoes breathing.

"And this," shouts Phariane at the far end of the tunnel, "is the mouth of Dragonkeep."

The Phoenix Prey step onto a bridge, a gneiss causeway stretching through a roaring forest of fire. But just as the Shadow is shadow and not shadow, so the fire is fire and something more. Huge columns of flame lick into the air, white or yellow or red, furious or serene. Liquid, streaming, fluttering, quivering stabs of blaze, brilliant but somehow not blinding. Yet although the cavern is hot, this is not a burning heat, at least not upon the bridge. Along the way, workers in ephods busily extend crucibles on long poles over some of the white flames, or pour the molten contents into moulds. When they see the Phoenix Prey they stop their work and stare.

"The white fire is used as forge heat," shouts Phariane as she leads them forward. "The yellow we take for the braziers that light Dragonkeep." She turns and faces them. "But the reason I've brought you here is the red fire." Cantilever strips of jet curl off the main causeway – like forks in a tongue. They lead into the hearts of some of the red flames. "This," she says, "is used for cleansing."

"Cleansing?" calls Gemmored.

"Perhaps not unlike your scabbard?" smiles Gel, leaning against his labrys.

Some of the crew from the dragonreme ships are emerging from some of the red flames. Their figures glow crimson for a step or two as they make their way back to the gneiss causeway.

Phariane indicates several of the cantilevers. "The red flame cleanses Shadow."

The Phoenix Prey exchange looks.

They have all been touched by the Shadow. Plunged into it. They remember its gelid burn. Still feel it.

Gel smiles again, the same fierce scorn of teeth as always. He yanks off his blanket. His body is almost as gaunt as his face. His colour has lost most of the unnatural flush it had held after the galley battle. The ribs and muscles cut ridges under the whitening skin. Wormings of Shadow cling to some of those ridges. Still keeping hold of his labrys, he strides onto one of the cantilevers and without hesitation into the red flame at its end.

Expressionless, Harnak removes his blanket and picks away one last unfeathered shred of maguey manta clinging to his skin. An old body, furrowed, wrinkled and veined, and also veined with Shadow. He looks down at it, then chooses another cantilever.

Gemmored tugs off his white bear pelt. It's matted with Shadow. Then he unbuckles his cuirass, vambraces and other armour. The nearest flame-workers look at each other, open mouthed, then edge forward, kneel, stroke the armour. "Iron is rare in dragonkeep," yells Phariane.

Swaths of Shadow weave among the other scars on Gemmored's huge body. Finally he unbuckles his belt and lays his scabbarded sword on the causeway. No one makes to touch that.

As he crouches he looks to Zantalliz. "Well?"

Zantalliz makes no movement. His blanket hangs on his shoulders. His strange eyes are still lost.

Gemmored looks at Phariane. She gives no sign. He goes over to Zantalliz and lifts off his blanket. Zantalliz' arms are still wrapped around his book, pressing it against his smooth chest. Then Phariane is there. Her guarded expression subtly changes, both hardens and softens. She gently eases the scallop shell from his arms. They unfold without willingness or resistance. The long, fine fingers slide against the ridges of the shell, the nacre clasp. For a moment his eyes sharpen from dream to concern. Then the oval tips of his fingernails lose touch. His arms slip to his sides.

Shadow stains him too, serpentining his skin.

Gemmored steps onto one of the jet cantilevers and turns. "Come," he calls to Zantalliz. "Come with me."

But Zantalliz stays still.

The cores of the flames chosen by Gel and Harnak give shrugs of undulation.

Gemmored looks back to Phariane, but her face is turned away.

Gemmored comes back, lifts Zantalliz without effort, and walks back into his chosen flame.

Phariane looks at the roof of the cavern. Something blazes there. Hovering. Unnoticed. It flickers with the same colours as the flames licking up and around the causey. White so bright as to be silver. Yellow so bright as to be gold. Red equally as fierce. Unlike the flames below, all mingled in a restless iridian plumage. And there's a fourth colour. Blue, as brilliant as the others, edges the shape's undulating span.

As Gemmored steps into his flame, it swoops, still unnoticed. It vanishes with a melting grace into the fires below.

"When the Phoenix chooses," says Phariane.

Even if the roar of the dragonmouth had faded to nothing her words would still have been lost.

Emerging from the throat of Dragonkeep, the Phoenix Prey wear fresh, simple himatia. Gel still holds his labrys. Gemmored has girt back his sword. They find the waiting throng thinner. Waiting at the foot of the shallow steps, are four horse-harnessed chariots.

"Why were we made to walk, before," Gel asks Phariane, "if you can provide these now?"

"To show us to the people," says Gemmored.

Phariane gives him a quick, tight smile like an ironic nod. "Just so." She takes the reins of one of the chariots from the driver and gestures at Zantalliz. He seems more alert since leaving the flame, his book restored to his arms, but still keeps silent. "I will take him."

But he stands still and for a moment they all do - the other Phoenix

Prey, the remaining crowd, Phariane with her arm out and the gesture frozen.

Finally Zantalliz' head tilts and his lips part. "I have lost many things," he says, in a voice soft but clear, "but not my hearing."

Phariane smiles again. This time without the tightness. "Will you come?"

Zantalliz climbs onto the chariot next to her.

Gemmored takes the reins of another chariot, as does Gel, but Harnak allows himself to be driven back to the archive.

There is a meal of bread and meats and fruits and wine and other drinks of such variety that all the Phoenix Prey are able to take something.

Then, on the table over the atrium well, lit by a small brazier of yellow flame, Phariane lays out a book. It's larger than Zantalliz', with heavy boards of wood. The front is skilfully incised with an Uroboros. Inside are sown pages of parchment. Phariane strokes the first page. "This is the book of Dragonkeep."

She begins to speak in a different tone and rhythm.

"The Shadow reached our realm hundreds of years ago. The sky clouded with darkness, cowling the sun and the stars. Eventually the darkness began to rise on the seas, over the isles and archipelagos, on the lands, over the fields, the plains, the valleys, the deserts, the tundras, the moors, marshes, fells, forests, jungles, fjords, fens, over the greatest of cities, over the highest mountains."

When Phariane speaks of a waste it becomes a moor or tundra or desert or whatever word and place the ear of each of the Phoenix Prey will recognize from the character of their own realm. When she speaks of a forest the word becomes a wood or a jungle or a marsh. And so on.

"When the sky cleared only the stars were left, and some said that even they were not the same stars, or at least that the patterns they formed were changed. But the seas and land were all Shadow."

Phariane pauses, head bowed, arms leaning into the table on either side of the book. No one else speaks.

"But the Shadow had risen slowly enough for peoples to consult and search out old knowledge. Only wyrms could float on Shadow, so quests were begun. Most fell. Ships were drowned. Companies broke apart or were simply lost. One found the last sky-wyrm, flightless, dying on the peak of a mountain. The word went out. Expeditions set out for the place, while the discoverers set about what had to be done.

"They cut their way into the wyrm. When a sky-wyrm enters the death-state its bone and flesh and vitals turn to rock."

"What of the blood?" muses Gel, almost too softly to be a question.

Phariane goes on as if having heard nothing. "The sky-wyrm's skin turns to jade. Its innards to granite, rhyolite, basalt, gneiss, to amber and sardonyx – but slowly. They sculpted. No common tools were allowed. Only hands and a few venerated instruments were deemed honourable enough to mould the petrifying innards into roads and arches, plazas and buildings... into a city."

"Leviathan!" The shout comes up from the floor of the archive. "Leviathan is sighted!"

Phariane lifts her head and something behind her face goes taut.

"There's still much to say, but tomorrow."

She turns her head and some dozen arrivals in plain linen shifts appear on the cloister behind her.

"These are Dream-ward," she says. "Choose one to guard your sleep."

Gemmored holds out his huge hand to a girl with a slender neck and long fair hair trailing down the back of her shift.

Gel holds out a hand and takes the hands of an older, dark-skinned Dream-ward. Her bristling hair is jabbed with silver.

Harnak lays his hand on the shoulder of a young tow-haired lad with an eager face, then makes a gesture inviting him to lead.

Zantalliz merely nods to another young woman, sallow-skinned and sloe-eyed, nervous and swallowing.

The unchosen bow their heads solemnly.

Each chosen Dream-ward leads each of the Phoenix Prey to a separate chamber on the cloister above. The other three couples enter, but Zantalliz stops on the threshold. He sends his Dream-ward away, tearful and bewildered, with another nod.

Only one of the Phoenix Prey sees Phariane slip urgently away.

Chapter Nineteen

In the transpicuous darkness Sstheness licks Rorn's ear, murmurs into it. She lies at angle to him, he on his back, she her belly, on the cold floor.

"They found the last sea-wyrm rotting aground an atoll," she says. "Some say in lost waters, some say in forbidden."

"The Shadow was rising over the sea and was lapping at the gigantic carcass. Sure enough, as the tale tells, the wyrm was lifting off the rocks, buoyed by the darkness, proving that the lore was true. That only wyrms could float on Shadow."

Rorn turns his head away but Sstheness lovingly winds her fingers into his straggled hair and pulls it back. Her lips brush his ear again.

"The fleet of questing ships were already sinking into the Shadow, but many reached near enough for the crews to make fall on the reef and cut their way into the wyrm. They knew there was nothing else to be done.

"They knew that when a sea-wyrm dies it dies forever, its boneless body locked between life and death, mouldering without becoming dust. They knew what they would find inside it. No bones. No vital organs. Not even blood. They found labyrinths."

Rorn shifts uneasily. The slick floor allows his shoulder blades to slide.

"Rotting, foetid, weeping labyrinths," she says. "A city of labyrinths."

An urgent echo ushers into the chamber.

"Dragonkeep!" it calls.

"Dragonkeep is sighted!"

And Sstheness is gone.

Chapter Twenty

Gemmored walks into his chamber. It's lit and warmed by another tripod of yellow fire, furnished simply but well - the style of Dragonkeep. A bed, a draped settle, other drapes on the walls and edging a window.

He unfastens his scabbard and lays it on the bed.

He remembers the reaction of the flame-workers in Dragonkeep's mouth when he laid his sword on the causeway - the expressions of hungry fearful reverence. He remembers something more. During the battle on the Shadow. The young Sword-Mariner he saw give his life to retrieve a sinking blade. He knows now the reasons for both actions. Steel. Dragonkeep has an armoury whose weaponry from before the Shadow fell is stored and guarded. There are no ores of iron to be mined from Dragonkeep. Steel is worth more than life here.

He lifts his eyes and stands looking out of the window.

He can see the avenue he and the others have walked to Dragonkeep's mouth. Another procession travels it now. Men and women carry pans of yellow flame, steadily, surely. Others join them from side ways, all carrying flame.

"May, may I help?" asks the young Dream-ward.

Gemmored doesn't turn. "Phariane says we will talk again tomorrow, but are you allowed to answer questions?"

"You are Phoenix Prey," she says. She edges forward and stands beside him, watching the yellow line gleam toward Dragonkeep's mouth.

"They have the careful pace of an important duty," says Gemmored, "but not the slowness of ritual?"

"Every night the flame is collected and returned to the mouth," she says. "Every morning it is taken back into the city."

"So the taking and returning gives you day and night," nods Gemmored.

"It, it is a ritual." The Dream-ward laughs, but the laugh contains the same tight anxiety as her words. "The task isn't usually so purposefully done. But your coming has changed... Your coming has changed everything."

"When the Phoenix chooses," says Gemmored. "What does that mean? What happens when the Phoenix chooses?"

Gel's chamber is laid out no differently to Gemmored's. "What happens when the Phoenix chooses?" he says. "What does that mean?" He winds his hand into the Dream-ward's wiry silver-scattered hair and prises her face to look up at his.

"It's for Phariane to say," gasps the Dream-ward, without rancour.

Gel bends his head down to her. "Why are we here, the swordsman and the old man and the little one with the book?"

"I'll answer whatever you wish about Dragonkeep, about -" he twists harder, "- about Leviathan, but the Phoenix's purpose is for the archivist to explain."

She speaks not only without rancour but without fear too, Gel observes. That angers him, amuses him.

He's curious about Leviathan.

He grins into the Dream-ward's face, pulls her onto the bed. He will ask about it later.

Harnak walks into his chamber. He turns before his tow-headed Dream-ward can close the door and raises his arm.

"If you call out or leave this room I'll kill you."

The Dream-ward shows surprise, but not alarm. He nods. "You are Phoenix Prey."

He watches as Harnak's old head wizens even more, the skin and bone of face and skull drawing in and sinking into the neck of his robe, the robe itself sucking in on itself and dropping to the floor, as a sable-dark cat darts from beneath the hem and out of the door.

The cat sleeks down the stairways to the floor of the atrium. Without pausing, it slips through the narrow gap between another door, this one bronze and ornate, and its frame.

Harnak pads soundlessly and surely down the bronze treads in darkness. The caracol winds down through vault after vault. Even a cat's vision can barely make out stone walls and the shapes of amphorae. The air is dank here, something he has not felt before in Dragonkeep. He can smell grains, seeds, soil, and other smells he can put no names to. There are not only words stored in the archive. This is no museum. No flame has lit these vaults for a long time, if ever. This darkness is settled, like dust. He can taste it. So the things stored here, the seeds of crops, of trees are not for exhibit. They can only be intended, someday, for sowing...

Harnak is not curious. Curiosity is one of many traits tortured out of him as a child. Or so he believes. But if that's so, why is he following Phariane?

She descended these treads just moments before. Harnak had watched her from the corner of his eye even as his Dream-ward had led him to his chamber, had seen her stride across the atrium and slip through the bronze door. Harnak wonders how she moves so swiftly, as swiftly as a cat, in the darkness.

He reaches the end of the winding stairway. Not in darkness. Nor in light. It's silvered, this cavern. The walls are incised with deep mysterious glyphs laid bare by the glimmering shed.

A fountain is set in the middle of this cavern, a bowl with a single delicate thread of silver arcing and falling back into the pool. The source of the glimmering shed.

On the edge of the bowl sits Phariane. Her carelessly shorn hair for some reason appears a little longer in the silver. She leans over the pool, hands cupped and raised to her mouth.

She sings or whispers to whatever she cups, or at least does something similar to singing or whispering. The soft sound is on an edge between breath and voice. There is pain in it. On her face too. As if what she holds stings. As if it burns.

Then her lips pause and her tongue licks them. "Harnak."

Harnak wills a change. He feels his blood begin to run in new patterns beneath his skin, feels his cat bones begin to flow.

He is a woman this time. Not old but young. With clumsily shorn hair. Another Phariane. The real Phariane doesn't even look, just resumes breathing or whispering or singing to her cupped hands. Then she stops again, and speaks.

"When Dragonkeep was made," she says, "the sky-wyrm's bone and flesh and vitals turned to stone."

"Granite, chalcedony, porphyry, jet," says Harnak. Even her voice is like the real Phariane's.

"But not the blood," says Phariane. Then she purses her lips and blows again into her hands.

Harnak comes closer.

The silver in the pool is clear, as much light as liquid. And there seems no system to propel the thread which still glitters up and falls back.

Phariane's hands hold a cupping of the same silver held in the fountain. The silver lustres her face as she purses her lips. The cupped pool ripples as does the pool below.

Harnak wonders if he or she should kill Phariane. There's much she doesn't understand since the Phoenix chose her, and assassination is a cool touchstone of what she does know, what she is. Harnak has never needed a reason to kill, only an order. Finally, finding she needs not even that, killing has become a token of freedom. But Harnak also thrives on change, of many kinds. Against the familiar sour despair that patinas murder she balances something new. Something different. She considers, while Phariane continues to sing or whisper or breathe into the cupped burning wyrm'sblood, sending urgent ripples across the silver bowled in her hands.

Chapter Twenty-One

After the woman is gone Rorn lies in the darkness, listening to dim shouts and laughter and the even fainter snapping of skulls' jaws. His mind turns back, with the drowsy unease of a troubled sleeper, to the Shadow.

He starts to remember the ponderous oceanic shifting beneath its surface, nuances of darkness eddying across the desolation. He finds it unnerving. The darkness of his own realm Nightwake is solidly simplistic in comparison. Rorn tries to pull away from the memory of the Shadow. He feels it pulling at him in return. But his thoughts are starting to sharpen and with them awareness of the now. Of lying on the cold floor of Leviathan's heart. A heart which is not really a heart. A heart which does not so much beat as shudder beneath his spine.

He listens to the dim shouts.

"Dragonkeep..."

That was the word...

"Dragonkeep!"

It spits into his ear this time, like hissing acrimony. The woman. She's returned. The taloned woman.

She pulls him to his feet and drags him to the wall of the heart chamber.

"Dragonkeep!"

She slaps a hand against the wall, curls her fingerstalls against it, then claws sideways. The stone splits open again like flesh. She shoulders through the vertical rip and pulls Rorn after her, bruising him on the stone-hard edges already sliding back together.

"Dragonkeep!"

She strides furiously through the labyrinths. Her hand still clasps his wrist. She pinches it, the fingerstalls scything harmlessly beyond the fingers. But the grip is unbreakable.

"Not this time, Dragonkeep..."

She pulls him through distorted slimed passages. She's robed now.

"...but soon."

They pass men, women, a child once, all scowling or smirking at him. Sometimes in the narrower passages he brushes against them and they make no effort to move aside, allowing elbows and knees to jab against his bruised body. The woman pays no heed to this but merely yanks him on.

"Soon," the woman says again. Still striding on, she turns to Rorn. "It will be soon. You, my lovely, are proof of that."

Some of the passages are strewn with skulls. Though these leave the woman alone they snap at Rorn's feet and ankles.

"Leviathan's time is coming... The twisting and twisted worm..." Her words echo.

She stops before another of the many wounds they have passed in the labyrinths, vertical slashes in the stillbirth walls, all rusted shut. She lays her hand on the scar, as she did on the wall of the heart chamber, and sweeps it open. Gateways, Rorn now realizes, to other chambers. And not rusted shut. Sutured with dried blood until the next time the wound is opened.

This chamber is different to the other. Much larger. Candled dimness, like the passages, not the transpicuous not-light of the heart chamber. And not bare. Furnished with a seat.

The woman talks lovingly of it. Its back is the spine bone of some massive deepsea beast, swallowed ages past by Leviathan when it still lived and fed in oceans of salt water not Shadow. The beast's ribcage has been prised open a little to allow access to the spine. More like a throne than a chair. A serrated throne.

Three figures await. Two skull-casqued warriors hold a leather-jerkined Corsair between them. He's shorter. A well-trimmed beard over a powerful jaw.

The woman mounts the throne. The space between the thing's ribs is still too narrow to allow passage without pain. She wrenches Rorn after her, gouging him on the cage as she has been. Her robe is open at the sides and he can see that the scores on her own ribs are laid over older marks – almost ruts. She thrusts him beside the seat and nestles her back with relish against the harshly jutting knobs of vertebrae. She still clasps his wrist.

Rorn is not sure, but believes that this is the moment when he begins to hate her.

Between the throne, slightly raised on a dais, and the three men, is a pit. A rectangular-hewn cavern which falls into gloom at an unnaturally shallow depth.

"Sstheness," says the Corsair.

The skull-casques wrench his arms but he twists a grin out of his grimace.

"Mistress Sstheness."

Sstheness. Rorn has a name for the woman now, a title for his enmity.

"Five of them, captain," hisses Sstheness. "Five chosen by the Phoenix. I gave you the command, told you where to take your quinqueremes, guided them to the place where the Phoenix would shed its prey one by one. Even sent the Pitspoor to aid you. Five."

The Corsair keeps his grin, but there's something in his eyes which keeps glancing at the pit even when he's not looking into it.

"Five Phoenix prey, captain," she goes on. "And how many do you see here?"

The woman lifts and twists Rorn's arm. Sstheness lifts and twists his arm. Bitch.

Something about the Corsair goes quiet. He looks at Sstheness steadily. His voice shrugs with a cold resignation. "Better one than none, Mistress, eh? Or doesn't this one satisfy you?"

Sstheness' head droops. Her face takes on an absurdly poignant sadness, then lifts again. Her free hand drifts to her shoulder and the talon fingerstalls gently rub against her robe. Then the movement stops and one talon lifts.

Rorn wonders if it might be the same talon that laid his cheek open.

The skull-casques pull the Corsair forward a step to the very brink of the pit.

Sstheness turns and bends and Rorn finds her mouth on his, her tongue in his mouth, slowly licking. It gives a last squirm and Sstheness withdraws. "He satisfies," she says. The Corsair makes no cry as the skull-casques thrust him forward. "But not enough..."

Rorn cranes subtly to look into the pit. There's movement deep within, slithering, juddering. There are gristly sounds, suckings, rippings. There are stiff, leprous-white shapes darting.

"But there's comfort in the darkness," says Sstheness, "the darkness that writhes and devours, the twisted and twisting worm."

The cut on Rorn's cheek stings coldly. He can feel the Shadow under his face.

Chapter Twenty-Two

Phariane wearily climbs the caracol through the vaults with Harnak following. Harnak no longer looks like Phariane, but is still a young woman. Phariane's steps have the heavy determined rhythm of someone drained in more than physical strength, and when she speaks, eventually, near the top of the stairs, almost at the bronze door leading to the atrium, her words have the same dull and negligent quality.

"What did you expect to find?"

Harnak's voice as well as her form remains young and female. "Perhaps a torment chamber," she says.

Phariane continues up without pausing or looking back, but her next step is slightly heavier still. "Why?"

"In my experience it's the way of things that such chambers are often found at the bottom of darkened stairways."

Then they're in through the bronze door and walking across the floor of the atrium. Most of the flames lighting the archive have been removed. A single remaining tripod glows soft yellow that washes rather than lights them. No more words are said between them.

A young sallow-skinned sloe-eyed woman hurries forward to Phariane as if she has been waiting anxiously. She murmurs to the archivist tearfully. Harnak goes up to her room.

She opens the door to find the young eager man sitting on the bed - not lying, sitting straight-backed, waiting. He runs a hand uneasily through his hair. Stands. There's wild puzzlement in his eyes, which he keeps unerringly on Harnak's young woman's eyes. He says nothing. Harnak smiles, more to herself than to the Dream-ward, and makes a cat's meow. She slips herself into the bed and closes her eyes.

Phariane carefully enters Zantalliz' chamber to find him gazing out of the window onto Dragonkeep.

"Your Dream-ward is distressed that you sent her away," she says.

Zantalliz says nothing. Phariane comes and stands by his side, looking out with him. His strange eyes look over the spearing avenues and narrower side roads and even narrower winding lanes, over archways and buildings and gardens and plazas. The procession of flame has ended. Only a few quiet pulses of yellow light remain. Night.

"This is one of the ways we tell time here," says Phariane. "How we mark one day, one moment's moving to the next."

Zantalliz keeps silent. Phariane sighs. Her voice is still flat with tiredness but struggles to offer something in its tone.

Zantalliz's strange eyes lift to Dragonkeep's sky roof. The porphyry has darkened, swallowing the purple mottling into a deeper lightless hue. Now and then something glitters star-like.

"Not rainbows," says Zantalliz.

Phariane looks across at him. She is half a head taller.

"The colours in the roof," he goes on.

Phariane smiles thoughtfully. "Bone and flesh and vitals to granite, basalt, jet, bluestone... To jade, amber, chalcedony..." She glances up through the window again. "But the dragon's ribs became crystal..." Her voice has become calmer reciting the names. "Emerald, garnet, spinel, sapphire, ruby, opal, carnelian, topaz, amethyst..." Still tired but softer.

"I presume it has something to do with death."

Phariane looks back sharply to Zantalliz.

"Why we have been brought here - the swordsman Gemmored, the one called Gel with the ax, the one who appears to be an old man,"

"Harnak," says Phariane.

"The lost one, taken by the other ships." He goes on. "We've been summoned to thwart death, or give death, or perhaps be given death."

Zantalliz turns to her and for the first time Phariane notices that he doesn't hold his book in his arms. It lies, closed, on the chamber settle. Her voice hardens again, her effort to reach Zantalliz turning sour.

"The Dream-ward have trained all their lives to perform their duty. To guard the dreams of a Phoenix Prey would be the highest honour. To have that privilege offered and then torn away, as you've done..."

"I have no need of a guard for my dreams."

Phariane stares at him for a moment, then steps away, not bothering to close the door after her.

Zantalliz knows that what he has done to the sallow-skinned sloe-eyed Dream-ward is cruel, but there is no sympathy in him now for any living thing. All he can do is mourn. He will not sleep.

END OF BOOK ONE.

Chapter Twenty-Three

"In order for evil to express itself it must take action," Phariane says the next morning at the table over the atrium well - the table of convocation as she calls it. "Thus Leviathan chases Dragonkeep."

"How long has that been?" asks Gemmored.

"Since the Shadow drowned the highest mountain in the realm and became a sea, leaving only Leviathan and Dragonkeep above it."

"How many years?" Gemmored persists.

Phariane gives a sniff like a jibe, her voice equally sarcastic. "Years fall from seasons. We tell time here by day and night, and generations. Generations of waiting."

"Awaiting what?" says Gemmored.

"Awaiting you," says Phariane.

She leads the Phoenix Prey out of the archive and through Dragonkeep. Pure silk robes have been provided for them this morning. A number of the hawk-helmed and gambesoned Blade-ward follow behind.

Harnak is aware that again their scabbards are pathetically empty. Iron is rare here, Phariane has said, and thus steel also. Warriors without blades. Harnak could kill them all.

But she also notes that Gemmored's scabbard, strapped over his gown, is full. And Phariane still carries her wavering-bladed kris in the belt of her tunic.

The city is, if not busy, not deserted. People stop and look at the Phoenix Prey as they pass, but there are no cries and few mutterings of "When the Phoenix chooses..." Faces still hold reverence, but a pensiveness has crept in.

Phariane leads them a short way, zigzagging through diorite-paved streets less wide and long than the dolomite avenues that took them from the docks to the towering archive or from the archive to the dragonmouth. The buildings are smaller here. Houses are of rhyolite. Walls are seamless, smoothed by the hands of Dragonkeep's ancient founders. The copper braziers they pass are again alive with light-giving yellow flame.

Phariane eventually guides them through an arched gateway into a vast amphitheatre. They stand in the centre before the rising curve of seating. They had thought it empty before they entered, but every iota of space on every tier is taken by men and women in chitons and himatia, and even children. Each one silent.

"The Phoenix has chosen," pronounces Phariane. And the roar starts.

A storm of gestures erupts. The audience jumps to their feet. The people of Dragonkeep are various. Most shorter than Gemmored; many taller than Zantalliz; some darker than Gel - now the flush infusing his skin from the galley battle has long since abandoned him; some paler than Harnak some not - though his colour now as a young woman is less bronzed than as a leathern old man. The architecture of their faces is as subtly varied as the styles of their homes. Questions are shouted, both down at the arena and across the theatre, all partly or wholly lost in the din. There's confusion, but excitement, even laughter, but resentment also, and something else. A bristling susurrus of anticipation. As much in the breath as in the shouts of the audience.

Phariane calmly holds up a hand and soon the clamour subsides, almost to the silence before. One or two of the children sob. The susurrus still hangs in the atmosphere. But if the Phoenix Prey are treated with awe, Phariane is given a respect which almost reaches awe.

One woman, from the high back of the amphitheatre, calls out her question. "Where is the other one, the one with the ax?"

It's a question Phariane herself has asked earlier that morning, in the archive. "Where is Gel?"

No one knows. Even his Dream-ward, who had slept with him in his bed, whose own sleep is trained to be light, had woken to find him gone.

Other questions are easier to answer.

The three Phoenix Prey in the amphitheatre.

Gemmored of Darkling.

Harnak of Aftermath.

Zantalliz of Voyage.

They each give their names and the names of the realms from which they've been taken. Even Zantalliz speaks. He no longer carries his book.

More curiosity is centred on Harnak's appearance. Many of the audience had seen a weathered old man the previous day. Now he's nowhere to be seen, and the Phoenix chosen are joined by a young woman much like Phariane. Who? Mutterings finally surface in a shouted question from a broad-shouldered man. Harnak gives no answer. Her lips smirk uneasily. But no one repeats any question. No one demands answers.

Some questions expect no simple answer and are aimed at Phariane.

How important is the loss of the fifth Phoenix Prey?

Are the Blade-ward ready?

How soon will the end come?

These questions spark responses from others in other parts of the amphitheatre. Arguments curve back and forth across the vast semi-circle. Authorities are cited. Scholars disagree. Disagreement turns to insult. Shouts become louder. Harsher.

The Blade-ward shift and lean and murmur to one another. Phariane half raises an arm again. Patches of audience calm. Hands are placed on shoulders of some who have angrily stood again.

Then another shout. Fierce. And then nothing can quell the roar, louder and more bitter. A new Blade-ward enters and runs across the arena and shouts into Phariane's ear. She nods, turns to the Phoenix Prey, and sees something no one else has seen.

Gemmored stands motionless, towering, looking down. A bloom of red is spreading across the silk of his robe, a knife thrusting from his massive chest.

Phariane yells to make herself heard to the Blade-ward. She gestures at the Prey. Take them back to the archive. Tend Gemmored's wound.

She runs from the arena.

She reins the chariot to a stop. Its wheels are wood rather than metal and no sparks fly from the brake. But they squeal. A waft of burn catches Phariane as she jumps from the car onto the plaza's sardonyx floor.

The masque is in full, swirling progress, or at least the performers are trying to execute their parts. Barefoot, in long gauze-silk drapes of black or white they dance. In exquisitely fashioned and painted masks they speak.

Phariane knows this masque. She watched it once as a child. It is rarely performed. A very special, elaborate performance of dance and song and poetry, intended for the most important occasions. It would be unusual enough in itself, but never before has it been executed without an audience. Those who might watch are either in the amphitheatre, or for whatever reason chose to have nothing to do with the arrival of the Phoenix Prey.

It is the largest of all masques. Dozens of dancers in black gauze frantically weave in and out of each other, occasionally weaving into an inner circle of fewer white-gauzed dancers who move in a simpler, counter circle. Masks ending just above the lips, the outer dancers hum a harsh monotone as they move - the inner dancers voice a softer, open-mouthed, swaying, soughing sound.

Between the two sets of dancers, at places throughout the circle, stand chanters. These are draped in crimson. "Blood and red slaughter." As the dancers eddy around them in precise sinewy movements they utter their cry.

"Blood and red slaughter,
Wield spear or blade,
Blood and red slaughter,
Against my rage,
Blood and red slaughter,
Furnish my hand,
Blood and red slaughter,
With a burning red gage,
Blood and red slaughter,
Blood and red slaughter and death,
Blood and red slaughter,
Wield spear or blade,"

... and round again, all in gauze and masks, all in harmony.

Or at least most.

Because at this layer of the masque's complex warp and weft of movement and sound, is Gel.

He swings left and right, twisting and darting, moving more wildly than the dancers. His movements disturb the flow of the masque's pattern. Dancers falter, half-trip, bump against each other. But no one raises a complaint or so much as looks askance at the tall, ghost-maned figure, one of the Phoenix Prey they perform to honour. He wields his labrys as wildly as his gaunt body. What was it he called it? Bloodbane. He spins its twin blades, sweeps it effortlessly in short and swift and weaving arcs, among the bemused dancers. He laughs as he does this, and the cackle is as wild again.

Phariane feels a deep, prowling thunder gathering inside her and walks forward into the outer black-gauzed circle.

The dancers adapt their steps to allow her progress - yet more disruption of the pattern, but only slight. After all, she is the archivist, perhaps the most respected citizen of Dragonkeep. Since as a child she was chosen as such she has known unrivalled deference. That is why she's resented the coming of the Phoenix Prey, resisted the awe that most of the city feels. And now, also, as she moves through the circle, she knows that she must earn that deference as no archivist before her has needed to do.

In the very centre of the dance two masquers stand back to back, a man, a woman, arms linked at the elbows. The woman keens "The twisting and twisted worm..." The man then sings "The twisted and twisting worm..." with as much joy in his voice as the woman had sorrow. Then the woman sings again, "The twisting and twisted worm..." but this time with joy, while the man then repeats "The twisted and twisting worm..." with sorrow.

Then the whole antiphony again, only with the woman and man exchanging phrase.

Then again, exchanging phrases again.

And on and on...

Even as the rest of the masque falters, even as Phariane reaches Gel and stands before him.

"...twisted and twisting worm..."

"Go on!" she shouts, not at Gel but at the masquers. Bare soles push on sardonyx. Uncertainly, haltingly, the circle starts to turn again, leaving a whorl of space around Phariane and Gel.

"Yes! Go on! Go on!" Gel shouts to them. Then he turns back to Phariane, breathing hard through a ferine grin. He leans on the long helve of his labrys. The silk robe he wears is streaked and clinging with sweat, yet his long lank hair does not slick to his skull but remains a wispy mass, drifting at the slightest movement of his head. "They dance prettily, do they not?" he says. "Though why they should dance is another thing..."

"...twisting and twisted..."

Phariane cups her anger and her fear and speaks with low, staring calm. "You left the archive this morning before we could talk. There was a meeting - an important gathering."

Gel whisks his fingers and sends the twin heads of his labrys spinning beside his face. "And what did you talk about at this meeting?"

"The future," says Phariane.

"...twisted..."

Gel laughs again, and makes a deep, sweeping bow. A dancer almost stumbles sidestepping his arm. "Come then, archivist Phariane! Lay wide the future like some worm-infested grave. Tell me my destiny!"

"There are no augurs here," she says. Gel stops Bloodbane spinning, one razored blade cantle a fraction from his cheek.

"The only place there are no augurs," he says, "is a place where there is no future. Is that why we're here? Myself and the others?" He kinks his head with the last question. Filaments of white mane shift and rise.

Phariane stares at him, and hates him, and thinks back to Zantalliz' words last night. 'I presume it has something to do with death. Why we have been brought here.' For a whiplash terror of a moment she wonders if these are, indeed, the true Phoenix Prey. But the books say that they will come, and they have. But far from comforting or calming Phariane they have the opposite effect - for this is all she knows. She has no idea who or what the five chosen are. Even telling Harnak in her new shape is only observation and guesses - the way his or her face is always subtly in flux, the cheekbones, eyes, lips, nose, skin, shading in shape or colour. For all Phariane's skills, all the words in the archive only reach this point in history. The chaotic roar of voices she left in the amphitheatre still echoes in her ears. She feels young. Very young. And afraid.

Gel's mouth is still drawn into a grin, but now it's fixed. As much a mask as any around them.

"A tide of shadow is washing over the universe," she says. "You have been brought here to turn it."

"So," he says, "there is to be war."

"Yes," says Phariane.

"And blood," says Gel.

"Yes," says Phariane.

Gel's grin stretches back to life.

The evening procession returning dragonfire back to the dragonmouth has begun before Phariane returns to the archive. The day has been filled with duties less intense than her confrontation with Gel but equally wearying and portentous in their ways. She climbs the steps and moves through the portico, nodding to the extra watch of Blade-ward she's ordered.

Within the archive, even at this late hour, there's more activity than Phariane has ever known.

Scholars hurry about. Each carries a small lantern holding a small precious tongue of dragonflame. They're checking their old studies, looking to confirm their old opinions. Others have been drawn here by the arrival of the Phoenix Prey, not even to read, just to walk through the cloisters, to look at the shelves of scrolls and tablets and books. Each visitor has a Blade-ward escort as Phariane has also ordered.

She goes to Gemmored's room. He's lying on his bed as she enters and swings to sit on its edge. Phariane kneels before him and eases down his robe to his waist. The knife wound has been dressed but seepings of blood still soak through the bandages. She carefully unwinds them. The wound still glistens.

Phariane takes the kris from her belt. She lifts her free hand to the head of auburn hair that has almost grown back to her shoulders in the space of a day. She runs finger and thumb along a single thread, stretching it out. She lifts the kris and guides the waving blade against the thread near the scalp. She cuts. Bringing down kris and thread, she holds the blade upright, the hair just above it. She watches. Metal and thread both sheen. The blade begins to pulse. The undulations of its shape become undulations of movement. The movement is always upward, craning toward the hair. The top of the blade lengthens, thinning as it stretches. It becomes a fine needle – a second sheening auburn thread.

Phariane's gaze moves from the needle to Gemmored's wound, then back. She lifts the hair a little higher. The needle responds, reaching higher, becoming even finer. When it touches the hair the tip parts, enclosing the end of the hair like an eyelet, seals around it. Now needle and hair are one. Only the stiffness of the needle betrays where they meet. It comes away from the rest of the kris.

Phariane brings the thread close to her parted lips. She draws it sideways until the whole length of needle and hair have moved through her breath.

Then she carefully if not gently puts fingers and thumb to each side of Gemmored's wound and draws the edges closer. As the needle passes through the edges the muscles around Gemmored's eyes, the grey of frosted steel, twitch.

"So Dragonkeep runs from Leviathan..." he says.

"Since the Shadow rose over the world."

"But soon now the chase will end..." His words are steady. There's no trace of flinching in his voice. His chest rises and falls a little more slowly and deeply. "It will end in a battle called the Uroborus..."

Phariane continues to ease the needle and thread back and forth through his skin. "You all learned much from the debate in the amphitheatre? Good. That's as had been intended."

"Was this intended?" Gemmored's hand closes over Phariane's - needle, wound and all. For the first time since she began stitching she looks him in the face.

"There are those who don't believe you are what you are," she shrugs. "Or perhaps want you to be what you are."

"Phariane?" says Gemmored. "Are we gods?"

Chapter Twenty-Four

The next morning Gemmored wakes, eases his Dream-ward from him, and looks down. Weakness, there still is, and a faint tickle of the pain that should still be jabbing into his chest. But he's not surprised to look down and find no trace of his wound or the auburn thread that had been woven across it.

His Dream-ward, who came to him last night as Phariane left, sleepily pulls her long fair fan of hair into neatness and smiles at him.

Through the window Gemmored hears shouts from outside the towering bluestone archive and lifts himself on his elbow. Taking Gemmored's movement as a signal the girl slides from the bed and stands. A smear of his blood colours her shift just below her breast.

He did not take her on their first night together, nor last night, though it's clear that he might if he wished. He wonders if the act is part of the Dream-ward's duties. The look in her eyes seems more than duty.

Does she think on him as a god?

"What are the gods?" says Phariane that evening, at the onyx table of convocation.

The day has been spent in different ways by the Phoenix Prey. Gemmored has rested as Phariane requested, sleeping under the protection of his Dream-ward.

Harnak and Gel have each gone out into Dragonkeep to explore the city. They had gone separately but both, even Gel, had agreed to a single member of the Blade-ward as an escort-come-guide.

Zantalliz has spent the day alone, still mostly silent, wandering the dim windowless recesses of the archive.

But Phariane, herself busy about the city with councils and other duties, has asked that they all return for this meeting.

"Zantalliz," she says. He seems not to be listening. "Zantalliz?

What are the gods of Voyage?"

He seems distracted by the activity around them. As last night scholars and others are moving about the cloisters and in and out of the rooms of racks and shelves.

"There are no gods in my realm," he mutters, "only my people and man. And now..." he lapses back into silence until Gel yawns, "...only man."

"What are the gods of Gnomon, Gel-a-Volquanon?" Phariane asks sharply.

"What is the purpose of all this?" he says. "If we're here to fight a battle, why not begin it and have done with wasting time?"

There are shouts coming from outside again. All day, groups have gathered to throw insults or threats or questions that might be construed as both - or even stones. Each group has been dispersed by the Blade-ward, only for another to gather.

"Before the Uroboros there must be four convocations," says Phariane levelly and carefully. "This is only the first."

Gel rocks back in his seat, setting a foot against the table edge. If not for the prop of his labrys he would topple. Restive breath pushes through his teeth. "The gods of Gnomon are young and fierce. There is Theedren the Hawk, Mareek the Spider Goddess, faceless Sarada, Geemass Lord of Ghosts, Tassess the Deathgiver... None of them have any love for mortals, or for each other. They're forever in theomachy and they use men to fight their wars." His voice dips thoughtfully. "They give men power in order to gain advantage, damning them as they see fit..."

"The gods of Darkling are not so young," says Gemmored. His hands are clasped on the table and his head bent to stare down at them. "...And men have learnt to bargain or trick or wrest power from them... And damn themselves."

Harnak seems about to speak. He's an ugly olive-skinned man now, with thick brows and full lips. As they part Gemmored speaks again. "Is it truly necessary to postpone the Uroboros?" The shouts outside have grown louder. His voice is also raised.

Phariane's is slower but somehow also impatient. "There are ways to prepare for when Leviathan and Dragonkeep finally meet, laid down in many of the texts here. As archivist it's my duty to interpret and judge how to proceed."

"So Leviathan chases, and Dragonkeep runs." A rumbling bitterness grows like a wave through Gemmored's sentence. It breaks into contempt on the final word.

In a lull in the shouting outside someone jeers. The yell resounds distantly through the atrium.

"But you control Dragonkeep, command its movements through the Shadow." Harnak smiles at Phariane. "I've seen you do it." Gel and Gemmored both look at her. "That's what it was, wasn't it, by the pool of blood in the deepest part of the archive."

Gel's eyes narrow and his grin is curious this time. His own words overlap the rest of Harnak's. "So you could stop this chase now? Bring this huge, man-hollowed eschar to a stop? Even set us on a course for this Leviathan?" Gel's words are more taunts than questions. Edging close to laughter, each is louder that the one before. A cloaked scholar with lantern emerges from one of the archive chambers into the cloister near the mezzanine. She pauses as she passes near the table. Gel, still leaning back on his labrys, swivels her a glance and she scurries on along the cloister. Gel darts his attention back to Phariane.

"The Uroboros will come soon enough," she says.

Gel is on his feet before his chair rocks back to four legs. He still grins, but something about his lips has shifted. The shouts from outside now clash with shouted orders from the Blade-ward. "For you, perhaps," he says, and strides away.

The next moment Gemmored pulls himself up, chair rumbling back, and also walks away.

Then Harnak.

Phariane suddenly stands and calls after him. "Harnak!" And again. Waveringly clutching at self-possession. "Harnak of Aftermath," she says, "what are your gods?"

Harnak turns. It's impossible for her to tell if the vagueness of his shape is entirely the gloom of the cloister. "They're dying," he shrugs, and slips away.

Phariane sinks back into her chair. Silence uneasily returns. Her fist slams the table.

Zantalliz hasn't stirred since his speaking. His head is slightly bowed, looking down so that his lids and lashes hide his eyes, forearms laid on the table, hands cupped one over the other.

Yellow castings from dragonflame lanterns dimly nudge from some of the chambers off the cloisters. Some scholars are still about but none of them ventures out after Phariane's shouts.

The disturbance outside has faded away. There's a listening silence throughout the archive, greedy, ready for the slightest echo.

Phariane's hand uncurls and slowly moves toward Zantalliz' hands. Long palms and fingers. Nails rounded and delicate. The skin looks silken. The veins hardly disturb their smoothness. As Phariane's fingers reach them Zantalliz instantly pulls them away.

There's a listening silence throughout the archive. Greedy. Ready for the slightest echo.

Chapter Twenty-Five

Long after Zantalliz has left the table, Phariane sits. She dwells on his hands. Not so much the pulling away but the manner of the pulling away. There was bitterness in the movement. Phariane has heard bitterness in his voice before. But what robs her of sleep that night is how sharply he reacted. Anger is something she had not suspected in him before.

Thus, when the call comes in that selfsame night that a Shadowfast has been sighted, she finds herself welcoming it. She frowns. Another token of strange times, of the approaching Uroboros. To welcome the sighting of a Shadowfast.

A party gathers at the archive, a dozen or so: two families, two men and a woman. They're petitioning Phariane, wanting to leave Dragonkeep for a new life on the Shadowfast. She does not ask why, perhaps afraid to. Perhaps some of them blame her for the coming of the Phoenix Prey, for the coming Uroboros. She's been honoured ever since she was chosen archivist as a young girl, and blame is a frighteningly unfamiliar thing to see in faces and hear in voices.

So she agrees. And she will go with them, to at least watch over their safety a while longer. She orders a dragonreme prepared and feels guilty for wanting so eagerly to leave Dragonkeep, if only for a while. She has spent the last few days in meetings with the various councils which regulate life in the city. Factions have erupted. Old racial and religious enmities not thought of since the Shadow came have reemerged. In the archive there are many works on the coming of the Phoenix Prey, even more on the Uroboros. But now Phariane realizes that there is little mention in any of them of the space between - the gap between the end of one world and the birthing of the next. So when councillors ask her what to do and she hears the fear in their voices, she answers questions with questions or prevaricates in a dozen other ways to avoid saying or screaming - I do not know.

So she lets the guilt fester and welcomes the sighting of the Shadowfast.

But even as the dragonreme glides toward it, a high rocky scar thrusting out of the Shadow, Phariane stands on the bowsprit and still dwells on Zantalliz' hands.

Behind her the twenty petitioners sit on sacks of possessions and provisions or stand on the deck, restless, staring at the Shadowfast or talking in whispers or casting anxious glances back to Dragonkeep. A child starts crying, is scooped up and comforted.

A wolf and its ward are also on the deck. Phariane has summoned them as an escort for the petitioners. The wolf is one of the hoar-greys – sturdier and thicker pelted than their black cousins.

This one looks up at the stars. Something howls somewhere in its eyes, but only its eyes.

The ward, in jerkin and leather gorget, has his thumbs hooked into the waist of his breeks. He looks now at Dragonkeep, now at the Shadowfast, now elsewhere, without particular interest in anything. His eyes skim but never drift.

When he boarded, Phariane looked at him for a moment, trying to decide if he was one of the Wolf-wards she's slept with.

Although there's a gauntlet on the hand that loosely grasps the wolf's leash, the leash is never taut. As the ward moves or stops, so does the wolf, without bidding or signal.

Phariane has also brought one of the Phoenix Prey.

She recalls making the decision. Weighing fire and ice - the different brutalities of Gel and Gemmored. Mulling over the elusive nature of Harnak. Searching her instincts, brooding over the Prey's actions, words, miens, since arriving in Dragonkeep. Refusing even to consider Zantalliz.

"Where are they kept, the wolves?" says Harnak.

Phariane turns to him.

"I've hardly seen any about in the city," he goes on.

"They may go where they will," says Phariane, "but they prefer the forest."

"Forest?"

Harnak has wandered Dragonkeep, usually at night as suits his assassin's instinct. He has flitted silently through the streets, past bathhouses and gymnasia and stables, and across plazas. He even knows of the cropfields that border the city on two sides. But a forest?

"It lies at the tail of Dragonkeep," says Phariane.

Harnak wonders what it might be like. He looks over to the wolf and ward on the dragonreme deck. Both somehow remind him of himself. Not their eyes that stare both outward and inward - Harnak's are far too guarded to stare. Their eyes hint at something lost while Harnak's merely suggest something missing. And although there is comparison in the sleek way of moving, what Harnak recognizes is something else.

It *is* the eyes. He remembers seeing a wolf and Wolf-ward walking in the city. The citizens of Dragonkeep looked on them with something of how his own people looked on Harnak. If the Dragonkeepers' eyes lacked the hatred, the contempt, if their eyes didn't spit on the wolf and Wolf-ward, they yet contained the same distrust.

The realization does not trouble Harnak. If anything it bores him. He turns to the looming Shadowfast. He draws a long breath and feels his robe swell about him, an enfolding tower of silk which is softly collapsing around him even as he darts up.

Up into the sky with only stars to distinguish its darkness from the darkness of the sea of Shadow below. His tiny wings drone, beating even faster, carrying him higher, until he halts, motionless, hovering.

Far below, for the first time, he can view the whole of Dragonkeep, poised as it is near the Shadowfast. He can view its enormous, sleek length, tapering gently into a tail and narrowing more sharply into a neck at the other extreme before swelling into a head. He can glimpse a sharply curved lace of crimson and yellow glimmer which is the chalcedony and fire of its mouth.

It lies on the Shadow, neither floating nor inhered, more still than any ship on any natural sea.

He can barely make out the far smaller speck of the dragonreme stroking toward the Shadowfast. And even the wooded top of this scarped tower of an isle is far below where Harnak hovers. His wings still blur to keep him aloft. He considers pivoting from the shape of a hummingbird into a bird better able to glide down onto the isle. A petrel? Or a poorwill? But no wind blows over the Shadow. There are only the shifting movements of illimitable distance playing on the senses, against the ear, the mute murmur of immensity...

Immensity does not trouble him. His own realm of Aftermath is swathed in vast pampas and tablelands. But Shadow does. The sky of Aftermath is without sun or star, only a sheet of dim crimson light, sometimes streaked by lighter vermilions or darker purples. Aftermath is always dusk. Shadow in Aftermath is a petty thing, carved by cressets out of the darkness only found in windowless chambers and dungeons. Harnak has been trained for such darknesses, to seek it, but Shadow reminds him of that training. It reminds him of shadows cast by hot coals porcupined with branding irons, cast by hanging strips of chain, cast by the coiling flickerings of whips. He relishes night but loathes shadow. But here, looking below, looking above, he cannot distinguish between the two. Sea, sky, everything is darkness and everything is shadow.

An uneasy realization.

He abandons it and plummets for the Shadowfast, still in the rainbow-plumaged hummingbird form, and starts to scout the top of the scar as Phariane has asked him.

He zigzags through the trees that choke the plateau. Some are thickly boled, others more narrow. The thicker trees splay out serrated, leafy boughs. The others shoot out furred and twisting branches, tipped with clumps of pricking buds. The branches and boughs sometimes entwine and Harnak has to hover, wings droning, making short dodges in the air, searching for a gap through the matted foliage.

Beneath is no undergrowth, no wildflowers or underwood. Sight is poor. The deformed canopy strangles out most of the starlight. All Harnak can make out is a floor of dark detritus, runneled with what might be roots or lichen. Or darkness drooling.

There are few trees in the city of angled agate spires, but Harnak has slipped through Dragonkeep's gardens, even sampling fruits from some and finding their tastes familiar.

Yet even the substance of the Shadowfast trees, he notes, is totally other. Their rinds are less like wood than some kind of diseased crust. Almost as if the trees are no longer trees but the shells of that disease.

Phariane has told Harnak that the Shadowfasts were thrown up, barely ahead of the rise of Shadow, by practitioners of powers gained from old knowledge.

"But such powers are close to madness and the Shadowfasts mirror such closeness..."

And then Harnak sees something.

The cliff of the Shadowfast is not quite sheer, and is rucked and cleaved.

Phariane climbs steadily. The sweat filming her springs from effort and concentration, not nervousness. She looks down at the dragonreme. The sweet stench off the tarnished scar is sickening, but she's almost at the top. She looks down at the dragonreme. Do they really want to make a home here? Is their fear so great? Has she failed them so completely?

A piece of the brittle yellow-grey face comes away at her touch. It skitters past the Wolf-ward who is climbing after her. His movements are less steady, less confident, but there's no alarm in his face as he looks up.

Looping each of their bodies, from shoulder to opposite hip, is a winding of silken rope. Once on the plateau a rope will be lowered and the harnessed wolf hauled up.

The three of them, four with Harnak, will scour the plateau until Phariane is sure of its safety.

As Phariane has told Harnak, the Shadowfasts were thrown up, barely ahead of the rise of Shadow, by practitioners of powers gained from old knowledge.

But such powers are close to madness, and the Shadowfasts mirror such closeness.

Below, beneath the Shadowfast's forest's thick, twisted canopy, on the runneled mulchy ground, Harnak sees something humped. Something of stone. Or rather something of stones, lumps of what look like greisen, piled on each other. A cairn.

Even with his sharp sight, Harnak might never have noticed it in the canopied gloom, if not for the movement. As he hovers in his hummingbird form, a second stone slides off the cairn. Harnak feels the hooded beat of an emotion he has encountered before. He darts away.

The children have stared unmoving since Phariane pulled herself up onto the top of the Shadowfast. While the Wolf-ward joined her. While he let down his rope and hauled his harnessed wolf up the cliff. It's only now, with the wolf freed, that they step forward.

They're some ten years in appearance, a boy and a girl. Their loins are hairless. Their smooth skin delineates their bones softly. Their eyes are dull, depthless, and Phariane doesn't believe they could ever be haunted.

The child figures come forward. The hoar-grey's hackles stir. Its ward places a steadying hand on its head. They come forward and Phariane and her companions have no way to move back. Instead they skirt sideways at the Shadowfast's edge. Wolf and Wolf-ward now return the child figures' stare as Phariane has done since her head lifted above the cliff. Feet and bodies feel inconsequential in comparison, as if the five are circling where their eyes meet. Phariane hopes her gaze has been as firm and unchanging as the child figures'. But the crushing sensation in her heart is veined with burning now, as she realizes that their gaze is changing. Something in their faces is sharpening. Something is stirring. Something is coming.

No wind blows over the Shadow. Harnak has accepted as much. But now something is following his hummingbird as he darts and veers between the tree boles. Something chill, slithering through the trees as if it stalks something.

Whatever is going to happen ripples in Phariane's perception, about to burst. The child figures' faces are now pinched wasp-like malevolence. The two groups - Phariane, the wolf and Wolf-ward - the brother and sister if brother and sister they are - have almost circled. The child figures now stand with their backs to the edge of the Shadowfast. The others have their backs to the forest.

The moment snaps like a sting.

The girl figure's eyes widen, and the wolf suddenly goes at her, flowing like hoar-grey quicksilver - and a hummingbird drills out of the forest into the starlight - and the wolf's jaw fastens on the girl figure's throat - and there is a sound, though it's impossible for Phariane to say if it's a snarl and which of them it comes from - and wolf and girl figure carry off the brink of the Shadowfast.

And still their stares stay locked.

The boy figure's own eyes, which were also widening, recede. Fade. He breaks his own stare, turns and leans over the edge of the cliff as if to watch. But he keeps leaning. Until his body, without twisting or flailing after balance, simply tips over and disappears.

Harnak stands for a moment, a lithe, rangy man now, slick with sweat, ribs and chest rising and falling. He speaks calmly but quickly to Phariane. He looks back at the forest and speaks of the cairn, and of how something has come from it. As he speaks a matted mass of canopy stirs in the distance and something soughs along beneath it, moving closer.

Phariane goes to the edge of the forest and ties a rope to the outermost bole. She takes the rope back to the brink of the Shadowfast and tosses the unravelling coil down. Its end comes to a stop, jouncing barely above the Shadow. The dragonreme nestles against the Shadowfast, a small pale disturbance in the vast ocean of dark.

Phariane turns and strides over to the Wolf-ward. He hasn't moved since his wolf plunged over. She reaches a hand to his shoulder. He turns without looking at her and both of them begin to descend the rope, feet scraping against the yellow-grey cliff, scuffling off more brittle sickly-smelling shards.

Harnak stands at the edge and watches them. He glances over his shoulder one last time at the dankly bristling patch of convulsion coming tearing through the trees and raises his long sinewy arms.

Phariane and the Wolf-ward are almost half way down the Shadowfast when they feel the feathery rush of a white tern diving past them.

Pulling away from the Shadowfast, stroke by surging oarstroke, everyone on the dragonreme can see the figure on the clifftop. It has a straggling eruption of hair like the forest itself. It has the shape and manner of an old, old man. And it rages. It shambles along the cliff edge, back and forth, back and forth, as the dragonreme slips further away. Its head jerks and twists broken-necked as it rends its monstrous hair.

And it screams, the cries ragged, their edges ripped.

Phariane and Harnak wonder if the old figure is the father of the child figures, or if indeed they are the begetters of the old one. Perhaps one or all three raised the Shadowfast long ago. Things are rarely as they seem in such places. The Shadowfasts are creations of powers close to, and sometimes more than close to madness...

All the way back to Dragonkeep the Wolf-ward says nothing. His eyes are open but hooded inwardly as is the way with his people. He hardly moves on the deck but, when he does, it seems as if he does so with a suggestion of something by his side - or missing from his side.

Once he tilts his head back and gives one piercing howl, crystalline with grief, into the stars. It ceases rather than fades. There's no wind to carry it away.

Chapter Twenty-Six

When the second stone slides off the cairn on the Shadowfast it is night in Dragonkeep.

Again he has stolen out of the archive. The Blade-ward are no challenge, more concerned with preventing entry than exit. And although he lacks the advantages of Harnak, he has the same stealth.

Also like Harnak, though less at ease within it, he loves the night. It comes only once in a generation to his realm. Darkness is treasured, hoarded in cool windowless chambers, but night, true unfamiliar night, is both worshipped and mistrusted.

He slides into it because he must. Because the hunger demands it. It begins beyond the fingers, then through them and the hand and the arm, and eventually the hunger soaks him. It feels like despair.

He restlessly prowls the city. Through streets and porticos and gardens, past water cisterns and over ramps and stairways. Passing motionless querns dotting deserted plazas. Stabled horses snort. He is crossing one of the few tells, the highest places in the city other than the archive and the amphitheatre, when he sees the glimmer.

There is meant to be little of that in the nights here. Light means dragonflame and dragonflame is a sacred thing. It's not darkness but day which is treasured here, and the flame gives it to the city. When the braziers are returned to the dragonmouth each evening few tongues of illumination are suffered to remain. The archive, because of its revered status, is allowed several. The Blade-ward in the present times of unrest, are also given possession. But he can see, as he steals closer, that these figures are not Blade-ward. There are some twenty, twenty-five, standing by one of the city's many arches. Only one holds a lantern. This is not one of the fine, silver cages in which flutterings of yellow flame are usually ported. This is a rough copper can. The light seeps from crude punctures. To steal dragonflame is sacrilegious, to keep it in such a vessel doubly so.

The figures carry long rods, and he waits, watches to see what they do with them. But his curiosity is already dwindling. He runs his fingers along the edge of something as sharp as the hunger. The expected sweet panic starts to bubble through his senses. He tastes blood, but not with his tongue.

When Phariane returns from the Shadowfast, it is still night within Dragonkeep. She stands wearily in front of the broken arch. In the light of the Blade-ward lanterns she looks at each piece of stone. She tries to put back together, at least in her mind, the frieze that lies in chaos at her feet. There are no statues in Dragonkeep. This was decided in the days of its founding. The body of the dragon was still softly and slowly transforming into rock and gem, into dolomite or granite or rhyolite, into jade and jasper and azurite and lapis-lazuli. The founders with little more than hands began sculpting the roads and then the buildings. But it was agreed there would be no statues. No idols to worship. No tall symbols of old faiths or old wars in old lost lands to stir unease in Dragonkeep. Instead they raised and shaped arches, decorated them with scenes of the time of Uroboros to come. Forewarnings. Reminders of the purpose of the city's people. A symbol of hope that one day the Shadow would recede.

Phariane stoops and takes hold of a stone. The arches are shaped of sarsen. Harder than granite. In time ancient before the Shadow, flint was whetted on sarsen. The Blade-ward, she is told, arrived too late to prevent the damage. But even if the desecrators had strong rare iron - tools stolen from the metal workings in the dragon's fiery mouth, "they should not have been able to do this to sarsen," she whispers.

But the Uroboros is close, she realizes. This is a time of change. What was not always stone may soften again. She remembers the faces of the child figures on the top of the Shadowfast – watching them change - how it reminded her of Harnak. She remembers, more unwillingly, how she recognized that something about them, about the power within them. How it reminded her of herself.

The Blade-ward around her are now panoplied from the city armoury in more than hawk-helm and gambeson. The golden lantern light sheens on the steel of pauldrons and cuisses and vambraces. For the people of Dragonkeep, her people, are changing too. This is not the first act of desecration since the Phoenix Prey arrived. But - she looks around her at the flesh-and-bone rubble strewn among the stone - these are the first deaths.

"Did you kill them?" she asks, for the lantern light falls on swordblades also, in the hands of the Blade-ward. Understandable if they did, she thinks, but no, they tell her. The desecrators were dead before the Blade-ward arrived. And she nods, because the human wreckage, the necks and limbs and torsos, have clearly been sundered by something even sharper than steel. And there's no blood.

Tears teeter in her eyes, for a crowd of reasons, but something colder than sadness stops them. She weighs the lump of sarsen in her hand. Dragonkeep itself is changing. Stirring.

Night has almost ended when Gel shoulders the doorframe of his chamber in the archive and gazes at his sleeping Dream-ward. A woman not old. Not young. The silver patterns in her hair dishevelled by the motions of her head on the pillow. She still angers him. Puzzles him. He's mocked her, hurt her, taken her with force – as is the way of princes in his realm. Yet she doesn't respond with fear in the way of slaves or even with hatred. She does not complain, or leave him. She stays. And if her duty is to guard his sleep why does she sleep herself?

Gel eases himself into the room and leans his body against the door to close it. Twin urges to laugh and sob shudder through his body. His robe is stained with blood, not drenched but rather finely sprayed as with mist. His skin is infused with a similar colour. The sweeping crescent heads of his ax, though dry and clean, almost glow crimson.

He leans on its pole and slides to the floor, not through weakness, onto all fours. Laying Bloodbane before him he strokes the crescent blades with the gentleness of a harpist caressing strings.

But the strains evoked only sound inside his mind. Screams. The cries of those whose lives the ax has taken that night. Ever since arriving at Dragonkeep he has kept the hunger in check - until tonight. He drives a hand against his gaunt but ruddy face, palm cushioning the pain, fingers clawing at the guilt. Suddenly a warm concerned arm is around his shoulders. And he knows that the Dream-ward is not asleep - was not asleep when he slipped out of their bed earlier - was not asleep on any of the other nights he slipped out of the bed.

But other voices, other screams rise to meet these newcomers. Bloodbane is old and has fed on epochs of blood. A thousand thousand ghosts swarm like flies about it, all screaming endlessly.

Chapter Twenty-Seven

"What is the soul?" The following evening, though still tired and troubled, Phariane asks the question at the second convocation.

There's no argument this time. No words at all. Instead Zantalliz, the last to leave the first convocation is the first to stand now, almost before the question is finished. With a quiet smooth swiftness he turns his slight shoulders and leaves the table. Phariane watches him go. She leans forward in her chair as if caught between staying or following him.

Phariane looks at Gel, but no snigger comes. He's unusually still. The uppermost prick of one of Bloodbane's crescents is laid thoughtfully beneath his throat.

Gemmored sits, fully healed, his scabbarded blade laid across his thighs. Unlike Gel, his glacial stillness is nothing more than usual.

Harnak's face, now the face of a wizened old woman, shows the subtle shifts in skin and eye and hair and bone that constantly play over her appearance, whatever it is. She too says nothing.

Phariane knows that her question about the soul has a meaning and a pain for each of them. The importance of it is not in any answer they might give her, but in the answers that they must silently give themselves.

With that, also silently, she answers a question for herself. She pulls back her auburn hair, which has now grown halfway down her back. She stands and follows Zantalliz.

Phariane goes along the cloister just below the mezzanine and enters one of the arches. One or two scholars peruse among the shelves. She ignores them.

The shelves she passes are stocked with leathern scrolls. The scrolls further on are parchment. By the time she reaches them she's beyond any light cast by the scholars' lanterns. Still she moves quickly and surely through the narrow passages crammed with words and symbols set on leather and parchment and papyrus and maguey and clay and velum.

She has no need of light, or to have seen the way Zantalliz went, to find him.

He stands before a section of lazuli tablets, holding one carefully in his hands. He studies its hieroglyphs with his strange eyes that need light no more than Phariane's.

She looks into those eyes and wonders what they might need,

hoping to see the same need she feels. She wonders how to tell.

Just a few days ago the arrival of Zantalliz and the others had the archive alive with eyes. Half of Dragonkeep it'd seemed. The coming of the Phoenix Prey had sent them scurrying here. Some came to consult texts they might have first studied years ago - chronicles, aetiologies, cosmogonies, eschatologies. Others came for the first time in their lives. But all searching for what's to come, for the truth, for hope. And now almost all are gone again. How quickly hope fades, thinks Phariane, or twists.

"Have you found what you were looking for?" she asks.

Zantalliz lifts his head and turns to her, responding without replying. "This is a fine library. Complex. Diverse. A good place for searching."

Phariane nods. Then, "There is a section I think may be of particular interest to you." She moves past Zantalliz for a few steps. Turns. He follows.

"There are thousands of accounts of times, places, lives, wars," she continues as she walks.

"Especially wars," says Zantalliz.

Phariane turns at right angle down a narrower passage of shelving. Scrolls and buckram spines.

"History is often blood," says Phariane.

"And legend is often darkness."

She turns again. Her hand trails lightly but not casually against metal tablets leaning one way on one shelf and the other on the next, chevrons of knowledge.

"There are thousands of languages collected here," says Zantalliz. "More than a single realm could contain."

"The archive is set out like Dragonkeep itself," Phariane responds without replying.

"Yes," says Zantalliz. "Avenues and streets..."

"Yes," says Phariane, "but Dragonkeep also has wynds."

Somewhere the shelving has strayed from straight, it now weaves. The change did not happen or begin, is outside happening or beginning. But soon they reach a part of the archive where the walls of books, tablets, scrolls and solanders bow out and recurve almost sinuously.

"Not many know how to find their way here," says Phariane. She stops. Her back becomes still. She pulls out a beresty manuscript of bark. Eyes lowered, she presses it against her chest and breathes. "These are my favourite," she murmurs. "They remind me of forests." She glances at Zantalliz. "The knowledge we both have comes from both book and forest." She holds out the long strip of ancient bark with its cuneal inscription, stares at it. Her mouth gestures with the barest of movements.

The sharp angles of the stylus marks begin to soften. To stretch. To change.

Phariane's lips close and the symbols shrink back and stiffen into their old shapes.

There's something new in Zantalliz' eyes.

Phariane hastily pulls out something from another shelf. A large gilt-edged book of bound vellum pages, almost as fine as silk. She opens it and offers it to Zantalliz.

The symbols on the vellum are looping and swirling in style. They intertwine with the border designs so intricately that not even the closest of study can be sure where illumination ends and text begins. Especially since both are laid not only in vivid inks but gold and silver leafs. Zantalliz brushes a hand down one page. Even the textures are pleasing.

He remembers the archives of his own people in the realm of Voyage. Regret, sadness, pain - none of these are tainted emotions, all might be allowed. Yet he has allowed no other since the Phoenix plucked him from Voyage. Since his people died.

Perhaps now...

The book reminds him not of forests, but the caverns and grottos of his isle, coraled with niches filled with scrolls of rayskin and tablets of bone and books bound in driftwood and shell. Nowhere in the Dragonkeep shelves has he found books like those.

But perhaps...

His lips slowly part, breaking a seal of dryness. Then, just as slowly, they start to move, hesitantly to shape questioning whispers. And although this book is leather and vellum rather than shell and silk, first the silver, then the gold leaf on the pages begin to twitch.

Oh.

These are indeed like his own people's scripts. The texts in the rest of the archive are fixed in the languages, the grammars of human knowledge. But these hold the strangely shifting knowledge that is his, and now he realizes is also Phariane's. Mankind desires yet fears it, calls it madness among other names, but it's simply that there is no order, no grammar to this thing.

Now the inks on the pages are becoming iridescent, swaying, reaching out from symbol to symbol.

Oh.

"Archives are places to search out truths," says Phariane, "but sometimes they can be used to escape them, to hide from them."

She regrets the words as soon as they're spoken, but then sees that Zantalliz hasn't heard. He stares deep into the swirling shapes on the book he holds. Phariane is unsure whether to be pleased or not. There is so much more she'd wanted to say. But perhaps if she waits.

There are things to say to the other Phoenix Prey, also. She believes that it was Gel who killed the desecrators of the arch and should explain to him that in Dragonkeep there is no punishment for one of the Phoenix Prey, no matter what they do. She knows that Harnak is also troubled, though in subtler ways. Even Gemmored. She needs to speak to them all. But not now. Now is her and Zantalliz.

He's moved one hand beneath the spine of the book and uses the other to turn the pages. His agile fingers brush the edges so softly, almost beckoning them rather than turning them. She reaches out and takes this hand. Still he stares into the book. On this page thin ribbons of interlinears appear, fade, reappear, coalesce into the other symbols. She slowly guides his hand towards her. Its back is smooth to the touch as well as the eye, with only the slightest ridging of veins. Slowly, slowly she brings the tips of his forgotten fingers to her lips and holds them there.

And then she hears something.

It's not so much a sound. Nor something glimpsed. Or detected with any other sense of the common five. But she's connected to the archive in such a way that she knows that something is wrong and knows where it's happening.

She runs headlong through the passages of shelves without disturbing so much as a single tablet or scroll or beresty. Without so much as brushing a binding of a book. Her breath is half pant and half sob, still stinging from tearing herself away from Zantalliz, furious at having to. Her kris is already drawn.

She turns a final corner and the anger vanishes.

He's so young. Hardly a man. Like the rest of the male Blade-ward, he has remained unshaven since the coming of the Phoenix Prey, sworn to do so until the Uroboros. Yet his jaw is barely feathered with beard. So young.

He kneels with a papyrus scroll in one hand and a small canister wrapped in cloth in the other. The top of the canister is hinged back and flickering out is a sliver of flame. White flame. It would not have been hard for him to steal it from the dragon's mouth, even in such wary times. He is Blade-ward. Trusted.

But Phariane can see from his face, his so young face, that he is scared, confused. Even if he could succeed in what he is trying to do, she could still forgive him.

He holds the flame under the scroll, almost touching it. Yellow flame, like the tongue in the lamp by his side, is for light. White is for burning. "Burn," he mouths, "burn," as if raising the archive, destroying every word here would turn back the Uroboros. "Burn..."

But the flame only forks, flows around the rolled papyrus.

The Blade-ward still is unaware of Phariane. His face is wet with sweat from the pure effort of willing the scroll alight. She waits silently, her breath quiet again. A dragon's fire will not burn the dragon, and the archive and every book and tablet and scroll in it are part of the dragon in a way Phariane understands. She waits for him to understand too.

Each step of Harnak's Dream-ward is carefully taken. Although he's transferred the yellow light-giving flame from the tripod in Harnak's chamber to a lantern, still he descends the steep caracol uneasily. He has never before been in the vaults underneath the archive. He wipes the back of his free hand across his damp forehead then pushes his fingers through his tangle of hair.

He steps off the stairway onto the floor of the third vault. Lifting the lantern he looks around quickly. Glazed amphorae fill this chamber as they do the two above. The young man turns back to the caracol as if to descend further, then pauses. Instead he steps deeper into the chamber, into the midst of the amphorae, which reach to his waist. He lifts the lantern and looks more carefully about.

After a moment he grows still. His eyes slowly drop to his other hand which rests on the edge of an amphora. A small black shape glistens there, but not with the sheen of glaze. Pincers twitch. A slim segmented barbed tail arches out of the back.

At the sight of the scorpion the Dream-ward takes in a breath. His mouth widens with delight.

In a moment, a naked version of the tow-headed Dream-ward stands next to the clothed. It leans a hip against the nearest amphora and folds its arms.

"How did you know that I wasn't a true scorpion?" says Harnak.

Immediately Harnak had transformed, the Dream-ward had turned slightly away and stared uneasily at the floor. Yet he jerks a moment's grin at the question.

"There are no scorpions in Dragonkeep?" Harnak continues.

"Oh yes," nods the Dream-ward, setting down his lantern, "and all in this chamber. But all of them sleep."

"One might've woken," says Harnak.

"No," says the Dream-ward as he pulls his plain linen shift over his still-averted head. "It's not time yet. Though soon."

"And where do they sleep?" says Harnak.

The Dream-ward picks up his lantern and makes a sweep of it toward the amphorae. Head still bowed, he offers his shift to Harnak and continues. "Have you seen trees in Dragonkeep?"

"Of course. Some like the trees of my realm, some very different."

"And flowers?"

"Again, some I know, some not."

"And cats?"

"And horses."

"And bees?"

"And tasted their honey."

"But there are many fruits and beasts of all kinds," says the Dream-ward, "that you've not seen."

"I know there are cattle because I've eaten meat. And I know there are silk-worms despite this," says Harnak, fingering the Dream-ward's linen shift but still not taking it. He has no need of it. He's not really naked. "But I thought most living things of this realm had been lost to the Shadow."

"Some," says the Dream-ward. "But many are stored here, in these chambers. In these containers."

They both look down into the nearest amphora, but even held over it the lantern light somehow fails to penetrate. From within comes the smell of the chamber at its most overpowering - moist, rich, but not the smell of decay. Harnak reaches a hand toward the amphora's mouth. The Dream-ward looks almost alarmed, but makes no protest. Nevertheless Harnak hesitates.

"Seeds? Eggs?"

"Seeds of a kind," says the Dream-ward. "Eggs of a kind. Life in abeyance. Biding."

"Awaiting the Uroboros?" says Harnak.

"Awaiting its outcome," nods the Dream-ward, "to see if there's any use for life..."

The Dream-ward slowly looks up at Harnak, for the first time since Harnak has retaken human form – the Dream-ward's form. He still holds his shift in his free hand. Still unaccepted, it leaves both of them naked. "Is that why you came here," he asks, "to find this out?"

Harnak shakes his head. "I came for what was here before you came, with your lamp. You've taken darkness and brought something else."

"Light," says the Dream-ward.

"And shadow," says Harnak. "One causes the other."

"I can take the light away," says the Dream-ward, turning, but Harnak takes hold of his arm.

He changes without letting go of the Dream-ward's arm. The transformation is not drastic. A slight melting of appearance. The frame becomes a little shorter and tauter, the shoulders broader, the hair sandy, the skin tawny. There are no subtle shifts as there are with other shapes he takes. No minute flickering of eye colour. No ghosting flux of bone.

Harnak no longer smiles. Now he really is naked.

He folds his arms across his chest, taking hold of his shoulders, then turns. His back is a mass of barely healed welts and cicatrix of older wounds like horizontal spines.

"Even if you took the light you would still leave shadows," he murmurs.

Chapter Twenty-Eight

Once again Sstheness sits on the serrated throne in the cold chamber with the murk-bottomed pit. Again Rorn, the fifth Phoenix Prey, lies like a beaten animal beside her. Again a figure stands before her. But this time it's a woman rather than a man, and no skull-casqued warriors restrain her.

Rather the woman stands still and calm before the pit. She's bare in the cold tallow candlelight. In front of her are placed boots, breeks, a plastron, a cape, and a sword shaped like a sickle.

"The Uroboros comes," Sstheness says to her, "and in that battle loyalty will be valued above all." Sstheness taps her face with her fingerstalls, the needle ends of the long sigils contemplatively pricking her chin. "Are you loyal, daughter of Leviathan?"

"I am," says the woman. Rorn gives a sound that might be a cough or a snigger, but is unambiguously bitter rather than defiant.

"Loyal enough to join those I trust most?" says Sstheness, ignoring him.

The woman nods, raising her head and letting it fall slightly.

One of Sstheness' sigil-thorns lifts from her cheek, leaving a pin wound of red. The finger stretches out, curls back. Beckons.

Rorn watches the woman walk around the pit. He glimpses the murk stirring as she does so - darting twitches of movement.

She bends to pick up something on the dais in front of Sstheness - a gaping skull. Her dugs pend forward as she stoops. If not fat, certainly not spare, considers Rorn. And not tall. Every skull-casque Rorn has seen in Leviathan has been these things.

As she reaches for the skull its mouth snaps shut. Her hands stop and there is a moment sharper than silence. Rorn is impressed that she does not look up at Sstheness. Then she takes it by the sides and the mouth slowly hinges wide again, as though mocking.

Rorn watches her retrace her path around the pit. No, he thinks, most certainly not spare. She stands where she did before, this time with the skull held over her head. As she lowers it Rorn searches her face for fear but finds none.

Sstheness leans over to him as if she knows. "Doubt," she says, "is punishable by death in Leviathan."

Then she turns to the woman and calls, "Who wear the clothes and sword at your feet?"

Before the jaw of the skull descends over her eyes she smiles. "Those of the Death'shead Cadre."

Then her head is encased by the skull to her neck. Her arms drop to her sides. She stands still and calm. Then the jaw snaps shut. Her throat jerks, a wild solitary movement of her body. Then a sound. A creaking. A creaking of bone. And then her hands fly up to the skull again and she's twisting and curling and arching as if the convulsion in her throat has exploded through her body. And catches her foot in the cape lying at her feet and staggers to the very edge of the pit and again its lost depths thrash. And her dugs and thighs quiver as she struggles. And blood trickles and bubbles from the skull's eye-sockets and jaw. And another sound weaves in and out of the creaking. A whine.

And then she falls to her knees. And it's over.

"And who are the Death'shead Cadre?" murmurs Sstheness.

The woman goes down onto her hands, reaches over for the sickle-sword and uses it to lever herself back to her knees. She lifts her skull casqued head and the jaw drops open again and moves. Her voice is different. Hollow. A resonance of echo.

"We are the skull beneath the skin, the steel beneath the skull..."

She climbs to her feet and Rorn sees that she is taller, sparer than before.

Then he feels the familiar prickling graze of Sstheness' sigil-thorns in his hair - finds his head wrenched up and Sstheness' tongue in his mouth.

"Hungry?" she says when she withdraws it. Without waiting for an answer she pulls Rorn to his feet and out of the ribcage surrounding the spinal seat. The ribs, curling inward, require even more pain in egress than in access. Wounds reopened, they leave the cold chamber with the serrated throne and the murk-bottomed pit while the new member of her Death'shead Cadre continues to dress.

The bloodless vessels and lifeless nerves, which make up Leviathan's narrow labyrinths, are even colder. Like the various darknesses Rorn has experienced since coming to this realm, there seem to be an equal spectrum of colds. The chill in the labyrinths is more active than that in the hollow varices, cysts and tumours that are the sea-wyrm's chambers. There's no draught as such, of anything as obvious - or wholesome - as air. But something makes it bitter. Something part of the mixture of decay, tumescence, slime, and razors that is Leviathan.

There is a spectrum of dread, too, that for Rorn is part of the wyrm-city. The one he feels now is not the greatest, but by no means petty. It is not the apprehension of an unknown but of a known. Sstheness has dragged him this way every day since he's been strong enough. Citizens of Leviathan who are licking the weepings from the labyrinths' stillbirth walls turn and leer at him as he stumbles past. They know where Sstheness is taking him. So does he.

Finally the twisting, gradually descending journey is done. They reach the longest vertical slash of any Rorn has seen in the walls. The tallest gateway. Sstheness tears it open fiercely and hurls him through into a chamber Rorn knows only too well.

Again there is a different cold. Bleak. Vast. Filled with moans. The chamber stretches into the distance, and throughout that length, hanging from the vaulty ceiling, are the same fleshy stalactites that strew the labyrinths. Except these are longer. And from them hang bare bodies. Men. Women. Children. Living. Moaning.

The tendril-things curl around their necks, holding them just above the floor. Others meander among them. Gazing up at them. Nudging them so that they turn slightly. Pinching them. Considering. Because these tendrils, unlike human umbilical cords, not only nourish but leach. They give life to the suspended ones but at the same time soften tissue, suck bone brittle - until the time is right. This is what they're considering, the free ones - if the time is right. Sstheness too, beside him, pushing him along.

They finally come to one. A young man, around Rorn's age, though with fair rather than the umber-dark hair of the Waste-Ranger. He's pallid, but all the hanging ones are pallid. Sstheness takes his hand. She looks up at him and perhaps he looks down at her. It's impossible to tell as his lids are drooped almost shut. Sstheness lays her other hand on his wrist and still his eyes don't widen. Her thumbs, just the thumbs, stroke. So gently. The sigil-thorns don't even touch the flesh. She smiles, and starts to twist. The sound reaches into Rorn's stomach and twists that too - the gristly stretching and ripping of human fibre. The stretching sound gives way to the ripping. The young man begins to moan. Softly. It remains soft even when the sound is joined by the cracking of bone. No scream. Of all the places in Leviathan there are no screams here. Only moaning, and the occasional laughter that echoes across this long chamber differently than through the labyrinths.

As the arm comes away there is only a piddling spurt of blood, the young man's heart being as enervated as the rest of him.

Rorn watches Sstheness bring the meaty bloody shoulder of the arm up to her mouth. He suspects that with her unnatural power she could well have twisted it off even if the hanging one had been strong and whole. In the middle of disgust he enjoys the moment's frisson of helplessness.

"We are all cadaverous fruit," she says, still chewing, "with a worm at the heart."

She swings the stump around into Rorn's face. An offer. He shakes his head.

Somewhere in this vast hall, once the intestine of the giant sea-wyrm and now the feeding gallery of Leviathan, a snigger spits into full laughter and echoes...

Before they can fade a messenger rushes up to Sstheness. A young girl. Spindly and flushed. She sprawls on her front, narrow back heaving in breathlessness. Sstheness discards the arm and hunkers before her, grasps her hair, pulls the girl's mouth up to her ear and listens to the spittle-lipped whisper.

Then Sstheness is gone. Rorn watches her rush through the hanging garden of living corpses, hurling or striking casual feeders out of her way, disappearing through the gateslash into the labyrinths.

He hears grumous jabs of chewing and sees the messenger urchin attacking the discarded arm. He turns to her. She stares back at him with feral apprehension, drops her meal and runs.

The fair-haired suspended one still moans, though faintly. The ragged shoulder has already stopped leaking. Soon, in a few days, the arm will begin to regrow - as it has done time after time. Why did they do it, Rorn wonders. When men first invaded and carved their city out of the sea-wyrm did the suspended ones volunteer for this fate or were they chosen and forced? To feed the populace of Leviathan forever, never dying.

Rorn looks at the torn arm and knows that eventually, like all other discarded flesh from the suspended ones it will be collected and rendered for the tallow that makes the candles that flutter in the chills and the darknesses of the city. But he knows another thing. That thought curdles in his mind and his stomach. He is hungry. And he will eat.

He looks up at the suspended one and asks a hopeless question, expecting no answer.

"Is the cold dark or the dark cold?'"

Sstheness strides fiercely through Leviathan. She runs the sigil-thorns of one hand along the walls as she goes. The fingerstalls are in a way part of her. They grow. The only way to keep them pared is to claw them against the stony surfaces of the sea-wyrm's heart chamber.

But apart from the spatter of viscously sharp scabs, the labyrinth walls are pulpy rather than hard. The talons simply sink through as they rake along. Even beneath is only a black crusty chitin that the sigils rasp against uselessly.

But Sstheness pays no heed to this. The message occupies her fully. Dragonkeep sighted again. So soon after the last. Evidence that the Uroboros grows ever nearer. But the sky-wyrm has not increased its speed or turned in its course. So it may be that though Leviathan has sighted Dragonkeep, Dragonkeep may not have sighted Leviathan.

So...

She might dispatch the Shadow Corsairs, but the Corsairs are wild and undisciplined, not given to stealth... The Death'shead Cadre are far more loyal... But there is another cadre at her command, beyond loyalty, beyond stealth.

Chapter Twenty-Nine

They stream out of Leviathan, out over the Shadow, rushing for Dragonkeep. They need no ships. They ride the storm. They are the storm. The storm is not lightning, or thunder, but moans and sobs and shrieks - and even these are silent.

As they pass, even the Shadow flickers for a moment.

They go swiftly, far more swiftly than Dragonkeep. The sky-wyrm moves differently than Leviathan. The sea-wyrm ploughs on changelessly, while the sky-wyrm - not home in sea or Shadow - pulses forward.

The storm is almost upon Dragonkeep now. They approach at the tail, but even if they rushed at its very snout, at the glittering chalcedony and fire snarl of the Beckoning Gate, or at the huge eye craters where watch is always kept, they would still not be seen.

They need no rams to breech the dragon. They will pass through jade scales unhindered, through streets and walls unchallenged, into the sleeping bluestone archive, infesting it, curling between strokes of ancient ink, sinking into the grooves of clay or wood or lazuli tablets, burrowing into the coils of scrolls, wrapping themselves around runes and symbols and sigils, and finally slip, unresisted, into dreams.

Gemmored:
Through a gnarling blizzard, Gemmored glimpses
one of the mighty ice-block fortresses of his folk,
high on one of the jokuls of the northern reaches of his realm.
Home. As a child he sits in its huge hall,
warmed by kindled blubber and furs and hundreds of kin,
aware of the winds bawling outside. Listening to words.

Stories of elder time. Stories of sombre gods.

As a child he sees those words seethe forge-red,
blinks at the splintery flashes that fling from the
thunderous blows of a hammer hard against an anvil.
He hears the words quieten as they describe the smith –
a dark giant figure with a brooding star of glimmer
beneath his brow. As a child he hears the words erupt
into cataracts of hiss as a candescent newborn sword
is plunged into water. Stories.

Now Gemmored sees himself as a giant, grown,
a bear-pelt horizoning mountainous shoulders,
a broad blade in his hands, ambitions of sojourning south
to fight in wars already forming in his young thoughts.
He sees himself undertaking that trek, but finding himself
lost in a lurking mist, known by his people of the ice-wastes
as the Shifting Despair. Few who wander within ever return.
He sees himself seeing the sword, settled on a cromlech
part ice and part eidolon, recognizing it by the pale scabbard
and the rubious gleam of gem that pommels the antler hilt.

Only possible in a dream,
he sees the look that formed on his face –
desire and terror.

He remembers remembering the story. How an elder god
in an elder war forged a blade for battle.
How huge and fine it was. How the god plucked an eye
from his head and set it on the end of the hilt.
How the sword would take from any it slew their battle skill,
pass the wiles on to the wielder of the warsword.
But also Gemmored remembers standing before the sword and considering
how stories are like rivers and sometimes tales fork.
How a different fork said that the elder god fixed
his soul upon the sword, that this soul was tainted,
and that it was this dark pupil-like defect within
which made it wear the semblance of an eye.

He remembers remembering how the two forks of the tale converge
to tell how the blade, through the eye or the soul,
takes into itself not just the battle skill of those it slays.

How it harvests their evil.

And how for this reason,
above all others,
the sword was named 'Doom'.

Gemmored dreams himself standing in the Shifting Despair,
before the sword in the cist of part ice and part eidolon.
He dreams himself balancing the desire and terror:
pride in the mythic past of his people,
descended from the warriors who fought beside the elder gods,
weighed against a presentiment that feels like
a shivering draught drawn across infinity.
He sees his hand
reaching for the sword.

Harnak:
Harnak has long believed that all his dreams have been tortured out
but among the dull scrawls of sense now seeping into his sleep
he dreams of his realm of Aftermath and the city of angled spires.

He dreams of the shackles biting his wrists, of the sweltering
odours of heated coals and cresset pitch, of streaks of fire
laid across his back, in the city of angled agate spires.

Harnak has long believed that all his dreams have been tortured out
in this way. This is the way, in the realm of Aftermath
that someone like Harnak is trained. Those who can shed their shape

in the city of angled agate spires, are shaped by the whip.
Each generation such children are taken. All but one put to death.
That one to become a servant, a weapon, ideal dreamless assassin.

Shape-shedders lack the secret inner part possessed by men
so can never know guilt. Nor loyalty. This must be taught by the whip.
In chambers such as the one that Harnak dreams of.

There are fifteen whips in the chamber beneath the palace of the city
and each is a different fineness of leather, he recalls,
each imparting a different nuance of fire, a different precept.

The finest teaches loyalty and is a favourite of the prince.

This is the way of the city – the lessons of the lash must be taught
by a prince of the city of angled agate spires.

Each whip has a different hiss as it slithers through the sweltering air
so even before the first stroke lands in Harnak's dream
Harnak knows the lesson his back is about to receive.

Harnak's screams are silent but they always echo the cries of
Harnak's parents, put to the sword by the city's guards while
their child is dragged away through the city of angled agate spires.

This is the one way that Harnak knows that this is a dream.
Because he stopped screaming, even silently, long ago.
And now the screams are not even Harnak's

but lacerating cries that sound as if they have prized open the air to be born,
keening shrieks swirling in the spireless ruin of a forbidden ringfort
pushing out of a pampa where not even grass would grow.

Harnak remembers then, standing inside that carious tooth of rubble,
wondering if the cries were of pain, or mirth, or something else...
and not caring.

Harnak remembers speaking, whispering, yelling
in the spireless ruin of the forbidden ringfort,
hurling at the voices til they quieted - and listened.

Harnak can see himself this time, of course, in the dream.
But he still cannot see the owners of the voices since
when he invaded their fortress his eyes were rammed shut.

He knew the lore of the place, knew what sight of the ragers would bring.
Oh, they asked him to look, he remembers, wheedled and threatened and cajoled
after he talked, after he struck his bargain with them.

All the while as he led them across the dust-pampa
toward the city of angled agate spires.
They tempted, taunted, pleaded for him to look.

But he had planned his vengeance for so long.
So he does not, did not look behind.
But he remembers looking down.

Under the sunless, perpetually dusky glow of Aftermath's sky
shadows are no more than dim stubs of circles around the body.
Yet the shadows of the voices stretched out across the dust like cold, black scars.

Chapter Thirty

Phariane's chamber in the archive is no different to those of the
Phoenix Prey. The measure is no larger. The furnishings are the same,
the bed, the settle, except for a table and chair. Except that the lick of
dragonflame hovers above her bed rather than in a tripod. The flame
is still, a smooth spindle of yellow which glows calmly in contrast to
Phariane beneath. She has always been a restless sleeper. Even before
the Phoenix Prey and all they've brought. She shifts vaguely in the
bed. Her hair, almost the length of her body, slides and fans and
tangles uneasily across books and scrolls abandoned on the sheets.

Then her head stops in mid-turn. Her bare arm, drifting across her
studies, goes still, and the dragonflame begins to quiver.

She sits up and listens.

Chapter Thirty-One

Gel:
Gel listens in his dream,
but does not hear what he expects.
Awake or asleep
he always hears them scream.

Ah, but he dreams of a time now dim
so perhaps that is why.
Before he found the labrys Bloodbane,
before the labrys Bloodbane found him.

He dreams of the Sun Skein,
a maze of electrum
above the cool onyx palace buried in the sands
where Gel is a warrior princeling thegn.

Gel dreams a rare sight –

the Sun Skein in darkness.
Such a thing happens once in a thousand sky weavings,
when all three of Gnomon's fierce suns have fallen into night.

The rays of even one of these,
reflecting and multiplying among the electrum,
is enough to turn the light too bright to bear,
the air too hot to breathe.

Only at a time of threefold setting
is it possible to enter the ancient maze.
Here the royal houses of the onyx palace beneath
place their dead, bedecked in jewelling.

And it is here,
on this long past night dreamed by Gel,
he sees himself placed –
not dead, but near.

In the onyx court intrigue is tradition. Poison,
both verbal and liquid, part of etiquette.
The stiletto an instrument of politics.
Venom takes many forms in the realm called Gnomon.

Dreaming Gel looks down as his cousins of House Volquanon
drag his body through the maze.
In one of the three-sunned realm's rare nights
they have waited until almost the first sun's dawn.

There are no guards to evade or bribe or kill.
In the near-perpetual day of Gnomon grave-riches are protected
by blazing mirrored heat; but in the rare night are sentried
by superstitions of ancient evil.

This is Gnomon - stories are despised here
but the maze is known to be older than the onyx palace
or the royal lineages within, or the arid land they rule,
or even the gods they fear.

Thus, as soon as they have dragged Gel's body
a little way into the maze,
Gel's cousins fling it down,

spit on it, and pad away quickly.

Gel looks down from his dream, feeling neither pity nor rage.
He waits for what he remembers will come next - watches
until his bloody body uncurls, twitching in weak agony,
and begins to crawl - crawl blindly - further into the maze.

And now the dreaming Gel can hear them scream,
whereas the dreamt Gel is only vaguely aware.
And the dreaming Gel knows something
he never knew before the dream.

He has always believed it was blind chance's fall
that led him further into rather than out of the maze.
Now the dreamer knows that the dreamt was summoned
- that there came a call.

In a dream's moment, through the Skein,
he has crawled on his belly for an age - along tall, twisting,
roofless electrum corridors and is almost within reach
of the ancient labrys Bloodbane.

And as the dreamt Gel reaches,
with the last motes of life trembling at his bloody fingertips,
the dreaming Gel realizes that he's no longer watching
from above, but also reaching.

Then a single trembling fingertip touch
on one of Bloodbane's blades and the summoning sound that has been
so soft smashes into his brain. Like a thousand raking slivers of noise.
No. A thousand thousand. Countless such.

Gel - the only Gel now both Gels are one, the dreamt and the dreaming -
twists. Something flows into him and at the same time out.
He feels himself grow stronger,
stronger than he has ever been, his wound closing and healing.

A convulsion close to hysterical laughter shudders through him.
But at the same time,
almost unnoticed,
something tears and slips away from him.

A rill of something infinitesimal
but unimaginably precious
trickles
or rather is sucked into each labrys sickle.

Gel stands now,
Bloodbane's haft in one hand,
the other stroking the blades.
They are bound now.

Part of Gel's soul is locked within Bloodbane,
together with the souls of others.
Countless others.
The souls of all those the ax has slain.

The labrys is older even than the maze –
indescribably old – from a time in Gnomon
before the third sun bloomed, when armoured warriors
fought beneath kinder skies, cooler days.

The whimper of Gel's fragment of soul
is lost among the others - they do not mourn,
they feel too much despair for that - they scream.
Endlessly howl.

He will hear them scream from that moment, he knows it -
from that moment, until the moment in another realm in a hollowed
corpse of a dragon in a chamber in a crypt of useless scribblings,
where he will sleep - and dream of knowing it.

But somehow Gel knows that this is more
than a memory,
more than a dream.
That death here would be more

than something to be waked from.
He is less than certain that this time he will escape
before the first sun brinks and turns the mirrored maze feral with heat.
He begins to run.

Phariane runs along the archive cloister. She has no time to give
thought to her nakedness, nor bother clothing it. She can hear them,

the stealthy invaders from Leviathan, sliding through the shelves and walls of the archive. Hissing among the cloisters. Curled in the centres of scrolls. Murmuring against the falls of stairways. She reaches the doors of the Phoenix Prey's chambers. Gemmored, Harnak, Gel, all have protection, but Zantalliz...

She throws open the door and sees him lying in his bed, a gracile form tossing mutely beneath fine sheets. Even distressed his breaths are soft. The sight throws an ache through her that makes her pause. Then she slips between those sheets.

Zantalliz' body is damp. She can feel it through his shift. Also the restless line of his spine. She presses against it, reaches her arms around him, and finds his hands. A tiny moan of sound escapes his throat. She entwines her fingers with his, gently pulls them against his chest. Caresses him.

She touches her lips against his ear and whispers.

Zantalliz:
Zantalliz watches his dream unfold. It
is woven of uneasy sights,
but many of his dreams in the past nights have been so.

So it begins with a dark temple, a
manytowered claw of lichened mortar
raking at a sky equally dark.

Dark as a forest, a
deep pathless light-forsaken chaos
of towering tangleboughed claws.

Claws the dream, flickers from the one sight to the other, like
a sail bellying about from one side to the other
in a squall that snaps that way and this.

This is Zantalliz' realm of Voyage before it became Voyage. When
what it was before, was ending.
When the Shadow began to fall.

Footfalls like whispers - a woman
glides through the streets of the temple precincts
or through the forest.

Forest or flagstone, her face and body are lithe and wild. She
has long sleek flaxen hair. She
twists and sprints and slips into alleyways - or thickets sometimes.

Sometimes she is a cat. Even when she is not she
has the eyes of a cat. She runs from pursuers
that Zantalliz can only see vaguely and he is glad of that.

That way in which she runs, so
tauntingly fearlessly, makes it almost seem that she is stalking them.
She is a god.

A god emerging from a sea tinted with evening, or
perhaps dawn, onto a corralled reef
that Zantalliz recognizes.

Zantalliz recognizes a young man, fine-boned, almost
as lithe as she, but not a god,
walking along the reef toward her.

Her body is bare, they both are bare. Unsure
if they were so a moment ago,
Zantalliz watches.

Zantalliz watches the
evening-dawn tinting their skin,
pearls of sea still clinging to them.

They pull each other gently down, and
Zantalliz knows what he watches.
This is the birth of his people.

People descended from the coupling of a god and a man on
a remote and nameless isle. Because of this,
knowledge comes to them in dreams.

Dreams set down in books bound in scallop-shell and
tablets of bone ledged among reef coral,
set down in squid-tapped inks.

Inks able to hold dreams, pliant

enough to bend and flow with the tides of their power.
Because of this birth, Zantalliz' people will believe,

believe they lack the taint in the soul, the
taint that damages everything human.
They will decide which emotions are linked to that taint,

taint them in turn, codify a culture of manners that forbid such
feelings. And they will hide on their nameless isle for
generations upon generations, until...

until Zantalliz watches the young man's back and flanks
above those of the she-god, swaying back and forth,
back and forth, on the reef, until,

until he no longer looks at the man's back, but
into the face of the she-god,
her sleek flaxen hair woven against the coral,

the wonderful bones of her cheeks, parted
lips sending out warm urgent breath,
the strange, strange eyes that look back into his, dreaming.

Dreaming Zantalliz pulls away from that look, slowly
turns his gaze away from the she-god's face,
over the reef, out over the sea,

sea no longer ocean but sail: the
war-ships have come.
They are generations early, but dreams have no use for time.

In the dream Zantalliz looks back to the she-god beneath him, his
loins still swaying back and forth.
But the face he sees is no longer hers.

Her hair against the coral is auburn, the
bones of the cheeks not quite as exquisitely sharp,
and the eyes are different. And Zantalliz...

Zantalliz can still feel warm breath on his face, but
that breath is Phariane's.
She seems to be saying something, but he can hear nothing.

Nothing but breath and he feels himself tighten within
the dream - an ominous sensation mingles unpleasantly,
confusingly with the growing sweet surge from his loins. Ah!

Ah! He wrenches his face away again, but
this time the view of the war-ships is pillared
between two boots,

boots that Zantalliz' gaze travel up, over
mail to a helmed head glaring down at him.
The grim jaw shifts and a grin appears formed of teeth,

teeth the colour of scar-tissue. A sleek spearhead, pristine
in comparison, is poised just beside the grin.
The warrior's shoulders tense and the grin widens at Zantalliz.

Zantalliz girds himself for the pierce of iron – the
anticipation is as painful as the blow,
which never comes.

He finds himself back in his bed in the archive. Plucked from the
dream. The she-god and the young man and the war-ships and the
warrior are all gone. The only thing to remain is the breath, no longer
on his face but against his ear. The realization is more terrifying than
any spear thrust. He plunges from the bed with a cry, away from the
warmth pressed against his back.

On the floor he glances back at Phariane, catches the last moment
of hurt on her face before she smothers the expression. He feels a
moment's guilt. She has, he senses, saved him from something
terrible. But then he dismisses it - sympathy is not one of the
forbidden emotions, but is to be reserved for his own people.

Phariane throws the bed sheet off and grasps his arm. "Come," she
says, probably hoping that the urgency of her voice and action will
disguise what he can tell has become anger.

Gel:
Gel still runs through the electrum maze
though time in dreams is outside measure,
he senses that he should already be free

of the maze.

He runs faster,
twisting and plunging through angular ambages,
darting past ancient charred jewel-bedecked bones.
Faster.

On each side of him other Gels slide
in the mirrors of the Sun Skein's walls. Each Gel looks up
and sees that the night sky is not quite so dark.
And faster yet they glide.

Then something whispers sharply, clear.
Not one of the souls
of Bloodbane's slain.
Something incalculably distant yet almost behind his ear.

He spins. A reflection of movement slides across electrum
and disappears into the maze's next jag of direction.
Again Gel runs. With every turn the same reflection
slides out of sight ahead - just seen, glimpsed then gone.

Finally he utters a shout
sees the reflection slide out of the entrance of the Skein,
exactly as Gnomon's first sun
sends its first ray out.

His heel lifts as the ray touches the first electrum mirror,
deep in the Skein.
Before the rest of his foot is off the ground
the ray has split into a thousand spears of blinding sliver.

By the time Gel has covered half the distance to the gate
each of those thousand has split into a thousand more,
and those thousands split yet again and again, raking
and swarming throughout the maze, a blinding torrid spate.

And as Gel is one step from escape from the ancient gyre
a ray of furnace catches him.
And as he bursts from the maze
he can feel his back blister into fire.

And as he crashes into the waiting arms of care,
of his Dream-ward whose whisper he recognized
from the moment of its hearing,
and as he buries his face in the silvered dark of her hair

and they fall out of dreaming
and into Gel's bed,
waking
he can still feel his back burning.

Outside the dream, Gel is bathed in sweat and his body heaves to breathe. He looks down at his Dream-ward beneath him, watches the lines of her no-longer-young face relax. He lowers his face to hers, then stops.

"Do you hear that?" he says.

"Out in the atrium," she replies. And then, "Do you want to go and find out what it means?"

Gel grins and shakes his head. "Not yet," he says, and lowers his mouth onto hers.

His back still burns, but this time with the sensual sear of fingernails.

Harnak:
Harnak's dream has returned to the lash.
He feels each stroke on his back,
feels blood flowing down his back,

dreams the bite of each stroke
shred and flow into the pulsing smart
of the strokes that have come before.

Dreams blood and pain.
Flowing.
Blood and pain.

Blood and the sight of his mother and father
butchered for refusing to give him up
butchered by the guards of the city of angled agate spires.

Dreams blood and being told that a shape-shedder

is no more than a soul-bereft thing.
Blood and being told it again and again.

Blood and the look in the eye of a beautiful young citizen
as Harnak walks the streets
of the city of angled agate spires.

Blood and the word spat at him by a citizen, young or old,
beautiful or otherwise, time and again year after year
in the city of angled agate spires.

Blood and pain, flowing, flowing.
And Harnak hears something as he waits, in the dream,
for the slither of the next lash:

hears distant cries that skirt pain and mirth without becoming either -lacerating
cries that sound as if they have prized open the air to be born – approaching the
city of angled agate spires.

The voices of the ragers from the forbidden ringfort.
The voices are coming nearer, coming for him.
That is wrong, of course, not what happened.

Harnak remembers – he was the one to free the ragers,
to lead them to the city of angled agate spires.
They came for the prince, not him.

Harnak knows that in a dream memory is malleable, that things which
never happened can happen, that things which happened can be twisted
to happen in different ways. But even so.

A thought enters his mind that this is not the kind of dream
that torture exiled from him long ago. That if the ragers were to reach him
his suffering would extend beyond the dream.

For a moment he considers if he would care.
Blood and pain, flowing.
He doesn't know. He hasn't known for so very long.

He simply waits.
For the lash. For madness.
For whatever will burn across his back.

Blood and pain, blood and screams,
blood and hopes and hatreds and fears,
flowing, flowing, flowing.

And then something is pressing against his back,
but it doesn't burn.
It is hard and smooth and warm – and not dreamt.

Lying in his chamber bed, though his eyes stay closed, Harnak feels arms holding him and knows that his Dream-ward has rescued his life. Even outside the dream, he's unsure whether or not he cares.

"So when you came to find me, in the vaults, beside the amphorae - you knew I was not a scorpion," he yawns.

"Yes," murmurs the Dream-ward into his ear.

"I might've stung you even so," says Harnak.

The Dream-ward smiles. "You are Phoenix Prey."

After a while, Harnak finally opens his eyes. "Do you hear that?" he says.

"Music."

"It seems very dream-like."

"But it's not a dream," answers the Dream-ward.

And Harnak peels back the bedsheet and rises.

Gemmored:
Gemmored's dream churns into memories of carnage,
relives the first time he slays an enemy with the sword
Doom, how the warskill of that warrior enters him,
merges with his own - the elation. Elation at how his arm
answers to subtly altered instincts.

Then the inevitable realization that the rest of the legend
is also true - that those instincts
are not only swifter, slyer, but more savage.
He feels a wingless flutter beating through his blood.
Feels it settle uneasily upon some secret inner part of him.
And he watches himself as the dream spirals faster,
in battle after battle, each slaying
piling martial skill upon skill but also evil upon evil.
Until he sinks the sword back into its sheath,

a pale scabbard cut and sown of the elder god's flesh and hair.
Each time he does this the scabbard screams
and Gemmored feels all the gleaned skill and darkness flow out of him.
But still the spiral swirls - battle after battle, blood and darkness,
blood and darkness until he becomes towering berserk death,
and must plunge sword into scabbard before the secret inner part of him
is damaged or diseased. And he finds the dream change
as he reaches down for the scabbard and finds it gone.

This is no memory. This has never happened in his life,
though he has feared it every time he has drawn Doom.
And still the spiral churns. Faster still.
Blood and darkness and fear,
blood and darkness and fear,
blood and darkness and fear...

Then he finds himself standing in the centre of the maelstrom,
watching his own life. And she is there too. Before him.
Long golden hair weaving about a slender young neck in a way
no real storm would shape.
She holds her hand out to him as he once did to her in the archive.
His Dream-ward. The expression on her face,
her smooth oval face is hesitant as ever, Gemmored sees,
but then something changes.
He senses his swordarm lift,
or rather feels the blade rise and bring the arm with it.
It points slowly up her body, slender as her neck is slender,
fragilely armoured in a sheer shift
as white in dream as it is in true life.
He looks along Doom's massive length,
its chevron watering sleek and shimmering –
rippling toward her ribs.

Now that 'something' shifts in the Dream-ward's mien,
as she lifts her other hand to join the first,
setting one on each side of the sword.
Gemmored sees something
appear on her face behind her apprehension.
He considers it could be courage.
Or perhaps, Gemmored mulls, it might always have been there
and he has failed to fathom it?
Her lips work but Gemmored hears no words,

since the dream spiral of blood and darkness and fear
and blood and darkness and fear
has begun to scream.

Chapter Thirty-Two

As soon as he leaves his chamber Gel feels a coolness in the archive. No bodily sensation, more a phantasmal instinct of vulnerability. It's nothing to do with the music he hears. Somehow his dream is still here, in the darkness, the cloisters, the walls. He nestles his gaunt cheek against the flat of one of his ax's blades. Bloodbane feels it too. He lifts his free hand to his lips. The fingertips still carry the touch of his Dream-ward's dark skin. He breathes in her scent and walks on.

Others are already sat around the table of convocation over the atrium. The brazier of dragonflame in the centre lights Harnak, Zantalliz, and Phariane, and one other.

He's a young man, hair uncommonly fair for Dragonkeep, silkily falling to his shoulders. His long smooth face is pale. The blue of his eyes are hardly even that. Nor is there any trace of line around or vein within them. Their lids are lazy. His mouth is kinked into a one-dimpled smile. One hand lolls on the top of the harp he cradles but ignores.

Gel asks, "Who is he?" as he slips into his chair. But his eyes stay on Phariane.

She knows why, knows that she hasn't bothered to fasten the gown that Harnak, unasked, has fetched for her, knows that it falls open. But she is far more concerned to hide any sign of worry than her body. It's always been so. One reason she's not taken a lover in so long, even one of the taciturn Wolf-ward, is an unwillingness to let anyone see how restlessly she sleeps.

This night especially, she keeps the mask tight. Zantalliz' disgust at finding her in his bed still stings. But there are more important matters.

"Who is he?" asks Gel.

She hears the harper introduce himself. But she knows that because of what he is everyone around the table hears a different name.

Then a fresh strain of music flows. And Phariane is grateful, because Zantalliz and Harnak's heads are drooping and even Gel's eyes are becoming heavy. Now they all look to the harp. The frame is sleekly curved. The swirling patternings on it are so smooth that they fall between engraving and grain. There are no strings. Nor does the harper move his hand. But something undulates in the gracefully cradled emptiness within the frame which is closer to wood than metal, nearer to bone than wood.

The movement is a ripple. Akin to the hackles of some animal stirring. The music has something of the same quality. One or two solitary notes quickly cascade into a longer timbre. Beautiful, but with a thrum of warning underneath, a subtle purr in the back of a throat, a memory of thunder.

The harper shushes it like a skittish animal.

"And what are you?" asks Gel.

The harper smiles. The hand on the harpframe lifts a revolving finger. "I am a Wheelwalker," he hums.

"And what might a wheel walker be?" asks Harnak.

The harper looks at Phariane. "How many of the convocations have your Phoenix Prey completed?"

"Two," she says.

He nods. "One, what are the gods and two, what is the soul." He looks around the table, words still more song than speech. "When you reach the fourth, you will know what a Wheelwalker is."

The harp stirs again, sending out another uneasy melody. The harper shushes it again, for longer this time.

"It senses the Coronach Storm," says Phariane.

"What kind of storm is that?" yawns Gel, now gazing down into the table's onyx patterns like Harnak. Zantalliz has rested his elbows on it and holds his temples up with his fingers.

"Leviathan has sent the Nightmare Cadre against you," says Phariane. Their weapon is the Coronach Storm. It cannot be seen gathering, or approaching, or heard breaking but it is here, in the archive, all around us, sucking us back into sleep. It's in sleep that the Nightmare Cadre strikes," says Phariane, her head also sinking.

"What do they strike?" murmurs Harnak.

"You know," says Zantalliz, the words struggling through a bleak drowsiness. "We all know."

"They enter the wounds in dreams," Phariane says. "They pry open the scars they find there."

"Scars?" says Gel.

"No mater how well hidden," says Phariane.

"Is there any protection?" asks Harnak.

"Stay awake," chuckles the harper, the only one around the table whose eyes remain clear.

"If we leave the archive..." says Gel.

Phariane moves her head from side to side. "The cadre would only follow." Then, after a moment, "Talk. Talking will stave off sleep."

No head lifts. Gel rests Bloodbane's haft against the table. The harper leans over and whispers to Phariane.

"They don't seem very talkative."

Phariane looks at him with disgust and something deeper, and he jerks his eyebrows in a soft shrug.

"The third convocation," says Phariane. "Earlier than I had wished, but..."

The harper smiles at her. He stretches the fingers of the hand on top of the harp, a gesture of offering. "I could play something if you let me," patting the frame with the other hand, "if she lets me."

Zantalliz lifts his head, draws himself up. "Give us the third question."

Phariane looks at each of them in turn, then says, "What is evil?"

"I know," comes a voice beyond the table. Gel and Harnak also lift their heads now. They all look.

Gemmored stands, towering, swaying at the edge of the mezzanine. Blood soaks down his shift and dapples his bare feet. Across his forearms, a mass of fair hair falling away from her face, throat arching upward, lies the still, bloody form of his Dream-ward.

Chapter Thirty-Three

Phariane watches as the galley is lowered on its chains into its groyned bay. The dockers strain powerful arms to ease the descent. The ship hardly sways. Then halts. In mid-air.

A gangway slides across from dock edge to galley. Several dockers cross onto the ship. Phariane steps onto the gangway. She looks down at the rock bed of the bay, up to the cavern roof, looks anywhere but behind her. She remembers sensing the Coronach Storm fade away, taking the Nightmare Cadre with it, leaving barely any time for sleep before the uneasy dragonflame procession and aubade and the start of her next day's duties. The drowsiness banished last night by the arrival of Gemmored at the table of convocation has not yet returned.

So it's not want of sleep that makes her rub her palms into her eyes. This first duty of the day is a bitter one.

The bulwark hooks groan softly with the weight of the galley.

Phariane turns in the middle of the gangway and finally looks at the twenty or so citizens of Dragonkeep who wait to embark. She places her hands on her hips, then raises them and runs them over her hair -anything but speak.

She remembers dressing this morning and catching sight of her hair in the mirror, seeing the striae of grey marring the auburn. It's not the translucent mist of Gel's mane, nor the silver flecks of his Dream-ward's hair - perhaps the reason why he chose her? It's more like a claw has raked ash through Phariane's hair from forehead to nape - a wound dealt by the Nightmare Cadre. She's shorn it close to her head again but has made no attempt to hide the cicatrix grey. The fear grey.

She studies the faces before her on the dock, looking for surprise, even sympathy, but finds none among the men, women and children - even children. The Uroboros is coming and everything is changing. Since the killings at the arch that night there have been more deaths, as if a key has been turned. Twisted. Streetfights. Rituals have been enacted, dredged from faiths lurking in wait since before the Shadow fell. So no pity. Good.

"It is your right," she says, "to go. But Dragonkeep was created for what comes. To keep alive the hope of life, to turn back the tide of Shadow from the realm..."

She pauses. The sound of laughter stabs her. It comes hawking from two Corsairs captured during the battle to save the five Phoenix Prey as they cometted from the sky. Two Blade-ward stand behind them but make no attempt to restrain them. The Corsairs too wait to board. Phariane stares at the people. Her people. Still no pity. The same concentrated look of fear and determination that fixed the faces of the group who wanted to leave Dragonkeep for the Shadowfast. But this ship is bound for no Shadowfast. This ship is bound for Leviathan.

"No one who has ever wished to renounce their citizenship has been prevented or punished in any way." She looks at the Corsairs again. One spits on the dock. For a moment she allows herself to want to kill him - kill both of them - wishes the law of the city was not that prisoners are returned rather than executed - wishes that the council that enforces such matters had fallen apart like so many others. She wishes all this and more. She wants to kill all the fine brave citizens before her who want to abandon their heritage, whose betrayal spits on Dragonkeep.

But all she does is nod to the dockers. The lock gates of the bay open. Below the gangway, around the pale hull of the dragonreme, nigrescence forms. The chains are loosed from the bulwarks and the ship sways, afloat on Shadow.

And all she says as she walks off the gangway is, "Just be sure you wish to place your faith in darkness."

Some of them move forward almost before Phariane steps back onto the dock. She silently counts. Twenty-two, twenty-three. Not as many as there might have been. More than she hoped. One would have been more than she hoped. One or two even brush against her as they pass, either from eagerness or resentment. She wonders which would be worse.

Then she sees a face familiar. The young Blade-ward who tried to burn down the archive. The coppery feathering of beard is still there, but the confusion has hardened into bitterness. He stops in front of her and thrusts out a stare.

Phariane makes herself wait for it to end. Then he passes.

Almost all have boarded when she sees another she recognizes. This time the vertiginous pang is even greater, almost overpowering.

A woman, young, cheeks still retaining the fullness of a child's, sallow-skinned, sloe-eyed. She meets Phariane's stare. No bitterness on this face, but a sadness just as hard to endure. Someone else Phariane has failed.

Their hands reach out, touch. The Dream-ward looks down as if in surprise, and without looking up again slides her hands free and boards the ship.

Phariane keeps her back to it. The only one standing before her now is Gemmored.

She has brought him in the slight hope that the sight of one of the Phoenix Prey might turn the mind of at least one of those wanting passage. But also to try and draw him out of the torpid state of trapped agony he has frozen into since last night. He wears a fresh chiton, but his vein-raked forearms are still streaked with blood. He looks down on Phariane with eyes the grey of frosted steel that are now not just bleak but tormented. Eyes that have watched without interest.

"Why do they go?" he murmurs.

"Why?" Phariane has told Gemmored about the Blade-ward, bitter because of his inability to find enough belief in either his city or himself to stay and fight.

"And the girl?"

"Do you remember the day you arrived in Dragonkeep? That was the Dream-ward chosen and then rejected by Zantalliz on the first night.

"I'd forgotten," says Gemmored.

"Yes," says Phariane, "so had I."

"And that's why she goes."

"After a lifetime's preparation, to have the chance to serve one of the Phoenix Prey... To be rejected..."

Gemmored nods. "Won't they be killed?"

"Perhaps, perhaps not."

"What does the law on Leviathan decree?"

"There is no law on Leviathan."

Phariane keeps her attention on Gemmored, even though there's pain in doing so - the wild deadness in his eyes, the deep graven despair in his voice. Is her pain concern, or something more selfish? Since their coming she has failed each of the Phoenix Prey in some way or other.

She listens to the dragonreme casting off. She knows that behind her it silently glides over the Shadow and if she speaks long enough the ship will pass through the puckered gate in the dragon's jade flank and she will not need to watch it go. Or, she admits, be tempted to wish that she was aboard.

"And the rest of them?" Gemmored intones. "Why do they go?"

Phariane's shoulders twitch between shrug and shiver. "Sometimes it becomes simpler to run onto the blade than try to avoid it. Sometimes it's easier to walk towards the night than wait for it."

Then she hears the cry and whirls.

The dragonreme is distant now, but Phariane is sure she can make out an arm thrashing above the sea, a head bobbing above the dark surface. Perhaps an argument and someone fallen or thrown overboard? No. There was no anger in the cry - only anguish. The cry of someone tormented but the cry of someone - even one! - turning from the night.

Then something huge rushes past her and plunges off the end of the dock. Gemmored. There's no splash or ripple - this is Shadow, not water. For a moment he's gone. Then his great back surges up, arrowing for the drowning figure.

Phariane remembers touching Gemmored's dream last night, hearing the sorrowing wails spiral around him. What is it that seems to have finally pulled him out of that nightmare?

Then she sees. The head struggling to survive is sallow-skinned. The hair is darker than Gemmored's slain Dream-ward. The neck equally slender. There will be some form of atonement if he can save this girl, this other Dream-ward.

If.

This is Shadow, not water. Even Gemmored's strength might not be enough to reach her and return to the dock.

But he must. Phariane knows he must. For now she believes more than ever something not all the books or scrolls or tablets in all the archive have convinced her of. That the key to the Uroboros is the

Phoenix Prey.

Since their coming she has failed each of the Phoenix Prey in some way or other. But one she has failed utterly. The one captured by Leviathan. She's abandoned him or her, even to having a name to call them by. She promises, as she waits on the quay, to ask that name. To hear the fifth Phoenix Prey speak it.

Gemmored grasps the edge of the dock and hauls himself and the Dream-ward onto land. The Shadow gives them up without sound or resistance, though it leaves rills of itself on their garments and flesh and hair. Both of them breathe in quick, struggling gouts.

Phariane waits patiently for this to ease. "Go to the dragon's mouth," she finally says to them.

Gemmored looks puzzled, but the Dream-ward looks up at him and nods. "To burn away the Shadow stains," she explains. And she takes his hand.

As she leads him away, Phariane calls after him. "Then prepare for a journey."

"To where?" asks Gemmored.

"To Leviathan."

END OF BOOK TWO.

Chapter Thirty-Four

As the dragonreme bears Phariane and the Phoenix Prey toward Leviathan, the talk is of evil.

"Evil is what casts shadow and what it casts shadow upon," says Gel, as ever leaning on his labrys. "Without the two there is no shadow..."

"Evil is therefore both outside and within us," muses Gemmored.

"So," Harnak says slowly, "good is necessary for evil?"

"And evil for good," Gel spits upon the dragonreme deck, "each defining the other."

"So simple," murmurs Gemmored, hand on the quillons of his sword.

"Not to say," interrupts the harper, "that both are eternal." The heads of the Phoenix Prey turn to him whenever he speaks, or plucks a few notes on his harp, as if they otherwise forget he's there.

"Some writings say that there's no evil – only fire and shadow." It's the first thing Phariane has said since the ship left Dragonkeep and took to the Shadow.

The harper smiles at her. "Good, evil, fire, shadow... The Uroboros will decide everything and nothing, as it has before."

"You talk like one who knows something of destiny," says Gel.

"Destiny," says the harper, "is more fragile than the augurs would have us believe."

Phariane looks sharply at him. He brushes the backs of his fingers over the space within the frame of his harp where the strings should be. No sound comes.

Zantalliz catches his eye. He gives Zantalliz a smile. A knowing smile. Zantalliz suspects that he knows some of the truth behind the harper's riddles. But out of dislike for him and - respect? - for Phariane he chooses to reserve judgment until the final convocation. He looks to Phariane. Respect? Yes, one of the Moon-Ghost is allowed to feel such for a human. No more. He looks away before she can notice his gaze.

Gemmored, the giant with the sword, is now once more accoutred in his cuirass and vambraces and jambes and other armour, all cleansed of Shadow by Dragonkeep's fire. He's taken for his Dreamward the girl that Zantalliz rejected. Zantalliz would be pleased for them both if compassion for their kind was not another of the emotions which the lore of his people decree unacceptable.

Zantalliz looks out over the sea. At night, he remembers that his people would emerge from their caverns and grottos and set out from their isle to fish from coracles. Always at night, hidden from sight of ships - hence the naming of his people the Moon-Ghost.

But that sea was nothing like this. There are no rhythmic foamy rustlings against the dragonreme's pale hull. Albeit this sea is not as flawlessly flat and still as when he first fell from the Phoenix's flames into it. Albeit momentary whippings of glimmer now bolt across the surface giving it some hint of the restlessness of the seas of Zantalliz' own realm.

No. This is no ocean of brine. This is Shadow. And Zantalliz, the last of the Moon-Ghost, is like wounded, sorrowing sea wrack cast upon the shore of a realm with no moon.

The voyage continues.

In the ship's bowsprit the navigator murmurs to the helm.

The harper meanders across the dragonreme deck. Sometimes he hums. Sometimes he strokes at the stringless harp and plucks silence. But sometimes it sings to life by itself. A ripple within the frame. A breath of sound. As if the harp has its own voice. As if the harp *is* its own voice.

Gemmored listens to it and hears the winds of the ice-wastes, the implacable snarl of his world.

For Gel it evokes the festering memory of the throatless scream made by Gemmored's scabbard when he sheathed his sword Doom.

Harnak is reminded of the drums of Leviathan's quinquereme galleys.

No wind blows across the Shadow, but when the harp sings something stirs across the dragonreme, whispering at hair and skin. A rumour of thunder.

Then Leviathan is sighted.

The navigator goes silent.

As the dragonreme comes toward it, so Leviathan comes toward them. Its face is as immense as Dragonkeep's, if not more so. Its wrinkled mouth, the only feature set into a smooth eyeless snout, holds no fire. The pucker opens wide, caverning in on itself, falling into blackness, teeth dripping strings of mucus and Shadow.

"Do we dock in that?" asks Gel, eyes narrowed to grimness.

"No," says Phariane, and instructs the oars to ease and the helm to angle the ship's course.

Leviathan moves on through the wakeless sea and the dragonreme slips down its flank. Across its leagues of back a spine of bony spikes stab out. On each spike is impaled a torn, livid body, an oriflamme of skin and sinew. The spike bores through the small of the back and up through the belly, bowing the body. Arms and legs loll down but not the heads. There are no heads.

"That," says Phariane, "is the Shrike Wall - Leviathan's sentry."

Harnak's lips twitch. "How do they keep watch?"

"And how," Gel sniggers, "do they give alarm?"

The dragonreme turns. Matching Leviathan's course. The oars pick up their tempo and the ship draws close to the sea-wyrm's side. Unlike Dragonkeep's sides, Leviathan's sides are not scales of jade but scales of charred weeping flesh. And while Dragonkeep 'pulses' across the Shadow, as if rowing, Leviathan surges in a ponderous unchanging motion.

Phariane strides to the dragonreme prow and tests the knot of the rope fixed there. She slides her hand along the cable's length as she comes back along the deck and picks up the harpoon fastened to the other end. She pulls back and flings the barb at Leviathan, sending its precious brass head deep into the scales. No reaction comes from the sea-wyrm.

So close to the monster, the Shrike Wall across its back cannot be seen. Nevertheless everyone on the dragonreme looks up and listens for a moment. There's nothing.

The oars on one side of the dragonreme have been withdrawn. That side of the hull is now flush against Leviathan's side.

Phariane moves over to Gel and speaks to him. He lifts Bloodbane onto his shoulder and moves over to the ship's rail. Not heaving but merely brushing one of the great bladeheads against the wyrm, its black scales part. Another effortless sweep and the putrid meat beneath gapes. Gel looks over his shoulder and smiles. Several more passes and weavings of the labrys and he skips onto the threshold to a short seeping tunnel of a wound. There's a slash of glimmer at the end. A glimmer with something sick about it. As if even the light inside Leviathan were a kind of decay. Before he disappears inside, Gel stands his ax on the pulp at his feet and bows to the dragonreme.

Phariane watches Gemmored follow into the tunnel. Gel is almost as tall as Gemmored, so the tunnel is of a size to admit even him. His pale scabbard is at his side. He rests an instinctive hand on the hilt of the sword sheathed within. Since the attack of the Nightmare Cadre Phariane knows better than to ask him to draw it.

When she slipped into Zantalliz' dream she touched all the dreams of the Phoenix Prey, heard the snickering ambivalence of the voices in Harnak's nightmare, the despairing shrieks in Gel's, the malevolent wails in Gemmored's...

She knows them all better now. Knows that Gemmored's Doom draws evil from whatever it penetrates, whereas Gel's Bloodbane draws souls. This is why she asked Gel to open Leviathan. The wyrm has no soul to rape, but there is still evil to tap. No, she will not ask Gemmored to draw Doom, at least not yet.

She runs her hand over her changed hair. Ashen. Still shorn close. Since the night of nightmares it no longer grows in the old way. No longer has the power to heal. Perhaps because she was touched by another dream that night - her own?

But she puts such thoughts aside.

Harnak is stepping into the tunnel next. He wears a Dragonkeep chiton. The rags that clothed him on his arrival were beyond even the dragon's flames to cleanse - yet another splinter of worry nagging at Phariane.

She follows him into the tunnel, then turns and waits for Zantalliz. He stands on the deck in his restored raywing cape - a fittingly exquisite garment - and returns her look with his strange eyes, then shakes his head. The sight scalds her. His eyes are not strange enough to disguise fear.

Phariane turns her back and Zantalliz realizes she has mistaken disdain for fear. He almost calls her back to explain. To endure talk of evil is one thing, but to be confronted with it so blatantly, so obscenely - the idea of actually entering this physical embodiment...

Phariane wears a cataphract of the same otherworldly mail as the ship's Sword-Mariners'. But this is not scaled as theirs, nor fashioned into jerkin and breeks, but clings sheer to her form as a skin. So delicate, he thinks. Making her seem more vulnerable than protected. For a moment Zantalliz almost follows her into the tunnel. But then he shudders and the possibility occurs to him that it might be he who's mistaken fear for disdain.

And then she turns again.

And the wound closes.

And Gel and Gemmored and Harnak and Phariane are gone.

Inside Leviathan is a livid gloom of a kind no candle should shed. Even candles such as those set into the wyrm's walls, fashioned, as Phariane has told the Phoenix Prey, of the rendered fat of the dead.

The four make their way through the bloodless vessels that form the wyrm's labyrinths. The first forking to the left is carpeted by skulls. Harnak looks to Phariane, who nods, and he turns toward this path. He appears to collapse but by the time his chiton drifts to the floor it seems for a moment empty. Then something moves within it. Something long. Squirming. Then a sleek brown cobra smoothly darts out of the folds of cloth, flows across the first of the skulls, and slithers away.

Gemmored is the next to go.

Chapter Thirty-Five

As Gemmored moves along the distorted, twisted passages, past the sealed varices, cysts, and tumours that are Leviathan's chambers, he listens. As expected, there are screams. And other, less identifiable echoes. But there is something unexpected, more disturbing than the rest. Laughter.

It's of a harsh, sometimes malicious kind, but laughter

nevertheless. And Gemmored realizes that he has heard more of it in a few moments within Leviathan than in all his time within Dragonkeep. He can understand the laughter of the Shadowsea Corsairs – Leviathan's warriors know that if captured they will be treated well, not tortured as their Dragonkeep counterparts. But there's more to it than that. He remembers Phariane saying that doubt is accepted on Dragonkeep but on Leviathan is punishable by death.

Then he finds *them* standing in front of him. Turning, finds more of *them* behind. Shaped like men, *they* stare at Gemmored with bottomless eye-pits. Something colder and sharper than ice stabs at his nape.

He draws Doom.

Harnak slithers wildly as a Death'sheadcadreman brings his sickle-blade down.

The sharp edge snicks the air beside the snake's skin, lifts over the grinning cadreman's skull helm, comes down again, as close again, boneshards flecking off one of the skulls carpeting the passage, lifts again and the cadreman's footing slips and he stumbles back a step and no longer grins and brings the blade down more fiercely than ever and the skull over which the snake slithers cleaves in two and the snake drives into the eye socket of another skull but before it has fully entered the blade comes down again and the snake's tail jerks, and an eyelet of skin oozes blood, but the wound and the rest of the body has vanished into the depths of the skull carpet before the blade comes down again.

Then everything is curses and wheeling and flailing steel and shattering skulls, but Harnak has gone...

Gel twists and turns as he makes his way through Leviathan's passages, looking this way, that, walking, trotting, his steps skipping sideways, backwards even. His shoulders jostle the walls. Sometimes an elbow jars an alcoved stub of candle. How different from Dragonkeep! Even the echoes - not clean and crystalline but smeared and glutinous. Not resounding against rhyolite and granite and dolomite and porphyry, but quivering through stinking fleshy tunnels.

Then a needle of pain rips his shoulder.

Looking down, he lifts the tear in his jehad swaddlings and touches the blood. His lips slowly curl and part like another wound opening. He realizes that the scabs that streak the glistening stillbirth walls are sharp as daggers.

As his eyes travel down the passageway they leave the walls and fasten on a mother and child. The mother is yanking her son along. Her hair is in slovenly ringlets, his head is shaved. Her face is pinched, his plump. Yet Gel presumes that is what they are to each other. There is a common look to the noses, to the eyes. And they share an expression that is brittle with resentment.

They stop. Turn to the wall. The child is snivelling. The mother pushes his face against the wall. He resists, squirms away. The mother clasps the back of his shaven head and rams his face to the wall again. This time, gasping and snivelling still, he licks. This is what they do here. Gel has seen others do the same. Phariane explained once that unlike Dragonkeep, Leviathan has no water. The citizens of the sea-wyrm slake their thirst with the weepings that slick her insides. This is what gives the taint to their skin.

Gel moves closer.

The mother is the first to turn and see him. Then the son, his head suddenly free, his mouth caught in mid-mewl like a bruised glyph.

Gel waits for their expressions to widen. For fear to flare. He's not like them. Taller. Pallid. The yawning hollows of his cheeks. The cruel jut of the bones. The hair.

Closer still, he touches the cut on his shoulder with the pad of his thumb, smoothes the blood across one face of his labrys. The smear fades at once and for a moment his skin is less pallid.

Still neither woman nor boy call out. Rather their stares dull. They merely turn back to the wall. The child's tongue reluctantly returns to its task.

Gel has met the same response when happening upon others in these tunnels, has not yet needed to kill to prevent an alarm being raised. He suspects he knows why. He suspects that despite all the shadows and talk of shadows in this realm, only here, within the sea-wyrm, is there no shadow of hope.

Decay and razors, razors and decay.

He skips down the passage, hardly able to contain his delight at this Leviathan and its people.

Chapter Thirty-Six

Gemmored pulls together the lips of the wound in the sea-wyrm's wall which have given him entry to the chamber. When he feels the blackened edges seal again he wipes the back of his hand over the wound raking his forehead. *They* had been sluggish creatures, but their nails had been sharp as any dagger.

He lifts Doom and turns it in the air. A scatter of powder slips from its flats. Its steel had bitten not into flesh and bone but dust. Its sweeps and thrusts had yielded not splashes of red but curls of grey.

Gemmored studies the gem that forms the sword's pommel. The flaw of black in its heart barely stirs... Shaped like men they may have been, but they had been nothing more than fragile envelopes of corruption and their evil just as ethereal. He feels it entering him like the shiver of wings, spattering his soul like smuts, but feels no urgent need to expel it by sheathing Doom in the pale scabbard at his side.

Instead he turns to examine the chamber he has backed into. It's almost bare. Only an ancient siege stands on the floor at the far end. It shows signs of a once ornate and impressive design, but the wood, of whatever kind, has rotted badly and rotted also any majesty. Its back is eaten to perhaps half its original height. Its edges are ragged. The legs taper like black stalactites. They could have supported nothing more than the rumple of soiled cloth piled on the seat.

Then the cloth twitches.

It might be a rat, a cat. For a moment Gemmored wonders if it might be Harnak in yet another form.The cloth begins to lift, to rise up as if an animal stretching after sleep. As the crumpled folds spread out it reveals itself as a hooded robe. Then it begins to fill out.

No. Not a rat. Or a cat. Or Harnak. This is not something squirming within the cloth. This is something taking the shape of the cloth - using it - something *becoming*. From the darkness of the cowl a face appears, not emerging out of the darkness but an extension of it.

The face is old - ancient. And it ripples, as if not a face but a nest of frantic maggots feeding on something which, unlike the siege, refuses to rot. And it speaks.

This is not the language of Dragonkeep, nor any language Gemmored recognizes. The sounds are not even words as much as malicious clatters of spittle. However Gemmored knows the meaning of them - the threat of them. He knows that if this arcane thing gnarled up in its filthy robe continues to utter them then he will never leave this chamber.

He lifts Doom.

But he understands all too well what will happen if he spits the creature. Its evil will rush through Doom's blade, into the hilt, and flood through his fingers, his wrist, his arm, and seek out his soul.

Perhaps from revulsion at this understanding.

Perhaps from despair at the memories of all the times evil has invaded him, tainting all the slayings he's made with Doom.

Perhaps from an instinct that if the arcane thing continues to spit sound then Gemmored will never complete the few steps needed to reach the siege and thrust the blade home.

Gemmored chooses to lift Doom higher and hurl it across the chamber.

It spears through the filthy robe and whatever matter inhabits it and thuds shivering into the rotting stub of the back of the siege. The flaw of black in Doom's pommel stirs. The voice stills. Then, slowly, the arms of the robe lift. From the emptiness of each sleeve a hand appears - like the creature's face, not emerging out of the darkness but extensions of it. They take Doom's chevroned blade. The watering wavers, starts to fracture. The flaw in the pommel dances wildly. Slowly, the hands pull. Doom comes free of the creature as smoothly as it entered.

Then there is a motion. The arms of the robe. Something rushes at Gemmored and carries him off his feet.

Sprawled on his back, looking down, he sees Doom, buried in his own chest. Then the pain comes.

Chapter Thirty-Seven

The pain sprays from the wound like poisonous spindrift. It soaks Gemmored's massive chest and spreads through him like capillaries of burn.

His back pressing against his cuirass as he lies supine on the floor is a distant pressure. He looks up at the steel spire emerging from the front of his cuirass. It ends in a crosshilt pommeled with a gem that sits on top like a rubious eye. He looks at the eye and the eye looks down at him. He remembers, then, that this spire is his sword, Doom, driven deep into his chest. He thinks perhaps that he can feel its point touching his spine...

Yes.

So the pommel is indeed an eye. An eye of an elder god of an elder time of Darkling Realm.

Gemmored looks into the eye and sees in its unfaceted depths the chamber he lies dying in. He sees the arcane ranting thing on the rotted siege. He sees himself, standing, facing it, with his sword in his hand.

Gemmored understands. What has happened in this chamber has happened and yet not happened. The scene in the gem is happening yet not happening. Nothing is settled until death. And Gemmored understands death most of all. He fixes his will on the Gemmored in the gem and the Gemmored in the gem takes a slow, dragging step forward.

Yes.

The Gemmored in the gem lifts the sword in his hand.

Yes.

But he does not hurl it. Not this time. He realizes the act will not do.

So another eternally slow awkward step towards the thing on the siege.

But the Gemmored who watches, who lies with his chest pierced and the wound still flowing, knows that if the short journey across the chamber is not completed soon...

Chapter Thirty-Eight

Each step is a battlefield strewn with howling, cursing dying. Yet finally Gemmored stands before the arcane thing on the siege. Both the Gemmored with the blade buried in his chest and the Gemmored he watches in the pommel gem do this - somehow they are one and the same now. The wound the first Gemmored sustained on his forehead drips the sting of sweat-salted blood into the eyes of the second.

Gemmored lifts his arms, hands clasped around his sword's antler-bone hilt - another endless battlefield - and wipes a wrist across his brow.

The arcane thing's harangue, louder with each step taken, now changes again, turns higher. The maggots rippling under its face become even more frantic. The rotting siege ripples too, infested with the same maggots. And Gemmored's arm is frozen.

Destiny balances on the moment.

Then Gemmored drops the sword and dies.

Then Gemmored plunges the sword into the thing.

Then Gemmored drops the sword.

Then Gemmored plunges the sword.

Then Gemmored.

Then Gemmored.

Then.

This is not like forcing the sword through brain and bone, nor does the thing's head offer only the desiccated resistance of the dust men outside the chamber. The chevroned steel bites into hate - the thing is fleshed and skeletoned with hate.

Its voice grows higher again. Piercing. The sounds are no longer words now - if words they ever were - but one sound. One endless cry in a scabrous language of one single sound.

Strands of dark blood, or dark that is blood, spatters and hisses along the blade. Gemmored realizes as it jumps toward him there is no difference - blood and darkness, darkness and blood, each a part of the other. He stands at the other end of the sword and waits for what he knows will come.

Not just pain but something else barbs through him. Vessels spawn through his huge body, twisting and twisted sewers - and then the familiar fluttering sensation sluicing through those vessels. He tastes the darkness that is blood, the blood that is darkness. He's felt it all before. But never this much. Never has he understood evil this much.

The sword's chevroned watering, the bridge between slayer and slain, quivers again, begins to crack again.

A strand of darkness spits off it into one of Gemmored's eyes. Yet another kind of pain. Blinding. Blood and darkness. Darkness and blood. Still he stands with both hands on the hilt, makes no attempt to withdraw the sword.

Nicks and scores appear on the edges and flats of the blade, making it as ancient, more ancient than the thing on the siege.

Then suddenly it ends. The thing shreds away like shrieks of saliva. The robe shrivels to a rag once more, sliding off Doom back onto the siege.

Gemmored staggers across the chamber. He pushes a hand into the crack of the entrance and tears it open again. Shouldering through, sword first, he finds other blades waiting. These are sickle-swords, in the hands of rangy cuirassed figures helmed in skulls. Some dozen members of the city's Death'shead Cadre crescent him, poised.

Gemmored notes the swords have edged pommels. He realizes then, that they cannot be fulcrumed on the wrist, which gives him an idea how they will probably be wielded. The knowledge is entirely his own. The thing on the siege passed no martial skill to him as it died - only darkness. Darkness he can still taste. Darkness that still blinds his left eye. Gemmored's mouth curls between smile and snarl and he lifts Doom. One eye will be enough.

Chapter Thirty-Nine

Phariane waits on the floor before the black knot that she knows is the heart of Leviathan. With her knees drawn up and her arms clasped around them she sits like a little girl amid the screams and laughter and other distant calls.

She knows that the harper is approaching along the scabrous corridor behind her, but she doesn't smile until he lifts the harp to his shoulder and adds its music to the echoes. Just for a moment. To Phariane it weaves between a lost lullaby hummed by her mother and a lover's bittersweet lament. Then, too soon, it stops. Phariane knows that for a moment more, after the harper's fingers have left the nothingness where his instrument's strings should be, the harp continues, itself unwilling to let go of the melody. Still behind her, the harper's fingers place themselves with equal gentleness on Phariane's shoulder. She lays her cheek on them.

"Your music betrays you," she says, "you were never meant for a world so dark and bloody."

"Sadly, I'm meant for every world. To walk the Wheel from realm to realm."

"But not to stay? Not even with the end so near?"

The harper's tongue nuzzles into her neck. "The Uroboros has come to other realms before."

"But perhaps this will be the last time - the ending that ends all the realms forever."

"Perhaps."

"And even if not the end of life," murmurs Phariane, "then almost surely the end of mine." She eases her face against the harper's hand. "Do you still care about that as you once did?"

"Once?"

"How long has it been since you last walked in Dragonkeep?"

The harper chuckles. "How do you measure time here?"

"Don't you remember? On Dragonkeep we measure time by the bringing out of the flame from the dragon's mouth to give us day and the returning of it to give us night. By the passing of generations. By the sightings of Leviathan as it pursues us. Some of us measure time by how long it is we've waited for our love to return."

"This," says the harper, "is an unlikely place to wait for me. Or is he in there, that missing Phoenix Prey of yours?"

They both stare at the black stony knot in front of them, watch the subtle rhythm of shuddering - Leviathan's sullen ghost of a heartbeat.

"No," replies Phariane. "He's not here. One of the other Prey will find him - Gemmored or Gel or Harnak. The Phoenix chose them all - the link will draw them to him."

"The citizens of Leviathan have merged in appearance," the harper goes on. "There's a taint to their skin through drinking the weepings from Leviathan's decaying flesh. Your Phoenix Prey will hardly pass unnoticed."

"Loyalty is disdained by Leviathane," says Phariane. "Only one of the Death'shead Cadre would raise an alarm, assuming they lived long enough. And how long would one more cry take to be recognized?"

They both listen. Screams and laughter and other echoes...

"So who do you wait for here?" the harper asks again.

"The one an alarm would be meant for," says Phariane. "But she's not here. I had hoped..." Phariane pauses and, looking over her shoulder, the harper sees the kris in her hands, the slim wavy blade balancing across fingertips. "...to meet her again.

"I've waited so long for that," she murmurs. "Longer than I've waited for you."

"Waited for?"

"The ruler of the sea-wyrm. The bitch of Shadow. Sstheness. My sister."

Chapter Forty

Kneeling behind Phariane, the harper lays his harp down, takes his hand and slides it around Phariane, stroking her hand that clasps the kris. Her hand remains motionless, but the blade stops undulating.

"And if you meet your sister," he says, "do you believe that would stave off the Uroboros? No," he murmurs when Phariane gives no answer. "No, you know better than that m'love. You won't have told your Phoenix Prey yet how the Wheel works, but you know..."

A single sharp note yelps from the harp and the harper turns his head. Behind him a broad, bearded figure in a blood-red lamellar jerkin is stealing up. Seeing him turn, the Shadowsea Corsair abandons silence and breaks into a run, boots slapping down hard, turning powerful shoulders and pulling back his sabre. Almost casually the harper takes his hand from Phariane's, reaches back and plucks - rather nips – the air cupped in the harpframe. No note sounds, but the Corsair jolts, stumbles and sprawls as if an invisible arrow has leapt from a phantom string. He lies still. The spittle on his lips still. No hint of sight in the eyes. The harper turns back to Phariane.

His hand comes back around her and takes her hand again, stroking it with his thumb. He presses himself to her, moulding his chest and stomach to her back. His chin nuzzles her neck, his cheek finding hers. His other hand moves off her shoulder and makes its way across the sheer otherworldly mail that allows the heat and scent of her body to escape, sheathing every swelling and curve and sinew, betraying every rise and fall of breath.

"You know the true nature of destiny," he continues. "If I die today, if you die today, if your sister Sstheness dies here and now, you know it would make no difference. The Uroboros will still come - and no act, nothing that happens before it comes will affect what will happen then..."

Phariane shudders.

The harp comes to life again - low, resentful jangles of notes prowling into being like musical hackles. The harper ignores it.

The cries and moans of Leviathan recede in Phariane's ears as she remembers the harper, no different than now, smooth, unblemished, pale eyelashes and paler insouciant eyes, in the forest of Dragonkeep. She remembers the girl with him. "Phariane," he says to her. The girl has Phariane's face, in some ways no different, but this skin has the subtle swell of child barely turned woman.

Behind them, the city glimmers, the yellow light is dimming as the evening procession returns the dragon's flame to its mouth. The young Phariane is already the city's archivist, mindful that she should return to her studies. Yet, hand in hand, she and the harper walk further into the forest, unable to tell which hand is pulling the other. And when night follows they lie on soft mossy ground and above the looming trees the roof of Dragonkeep is nothingness punctured here and there by a spark of emerald or garnet or amethyst. And a wolf bays out. And the girl eagerly pushes herself up against the harper's weight.

"Promise me," she whispers.

"Phariane," he says.

And not even his heavy-lidded voice has changed.

Phariane's voice though, has become harsher, weighted with time and hurts and fears. But here, in Leviathan, still sitting and staring at the black stony knot at its heart, the harper's hands running over her, her words are the same. "Promise me."

Quivering out. More gasp than speech.

"Promise me," she says. "Promise not to leave me this time." So easy. So easy just to stretch out on the cold sea-wyrm floor and push her body into his. Even so she forces herself to ask again. "Promise."

But instead the harper's hands grow still. There's the warmth of a sigh brushing her ear. Then the hands move again - softly - caressing even as they leave her. Phariane knows better than to listen for his fading footfalls.

She sits alone, listening to all the sounds dimly trickling through Leviathan's passages. Calls. Threats. Sobs. Snickering. Moans. Shrieks. And something else. Something she realizes has been there all along. The sound of breathing, long, deep but quick nevertheless, and quickening. And inlaid within the breathing, riding it, is another kind of moan. A woman's rhythmic moan, violent, hungry, and growing louder.

Phariane recognizes the throaty mockery of lovemaking. Recognizes her sister's voice. She measures its intensity, the nearness of climax. There may still be time. Sstheness might yet sate herself and return here to Leviathan's stone tumour of a heart before one of the four Phoenix Prey finds their missing fifth. Or she might return before the alarm is raised at last and Phariane and the others have to flee the city with or without the last of the Phoenix's chosen.

She looks away from the heart, her eyes paining after being fixed so long. She blinks down at the kris. It too recognizes the moaning, undulates in her hand. There might still be time for it all.

To kill Sstheness,

To find the fifth Phoenix Prey.

To escape to Dragonkeep.

But Phariane no longer cares. She climbs onto stiff legs and hobbles down a passage she barely chooses, leaving the Corsair's corpse and the kris behind. And even some way along the winding length of razors and decay, when the suppleness returns to her legs, she moves no faster.

Chapter Forty-One

The Death'shead Cadre guard shrieks as venom sprays through the orbits of her skull helm and turns her eyes to fire.

The snake lowers from its rearing and Harnak uncoils into a man, scoops up the staggering guard's sickle-sword and cuts short her cry.

All assassin-swift. A few flecks of candlelight squirm.

Harnak knows that this is the chamber. Knows that the staring figure he turns to, huddled against an empty serrated ribcage throne, wrapped in a blanket like a broken animal, is the fifth Phoenix Prey.

Equally swiftly Harnak moves to the guard's body, lying at the edge of a murk-bottomed pit in the centre of the chamber. His hands dart at cuirass straps, wrench free boots and breeks. Soon the woman is naked and Harnak is clothing his own nakedness. As he dresses, his body subtly narrows, lengthens, adjusts to fit the garments more exactly. Finally, she reaches down for the corpse's skull helm.

The fifth Phoenix Prey, still huddled against the throne, pulls in a breath, his stare less dead for a moment.

Harnak tugs. The corpse jerks but the skull casque remains firm. Harnak lets go, straightens, and her head, having just made the slight transition from male to female, begins to change again. Her hair drifts in thick locks to the floor. Then the skin begins to fade - a gentle, ghostly flaying. Flesh melts into bone and eyes recede deeper into sockets and Harnak's head is now a Death'shead Cadre helm.

Picking up the sickle-sword again, she moves over to the blanketed ruin. "What are you called?" she asks.

Standing over him, in the silence slurred by the echoes roaming Leviathan's passages and chambers, Harnak considers whether to kill him. Not for mercy, though it would be such. Harnak has moved through Leviathan with the stealth of a murderer, the role she is trained for in body, mind, soul. The call of blood still murmurs in her.

Then, raking through the city, a new ululation enters the chamber. Shrill. Vibrant. Ripping through yearning and despair and terror and fury and most of all ecstasy.

And the staring face of the fifth Phoenix Prey wraps itself even more tightly in the blanket.

Harnak bends and pulls him to his feet, neither gently nor roughly, meeting neither resistance nor help. As she guides him to the chamber entrance they nudge the Death'sheadcadrewoman's body. Her arm lifelessly pendulums over the edge of the pit. The murk below twitches.

Chapter Forty-Two

Slick with crimson, Gemmored stands among the juddering sprawl of dead and dying cadre.

A head struggles to lift and arms fight to prise themselves out of the debris of skull-casques and cuirasses and sickle-swords. Gemmored pulls back Doom with the slowness of an archer stretching a bow-string, relishing the gathering of power before its release.

Then, just before the stroke, something else is released. A sound rather than steel, but just as powerful. From some distant place in the city it knifes through the passageways, exultantly raping its way higher and higher through yearning and despair and fury and ecstasy and most of all terror.

As he listens, death remains taut across his shoulders and arms - then he allows it to slacken.

Gemmored lowers Doom.

Even before the ululation starts to fade he strides away.

Chapter Forty-Three

Gemmored is not the first to emerge through the crusted cut in Leviathan's side. Murmurs edge through the dragonreme's oarcrew as he appears, wounded and bloody and changed in other ways. Other murmurs had travelled through the banks when Phariane had appeared, not wounded but also changed. The whispers that greeted

Harnak's return were not because of his shape, though it was still that of the Death'sheadcadrewoman. They were for the hunched shape that accompanied him.

The fifth Phoenix Prey had been barely able to keep his feet. Harnak had sat him down on the galley deck and crossed his legs for him. Then, like Phariane, she stood, silent, apart.

Head still bowed, Zantalliz had not moved since refusing to enter the sea-wyrm.

Gemmored is not the last to emerge.

He strides over to Phariane, Doom still in his hand. The few Sword-Mariners aboard tighten their grips uncertainly on their own blades. Phariane watches him come, her arms wrapped vaguely around her sheer-mailed body, face fixed. "Where's Gel?" he says.

"Still within," she answers.

"Leave him," says Gemmored.

Another murmur goes through the dragonreme. Although Phariane looks at Gemmored she gazes at his cuirass, as if she lacks the will to tilt her head to see his face. Through the skin-sheer mail the hollow at the base of her throat deepens and shallows as she speaks. "A little longer."

"Are you so sure of his return?" says Gemmored.

Another murmur.

The fifth Phoenix Prey sits in his blanket and stares at the sky. There are stilettos of light. In his own realm of Nightwake the sky is a dark, starless waste. He remembers the Phoenix, all fire and infinity, rising out of the prophecy vats, plucking him from his world and plunging him into another. The stars are terrifying - they only make the darkness darker. For a moment he remembers his name, then forgets it again.

Then Phariane does lift her head. Slowly. As if pain makes her ancient. She looks at Gemmored, at the wounded eye. It bulges. The lid strains over something inky, bolused within the socket that's no longer an eye. A discharge of Shadow trickles out of it.

"I cannot heal that," she murmurs.

"I know," says Gemmored. "Nor heal as much as a splinter in a child's finger. Not since the Nightmare Cadre paid us their visit and gave you this." His hand reaches forward and sinks into Phariane's hair, tousling the ashen streaks. His voice creeps louder. "Dragonkeep will have to make do with henbane and opium and propolis, now. They all know it."

The dragonreme is taut. The Sword-Mariners stare, straining in their stillness.

Gemmored clutches Phariane's hair and brings his head down toward hers. Almost as if to kiss her. His voice lowers again. "The Nightmare Cadre touched us all that night. Perhaps some more than others. Perhaps Gel most of all. Perhaps he prefers Leviathan." His mouth forms the words savagely, spittle jumping like sparks. "Leave him."

A droplet of Shadow from his ruined eye slides into his mouth and leaps with the last word onto Phariane's face and she winces.

A hand closes on Gemmored's wrist, small, slender fingered.

Gemmored turns his head to stare at Zantalliz.

The blister within the eye socket shifts.

A shout.

Bloodbane's twin blades slip smoothly down the slit in Leviathan's side which the ax had itself first opened. Gel follows, smiling. "I believe the alarm is raised," he says.

Without taking his hand from Phariane's hair or his stare from Zantalliz, Gemmored lifts and points Doom at the brass barb fixing the dragonreme to Leviathan's flank. "Cast off," he roars.

The Sword-Mariner entrusted with the care of the barb tugs at it. He works it back and forth, twisting it in the sea-wyrm's scales, but it stubbornly holds. Doom still points unwaveringly. As blood-splashed as Gemmored, strands of thickening crimson stretch down from the blade. The Sword-Mariner's efforts become more frenzied as Gemmored's head turns in his direction.

Gel takes a stride of his long legs, swinging his labrys up.

The sweeping blades climb high and fall in a blurred crescent. They stop impossibly a fraction above the deck, having lazily severed the barb's shaft.

Immediately Leviathan and the dragonreme begin to pull apart.

The ship's withdrawn banks of oars shoot back out and into the Shadow. All three tiers of oars on each side pull. One stroke. Nearly two hundred pale-bladed shafts hauling through oceanic darkness... lifting... swifting back... plunging down for a second stroke... a third... each faster than the last... each a sinewy response to the urgent notes of the pacemaker's flute.

The dragonreme quickly pulls away and ahead of Leviathan, but the oars continue to strain. Gel, Harnak, Zantalliz, Phariane and Gemmored stand at the stern, watching Leviathan's massive puckered maw ploughing after them through the wakeless Shadow.

The fifth Phoenix Prey sits on the deck still, beginning to rock. A question which is perhaps a memory has wrapped itself around him. Is the cold dark or the dark cold?

"What will be sent after us?" says Harnak, whose face is still a skull.

Gel glances at her. "Perhaps the Death'shead Cadre, eh?"

"More likely the Corsairs," says Gemmored. "Or the Pitspoor."

Harnak nods. "The Corsair ships are slower than a dragonreme. The Pitspoor are winged and swift enough to catch us." He turns to Phariane. "Or might it be something else?

She makes no reply but something is emerging from the dark cavern of Leviathan's mouth.

It spits out. Spewed in shreds. Once out onto the Shadow, rather than sinking, the shreds flurry in front of the sea-wyrm. They swarm. Then they turn toward the dragonreme.

The pacemaker's flute springs almost to frenzy and the oars obey. Pale blades lift. Shimmers of dark cling on them for a moment then slide away. The oars dart and dip again. The ship speeds forwards and Leviathan seems to fall further behind with every stroke - but the spewings still gain. They seem to neither swim through the Shadow nor fly over it. They look, like the dragonreme, to be travelling upon its surface. But not, like the dragonreme, to be skimming. They run. Each shred is now clearly a horse and rider. A threatening paean drifts before them.

"What have they sent after us?" asks Harnak.

"The Wyrmshod Cadre," murmurs Phariane.

The oarcrew continues to row with disciplined savagery, but their heads and eyes strain to look behind. Soon, terrifyingly soon, they have no need. The Wyrmshod Cadre are all around the ship.

They outstrip the dragonreme almost at will, it seems, taunting its speed. The horses are clearly too wild to bear saddle or bridle, are held by the riders' knees, guided by a hand clawed into the mane. They wheel and even rear on the Shadow, allowing their quarry to spear ahead again, then gallop back along its sides.

Riders and mounts are equally manic. The paean has become a battle yell. There's something of the mocking call of Leviathan's Corsairs in the sound, but this is closer to panic than laughter. Like panic *in* laughter. One of them surges ahead again, wheels again, brings a hoof down on a splintering oar.

Gel wonders how they ride on Shadow. The dragonreme is hulled with parings from the dragon's talon. The Corsair quinqueremes, he's heard, are coated in the grave-wax that seeps throughout Leviathan. But these horses...

But as this horse rears, Gel glimpses its shoes, recalls the daggersharp scabs veining the sea-wyrm's stillbirth halls. Of course. These horses are marvellously shod with the selfsame razors!

And what horses. Sinewy slicks of tremulous ferocity, unnaturally loosely jointed, eyes bulging and darting through bone chamfrons. As he admires them a cry breaks from the other side of the ship. A Sword-Mariner staggers away from the rail then jerks back toward it, hands clawing at his neck, blood spitting from his throat.

Harnak is the nearest of the Phoenix Prey and for an instant is the only one aboard the dragonreme who knows what is happening. From the moment they emerged from the distance into warriors she has wondered what weapons the cadre bear. Swords such as Gemmored's or the sickle-sword Harnak carries in her present Death'sheadcadrewoman shape would be useless to them. Throwing blades or axes would be almost as futile, spent in a single cast. Bows would be the natural choice, but she remembers that, unlike Dragonkeep, there is no wood on Leviathan. No tree would survive in such a place, and timber from before the Shadow fell would be as rotten and frail as kindness.

But just before the Sword-Mariner's cry goes up Harnak knows what their weapon is. Cold vertigo leaps and twists in her heart. She sees the riders unwinding the coils of rawhide cord they wrap around hand and bazuband and elbow. She sees one snap forward an arm. Sees the cord wrap around the Sword-Mariner's neck and wrench taut. And the blood? Harnak sees the specks of white, woven into the cord. Teeth, she thinks, filed to needle points. Of course. Not only whips, but barbed whips.

Harnak lifts her sword too late. The Sword-Mariner struggles against the ship's rail for a moment, then pitches over the side. The Shadow swallows him without sound, without ripple or splash. The Wyrmshodcadreman yanks his mount to a halt. Razored shoes skid on blackness. As the dragonreme speeds on, he snaps his arm in jerky, elbowing twists, and the end of his whip, plunged into the Shadow with the Sword-Mariner, emerges free. Streaks of blood and Shadow cling to the rawhide.

The Wyrmshodcadreman snaps his arm again and the cord curls back to him. Releasing the horse's mane he catches it expertly with the freed hand. He digs his knees into his mount's sides. It spurts after the dragonreme again. The rider's bazubands cover forearms and elbows, but the hands are unprotected. The cadreman ignores the barbs which tear and bloody his fingers and palms as he winds the whip back into its coil.

Around the dragonreme others are wielding their whips now too. Barbed lashes crack out, wounding and blinding oarcrew. Once again one of the cadre holds her mount in mid-rear, waiting for one of the dragonreme's oars to sweep past, then brings the hooves down upon it.

Another does the same.

Another.

Even if the wounded oarcrew row on, little by little the Wyrmshod Cadre are crippling the ship.

One, even more frenzied than the rest, urges his mount at an oar bank. But rather than rear and drop onto a single oar, he leaps it onto the bank, riding a plunging splintering path across them, then lunging onto the dragonreme's deck.

And now the mount does rear. And wheel. And lash out with its front hooves. And the rider also lashes out, twisting left and right with his whip. He screams his warcry, lathy torso and limbs bristling with ferocity and swirl-patterned tattoos. An unmorioned Sword-Mariner charges him and he bends and sweeps his arm. The Mariner staggers back, face ripped open. Iron is as precious to Leviathan as to Dragonkeep, but the riders' bazubands are woven with shards of it - the riders, as their mounts, are shod with razors.

The cadreman pulls on his horse's mane. It rears again, over an oblivious blanketed figure hunched cross-legged on the deck.

The fifth Phoenix Prey is looking up, but not at the hooves. At something above. Something flickering, he thinks. No. Not the stars.

As the horse stamps down toward his head, a bolt of bloody steel sweeps from the side. Gemmored. Doom. The horse nickers in outrage, staggering sidelong. The rider splashes onto the deck, almost severed through the middle. His warcry turns liquid in his throat before stuttering to nothing. The tattoos on his body begin to unwind. They run down his skin onto the deck and scuttle crazily away, ratstails of Shadow.

Gemmored, tall as the horse, steps forward and reaches for its mane. It shies away and almost stumbles again as another blur of steel hurls at it, this time from behind - and Gel is astride its back, lofting his ax and laughing. The mount yanks its neck to and fro, muzzle peeled back in outrage and teeth snapping. Gel stabs a hand into its mane, rams his legs against its ribs, and sends it racing for the galley's side.

It slides a splintering path down the oars and back onto the Shadow. Both mount and rider twist and jerk for balance. Both achieve it in a moment. And then Gel begins to whirl Bloodbane.

Zantalliz has watched Gel go. He's pulled Phariane away from the ship's stern and huddles kneeling with her on the deck, an arm around her shoulders as the barbed whips cast and snap overhead. He watches Gel disappear over the side, melded and matched in ferocity with the Wyrmshodcadremount, Zantalliz finds himself wondering if

Gel goes not to slaughter but to join his new brethren?

Gel is a joyous snarl of motion. Hair a savage translucent pennon. Some of the Wyrmshod Cadre break off their attentions to the ship and close on him. Whips lunge at him but the labrys, whirled by the thong at its end, shifts its path to meet and slice the cords. One of the cadre edges his mount too close. Bloodbane's humming arc swoops and the horse's foreleg vanishes. Its shoulder plunges wildly and its rider falls, swallowed instantly by the Shadow. His whip licks the darkness for a moment and is gone too. The horse bucks and screams away in agony.

Bloodbane whirls.

It knows its way, the familiar swooping and soaring way through limbs and skulls and spines - a fragile way, for all things part like ghosts at the touch of Bloodbane's thirsty crescents. This is the swathing. Steel and stone are flimsy as flesh and bone, flesh and bone frail as straw. And with each passing the numberless souls locked within Bloodbane scream again. Even, faintly, the sundered fragment of Gel's essence whimpers. And after the labrys passes, a wake of blood and soul follows its weaving flight.

This is the swathing.

This is Gel's delight.

And even this is barely enough for the labrys. It yearns for something to challenge its bite, defy its swathe – this is its true hunger. The bansheeing of the souls in its keeping provides no more than consolation.

This is the swathing.

This is Gel's delight.

Blood and soul and scream.

Somewhere, in the distance, still torn at by Wyrmshod Cadre whips, the dragonreme drags itself on.

Chapter Forty-Four

Sstheness rips open the blood sutures of the entry and stumbles into the chamber with the serrated throne and the murk-bottomed pit. She steps, wearily, upon the dais and scrapes herself through the ribcage and slumps onto the throne. She has come, breathlessly livid, from the things she calls her husbands, still covered in the slime of her pleasures. In the candled dimness her flesh glistens.

Far away, in some coiled lonely winding of Leviathan, her scream still echoes, but only she can hear it now.

"Do we have them?" she asks.

Beyond the pit stand a Shadow Corsair and a Death'shead Cadre warrior.

"They row the Shadow," says the Death'shead.

"Still within sight," says the Corsair.

"But too fast for quinqueremes to catch," says the Death'shead.

The Corsair spits a look at the Death'shead warrior. "Not so swift now."

"The Wyrmshod Cadre are on them," says the Death'shead. "The dragonreme is almost crippled."

Sstheness has covered her face with a sigil-taloned hand. The tips of the sigils are buried in her hair. "The Wyrmshod won't take them," she coughs. She bends forward, slithers through the ribs of the throne onto the dais on all fours, throws out a spatter of blood-streaked vomit.

Several beads drivel over the edge of the pit and into the murk.

Sstheness' matted hair curtains onto the mess until she lifts her head.

"The Wyrmshod will fail," she says, "but we'll still have them."

Chapter Forty-Five

On the dragonreme the ratstails of tattoo Shadow still scurry about the deck, over planks and feet, but always around, never touching the fifth Phoenix Prey. He still watches the sky as if it might swoop.

No one else looks up. He's the reason the others on the galley have risked their lives on an unthinkable voyage but now no one gives him a moment's attention.

The oarbanks on each side of the ship still row, but a good half of the oars are damaged, the wood broken or the pale end-blades gone.

Wyrmshod Cadre whips crack and lunge all around. More of the Wyrmshod Cadre riders have taken the same suicidal route onto the ship as the rider slain by Gemmored. They lay about with whips and hooves among the banks. Some of the oarcrew are hampered by weals and cuts. Some are broken like their oars. Some are dead. Several have lost eyes to the barbed lashes. Not one leaves their station on the benches, but even the unwounded are exhausted, their strokes shuddering with effort.

Gemmored wrenches Doom from the dying chest of a wyrmshod horse. The rage of its eyes dim. As it adds its blood to the crimson wash on the carcassed deck, the swordsman turns in the mess and roars at Phariane.

"They have us!"

Zantalliz still kneels beside her, his cloaked arm protectively pressing her against him.

Her head stays bowed but her lips move.

"What does she say?" yells Gemmored.

Her lips motion again. Zantalliz brings his head even closer to hers, their foreheads gently touching, his fine-boned face squints with concentration. Then he looks up.

"She wishes us to unfurl the sail," he calls back.

The ship goes still.

The pacesetter's flute goes quiet at his mouth. Sword-Mariners halt. The helm pauses at the rudder. The oarcrew's leaden pulling stops for a moment.

Gemmored and Zantalliz exchange a stare. When the Phoenix flung them into this realm, the furled sails on Dragonkeep's triremes had puzzled them both. A mystery too petty to give thought to. Until now. Why a sail? No wind blows over the Shadow.

Then life returns to the galley. The oarbanks row on. Sword-Mariners race to the lines fixed to the deck and running up to the yard crossing the single polemast. Wyrmshod Cadre whips fly at them. Most narrowly miss or harmlessly slap against helmets or the tunics of otherworldly mail. One or two find and rip open necks or faces, but even these Mariners stay hunched over their task.

One side of the sail comes down a little. It floats deckward rather than drops. The canvas behaves as if thinner and lighter than canvas - almost ethereal - and it glitters.

On the opposite side one final line is proving troublesome. Finally the Sword-Mariner frees it but as he does a Wyrmshod Cadre whip snakes up and wraps around yard and sail before it can unfurl.

Without hesitation another Sword-Mariner springs to the mast. Taking a dagger from his belt, he takes it between his teeth and climbs.

Almost at once the Wyrmshod Cadre riders circling the ship bend their whips on him. Twisting and wincing, he manages only a short way up before a vicious lash-wound on an arm loosens his grip and he falls to the deck. A second manages more than half-way to the trapped sail before barbed rawhide curls around his thigh and he's dragged off the mast.

Without the pacesetter's bidding, as if their hearts have decided as one, the oarcrew pull with new desperation. The Wyrmshod Cadre rider whose lash traps the sail is caught by the spurt and is jerked from his mount. He flounders a moment in the Shadow, keeping grip on his whip, pulled along by the dragonreme, then vanishes. But still the rawhide cord, trailing in the dark ocean, traps the sail to the yard.

Harnak, still in the shape of a Death'sheadcadreman, turns her skull-casqued face to the mast.

The casque starts to change. The grey colour of bone becomes the colour of skin. But not human skin. She drops her sickle-sword, bloody with Wyrmshod Cadre blood. Her hands tear at and release the straps of her cuirass. They're already shrinking and growing fur.

By the time Harnak has bounded up to the mast the change is complete. The monkey scoops up the dagger of one of the fallen Sword-Mariners and, as the Mariner had done, places it in her mouth and scurries up the pole.

Whips snicker at her as she climbs, but this is a smaller and more agile target than the Mariners. Reaching the horizontal yard she scrambles along it to the rawhide wound around the sail and grasps the dagger.

Now still, Harnak is a better target for the Wyrmshod Cadre

riders' lashes, but her tiny hands are as agile as her long-limbed body. In a moment the sail unfurls.

Chapter Forty-Six

In the candled dimness of the chamber with the serrated throne and the murk-bottomed pit, Sstheness kneels low and forward, thighs folded onto calves and ankles, her forearms flat on the stone floor - like a cat - like something about to pounce. She watches the spatter of blood-streaked vomit between her forearms, waits for it to congeal.

Chapter Forty-Seven

The unfurling is accompanied by breaths of relief and awe and dismay.

Phariane does not need to look to know the sail is freed. She can hear the shame in the voices. She shares it. If they manage to return to Dragonkeep she will, no doubt, shoulder the blame as she has for everything else since the Phoenix Prey's arrival. She no longer cares but some, she knows, will consider this unfurling blasphemy.

Dragonkeep has always been riddled with guilt. Guilt over surviving as the rest of the world perished. Guilt over maiming the dragon, most glorious and sacred creature of the skies, vast as aurorae, all fury and sunrise and corona and starlight. Shame over mauling and twisting its dying, transmogrifying vitals and humours for man's own selfish use. The triremes are the embodiment of that guilt. The pale plates of their hulls, the plates that enable the ships to breast the Shadow instead of sink beneath it, the blades of the oars too, are parings from the heaven-raking talons. The sheer scaled mail of the Sword-Mariners' jerkins and breeks, harder than metal and more supple than leather, are woven from crescents of haw, the filmy inner eyelids of the dragon.

But the sail is the most terrible shame of all.

The populace of Leviathan feel no guilt. No guilt in the price they pay for survival. No disgust in walking the wyrm, in sustaining themselves on the diseased weepings of its eternally rotting walls. No unease in spawning to the rhythm of its still-shuddering heart. Their Corsairs give no thought that their quinqueremes can only ply the Shadow because their hulls and oars are slathered in the sea-wyrm's gravewax. On Leviathan guilt, like doubt, is forbidden.

Often, latterly, Phariane has wished as much of Dragonkeep. Now she no longer cares. But still she does not look at the sail.

But Zantalliz does look. The last of his people, the last of the Moon-Ghost, the Phoenix Prey who refused to enter Leviathan, he churns with shames of his own. But this is not one of them. His view untainted with remorse, he stares.

The sail is square-cut. Not canvas, no more canvas than the Sword-Mariner's mail is iron. More sheer than that mail, the sail flows down from the yard without a crease, a delicate, iridescent membrane.

A dragon's wing.

So beautiful that for a moment Zantalliz fails to notice that no sooner has it unfurled than it has begun to billow.

No wind blows over the Shadow. As far as Zantalliz knows no wind ever blows over the Shadow. And the sail does not move as if caught by some stir of air. No sooner has it gracefully arched away from the polemast than it begins to flatten again, no sooner flat than arching out again, rhythmically, smoothly flexing, in, out, in, out, colours shifting and shimmering as the membrane swells and sinks and swells.

Not like a sail.

Like a wing.

Like a beating rainbow.

Almost from the first beat of the sail the dragonreme noses forward with renewed speed. The Wyrmshod Cadre riders shout in surprise. They urge their mounts harder. Their whips spit out with even more frenzy.

Swelling, flattening, swelling, flattening...

And not just renewed speed.

Billowing, sinking, billowing, sinking, billowing...

After several beats the galley starts to rise. After several more it parts from the Shadow, cleanly, without a speck of darkness clinging or trickling from the ship's pale hull.

The remaining oars cease motion. As they withdraw one Wyrmshodcadreman makes a last wild charge onto the sloping sweep of oar shafts but immediately his mount skids, loses balance, and falls.

The sail gives another, almost triumphant, swell. The galley picks up both speed and height with each beat.

Impossibly, on one side of the ship, comes the sound of steel slicing into the dragon-paring plates of the hull. Gemmored speeds to the rail. Crimsoned sword poised, he looks over to see Bloodbane buried deep into the plates. Below it, hanging onto the labrys' haft, Gel fleers up at him. In moments he climbs effortlessly onto the deck and prises Bloodbane free with equal ease.

The dragonreme is soaring now, far ahead of and above the Wyrmshod Cadre. Far below they whirl their whips in the air, impotently hissing strips of maelstrom.

But the crew of the dragonreme stays silent, notes Zantalliz. Though their bodies, exhausted, some injured, slump with relief, they still owe their escape to the butchered square of wing. Their silence is their token of thanks, of repentance. Zantalliz is surprised to find himself impressed. They carry their guilt well.

Even so, only the Phoenix Prey look to the sail. And of these only Zantalliz gives it more than a glance. But still it beats. The dragonreme speeds on, not pulsing forward as Dragonkeep across the Shadow, but with a pure, soaring flow. Like a dragon.

Quickly the Wyrmshod Cadre are almost lost to sight. Eyes turn to look towards and beyond the ship's prow, watching for the jade scales of Dragonkeep to appear on the horizon formed of dark sky and darker Shadow. Other eyes glance to the stars. Others are occupied with the wounded and dying.

Not Phoenix Prey, nor Sword-Mariners, nor oarcrew see that the fifth Phoenix Prey, still heaped in his blanket in the middle of the blood-drenched deck, is no longer looking up as if the sky might swoop. Is no longer looking up, but ahead.

And the ship smashes into nothingness.

Chapter Forty-Eight

In the candled dimness of the chamber with the serrated throne and the murk-bottomed pit, the patch of grume-streaked matter between Sstheness' forearms has shrunk, thinned and dried to a wafer. She nestles her chin on the cold dais and purses her lips. She blows. Softly.

The edge of the wafer lifts, flaps. She blows harder and the wafer flips over. Even as the last glisten of moisture fades from the underside, a pictogram is resolving.

Lines appear, funnelling in and splaying out from a centre. Others emerge and demilune between them.

Sstheness' chin stays on the dais. A speckle of vomit has dried on her lips. It falls as she smiles.

Chapter Forty-Nine

It's as if the ship's hull has run aground some reef of void in the sky. Those standing are nearly all thrown onto the deck. Those lying wounded are flung painfully about. Those dying are jolted a little nearer death. But the dragonreme does not stop instantly. Whatever the ship has crashed into, yields slightly. Even once the ship steadies, it saws fractionally back and forth in the air.

Almost at once the sail begins to beat again, adding to the swaying, but whatever holds the dragonreme holds it fast.

Then, slowly, perhaps brought to life by the ship's struggles, it starts to reveal itself. Like a flower opening. Like a beast uncurling. Like annihilation stretching out.

Capillaries of silver spread out of a point of nowhere, bleed smoothly away from each other like languorous, fluid lightning, out into the sky. Other capillaries fork out of these, not smoothly but erupting like brittle splashes of lightning. These leap and curl and weave between the straight threads, creating ever widening luminous traceries. The straight threads all spoke out on the same plane. Immense as it is, *Annihilation* is flat. Not perfectly vertical, it tilts back a little. The dragonreme has run into it just above the centre, ramming into one of the traceries.

Harnak remembers glimpsing flickering patches in the air on the journey to Dragonkeep after the Phoenix dropped him into the Shadow. And on this voyage too, to Leviathan.

Gel recalls the same flickerings, but also remembers dismissing them as some trifling mirage of the realm.

Gemmored has speculated on their nature. Some kind of bird? Perhaps roosting on the rare Shadowfasts which rear up into the sky? Perhaps Pitspoor of the kind which attacked on the Phoenix Prey's arrival?

But only Zantalliz realizes what this is.

Harnak's monkey-shape still crouches on the dragonreme's yard above the sail. The dagger used to cut it free is still in her hand. She replaces it between her jaws and darts head-first down the mast. Reaching the deck she scurries on her four long limbs for the prow. The intention is obvious to the crew. She's cut the ship free once...

Though the trireme's ram is buried in the luminous threads there's a space between them and the higher front rail. Harnak jumps the gap without pausing. She lands surely. The threads flex slightly under her weight. It takes a moment for her to judge the give, then she scampers over the silvery disk. Her movements are sure, but erratic, darting across one patch of tracery, then swinging to another, then double-backing. Then she halts, as if some instinct has decided that this is the place to start - almost exactly above the dragonreme's ram, nearly level with the prow deck rail. She grasps one of the threads in one front paw while the other reaches for the dagger.

Zantalliz gently detaches himself from Phariane and stands. She makes no protest, but even so he feels something tear in him as he moves. But he knows he must. He moves to the prow. He's the only one to look for it, the first to see it, the first voice to shout. But even he is too late.

It looks like a dark break in one of the glowing tracery threads below

Harnak. Yet even after it appears, the line doesn't fall apart. So not a break, it seems, but a glaucous bruise of some kind. Then it moves. It speeds along the tracery line, onto another more twisting, another more curved, then darting along one of the straight radial lines, then jagging back onto the haphazard traceries, but always moving up, always rushing nearer Harnak.

She's sawing at her first chosen thread when Zantalliz' shout goes out to her. The gleaming lines are not irresistibly strong, yet their give makes them difficult for the dagger to sever. Harnak holds it with her other front paw, pulls it taut for the blade. In a moment more the line breaks. She reaches for another but other shouts are going up now.

Even as her head lifts, the glaucous bruise reaches her.

As if struck by a catapulted missile, or even lightning, Harnak is hurled off the disk and back over the prow onto the dragonreme's deck. Several Sword-Mariners cluster around her. They kneel or stand in keen bow, exchanging confused, concerned glances. One or two extend a solicitous hand, but these waver short of touch.

Harnak fidgets dully like a troubled or fevered sleeper - as if the bruise has stung as much as struck her - as if the darting glaucous patch was not a gap or a bruise but some kind of cunning stalking venom.

And it is exactly that. Zantalliz knows. His people, the Moon-Ghost, wrote of such things in their grotto-archived books. He remembers these books, remembers the deep fear which always came in the unlocking and reading of them, the fear that beckons to the heart and can always be recognized but never known. He feels that same fear now. Recognizes it.

This fear is his heritage. His race sprang from a young, fine-boned man on a corralled reef fringing a nameless isle and a lithe and wild she-god with the eyes of a cat.

But after a time the human half came to be considered tainted. The fear considered part of the taint. It was then that the race took the name of The Moon-Ghost, created a lore which forbade the knowing of that fear, demanded the shunning of it.

Before this, the race had another name.

Zantalliz turns from the prow and goes back to Harnak. The body of the shape-shedder is fitfully swelling and shrinking, from the size of a monkey to the size of a human and back again. Patches of singed fur dissolve, regrow and dissolve again. The monkey muzzle melts back into a woman's nose and mouth and jaw. Then the flesh itself melts into the bone of a death'shead helm. Then grows back again, this time into a man's features. Then bulges again into muzzle.

Zantalliz' eyes squint concern for a moment, then he kneels and gently eases the dagger from Harnak's twitching hand. He lifts it to his mouth and starts to speak. No sound comes and the motions of his lips seem to stop short of fully forming language. He passes one flat of the blade before his breath from tang to tip, then turns it over and does the same to the other flat. He extends his other palm beneath. The dagger changes. Its shape becomes molten. The blade shifts both like Phariane's kris and yet unlike. The bronze forks and bristles rather than undulates – almost more like the traceried threadwork of the disk. Almost more like a bronze barracuda skeleton. No longer just a dagger.

Zantalliz passes the dagger over his other hand and a line of blood appears across the unwounded palm. The line curls for a moment into something like a symbol, then sinks back into undamaged skin. Zantalliz draws his slender fingers into a fist and turns back to the prow.

With a sleek movement he vaults onto the ship's ram.

He stands without wavering, lifting both the hand closed into a fist and the hand holding the dagger. The glow of the disk flickers in his face, and the fear gathers around him. When he stood before Leviathan he refused the knowing of it. This time he accepts the knowledge, allows the fear entrance. Feels it enter his heart.

The slender fingers locked into a fist uncurl and reach out. Zantalliz steps forward and springs.

The threads sway beneath him as he lands lightly on the disk but he holds firm. Then he climbs. So that both hands can grasp the threads, the barracuda dagger is held between thumb and palm. Zantalliz guards it carefully. This is the only chance of freedom for the ship. Below, now far below him, the dragonreme sail beats more slowly than ever, sluggishly, like the fading memory of something once vast as aurorae and furious as storm. The silver threads hardly distort as the ship pushes against them. *Annihilation* cannot be torn. It can only be severed. Zantalliz finds a certain thread. The dagger no more than strokes it and it breaks. As it falls apart Zantalliz is already climbing for another. He moves almost as nimbly as Harnak's monkey and just as surely, almost as quickly as a spider and far more fluidly - like a cat.

He cuts another thread. Turns. Climbs. Knows unerringly the next place on the disk to aim for. Zantalliz feels laughter bubbling up like so many times when he has spoken the contents of the books of his people. But this time the feeling is different - not maniacal but cool, cool within him. This is how his people must have felt before they shunned the fear and so much more and became the Moon-Ghost. The laughter stays silent, yet it courses through him like a kind of terrifying joy, even when shouts fly out again from the ship.

The venom sac has appeared again. Zantalliz knows it without the shouts, without seeing it. He knows he must work faster, and not just because of this. The luminous face of spokes and weaving tracery threads is no longer a disk. It curves. The threads above him are vertical now, harder to traverse. Zantalliz has expected this. He knows the nature of the thing he climbs. Knows it is part sky, part lightning, part star, entirely predator. It is a plexured tumour, turning conic, slowly enfolding the dragonreme.

One of the stalking sacs approaches Zantalliz. He cuts another thread. Not the thread along which the poison travels. From the ship it seems an apparently random cut, yet the sac shrinks and fades.

Zantalliz understands the threads. That they're not silver but a kind of silk spun of Shadow, their glow the sheen of darkness. But darkness is as much a part of Zantalliz now as the fear, as it was part of his people before they called themselves the Moon-Ghost - when they called themselves the Shadow-Dancer.

As the disk becomes a cone the threads above him are overhanging him now. His foot slips and he hangs by his free hand. The barracuda dagger almost slips from his other. The spokes funnel down to a core of nothingness, the centre of *Annihilation*. If the threads enfold the dragonreme much more...

Another of the venom sacs makes toward Zantalliz. Despite it all, the fear is still cool within him. The Shadow-Dancer finds new footholds, cuts another thread, clambers through the gap to the other side, slices another thread and the sac hesitates and starts to fade.

Now the cross-webbing begins to change. Brighter shapes appear in their weave - pentacles and runes and almadels form and melt like brilliant hoar. Zantalliz knows that the shapes are no brighter than the threads were moments ago. It's the threads that are dulling. They're weakening. The shapes are not forming on top of the threads. The shapes have always been beneath. Like bones. Like entrails.

More venom stalkers swell into being. They move in frenzy this way and that, darting, hesitating, even moving back on themselves. Zantalliz knows, even the dragonreme crew can guess, this is panic. The mandalas twist. The pentacles disfigure. All the glowing diseased arabesques maim themselves. As the Shadow-Dancer goes about his task, the venom stalkers finally all go still, then rush at him as one. But even as they do, Zantalliz knows they're too late. He reaches for the last thread he must cut - not a spoke thread plunging down into the core of nothingness and out into infinity, rather a tarnishing trickle of a tracery thread, splitting into two before it reaches its opposite spoke. But Zantalliz is sure. Fear and darkness meet in him now, and he feels the same in the thread. The first of the venom sacs reaches him as his dagger touches the thread.

Annihilation goes instantly dark. All its fading rigging collapses into aether.

The dragonreme plunges toward the Shadow for a moment, drowning in its sudden freedom. Then the sail stirs with renewed force. Within two vigorous beats the ship is climbing again.

Soon it's holding its steady course for Dragonkeep between sky and Shadow.

Like Harnak, like the other wounded, Zantalliz lies on the ship's deck where he has fallen. Sword-Mariners kneel and minister to him. Phariane still kneels where he left her, head still bowed.

END OF BOOK THREE.

Chapter Fifty

Even when the glittering line of the Beckoning Gate, the jagged light escaping the dragon's mouth, is sighted, there's little elation aboard the dragonreme. A stir of relief. No more.

As the ship descends, the crew manages a crippled murmur of the hymn of greeting.

"Dragons were before land..."

"Before land..."

"When the world was only sea and sky..."

When the pale hull touches the Shadow the oarcrew slumps back to their task. They've tasted what a dragon used to be, a glimpse of starlight and storm and corona. Their oars are awkward embarrassments, distasteful to ply.

The ship forlornly manoeuvres along the jade flank of the dragon and into the immense puckered entrance to the harbour.

Even the vaulted rainbowed roof-sky... purple porphyry inlaid with emerald, garnet, spinel, ruby, sapphire, opal, carnelian, topaz, amethyst, jasper... does not lift the heartsickness.

A crowd awaits on the quay. Not the throng that met the Phoenix Prey on their first arrival. Men, women, a few children. None as feverishly expectant as on that first time. Still respectful in stance and gaze. But calm. Eerily so.

Dockers execute their tasks, with derrick and boom and chain, equally calmly. The rhyolite lock is closed. The Shadow beneath the ship fades. The gangplank extends. The dead and wounded are disembarked. Then the rest of the crew. Then the Phoenix Prey. There is no turmoil in the crowd. No chant. No jeers. A child, held in a father's arms, grizzles. A chariot horse restlessly sidesteps. There are six chariots.

Harnak, weak but recovered, now a tall narrow-shouldered man clutched in a blanket, searches for the face of a young tow-headed man.

Gel spies his Dream-ward in the crowd. He strides over to her, pulls her against him, draws in her scent, dares her eyes to meet the want in his.

Gemmored also sees his Dream-ward. Still blood-grimed, he strides to his chariot. The young Dream-ward, his second, looks up at him, puzzlement dawning across her expectant sloe-eyed features. Gemmored ignores her. He hauls himself aboard the car, pushing the driver off almost by his thrust alone. The horse starts in a half-rear. Gemmored snatches the rein and turns to Phariane, the last to disembark.

"Well?" he shouts at her. "Are we gods now?"

He yanks on the horse's rein, even as his Dream-ward, still unacknowledged, climbs beside him. He sends the chariot in the direction of the cleansing flames of the dragonmouth.

Only Gel matches his vigour, lifting his Dream-ward into his own chariot before boarding himself. Gel has little interest in purification - his most urgent need is for another satisfaction. The other Phoenix Prey and Phariane climb wearily onto their chariots. Their most desperate need is for rest. Cleansing will wait until tomorrow. Their drivers turn their chariots toward the archive.

The fifth Phoenix Prey, the very cause of the journey to Leviathan, is neglected for a moment. He stands as if he should be swaying, rapt in void. A thought flickers and he remembers and then again forgets his name.

Chapter Fifty-One

Harnak's chariot is the first to arrive. Strength returning rapidly, his frame is stout now, his legs more powerful. He jogs up the wide shallow steps into the archive. In the atrium he halts on the turquoise and amber tiles, staring up at the tiers of cloister above, all lit fitfully by yellow brazier flame. He shouts the name of his Dream-ward. He shouts again and launches up the basalt stairway into the echo.

But his recovered strength is fragile. By the time he reaches the fourth cloister, the one containing the Phoenix Prey's chambers, he can barely stagger into his own to find it empty.

He emerges and leans his back against the doorframe. His breath despairingly comes and goes. Gel and his dark-skinned Dream-ward appear at the end of the arcade.

She turns to Gel, lays a hand on his chest, and speaks quietly. As she moves away from him, Gel reaches out a rangy, lazily protesting arm and grabs her shoulder, but she eases free and walks over to Harnak. She moves close, her face going gentle and sad as she speaks. Harnak's begins to change also. The skin shrinks on the skull. The skull itself sharpens, the eye sockets plunging deep and blackening. He lifts his arms and the blanket slides from his body as the shoulders narrow again. His hands slowly claw from his temples to the back of his head. Then he claws at the Dream-ward. His fingers sink into her neck.

Even as her back arches and her hands splay Gel is between them, prising Harnak free and flinging his gibbering frame over the cloister edge into the atrium well. The Dream-ward gives a cry and staggers to the edge. Even as she does a fluttering sound rises. As she looks down a bat is frenziedly swirling around the brazier-lit well. It weaves madly into and out of the cloisters and in and out of shape, rippling out of bat and into bird into hornet then back to bat, slamming against the walls in one shape and thrashing away as another. Finally Harnak slumps onto the mezzanine just below.

Zantalliz and Phariane arrive in time to see a shivering sprawl-winged raven fall onto the table of convocation.

Each leans on the other, Zantalliz still weak from his injuries, Phariane still wrapped in her drifting sham of awareness. Nevertheless she moves as if wanting to go to the table. Zantalliz supports her. Sinking into one of its chairs she's within easy reach of the raven, still brokenly twitching in a spatter of its blood, but she makes no effort. Instead she slides her forearms onto the table and together. Just before her head nestles onto them she nudges a hand in a torpid gesture of dismissal at Zantalliz.

He stands for a moment, breathing, then turns away.

Chapter Fifty-Two

Zantalliz steps into his room. A hand reaches up to a sharktooth brooch and his raywing cape slides off his shoulders to the floor. Would that he could shed the weariness pressing onto his body and heart.

The tripod is bereft of the yellow fire that once lit the room. An unthinkable neglect, but he feels no surprise. Dragonkeep has changed. Perhaps as much as he. And as with Zantalliz, there is a calmness and strength about the change.

His eyes adjust to the dimness and he sees something placed on his bed. His book. Another neglect, the bed is only roughly made. The scallop shell rests among rumples of blanket as if lying on a slovenly seabed.

Zantalliz feels a thought touch him fleetingly. Before he can grasp it he finds himself kneeling before the bed and pulling the book to him. He rests it on his thighs and releases the nacre clasp. He gently eases the scallop covers apart and the pages, even finer than his cape, swell at the spine and part and stretch open.

Still blank.

Then, as he watches, neither expecting it or surprised by it, like a tentative shooting star, a rill of colour slips down one page. Even for Zantalliz' strange eyes, it's too difficult to tell in the dimness if the rill is the colour of blood.

Chapter Fifty-Three

Heat and flesh and bone and breath...

In Gel's room Gel and his Dream-ward gasp and snarl, sinking into each other, straining, his misty mass of hair spreading over the bed, her wiry mass of dark and silver hair roiled in his darting fingers.

Heat and flesh and bone and breath...

Gel needs her nails in his back, needs razors...

On Leviathan, among echoes of laughters and sobbings and groans and threats he felt comforted. Even Sstheness' scream, both climax and alarm, whetted sharp on the barbed passages of the sea-wyrm, cloaked those in his head. The thousands of raking slivers of despair.

He still hears Sstheness' scream, still wants to hear it, beneath the scream of his Dream-ward who clings and claws. Even his Dream-ward's petty cry of pain and joy comforts him.

All the time one long arm caresses and wrenches and crushes her body, the other trails off the edge of the bed and tenderly fingertips the haft of his ax.

Chapter Fifty-Four

The chamber which Rorn is carried to is only slightly different to the chambers of the other Phoenix Prey. A small tongue of yellow dragonflame has been left in this chamber's brazier, offering a tender and soothing glow. The drapes over the walls and window are thicker, though despite this the cries of Gel and his Dream-ward, albeit distant and muted, still seep into the room.

The bed on which he is laid is deeper, kinder. The covers placed over his body are softer.

The two chariot drivers who carefully lifted him into the archive and up the stairways leave. Only Rorn and a woman remain.

In place of a comfortable settle is a bare, harshly carved chair. The woman sits. Tawny-eyed and skinned. Her hair is scraped back and all expression with it. Her brows and her mouth are set watchfully. Rorn had not been able to choose his own Dream-ward. She's chosen herself.

She sits with the blanket on her knees that has swathed Rorn on the journey to Dragonkeep. The blanket from Leviathan. She looks down at it, smoothes it on her lap with her thumbs. It reeks. There's piss. There's something else too, that smells of chill. Smells of taint.

There are echoes inside Rorn, beside his name. The covers over him are warm, the bed forgiving. But there are echoes inside him which are neither.

He sees a face, a mordant smile kinking the handsome features, reflected in the wafer-quartz of a window. As he stares he drifts closer to the face, drifts *into* it, and suddenly the face is gone. He drifts on, across a wreckage of utter unending night unsullied by moons or stars, prowled by things suited to blindness and ruin. In this *somewhere* man clings to survival. Only a few can and do step outside

150

impregnable noctilucent mansions to carry messages of possibility and comfort.

Presently he sees, or possibly hears, perhaps even tastes, one of the prowling things. He drifts on, becoming aware that he is following *it*, stalking *it*. He glimpses or hears or tastes *it* twist in the wreckage of night, arch like something without a spine and uncoil away further into blackness. He follows. *It* claws and squirms and swims through the blindness of the landscape. And as the one who has forgotten his name drifts after *it* he realizes that the face, the face that had been reflected in the quartz window, that mask of skin and cynical eyes and mordant mouth, is not gone. It's instead adhered to his own - over his own... or... rather... he realizes his mistake... this face *is* his own. Except for one lineament. A faint white scar, the merest delicate indent, on its... on his... cheek.

He remembers a woman. A long talon of a fingerstall. He remembers a needle of icy burn drawing down his cheek. He can feel it now, and feel something below it, something which slithers beneath his face much like the prowling thing he still follows slithers across the ruined face of this realm.

And just before it vanishes, the one who has forgotten his name almost wonders if the thing was the name he has forgotten.

And he groans.

The Dream-ward beside Rorn's bed lifts her head at the sound. She lets the tainted blanket drop to the floor as she stands. In the gentle brazier light she watches him shift in a forlorn shred of restiveness. She studies the pale etch that runs just below his eye to the side of his slack mouth.

She reaches forward and lifts the bedcovers and eases herself beside him. He groans again. She stretches her arms around him, still tracing the path of the scar.

Chapter Fifty-Five

After Phariane lifts her head from her arms and stands and leaves the table of convocation, Harnak sheds the bloodied feathers of the raven and stretches into a man. This is his true shape. Young but not youthful. Strong shoulders. Lean but not thin. The skin bears the scars of his training in the torture vault of the prince of the city of angled agate spires.

He remembers revealing the scars to his Dream-ward. Offering him true nakedness. Baring the seals of the blood and pain that disfigured his heart into an assassin's. On the table of convocation he leans forward and loops his arms around his knees, feeling the cicatrices stretch on the rack of the skin of his back. He bows his head. To reveal them now is not to make an offering. He is not sure why he reveals them.

Perhaps because of what Gel's Dream-ward has told him - that Harnak's Dream-ward was not waiting for his return because unable to bear the presence of one who's trodden Leviathan. Harnak searches his memory for some hint, in gesture or word or voice or eye, that would explain the change, the betrayal. Perhaps this is why he allows the scars display. Because other fresher scars make them less important? Less precious?

Harnak thinks of Gel's Dream-ward, Gemmored's Dream-ward, the tawny Dream-ward who has offered herself to the ruined Phoenix Prey brought back from Leviathan. An appetite stirs within him, familiar, if not as comfortable as once. The taste of killing.

He remembers Phariane walking away from the table, wearily stumbling her way to the back of the mezzanine and down the stairway. He remembers that shortly afterward came the sound of the bronze and ornate door on the floor of the atrium, the door to the vaults below.

He feels the need to follow. He slides off the table. Whether he wishes to talk to Phariane or kill her he will consider on the way.

But before he goes...

Instead of taking the stairway down Harnak climbs again to the next level. He sees the blanket that slipped from his shoulders in the exchange with Gel's Dream-ward. Lifting it he uncovers what fell, unseen, with it. It lies in rawhide coils. He picks it up. Pale needles of teeth are woven along its length.

Recovering his senses from his fall, Harnak had found the whip by the corpses of a Wyrmshodcadreman and his mount on the deck of the dragonreme. He had slipped it beneath his blanket, fingering it secretly on the voyage back to Dragonkeep, fingering it secretly.

He fingers it now, still not knowing why.

He turns and makes for the staircase, allowing the whip to uncurl behind him. The teeth barbs click on the basalt steps all the way down to the atrium floor. It eels after him along the tiles and through the bronze door where garnet, emerald and amber give way to metal treads and darkness.

Harnak does not have the sight of a cat. He makes his way slowly down the vaults. The smells in the damp air are the same as before - grains, seeds, soil. These give way, as before, to the other smells he can put no names to. He stops now. Moves off the stairway into the vault - the third, forth down? He's neglected to count. Around him are the dim sheened outlines of the amphorae. He sinks down against one, bare back against cold glaze, running the whip over a palm.

Waiting for the silence to turn against him, his flesh wafts from male to female. Young but not youthful, high breasts, lean but not thin. No minute flickering of eye colour, no ghosting flux of bone - this is also her true shape. Scars still swathe across her back.

She realizes that she's listening for footsteps descending the stairway, watching for a yellow lantern glow. Something twists even more inside her.

Looking down she sees her hand crushed into a fist around one of the whip's barbs, blood wetting the squeezed channels between the fingers. This, too, is a realization.

She takes a length of the whip between her hands and lays it across her back, from one shoulder to the opposite hip. Then she starts to saw, slowly, back and forth. The barbs cut across the sometimes ancient paths of the scars, and the not so ancient, ripping their calloused seals and releasing the pain again.

Yes.

Now she knows why she took the whip.

This pain, this old pain, this pain feels like faith.

Chapter Fifty-Six

Not in darkness, nor in light. The cavern at the bottom of the bronze caracol is the same as before. Silvered. Walls incised with deep mysterious glyphs. A fountain set in the centre.

But this time Phariane does not sit on its edge. She has struggled out of the sheer otherworldly mail of dragon's membrane and left it slumped wearily on the ground and stepped into the pool.

She dips her hands into the path of the arc of silver rising out of the pool and lifts it onto her bare shoulders. It runs glimmering down her back, her breasts, her belly. It burns.

As she once told Harnak, this silver is sky-wyrm's blood. She did not tell Harnak that a sky-wyrm's blood is fire. Unlike Leviathan, whose inhabitants still walk the vessels that once contained its blood, those who found the dragon found no veins, no arteries. A dragon's life is fire. Dragonkeep still lives in the furnace of its mouth, but also here. In this pool. This silver is also fire. Cooled and distilled but still fire.

And it still burns.

Good.

She wants it to burn.

She wants to care that it burns.

She wants to care that it is her fault, all her fault that all they have brought back from Leviathan is a half-dead shell of a man and hopelessness. She wants to feel anger for the toll the voyage has taken, the damage done to Gemmored and Harnak. To feel disquiet at the changes in Zantalliz and the lack of changes in Gel.

She delves for the old nagging fear born on the night of the Nightmare Cadre's attack - the suspicion that the cadre has left some taint on one of the Phoenix Prey, a diseased seedling of betrayal waiting to burst at the Uroboros. That fear has gone. A dripping hand strays to her ash-clawed hair. Even the dread that such a seedling might have been planted in her - even this is gone.

Most of all she wants to feel pity for herself.

But no.

She cups more scalding silver fire onto her shoulders.

As the pain trickles forlornly down her body, she hears something behind her.

Chapter Fifty-Seven

Phariane knows the sound for the tremor of a phantom harpstring.

She does not turn around.

The tremor clings to the air in the cavern, not desperately, but with a crafted firmness, a sweetness. It holds just long enough to open the way for another note, and another, cascading now into melody.

It breaks over the silvered walls, washing the glyphs, draws back, surges again.

Winds murmur in the timbres, or maybe sough between them, in shrills, flourishes and broodings of sound. Sometimes there is a wanting of a voice in the harp music, and sometimes what comes needs no voice, and sometimes it seems that the music cadences into a lost language that dances between the two. Then the music gathers and glissades back from the walls for a soft stroking moment, single samite pangs of sound, only to sweep out again, lazily carrying with it skies and seas and oceans of skies and plains and cities and gardens and mountains and forests.

Most of all, Phariane hears forests, but she does not turn around.

And realm glissandos over realm, languorously and sweetly.

And there are storms in the promise of some melodies, and in the foreboding of others, and in the melodies where promise and threat meld into one, and the echo of storms, and the memory of storms.

And Phariane draws in her breath, deeper and deeper. The harp sowings tremor along her spine. They taunt and coax through her, plucking at her misery. But still she does not turn around though her will tears at the effort.

Then something touches her spine, her back. Warmer than sound, it moulds to her from shoulder to flank, harder and more urgent than song. Skin. Another body pressing against hers.

"Come with me."

The voice comes, as she knew it would. The harping purrs lower, but the voice also holds storms and the echo and memory of storms.

"Come with me."

And hands slide along her body, a touch so light and smooth that they seem not to have been laid on her skin but simply to be. They slip from her thighs, across her belly, over her ribs as if they were harpstrings, and on.

"If I die today, if you die today, if your sister Sstheness dies, you know it would make no difference. The Uroboros will still come - and no act, nothing that happens before it comes will affect what will happen then..."

Phariane's voice is a stranger. She waits to hear what it will say.

"If the Uroboros is lost there will be nowhere to go."

"Only if it is lost. And you know that even if the Uroboros is won then Dragonkeep as well as Leviathan will die, and most of the dwellers of the wyrms, even your Phoenix Prey, m'love, even you. And you don't care any more, m'love, I can tell. Come with me..."

Breath winds into the whorls of Phariane's ear. It's true. She's changed. She remembers that not so long ago she considered the damaging of one of Dragonkeep's arches more tragic than the deaths of those who committed the damage - perhaps that's when it began, when she began to edge away from her duty. She would not have considered an arch as important as a life when she was younger, even though fresh with belief in her calling as archivist of the city, as its protector. She would not have thought life less important than stone when she first met the harper. When he first walked into this realm as he walked so easily from another. When the Uroboros was not so near, or so certain.

"Come with me."

If he had asked her then, would she have gone? No, that at least is sure. Nor if he had sauntered back into her realm when the arch was broken. Even then with her duty, twisted away from care for the flesh and bone of Dragonkeep to care for its petrified corpse, even then she would not have gone with him.

But now...

"There's no care left in you." The harper's hands still play over her nakedness, his own pressing against her. The harping has slid again into a timbre needing a voice to complete it. But the harper's voice in her ear, Phariane realizes, is that voice. As her own hands stray back to the harper's thighs, she realizes that it always has been. Voice of harper and of harp are one and the same. Purring. Prowling with storms.

The storms gather around her more tightly, soft and sweet, and unending, and none bring with them blood, or darkness, or fear.

Or anything.

She arches and strains to hear anything beyond the sweetness. She finds nothing. The harper, the Wheelwalker, has walked, sauntered, meandered countless realms without care. And there is no care in his voice, in his lazy touch. Not even for her.

"Not even for me."

As she says it the harpsong dies away but the voice continues. It says, "If you won't come with me, perhaps the other one will. The ruler of Leviathan. The bitch of shadow. Sstheness. Your sister." The voice laughs. Lazily. Mockingly. A shrug of a snigger echoes into nothing and she knows the harper has gone. Her back is naked again. Alone. Already beginning to cool.

Even now she doesn't turn.

Chapter Fifty-Eight

Harnak stops raking the barbed whip back and forth across her back.

She hears footsteps.

For the span of a pang she holds her life frozen as she listens. Harnak struggles to turn the sound, change its quality as it reaches her ears. But the footsteps are too soft, too sure, too feline. Not the footsteps of her Dream-ward. She listens to them descend the metal treads, reach the vault where Harnak sits, continue down without pause.

Before they fade she begins to ease the barbs back and forth once again.

Chapter Fifty-Nine

Phariane stands in the fountain, in the light shed by the delicate thread of silver arcing in front of her.

In the emptiness left by the harper there comes to her a footfall - graceful, silent, and unmade. After a moment's eternity her shoulders straighten. She turns and looks at Zantalliz.

Climbing from the pool she moves closer. He's changed into a fresh shift. Phariane takes hold of it, grips it in her fists and tears. Then she takes his fine-boned hands and twines her fingers with his and brings them to her breasts. She drives them hard against her. His strange eyes watch her. Then she frees her own hands and takes his face in them and draws his mouth to hers. Then they draw each other to the cavern floor and she rams herself down onto him. And again.

She wants it to burn.

She wants to care that it burns.

Chapter Sixty

Gel awakes in the morning. His Dream-ward is warm and still. Pouting, he studies the path of her spine, stretches out a finger and traces it without touching. Thought touches his eyes. He wends the finger back.

He can still feel spits of Shadow on his body from the voyage back to Dragonkeep. They squirm about the dried Wyrmshod Cadre blood stiffened on his skin. They slide over the scratches on his back still fresh with sting from the night. In the bed the Dream-ward stirs, awkwardly, as if something nags her sleep. He glimpses specks of the same dark amorphous lice on her back.

He knows what he needs to do, where he needs to go.

He suddenly glides out of bed, disturbing neither sheet nor Dream-ward, and straightens. His labrys is already in hand. His hand has never left it through the night. He winds on his jehad swaddlings. Moving to the window, he pulls back its drape.

Morning in Dragonkeep, but unlike any Gel has known before. The pensive quiet which settled over the city last night remains. The avenue stretching to the dragon's mouth flickers with yellow flame, but it seems that almost half the wayside braziers are empty. This dawn is more a pallid twilight.

On the table of convocation food has been laid. Cold food. There is a bowl of fruit, some that Gel recognizes from his own realm Gnomon, some not. There will be no more fruit from Dragonkeep's trees. Gel remembers seeing the hacked stubs of orchards from his chariot on last night's ride to the archive. The wood has gone to fashion staffs, tonfa, arrow shafts, hafts for hammers. There are a few plates of cold meat. The animals in Dragonkeep have been slaughtered. The bread is stale. No cults or gangs set fire to the fields for malice or some ancient desperate ceremony anymore. Not that anyone tends crops now. There's no more time for husbandry. The Uroboros is coming. The city has accepted it.

As he walks along the avenue he sees that the city is by no means deserted. People are about. They move quietly, but they move purposefully. There is a look to them. Every one of them.

On his way Gel passes one of Dragonkeep's armouries. Throughout the troubles since the arrival of the Phoenix Prey, the city's hawk-helmed Blade-ward have needed to guard them day and night. They still station themselves around this armoury, but the gates are open and they're passing out the panoply within. Iron and steel. Worth more than life here. Ancient swords and daggers, tridents and halberds, and axes and javelins of varied lengths and shapes, shields and helms and armours of many designs. The citizens who wait stand calmly and orderly but nothing disguises the awe on their faces.

For some reason Gel turns down a side street off the avenue before he can be seen. Perhaps the awe on the faces disturbs him. Perhaps he wishes to avoid such expressions turned onto him. Perhaps he feels it best not to risk the lack of such expressions when the citizens' eyes fall on him. Perhaps he simply wishes to avoid delay.

The lesser streets and wynds of Dragonkeep are emptier. Gel moves quickly. Then he happens upon a plaza flagged in sardonyx. He slows. He finds it familiar.

The plaza is quiet now, but he remembers it swirling with masked dancers in white and black and crimson gauze. It was soon after the Phoenix Prey arrived in the city.

And there was a song, an antiphony.

'The twisted and twisting worm...'

'The twisting and twisted worm...'

Yes, and there was a chant. He smiles.

'Blood and red slaughter.'

He remembers laughing.

In the middle of the plaza is a single figure. A woman. Young. Dancing. If she notices him she gives no sign. He comes close to her, Bloodbane across his shoulders, his wrists resting over its pole.

She's dressed in black gauze, the colour of the most frenzied of the dancers. But this dance is different from the dance of the masque. Her eyes transfix the flags. She sways and turns differently, her steps abort, gestures pull short of flow, movements turn in on themselves. He's close enough now to see the blood flushing her cheeks, hear the breathless murmur on her lips. Still she doesn't look at him.

Gel grins. He has always been able to recognize madness, always been drawn to madness, always been beguiled by madness.

He skips around her, bowing, bending his face near hers. Her blood flushed face.

'Blood and red slaughter.'

Still she doesn't look up.

Blood and red slaughter.

And the murmur on her lips.

"The twisting and twisted worm," she breathes, "the twisted and twisting worm."

And he can taste the echo of blood on her murmur.

But he knows what he needs to do, where he needs to go, and he backs away, sliding his feet across the sardonyx, and turns away for the dragonmouth.

Chapter Sixty-One

Gemmored is unaware that morning has come to Dragonkeep. He again shifts his stance on the gneiss causey stretching deep into the fiery cavern of the dragon's mouth. He steps forward, back, side to side, diagonally, pivots on one leg, then the other, time after time. His right hand is close to the hilt of his sword, the left underneath. Twists of sheen spasm along the blade. Each cut is strong, whether born in shoulders or elbows or wrists. Plunging cut, shifting cut, crooked cut, the cut of wrath. Each guard and ward and thrust too, is powerful, swift, though he's performed these movements throughout the night. The old dance - renewing and refining the bond between arm and steel. The familiar pride is still there. Somewhere.

Even the evil coursing through his body like the hiss of wings is something he's known before. But not so much. Not for so long.

Before, when he's slain enemy after enemy without cease and felt the evil build in his soul to a pitch, he has sheathed Doom. Even in mid-battle he has sheathed his sword in its pale scabbard and heard it shriek and felt the evil drain out of him. But now the scabbard is gone. Now he can sense the evil rooting vessels through his whole massive body. He can feel the darkness on his tongue but has no word for the taste.

Beneath and all around the causey is breath as dragons know it - fire. An immense roaring inferno of life, writhing forest of flame, pirouetting branches and leaping buds, furious and licking and undulating tongues of yellow and white and red. The yellow gives light. The white bestows the heat used to forge or to kiln or to cremate the dead. And the red is the cleanser - the unShadower. When he came here last night, before beginning the old dance, he'd stepped onto one of the cantilever strips of jet leading off the main causeway into the hearts of some of the red flames. He did not complete the walk. Smears and flecks of Shadow still matt the fibres of his bear pelt, stain his cuirass and vambraces and jambes, lurk in the clefts and pits of his body. If Gemmored steps into the flame he knows these stains will all burn away.

But afterward, would his ruined eye still be abscessed with darkness? Would it still see things in its slurred vision that only dying minds have a right to see?

Would bathing in the flame unShadow Doom? purge it as the lost scabbard did?

He stops the dance and looks at the blade.

Or is he always destined to be Doom's suckling? Destiny? Is it more than chance that he happened upon the arcane thing on the rotting siege in Leviathan and slew it and lost the sword's pale scabbard? What was it the harper had said about fate? Has he been chosen to set the Uroboros in motion? Or to turn the coming battle in favour of Shadow?

Anger surges and breaks within Gemmored. All the talk of shadows, different darknesses, the words themselves shadows within shadows...

He walks to the end, the edge of the causey, and stares down. He holds Doom out and turns it, kinding glims of indigo - like brooding blood - and silver. Should he -

"Throw the blade!"

Gemmored turns. He's not surprised to see Gel, smirking, wrapped around his labrys like a whore.

Gemmored strides away from the end of the causey without discovering if he would, or could, or even wanted to loose Doom.

Standing before Gel, he presses the sword's tip onto the gneiss and leans lightly on the crosspieces. Beneath Gel's mist of mane, squirms of dark maggot across his scalp. More shadows. His smirk is jagged. He shakes his head.

"You serve your blade," he says, "bound to its hunger. As," he caresses Bloodbane, "am I to mine."

"So why," says Gemmored, "do you come here?"

"Perhaps," says Gel, no longer smirking, "I came to do what you can't. To throw my blade into the fire, to be rid of it. Perhaps I've tired of it."

"So you don't come to be cleansed."

Gel walks past Gemmored. Gemmored does not move, doesn't watch him stand where Gemmored had stood, at the end of the causey.

The thundering forest of fire columns up before Gel. He talks into void and flames. "Why bother to wash away a piddle of darkness?"

Gemmored starts to stride away down the causey, toward the city. He knows where he needs to go, what he needs to do, even before Gel calls out to him.

"We are all shadow. Shadow to the bone."

Chapter Sixty-Two

Phariane and Zantalliz lie, spent, on the stone floor of the cavern in the depths of the archive. The glimmering rill of silver, arching from the pool, veins through the silence. They gaze at the roof of the cavern.

Zantalliz thinks of the reef of the isle in the nameless sea. Of trails of moonbolt over the water.

Phariane remembers the forest, soft mossy ground and the roof of Dragonkeep pricked here and there by a spark of emerald or garnet or amethyst.

"What do you know," she says, "of the way of Dragonkeep and Leviathan?"

"Dragonkeep flees, Leviathan pursues."

"Dragonkeep flees, Leviathan pursues."

"Across the Shadow."

"Across the Shadow," says Phariane. "Bound."

The silver light burrows deeply into the glyphs on the cavern walls.

"Do you know how the bond is formed and sustained?" asks Phariane.

Zantalliz stretches out a reply. "Your sister?"

"Dragonkeep has its archivist, its healer. Leviathan its…" Phariane's voice trails. "When the time comes to choose them, it must be twins. The binding must be blood. Sometimes they're found on the sky-wyrm, sometimes on the sea-wyrm. Never grown. Always just old enough to remember the parting. Sstheness and I were born on Dragonkeep. I remember her crying. Her mouth wide. Wider than madness. As though her pleas were splitting her face. My fingers sliding over her fingertips and then over nothing. I remember the fury in her screams as a dragonreme pulled away from the harbour, taking her to Leviathan."

Chapter Sixty-Three

Sstheness lounges on the throne in the cold tallow-candled chamber with the rectangular-hewn murk-bottomed pit. Her eyes brood. One foot rests on the seat. A thigh juts out from the coarse mantle that slovens over her. Her teeth vaguely gnaw on her lip.

Equally vaguely she runs a long pale sheath back and forth through the sigilstalls taloning her fingers. A keepsake – something left by one of the Phoenix Prey. She knows what it is.

The chamber is crowded. Eyes dart. Shoulders bunch. Elbows twitch. A Shadow Corsair yelps and drops into the pit.

There's movement deep below. Slithering, juddering. There are gristly sounds, suckings, rippings. Stiff, bone-white shapes dart.

The chamber is full of Corsairs and Death'sheadcadre and others who are neither. Sstheness' gaze sharpens a moment and picks out one of these - a woman - the pinched-faced woman with the child that Gel once passed in Leviathan's passages. She's levered forward to the edge of the pit, whimpering. She looks up at Sstheness in the last moment before she's pushed, but Sstheness' sight has already drifted back into sulky abstracted wanderings.

Presently, her gaze sharpens again.

This time another Corsair, this one struggled forward by one of the Death'sheadcadremen. The Shadow Corsairs are freer than the Death'shead Cadre, whom Sstheness treats like puppets - each hates the other for this. This delights her. The Death'sheadcadreman wrests the Corsair over the pit brink, but the Corsair keeps his own grip. Both topple into the murk.

Slithering, juddering, suckings, rippings, dartings.

This doesn't matter. It doesn't matter that neither had any part or blame in the escape of the Phoenix Prey from Leviathan. It doesn't matter that the pinched-faced woman had.

There is no justice on Leviathan.

Sstheness is punishing because she must punish. Reason would only blemish what she does here.

She sighs and tosses Gemmored's lost scabbard into the pit.

Chapter Sixty-Four

"We are all shadow. Shadow to the bone."

Gel waits long after he's shouted the taunt over his shoulder to Gemmored. Long after Gemmored has gone. He stands on the edge of the causey. Looking over the blinding molten havoc. Listening to the dragonmouth roar like volcanoes breathing.

Then he holds his labrys out over the flames as Gemmored did his sword. He balances it by a finger under the long haft, flawlessly unswaying. Perhaps he should have wielded it on Gemmored, as he'd intended, added his delightfully tormented soul to the screaming horde within the twin blades. He still feels the hunger, part his and part Bloodbane's and unable to distinguish between. It's true, what Gel said. Both of them are bound to their blades.

And yet.

Gel's head tilts. He listens to the screams carefully. Picks among them like carrion for the sundered fragment of his own soul among the howls. Searches without finding. Has the misbegotten whimper of essence died? Or, unnoticed, returned to Gel? Or, less fanciful, he sneers, has his entire soul, unnoticed, migrated to the labrys?

And. If any of these imaginings are true...

Gel's gaunt face hardens still and deep with an alien look.

Could he be free? His finger lifts Bloodbane higher. The flames light the blades but don't dance over them as they did over Gemmored's sword. Could it be? Could there be a time where he can be sure where pleasure ends and despair takes its place?

He brings Bloodbane back on his finger, slowly, like beckoning. He takes a step backward. Stoops. Bows? Abases? Eyes still fixed on Bloodbane. He lays the labrys, the violent god he no longer loves, slowly, slowly, on the edge of the causey.

And slides his finger away.

He takes another step back.

Another.

Gel kneels.

He can still hear the screams, but not so intimately, so painfully, and fading. Could it be? A fog descends on him, on his sight, his hearing, on all his senses, like a cataract over existence, like a concentration of mystery. And the screams are distant, are gone.

And then something emerges from the fog.

Chapter Sixty-Five

"We are all shadow. Shadow to the bone."

Gemmored walks down the causey away from Gel's taunts. He passes the deserted ironworking tools - swage blocks, mandrels, crucibles - beyond the dragonmouth and through the dragonthroat. Finally he emerges onto the long shallow stairway leading into the city.

At the foot of this his Dream-ward still waits. She raises her head from the rim of the chariot where she slept. She smiles. Her sloe eyes search Gemmored - see the smuts of Shadow still spattering him - become uncertain.

She steadies the horse with the reins. Edges to the side of the chariot. But Gemmored walks past, starting down the wide straight avenue arrowing to the heart of Dragonkeep - to the archive.

He passes through vaulted arches petroglyphed with sinuous and angular stories, unknown but familiar.

Blind to them.

He strides past brazier after brazier.

Not noticing that many of them are empty of flame, that the day is dimmer now in the city.

A shout goes out from somewhere along the streets and wynds off the avenue. Once it would have reminded him of other shouts in other cities, on battlegrounds of his own realm Darkling. But not now. The pensive quiet that the shout slices through he ignores also. There is a feel to the city. The Uroboros is coming.

But there is something he must do first.

He walks on, Doom in his hand. His Dream-ward, no longer smiling, nudges the chariot along behind.

Inside the archive Gemmored sweeps the bowls and plates and cups from the onyx table of convocation. He sits and lays Doom down. Even on the journey from the dragonmouth he's felt the dark strengthening within him, the feathery, leathery, liquid, barbed wings of it surging. He feels the old pride, the honour, souring like bile.

He runs his eyes along the sword. The once fluid watering of its sleek grey flats is now ruined, the chevrons cracked and distorted as if the metal has wizened. This has always been the way of it. The more Doom has slain, the more disfigured the watering has become. Until Gemmored has sheathed it in its pale scabbard and the throatless scream has crescendoed. And when Doom has been unsheathed it has always emerged pristine and pure again. Pure.

Gemmored's gaze reaches the sword's pommel.

To his surprise the dark core of the gemstone is not flurrying wildly. It no more than stirs. A pupil-like flaw.

He remembers lying in the chamber with the rotted siege in Leviathan. Remembers staring into the gemstone and seeing himself – seeing himself and yet not seeing himself. He stares at the gemstone with each eye - his whole eye, still the grey of steel, and the wounded eye. The wounded vision sees differently. Gemmored has begun to understand. There may be no difference between blood and darkness, darkness and blood. Dark may be blood, but dark is not shadow. Shadow is something cast. A promise of darkness. Shadow is a mixture of light and pain and something else.

Gemmored takes the sword, lifts it by the crosspieces, and brings down the hilt on the table. He lifts it again. The gem remains on the onyx. It glimmers.

He lays Doom down again and takes up the gemstone.

He draws a breath into the jokul scarp of his chest. A shivering blade of breath drawn across eternity.

His other hand lifts to his face, to his wounded eye. Pushes at the bulging lid. Shadow trickles out. Presses harder, pushing the lid up, fingers digging. Feathery, leathery, liquid wings flicker blindingly around the pain.

One final wrench tears out the last of the dark pus from the socket.

His other hand, trembling, holding the gemstone, starts to lift.

As it nears the empty socket, Gemmored almost glimpses something.

Light and pain and something else.

Chapter Sixty-Six

Sstheness still lounges on the serrated throne. The cold tallow-candled chamber with the rectangular-hewn murk-bottomed pit is not so crowded now.

A child, a girl, thrashes and squeals above the skull helm of a Death'sheadcadreman before being flung into the pit.

Sstheness yawns.

Now she runs something else back and forth through the sigilstalls taloning her fingers. It had been found in the same room as the scabbard. A soiled, rumpled shred of cloth.

She knows what it is.

She presses her sigilstalls closer together, stretching the shrivel of robe taut.

The Death'sheadcadrewoman who brought it to her is the next to drop into the pit.

Juddering, suckings, rippings.

Sstheness cranes her neck, peers into the murk.

A Shadow Corsair snaps into frenzy. Wrenches his sabre blade free. Flails.

Sstheness' eyes thoughtfully shift from the pit to the shred of cloth. She crumples it between her hands, cups it to her face, buries her nose in it, breathes. Her eyes pass through terror and pain and fury and desire and as she stands they still waver.

She strides off the dais. Even though the men and women and children in the chamber roil, splashing cries and blood as the berserker Corsair lays about, they make a way for her. Someone topples into the murk-bottomed pit.

She pays no attention to this. To the berserker Corsair being dragged, sniggering and weeping to the pit. To the scuds of thrash in the murk. She rends open the entrance to the chamber and slips out.

Chapter Sixty-Seven

Above all the bone echoes and meat echoes of Leviathan's labyrinths, Sstheness walks the sea-wyrm's back.

She weaves thoughtfully between the spikes of the Shrike Wall. One hand trails across the oriflammes of skin and sinew hanging from the torn headless bodies impaled on the spikes.

Finally, she stops.

She looks down at the soiled, rumpled shred of cloth she's carried from the cold tallow-candled chamber with the serrated throne and the murk-bottomed pit.

She looks up over the Shadow that Leviathan ploughs through. Vast. Pendent. But no longer flawlessly level. There is a suggestion of movement, of sway, of swell, of sink. Restlessly serpentined with whippings of glimmer. Neither sea nor sky. It is Shadow.

She lifts the rag. Caught between anguish and anger, with her other hand she drags the carelessly shouldered mantle away and tosses it onto the charred scales carpeting Leviathan's back.

No wind chills her naked body. No wind ever blows over the Shadow, but the oriflammes on the Shrike Wall suddenly stir.

There is a sound behind her.

Sstheness knows it for the tremor of a phantom harpstring.

She does not turn around.

The tremor hovers in the air. A crafted sweetness. It remains just long enough to open the way for another note, before it drifts out over the Shadow.

And as the notes cascade into melody there is wind. It murmurs in the timbres, or maybe soughs between them, in trills, flourishes and broodings of sound. Sometimes there is a wanting of a voice in the harp music, and sometimes what comes needs no voice, and sometimes it seems that the music cadences into a lost language that dances between the two.

It sweeps out, over the Shrike Wall, lazily carrying with it skies and seas and oceans of skies and plains and cities and gardens and mountains and forests.

Most of all, Sstheness hears gardens, but she does not turn around. She knows there's no need. She knows what will happen next, waits for it.

Something touches her spine, her back. Warmer than sound, it moulds to her from shoulder to flank, harder and more urgent than song. Skin. Another body pressing against hers.

"Come with me."

The heavy-lidded voice comes, as she knew it would. The harping purrs lower. Like the harpsong the voice carries the memory of storms, the threat of storms. She loves storms.

"Come with me."

She says his name, the name she heard from his mouth so long ago. It's a lie. Every ear that hears his name hears a different name. Every one a lie.

The Shrike Wall twinges again.

And hands slide along her body. They slip over her scars as if they were harpstrings. And the music glissandos to a sweetness like wounds.

It's been so long since the Wheelwalker last came to her. Promising her. Teasing her. Lying. Laying her down and taking her in the dank messes of the knot at the heart of Leviathan. Swearing to stay. Leaving.

"If I die today," he says, "if you die today, if your sister Phariane dies, you know it would make no difference. The Uroboros will still come - and no act, nothing that happens before it comes will affect what will happen then..."

She arches her back, laying her cheek against his, and whispers.

"Good."

Sstheness brings the sigil-thorns of one hand to her neck. Her thighs, her belly, her breasts, arms, shoulders, face, every part of her is etched with scars. Except her neck. Flawless and swan-smooth, it throbs. Then she whips the hand across, snapping her head the other way to the cut as if in disdain.

She doesn't draw a single sigil-thorn across her throat, slit a thin, delicate, swelling gorget. Instead she rips it crimson wide. In the glistening wreckage tiny verminous things squirm.

She drops to her knees.

The harpsong stops.

Sstheness smiles with bloody teeth. She wonders if her sister, Phariane, with all her scrolls and tablets and books, has ever suspected that the harper might always appear in each realm as each reaches its Uroboros? And if he does if it means anything. Means anything beyond a gibe.

There comes an unmusical sound like a snort from behind her and she knows the harper has gone.

She takes the rag she still holds and smothers it in her throat.

Peeling it away she tears the soaked cloth once, twice. They're long, careful tears, more gently ripped than her flesh. She impales each piece onto the sigil-thorns of one hand.

She crawls away from the Shrike Wall, across the breadth of Leviathan, towards its edge.

But Leviathan is as wide as a city. Sstheness knows she must hurry. She can see, beyond the sea-wyrm's horizon, that the Shadow has already begun to change. No longer flat. No longer still.

And Leviathan has no real edge. Its back slopes away. After a time Sstheness' hands and knees start to slip on the charred yet weeping scales. She slides. Halts. Slides again. The steeper the back becomes, the further she flounders. Massive scales break loose under her like squarrose brash. She sobs. Though the verminous things have gone from the tear, the sound is mangled by the journey through her throat.

By the time she reaches the place she needs to be and kneels, the tsunami has already risen. It rushes for Leviathan's flank, faster and higher than the sea-wyrm - a great, flowing, inescapable precipice of blackness.

Sstheness picks each piece of what was once robe from her sigil-thorns, crumples each tightly and throws it. Each toss is a weary convulsion. With each her knees judder liquidly further down the slimy fell of sea-wyrm. None of the rags reach far. But each lands on the sloping scales and rolls on and down and finally into the Shadow.

As the third rag disappears the tsunami halts, poised over Leviathan, blotting out the stars. Then, as Sstheness watches, from the arching crest of the wave fall three drips of Shadow. They fall beside the Shrike Wall.

Sstheness digs the sigil-thorns of her hands into the sea-wyrm and climbs. By the time she looks up again there are three robed and cowled figures, hunched like ancient fears, beside the Shrike Wall.

She continues to climb, clawing and slathering and gasping her way up. Her savaged throat has almost closed now, but blood still dribs. She looks up again, peering at the Shrike Wall as if each spike is a pierced prophecy. There's no wind over the Shadow, but the impaled cadavers undulate.

The scars on her body burn. She loves how they burn.

One of the cowled figures raises an arm. The tsunami begins to fall.

Chapter Sixty-Eight

Gel writhes and thrashes on the dragonmouth causey. Spittle erupts from his mouth and slithers across the gneiss. His spine whips and convulses, cracks on the stone.

The fog still swathes him, his sight, his hearing, a cataract over existence, a concentration of mystery. His being is fastened onto a single sense - an awareness of where he ends and Bloodbane begins. The sense of separation is entrailed with dismay and pain. Is this what he wished for? What he hungered for? He wonders when he began not to love the indescribably ancient labrys, its long slender helve and sweeping crescents of blade lying so near on the edge of the causey.

It has taken with it the screams. Silence bathes him like darkness, or blood, or fear. For a moment he imagines he hears the bone echoes and meat echoes of Leviathan flitting through his torment. He listens again, in shreds of memory, to the ululation of alarm that raked through the sea-wyrm when the Phoenix Prey invaded its passages. He strains to keep the shrill and yearning and furious sound inside him. Anything but the silence.

And then the fog vanishes. Sight crashes back. And touch. His clawing, floundering fingers have brushed a razor, a sweeping crest of keenness. Bloodbane.

And his long lithe body snaps away, a rolling, squirming, jerking, kicking, howling, gasping, frenzy. Bone glancing on stone. Vision maelstroming. The causey. The dragonmouth roof. Colossal veins of flame streaking up into the air. He glimpses fragments of all these as he writhes and tumbles, and one thing more. A woman. No longer young. Dark bristling hair jabbed with silver. Gel's Dream-ward. Staring.

Gel keeps rolling. The next glimpse of the Dream-ward allows him a suspicion, the next confirmation - that she is not staring at him but at something else. When he stops tumbling he comes to rest on the far side of the causey. There, on the very other edge of the gneiss, he sees what transfixes the Dream-ward. He gazes into the dragonflames, the burning whites, the brilliant yellows, the languorous reds. Among all the flurrying colours there is one more. Something new. A single still blue flame like a gigantic lambent fang.

The Dream-ward breaks her stare. For a moment her eyes meet Gel's and anguish settles in them. Then she wrenches them away. She runs down the stone dragon-tongue, stumbling towards the dragonthroat and the city beyond.

Sprawled on the causey edge Gel watches, confused, disbelieving. He raises a numbed and bruised arm and reaches out to her until she disappears into the distance. Only then does his arm fall back, not onto stone this time but emptiness.

Chapter Sixty-Nine

In the archive Harnak, the shape-shedder of Aftermath; Zantalliz, the Moon-Ghost turned Shadow-Dancer of Voyage; Gemmored, the swordsman of Darkling; sit around the onyx table of convocation with the archivist Phariane.

It's morning. Outside, Dragonkeep is still. Has stilled while the Phoenix Prey has been away.

There are no more fires stolen from braziers or from the dragonmouth itself. No more fires are lit for malice. Once, not so many days ago, a stolen dragonfire had been spilled in the amphitheatre. The act had been thought of as nothing less than blasphemy. Now the Blade-ward no longer even guard the braziers. The youth bands who had drunk and insulted the Phoenix Prey and ran riot, have drifted apart. Those who blamed Phariane for the coming of the Phoenix Prey and all it heralded have forgiven or at least fallen silent. And those who refused to believe that the Phoenix Prey signalled the beginning of the end have long since succumbed and admitted the truth.

"The Uroboros is coming," says Phariane.

Harnak sits calmly. She finds it amusing that no one notices that the tiny shifts of skin tone or bone contour or eye colour have stopped. She's clothed herself in a new robe. Beneath it, her old scars and the new ones from the barbed whip still swathe across the skin of her back. Both old and new are still open, damp if not flowing. The silk sticks to and stings her back, but no blood seeps through.

The desire to kill Phariane has receded but still pulses. Harnak balances it against other desires inside herself as she listens.

"Leviathan will soon reach Dragonkeep," Phariane goes on. "The hejira is nearly done."

Zantalliz nods. Fear and darkness are still met in him, as they were in the battle with *Annihilation* in the sky above the Shadow. He allows himself to want the Uroboros. He also acquiesces to concern for Phariane. Both feelings are meldings of fear and darkness, and also something more. But not the same something.

Phariane glances up at the next level of the archive. "The fifth Phoenix Prey is still bedbound and broken. Gel is nowhere to be found."

Gemmored knows where Gel is to be found, but says nothing. The others around the table have eaten. They have bathed and put on clean robes, even though remnants of Shadow still streaks their bodies. But Gemmored has sat at the table since early that morning, without food, without sleep. Dark and red stains grime his face and vein-raked arms, the chest of his cuirass. His bare unpommelled sword lies across his thighs. Doom's gem gleams in the socket of his eye. He can still almost glimpse something through it - blood, and darkness, and something more.

Phariane pauses as a bowl of seeds is placed in the middle of the table. She takes a few, caraway, luffa, poppy, pomegranate, and swallows them. They are a symbol of the time. "Time," she says, "for the last convocation." But as she takes another breath, a shout comes from the stairway and the words stay lodged heavily in her throat as they have since the Phoenix Prey came.

All those sitting around the table turn. Gel's Dream-ward, breathless, torture-mouthed, staggers across the mezzanine. Too exhausted for deference, she slams her hands down on the onyx. Her arms prop her, head hanging.

After a while, speech comes. "The dragonmouth." And soon after that, "The blue flame has returned."

The Phoenix Prey look to Phariane for explanation. But all she does is stand. All she says is, "Come."

She leads Harnak and Gemmored and Zantalliz down to the floor of the archive's atrium and towards the entrance. Then she turns to Harnak. "You must stay," she says, and looks toward the ornate bronze door leading down into the vaults and finally the glimmering cavern. She places a hand on Harnak's shoulder.

Harnak looks into her eyes and sees them still cold, but the action is that of another Phariane. Not the cool and even haughty Phariane from when the Phoenix Prey first arrived. Not the woman distanced by her archivist's duties, weighed down by them. Not the woman haunted by the harper, his coming and his vanishing. Perhaps the woman from the cavern below the archive, singing to the silver blood from the fountain?

"If we don't return, the battle will come without us," Phariane tells Harnak. "Guard the ovary chambers."

This is the first time Harnak has heard the term for the vaults below the archive. It may well be that the dank amphoraed vaults are shaped from the spawning parts of the dragon. But she knows the name means more. She remembers the bowl of seeds placed on the table of convocation. She remembers her Dream-ward's words about the contents of the amphorae - life in abeyance, awaiting the outcome of the Uroboros.

Phariane's trust is vertiginous.

Harnak manages to nod.

As Phariane watches her slip through the bronze door, Zantalliz speaks. "What of the last convocation?"

"There may be no convocation," says Phariane.

"Does that mean there may be no Uroboros?" asks Zantalliz.

Phariane wonders. The blue flame has furnished her with a chance for the words of the last convocation, still waiting in her throat, to die there. A chance for her to discover what she and all the previous archivists have sought: a way to put back the Uroboros, perhaps forever. She feels no hope, but a kindling of something like a scrape of ice.

Perhaps.

But as she leads Zantalliz and Gemmored out of the bluestone archive, through the portico and down onto the vast esplanade, she hears something coming from the distant forest. The wolves have begun to howl.

Chapter Seventy

Phariane leads the two Phoenix Prey through the dragonthroat. This time, the tunnel is silent. The gneiss bridge stretching into the mouth above the flames is the same. The flames still rage, as terrific and soaring as ever, but soundlessly. Even though Phariane has no need to shout now, she says nothing.

As they come near the end of the causey, they can see Gel. His head and shoulders hang below the edge of the gneiss. His ribcage, ridged high beneath his jehad swaddlings as his body bends back, is still.

Phariane steps slowly toward him. Gel's Dream-ward has told her how she came to the dragonmouth to find him. How, before seeing the blue flame, she had found him. Because of what she had seen she has not returned here with the archivist and Zantalliz and Gemmored. She had, she sobbed, seen Gel dying.

But as Phariane moves forward, Gel rises. His shoulders and head and finally arms leisurely lift up. His ghost-fine mane is singed. In his hands is the long haft of Bloodbane. He grins.

Then he speaks. "Is this silence a herald of the Uroboros?"

Then, finally, Phariane speaks. "No," she says. She gestures to the blue flame, beautiful and lambent and steady, in the midst of the restless forest of other plumes. "The dragon always falls dumb when the blue flame appears."

She and Zantalliz and Gemmored and Gel moves to the edge of the causey closest to the new plume. Ethereal sapphire. It hovers just a few feet away, but there's no cantilever strip of jet leading into it as they lead into the red flames. "Yellow is the flame of light," she recites, "white of heat, red is the cleanser, the unShadower..."

"And blue?" says Zantalliz.

"Blue is the flame of rapture," says Phariane.

"What is the purpose?" says Gemmored.

"It takes," says Phariane. "It transports. It is the carrier."

"A means of escape?" asks Gel, with a start of amused interest, "from the Uroboros?"

Phariane shakes her head. "The blue plume always calls back those who travel through its gate."

"But where does the gate open?" asks Zantalliz.

"Into Leviathan?" asks Gel.

Phariane shakes her head again, and turns to the three Phoenix Prey. "Much further," she says, "though not as far."

"Other realms?" asks Gel, no longer amused.

"Any realm where dragons abide," says Phariane.

"Living or dead?" asks Gel.

"Even when a dragon's body turns to stone and gem that dragon still lives," murmurs Zantalliz, "as long as its fire still burns."

"A dragon *is* fire," says Phariane.

"My people kept their own archive," says Zantalliz. He remembers books bound in scollop shell and tablets of bone ledged among reef coral, browsed by rays and sharks, wandered by sea stars and crabs. "Much was written of dragons," he goes on, "among which was that each dragon has many heads."

Gel laughs. A shriek. It spears the cavernous quiet of the dragonmouth. "And I have only noticed one," he says.

"The fire is the true head," says Phariane. "And that fire is spread over many worlds, housed in the maw of a different sky-wyrm in each different realm."

"So the jaws of Dragonkeep," rumbles Gemmored, "the Beckoning Gate, is a gate that does open after all, in a way."

"When the key can be found to unlock it," nods Phariane, turning once more to the blue plume. "It appears from time to time, and every time a party is led by the archivist into another realm."

"If not to escape then why?" asks Gel.

"Here in Dragonkeep we grow and rear our own food. But there's one thing we can't husband."

Gel remembers the denizens of Leviathan suckling on the weepings of the sea-wyrm's stillbirth walls. He smiles. "Water," he says.

"We crush and drink the juice of fruits," Phariane replies. "But to replenish the city's water, it must be brought from the rivers of other realms."

"But why does the archivist go?" says Gel.

"Because they are the archivist," murmurs Zantalliz.

Gel shoots him a questioning look.

"There are books, scrolls, tablets, writings of knowledge in most realms," says Phariane. "While the others hunt out water, the archivist looks for lore."

"More stories?" says Gel. "Does Dragonkeep need more stories?"

"Not more," says Phariane. "All realms have their own legends, but all realms also share the same tales."

Gel shakes his head. His mane wafts uneasily. "Why do you want stories you already have?"

"The tellings are different," says Phariane. "It's the tellings that Dragonkeep's archivists and scholars have always scrutinized, comparing names, studying what is the same and what is almost the same and what is found in some tales and missing in others. Chronicles, aetiologies, cosmogonies, eschatologies... Myths, matters, cycles... Tales of beginnings, of battles and wars, of endings.

"Particularly," she goes on, "tales of endings. We look for clues, hints, ways of holding back the Uroboros."

"Why would other realms know of the Uroboros?" says Gel.

It's Gemmored who answers. His new eye glimmers. He suspects Zantalliz knows too, but Gemmored's glacial voice is the one that says it. "Uroboros comes to all realms in turn. The name changes but the end of all things is unavoidable fate."

"The harper used to talk about fate," says Gel, and Phariane winces and drops her head.

"Not all endings are the same," she murmurs. "Some are as much victories as defeats."

"So the blue flame offers a kind of victory?" says Gemmored.

"If it can be found," says Phariane.

"Will the search be through blood?" asks Gel.

"And darkness?" asks Gemmored.

Flames tremor on their faces, darting hammerings of light.

"History is often blood," says Phariane.

"And legend is often darkness," says Zantalliz.

Gel turns to Gemmored and extends his labrys toward a red flame, one of the cleansers. Shadow rills still swarm along his arm, weaving in and out of his jehad swaddlings. Similar rills coil over Gemmored's stained cuirass, his blood-grimed face. "Will you cleanse yourself before the journey?" asks Gel. Gemmored says nothing. Gel leans his head closer to Gemmored's. "Shadow to the bone," he whispers.

And he leaps from the causey into the blue flame and vanishes.

Gemmored stands, watches, glacial, specks of Gel's spittle glistening on his face. Then he leaps too.

Zantalliz slides a foot to the brink of the causey in preparation, but Phariane puts a hand on his shoulder. He turns and she slides her hand down to his hand, draws him away from the edge. "No," she says, "not you."

She backs along the causey. Her arm stretches out. Her fingers slide across Zantalliz' palm. When fingertips touch fingertips Zantalliz follows her, sustaining the touch. "If there is an archive in the other realm," he says, and she nods, "I can help you search."

She keeps moving back, looking into his strange eyes. "There is still a chance that what might be found might be found here. I need you to search here."

"In the archive? Where every text has been poured over by generations of archivists and scholars?"

Zantalliz stares into Phariane's eyes, but knows that her feet have stepped off the very end of the tongue of gneiss into air. Onto air. He follows her.

"There are other texts," says Phariane. "Texts which only a few, even among archivists, have had the skill to study."

Zantalliz hears something ahead, something murmuring, and he understands. The cavern is not entirely silent. There are other texts in Dragonkeep. Secrets written on air rather than page, in voice rather than ink.

He delves more deeply into Phariane's eyes and finds nothing, and understands something else. Her hand drops away from his and he allows the touch to break. He nods.He walks past her, into the raging fires of the dragonmouth, into the ethereal archive of sounds housed in the flames. The voices enfold him.

Phariane steps back onto the causey and walks back to the blue plume. She thinks of Zantalliz' lips on hers, his body against hers in the silvered cavern below the archive. But she does not look back to watch him glide deeper into the dragonfire, does not want to. She wants to be shamed at her betrayal of his care. Wants to feel pity for Gel's Dream-ward who abandoned her charge to bring the news of the blue flame to the archive, who Phariane last saw slumped at the table of convocation with suicide in her eyes. She wants to burn and care that she burns. But no. Zantalliz couldn't give her that. Not all the Wolf-wards she's bedded over the years, not all the flames here in the dragonmouth, could give her that. There is nothing inside her now but a cold lingering sweetness like a harp's whisper, like forsaken storms.

She looks at the blue flame. What she is about to do she will not do for the sake of hope.

She leans forward, lifting her arms, feet tilting over the edge of the causey.

A distant call reaches her from the dragon's throat. Leviathan has been sighted. But even if she could halt her dive into the blue flame she doubts she would.

Chapter Seventy-One

Sstheness has crawled her way back through the bone and meat echoes, through the barbed, glistening passageways of Leviathan. Her torn throat has closed entirely now. The tears have resolved into scabs that resemble the sigils on the fingerstalls that made the tears. All that bleed now are her hands and knees. She has pulled herself over snapping carpets of skulls away from the roar of the Shadow tsunami. Sstheness knows there is no stillbirth wynd of the labyrinths deep enough to escape the sound, but she crawls on.

One last twist around one last corridor, and it stands before her. A glistening black barrier. A swollen knot of stone.

Sky-wyrms have hearts of fire. Sea-wyrms, like Leviathan, have this.

She drags herself to it, climbs against it, flattens hands and belly and breasts against it. She can feel the pulse of Leviathan. The familiar sullen ghost of a heartbeat. Is it faster now? The motion of Leviathan is different now. Not ponderous but driven.

She smears her cheek against the chill and hardness of the knotwall and its curve distends still further. Top to bottom, a split appears. Sstheness sucks in the foetor from within. It bitterly delights her. The cleft opens into a gelid hollow darkness. The special darkness, different to any other found in Leviathan. A darkness which welcomes the eye - transpicuous. She is about to press against the cleft, knowing how it will soften, widen, allow her through, when she catches sight of a movement in the corridor. An undulation on the floor. A squirm in the dimness.

She slides off the knot and reaches for it. It twists sluggishly away but Sstheness' fingertips are already on the handle. Her sigil-thorns curl as her hand closes on it and picks it up. The slim blade continues to weave in the air.

Phariane's kris.

Sstheness holds it in front of her face. She can smell her sister on it. She turns it and clasps the blade between her lips. Can taste her too. She stays there awhile, supine, until she again becomes aware of the roar of the tsunami, and a distant call winding nearer through the labyrinths.

She staggers up and back against the fissured knot. The cleft splays. As she slips inside she hears that Dragonkeep has been sighted.

When does the Uroboros begin? Some of the books and scrolls and tablets of the archives across the realms maintain that it is the moment when the tsunami begins to fall.

But in a way it has always been falling. It began to fall from the moment it first reared, since one of the three robed and cowled figures on the sea-wyrm's back raised an arm.

It's behind the sea-wyrm now, rather than at its side. Leviathan, longer than a city, has continued to plough on, beneath the arching of Shadow. The tsunami, longer than fifty cities, pushes it on by its fall.

Its perpetual fall.

It perpetually falls as Leviathan perpetually rots.

Now Dragonkeep is sighted.

A distant nub of jade jagging the smooth horizon of dark sky laid hermetic against dark ocean.

Leviathan pushes nearer, closing the distance between the two wyrms as never before through the tsunami's urge. Leviathan approaches Dragonkeep from the rear. There is no wide glittering line of light beckoning, no crimson-yellow flames flickering between bared dragon teeth the size of spires to chase. But the wyrms are linked by deeper forces than sight. Gradually Dragonkeep's immense tail, climbing to even more immense trunk, becomes a mountain. Jade scales become the size of galleys.

And now the tsunami truly falls.

Chapter Seventy-Two

In his chamber in the archive of Dragonkeep, Rorn still dreams.

In his dream he again walks in the perpetually dark wastes of Nightwake, his realm. He feels the ash bunching beneath the heels of his boots. He's reached the point which a Waste-Ranger will always reach, when setting out from an impregnable noctilucent mansion. It is the instant when the last of the restless uranic gargoyles squatting on its roof abandons its last luminous glimmer to the distance. It is when, utterly blind under the moonless and star-forsaken sky, Waste-Rangers know they are home.

Rorn knows he is home.

He has even remembered his name.

The dwellers in the noctilucent mansions have no conception of real night since the Dark March into sanctuary. At best all they know is the pathetic enervated twilight when the generators damp for sleep. Nor can they imagine silence, the windborne boundless silence of the wastes. Instead they chatter.

Rorn has attended their banquets and yawned through their chatter. The pretty compliments strewn amongst themselves, glittering phrases wound round perfumed necks, brightly coloured words bedazzling the ear.

But now, watching as the last scintilla of light fails in the distance, he waits for the feeling that always comes. The perception of something lost, something passed, something gone. But that passes in a moment. He turns, pulls his heart tight, and plunges on into the wastes. Only the Waste-Rangers can do this, this scourging of feelings. Only the Waste-Rangers must do this. In the blackness between mansions, emotion and imagination kill. The blackness breeds them into fear. Once the fear takes root the whispers come. On the wind. Out of nothing. Then even a Waste-Ranger is lost.

And so Rorn plunges on, unwaveringly, unerringly, across a land where even the gods have become unrecognizable and unknowable gibbous things.

And on.

The only concession he allows his introspection as he travels is a relished smatter of a sense of transgression. It warms him under the cloaked sky.

And on.

Until he skids to a stop. Teetering. Confused. On the brink of a chasm. He looks down. The shifting depths at his feet have no place on Nightwake. They do not move with the elegant entwining of umber and magenta and cyan and ochre and celadon of the mansions' prophecy vats. This darkness twitches. Slithers. Judders. Is not darkness at all.

In his dream, Rorn recalls the pit in the cold candled chamber with the serrated throne in Leviathan. The murk of that pit was not darkness either.

Nightwake's blackness is vast but utter. Clean with utterness. But the blackness of the chasm before him, the blackness of the pit in the chamber in Leviathan, the blackness that oceans the realm that the

Phoenix carried him to... that is no darkness but a compound of many darknesses. There are currents within it, nuances and glimpses and eddies and echoes.

And at last Rorn realizes, understands, the difference between darkness and shadow.

The darkness is all around him, full of prowling things, but the Shadow is not just enchasmed at his feet but is within him, prowling within him.

He feels it, searingly chill, twisting and arching and uncoiling. He reaches for it.

In his bed in his chamber in the archive, Rorn stirs again. He tosses suddenly. A deep moan escapes. His watchful self-chosen Dream-ward, still holding him, tightens her arms. His legs jerk, threatening to dislodge the bedcovers.

Still lost in sleep, his hands reach for his face. They tremble each side of the faint white scar. They pull. His Dream-ward straddles him, clutches his wrists, resisting. She whimpers but has no more strength to spare her voice to shout for aid.

Rorn is silent. His eyes still closed. His fingers sink deep into his cheek. The skin each side of the scar stretches. The faint indent between eye and mouth is no longer pale but livid.

The tongue of yellow dragonflame in the brazier glows gently.

The tainted blanket from Leviathan that swathed Rorn on the journey to Dragonkeep lies on the floor.

Desperation edges into the Dream-ward's whimper.

The scar begins to tear.

Scrawls of sense touch what remains of Rorn's mind. Sobbing... Fire and darkness... Something falling. Something passed, something gone... Something slithering beneath his face...

And he feels a shudder of joy as he realizes that he has again forgotten his name.

And the scar bursts open.

Chapter Seventy-Three

Leviathan leaps from the fall of the tsunami, spurted forward by the force. The Shadow is no longer mirror-still obsidian, but all whipping flickering movement. Leviathan drives through it. The great wrinkled mouth in the smooth, eyeless snout opens, then closes on Dragonkeep's massive tail.

Some of the books and scrolls and tablets of the archives across the realms maintain that this is the moment when the Uroboros truly begins.

And on the top of the sea-wyrm's leagues of decaying back, the torn, headless bodies impaled on the Shrike Wall go mad.

And within the sea-wyrm all the skulls cobbling its labyrinths open their bony jaws and shriek.

And within those same windings and within the varices, cysts and tumours that are Leviathan's chambers, the members of the Death'shead Cadre halt. From deep inside the eye-sockets of their skull helms, below the skull beneath the skin, below the steel beneath the skull, something begins to glow.

And within Dragonkeep a tremor passes through the city. It shakes the forest, the cropfields, it shivers the city, the wide dolomite-flagged avenues and wynds, the sardonyx plazas, colonnades, ramps, tells, the braziers both empty and enflamed, and the arches petroglyphed with sinuous and angular stories. Cracks appear. Shards fall. The shock is not just the ripple of vibration of Leviathan's jaw closing on Dragonkeep's tail. This is something deeper. Something ancient.

Even the great amphitheatre quivers.

Even the archive.

In the moist dark of the lowest underground seed chamber, the dense array of glazed amphorae judder against each other. Harnak the shape-shedder lays his hand on the nearest and looks up.

Above the vaults, above the tegular floor of the atrium, above the mezzanine and the table of convocation and the cloistered chambers of the archive, above the purple porphyry of Dragonkeep's roof, the dragon's jade scales strain onward.

For a time the sky-wyrm slides on over the Shadow. The sea-wyrm, locked on its tail, is pulled along. The narrow whole is longer than two cities. Jade scales the size of galleys give way to decaying scales of charred flesh, just as huge. Within the sky-wyrm's mouth, the flickering crimson-yellow flames between bared teeth the size of spires, flare even brighter. The Beckoning Gate the people of Dragonkeep call it. A sign to Mariners on the Shadow, a call home. Now it beckons even more strongly. But not to ships.

On the back of Leviathan, the spine of the Shrike Wall still squirms with the frenzied throes of the impaled, from the nearly whole cadavers to the petty oriflammes of flesh. Beside the bony spikes only one of the three robed and cowled figures remains. Now it raises an arm.

And now the mountainous head of the sky-wyrm, the hollow amphitheatre eyes, the snout ending in the Beckoning Gate, starts to move. Begins to turn.

And the rest of the body follows. For the first time since it died, since the last of man discovered it and founded a city within its petrifying bones and tissues, the dragon twists.

And the sea-wyrm, too, begins to turn. Its blackened length starts to curl sluggishly, like some vast rictus. Its tail begins to turn toward the dragon's head.

And the dragon's chalcedony teeth the size of spires yawn apart. And the fire within the mouth, fallen silent, begins again to roar.

Within the mouth Zantalliz hears it. He walks on air and through flames still, musing, listening to the voices of the ethereal archive. The flames don't burn. He's a Shadow-Dancer, and fire and shadow, after all, are much the same. It is a lore once set down in his people's books. Shadow-Dancer and then Moon-Ghost, they would read the secrets written in the blood, in the air, under the sea, in the sobs of sirens and the murmurs of krakens. His heritage allows him to hear the words spoken here too, to understand that the echoes are not so much echoes as palimpsests of other and more distant voices. He searches for a word, a truth, a key, a meaning, to even now turn back the Uroboros. One voice – perhaps the same, perhaps different, tells him that he has been betrayed, that he should kill his betrayer. He continues in his task. Listening. Pondering.

Now the flames erupt into deafening thunder. But even though the words are drowned Zantalliz can still hear them, like the sorrowing of a siren or rumble of a kraken an ocean away. All he says is one word.

"Phariane."

Chapter Seventy-Four

Phariane is fire. Blue fire. Cold and infinite. She flickers through realm after realm, raptures as many times before, knowing this to be the last time. She tumbles through thunderous cavern after cavern of inferno, part of each, each part of her.

When she reaches her destination she knows.

She spits out of the final cavern into the day. Above her the sky is wings and scale - the sky is dragon. Each cavern on the journey has been the mouth of a dragon, each inferno the same inferno, a step on the way. And then the sky-wyrm is gone, vast as aurorae, all fury and sunrise and corona and starlight, soaring for the horizon.

Still falling, Phariane realizes that the pluck of sadness she has always felt at this sight is gone. Something else lost.

Then her shoulder hits stone. She rolls. She stands in a new world for the last time.

The stone this time is limestone. The realm is karst as far as she can see, a shattered pavement of clints, runnels, pits, pans. A few trees tear the flatness of the landscape. They jab out of the fissured limestone and splinter into barren branches, gnarled sculpts of brittle lightning. The wind twitches them.

The wind.

No wind blows over the Shadow. Phariane remembers it has always disconcerted those who've raptured from Dragonkeep into other realms - even her. And always the wind is different. It's anxious here, shifting, gusty. The wind is always the first thing Phariane notes.

The first thing Gemmored noted of this realm were the clouds. Bruised omens of storm.

For Gel it was the light. The bleakness of it.

The second thing either became aware of was the other.

Then Phariane becomes aware of them. She stands between them.

They stand apart, not close but not shouting distance. Gemmored's blood and Shadow spattered bear-pelt ruffles in the wind. His great sword, similarly soiled, he holds out double-handed in front. On guard. Towards Gel.

Gel stands as though on the brink of pouncing: hair whipping about like rips of quicksilver, the slender haft of his twin-bladed ax held at a mocking angle. Towards Gemmored.

Phariane looks from one to the other. For the first time she wonders if not one but two of the Phoenix Prey might've been infected by the Nightmare Cadre, that both of them may be destined to betray Dragonkeep and decide the Uroboros. If one were to kill the other... If each were to kill the other...

Then something dark flickers nearby.

A raven perches itself on a barren tree branch. Two jagged shapes fused.

Gemmored lowers Doom. There's the merest drift of the blade across his body, as if the old instinct for sheathing it still remains even though the pale scabbard is gone.

Gel lets Bloodbane's pole swing down.

Phariane feels death recede. Breathes again.

"What do we look for?" smiles Gel. "Water or lore?"

"Lore," says Phariane.

"Where?" says Gemmored.

Phariane turns to look into the flat fissured distance. She has no foreknowledge of what she will see - only that she will see it.

Gemmored and Gel also turn. No castle, or temple. No amphitheatre. No tower. But there is a building. Not close but not too distant for sight. It's broad rather than tall, a kind of flat-topped mound. The sides glimmer.

"It bares no resemblance to your archive," says Gemmored.

"Nevertheless," says Phariane. She starts to walk and the other two follow. Gemmored lifts Doom easily in one massive hand, resting the stained flat on his shoulder. Gel swings Bloodbane lightly onto his.

"Do you think you'll find it?" he asks Phariane. "Victory?"

"No one ever has," she replies. "Every archivist has searched for a way to postpone the Uroboros, to hold back the tide of Shadow... Something hidden in a book, a scroll, a tablet, in the tales told of the last Uroboros."

"So it's happened before?" says Gel. His stride almost falters.

"There're such tales in my realm," says Gemmored, "in Darkling."

"Not in mine," mutters Gel sourly, almost angrily. "In Gnomon such things are held in contempt."

"Some realms eschew story at times," says Phariane. "It's a way of denying the truth."

"The truth?" snaps Gel.

"That all realms travel toward the final battle," she replies. "All realms are part of the Wheel, and the Wheel is turned by the Shadow, carrying each realm in its time to the Uroboros."

"There's no Wheel in the cosmogonies of Darkling," says Gemmored.

"The Wheel is a symbol," says Phariane. "With some realms other symbols are chosen."

Gel hawks and spits on the limestone. "The harper said he was a Wheelwalker. Is that what he was? Someone who moved between realms without the aid of a Phoenix or a blue dragon's flame?"

Phariane speaks as if forcing breath into words. "He was. He is." Within her, over and over, the only echo of feeling left in her, the sweetness of harpsong...

"He also spoke," says Gel...

"If vaguely," adds Gemmored...

"Of fate. Is that what archivists really search for? Prophecy?"

There's silence for a while as they walk.

Gel eases Bloodbane behind his ghost-maned head, across his shoulders, wrists dangling from the haft.

"There is no prophecy," says Phariane eventually. "Because nothing is certain. All there is, all there can be, are stories of what has been, because many things that have happened will happen again. Not all things, not always in the same ways, but always the Shadow rises. Always a final battle is reached."

"And then?" says Gemmored.

"Each realm faces the Uroboros in turn," she goes on. "Each time the darkness is thrown back. The realm is laid waste. Its people devastated. But the darkness recedes, and the realm is freed - but freed only to take its place at the lowest point of the Wheel. Only to wait for the Shadow to rise again. That is the cycle."

"So the darkness is always thrown back," muses Gel, something puzzling nagging his words.

"Some writings seem to say not so much thrown back," Phariane replies quickly. "Rather that the realm passes through Shadow to a new beginning. At least to begin the cycle anew. But all agree that the tide has never been turned."

"So why did the harper say to me that destiny is fragile?" Gel's tone is prodding and uneasy. "And why have we come here to find a way to postpone a battle that always comes and that is always won?"

And then the three reach their destination.

The archive is like a dolmen. Pillars of brick raise it off the limestone and a timbered ramp leads into the building. A rotunda. The sides have no corners. The walls are slightly angled sections. They sheen because they're glass. Stained glass. Tall rectangular windows allow no views inside. Instead they depict latticed multicoloured images, vistas and figures and battles in pigment, all at the same time unfamiliar and familiar, hinting at meaning, much like the petroglyphs on the arches of Dragonkeep.

Gel stiffens. More stories.

The three move up the ramp.

"The ground is solid and high," says Gemmored. "Why is the archive raised on piles?"

"I don't know," says Phariane.

The metal door at the top of the ramp is wide and twin-valved. And unnaturally thin - almost bract. It swings inward smoothly.

"Why is there no lock?" says Gemmored.

The interior is one spacious chamber. Like the karst outside there's no sign of human life.

"Has it been abandoned, then?" asks Gemmored. His voice is no longer battered by the wind. Here it resounds. Cupped and held by the harsh interior surfaces of the rotunda rather than flung away.

Gel's voice is the same. He swings round the haft end of Bloodbane, presses it gently to the cleft between Phariane's jaw and neck. "I asked, why bother to postpone the Uroboros." Then he smiles. "And what could you find here to do it?" There are no books or scrolls or tablets to be seen. The rotunda is empty except for an array of slim pedestals on each of which perches an elegant, delicately incised or stippled crystalline vase. "Where are your words to turn the tide?" Gel starts to laugh.

He stops as something smashes against the haft of his labrys, and Bloodbane whirls away from Phariane's throat. Gel lets the pole spin about his fingers and then brings it to a halt.

Gemmored's sword blade is poised double-handed in front of his cuirass.

Gel smiles again. His fingers twitch and Bloodbane spins again, the twin blades arcing at Gemmored's head. The swordsman snaps up and angles his blade and the ax sheers over him. His face stays cold.

Then it begins.

Gemmored and Gel silently weave between the pedestals, Doom and Bloodbane a tapestry of flicker. The stained glass of the rotunda colours the bleak light of this realm as it passes into the archive, but leaches what strength it possesses. Yet Gemmored and Gel move through the dimness without stumble across the tiled floor. Gemmored is broader, but still surefooted, the slenderer Gel gliding between the pedestals and crystal vases. Both could simply smash their way through the battle, but this is as much a pitting of skill as of power.

Gemmored switches from one to two hands, Gel stays with one.

Doom arcs and thrusts and stabs and angles and cuts.

Bloodbane arcs and swoops and whirls and soars and spins and sweeps. Now and then it scythes through one of the exquisite vases, but purely through its wielder's design. Gel relishes the joy of the shatter, makes it a part of the rhythm of the battle.

When ax blade meets sword blade, a sound like a metallic snarl sheers away with the spark.

Gemmored is still a supple, cuirassed, bear-pelted berg. But Doom's once sleek chevroned watering is a crazed ruin. Where the red gem formed its pommel is only a dewclaw of antler bone jutting from the end of the handle. Gemmored is aware of the damaged balance of his weapon with every movement. The forces that Doom has gathered with each slaying are still within him since the gem is not lost but socketed in his face instead of the sword. He remembers battles long gone where the martial skill of those he slew entered him, merged with his own. He remembers the elation. The evil that entered him at the same time could always be borne as long as he could finally sheathe Doom in its scabbard and free himself. But the scabbard is lost. And the things Gemmored has slain since its loss have yielded far more evil than skill. And even in the midst of the battle with Gel, the gem still beguiles and distracts him with sights just beyond his grasp.

Blood and darkness and fear.

Blood and darkness and fear.

And something more.

Gemmored still moves as one with his sword, like a war-wise storm. His wards flow into attacks, but Gel is all flow, defence and attack all at once. One of Bloodbane's slaying crescents sweeps across Gemmored's throat and crimson ribbons after the blade. The battle flickers on. Gemmored's face is still cold - one eye the grey of frosted steel, one crimson and unfaceted.

Again ax blade meets sword blade. Again the clash is a metallic snarl, and sparks stab the dimness, glimmer over the glass of the vases.

It's this sound that brings Phariane forward.

She should rush, she knows, but she simply walks steadily toward Gel and Gemmored. As she nears them Bloodbane sweeps through another vase and shards of crystal spray at her. Her sheer cataphract of otherworldly mail is still in Dragonkeep. She wears a sleeveless tunic. Her right arm turns red with cuts. She doesn't care.

It's not through eagerness to end the battle that she doesn't wince at the pain. Nor because of the urgent need to explain that she's seen the secret of the rotunda. Nor through any wish to stave off the Uroboros. Not through any desire. She has come to this realm because this is what the archivist does. She watches herself performing what the archivist does. She watches herself doing what others have done before, moving through the Shadow Cycle. Phariane's arm is raked with tears. But Phariane is dead. She imagines her sister, Sstheness, her entire body covered in scars, curled up in the darkness of the heart of Leviathan, shivering with ecstasy, shivering with dread, febrile with anticipation.

Gemmored and Gel stop and turn to her as if their battle had never been.

"Bring the blades together again," says Phariane. Gemmored and Gel look at her. "Over one of the vases."

Gemmored and Gel place themselves either side of one of the pedestals. A glance between them, and warsword and labrys clash again. Again the sound resounds through the rotunda. Phariane stares at the vase below the blades. The engraving on its surface shivers, then returns to the original design. Phariane nods, and kneels before it.

She hums, softly, almost beyond softly, somewhere on an edge between breath and voice. The air vibrates. Phariane cups her hands around the vase. It too hums. Those nearby also start to hum, then those near them, growing louder all the time, until the rotunda is alive with plangent shrill. The design on each vase stirs, first quivering, then undulating like delicate tendrils.

Phariane stops her hum. The silence spreads from the vase in her hands to each of the others, until quiet completely returns to the chamber. The engraving on each vase also stills, but the designs are no longer swirls or spirals or arabesques. They've reformed into other patterns. Logograms. They've become language.

"So it *is* an archive," says Gemmored.

"No leather or parchment," chuckles Gel. "He picks up a vase and juggles it carelessly. "No books or scrolls or tablets..."

Phariane comes forward and pulls the vase from his hand and turns her back on him. She cradles it, gazing down at the writing on the smooth crystal as she walks away. "Is it here?" Gel calls after her. "The secret? The words to turn back the Uroboros?"

Phariane gives no answer.

The wind blusters over the karst and jostles the stained glass windows.

Phariane listens to it. She has no answer for Gel, does not even know what she wishes the answer to be. Then she hears something picking its way through the wind. Numerous sharp clops tapping ominously on limestone.

And she knows then that Gel's question has lost all meaning. That the Uroboros has come.

Chapter Seventy-Five

Dragonkeep and Leviathan are fused now. They form a single squamous torc of swirl.

Outside the immense circling atoll of wyrm the dragonremes of Dragonkeep have taken to the Shadow. Leviathan's quinqueremes have also launched. These traditionally emerge through the Beckoning Fear, the sea-wyrm's mouth, the puckered maw of mucus and Shadow. Finding that the mouth is now clamped to Dragonkeep's tail, the Corsairs have hacked open Leviathan's blackened side.

Both fleets struggle not just with each other but with the Shadow. No longer mirror-still obsidian. Now roiling phantom jet.

Prows shear through rearing black spume. Oars flounder. Galleys heave and lurch. Hulls clash and cave. The agile speed of the dragonremes and the surging power of the quinqueremes are both useless, boarding planks and catapults equally futile. There can be no aiming of either.

Lamellar-jerkined Corsairs leap laughing from ship to ship. Some slip, fall, and disappear. The Shadow swallows body and voice instantly. But as they fall even their screams are mocking. Otherworldly-mailed Sword-Mariners and wolves grimly meet the Corsairs who manage their leap. Swords sweep and thrust and wound haphazardly as the decks jerk and roll. The decks are slick. Fluid fragments of Shadow flit through the air like black spindrift.

And still the wyrms swirl.

Not only do they turn, they twist. The Shrike Wall on Leviathan's back is now a coil rather than a straight wall of spines. There are no more robed and hooded figures standing beneath them.

Inside the turning and twisting torc, the Shadow is neither mirror-still nor roiling.

Within the circling wyrms, the Shadow is an endlessly deep conical void, spinning far more wildly than Dragonkeep and Leviathan. A maelstrom of dark.

At its lost pinprick core, somewhere beyond distance, something seethes, convulsing like a swarm of talons, and climbing.

Chapter Seventy-Six

Hooves stamp on the metal doors. The wide twin valves crash inwards. The horse slides and clatters onto the smooth floor of the rotunda archive. Its rider yanks viciously on his reinless mount's mane to steady its frenzy. His brawny tattooed arm, above the bazuband, ripples with the strain.

But Gel is there already.

Bloodbane's blades shear up through the horse's breastbone and into the rider's. Both ruined bodies shudder to the floor. The manic paean on the rider's lips falters.

Gemmored is there too, past the corpses and on the ramp sloping down to the limestone. The next charging rider fails to reach the doors. As does the next. Blood begins to soak the ramp. Gel joins Gemmored. Crimson erupts into the wind.

With each sweep or thrust Gemmored grows more familiar, more content, with Doom's flawed balance. The pommel gem nestles in his skull as if it has never rested anywhere else. Sword and swordsman more one than ever. As Doom reaps, the ancient wingless spasm beats through Gemmored's veins.

Gel moves like dancing razors. His time writhing on the dragonmouth causey, impaled on the agony of his separation from Bloodbane, is barely a memory now, hardly a smatter of unease amid his elation. Only the sour twitches of his lips, like slashes of cirrus in a desolate sky, betray the last remnants of fear.

Inside the archive Phariane still stands at the stained glass window. She watches the Wyrmshod Cadre circling the rotunda as they once circled the dragonreme as it fled Leviathan. She remembers them emerging from the dark cavern of the sea-wyrm's mouth. Spat out. Distant shreds gradually becoming riders and horses. She recognizes the riders' ululating paean. But the sound of the hoofbeats is new. The cadre is shod for Shadow. Shod with the daggersharp scabs which vein Leviathan's stillbirth halls. On Shadow they make no sound. Here the impact of scab on limestone lacks the clean ring of farrier metal. The hoofbeats are dull. Scuffed. Tainted.

Phariane imagines the same sound on the Dragonkeep causey as the cadre must have thundered along it, until coming to the blue flame. Until rider and mount must have flung themselves into it, one after another. Perhaps some jostled, slipped in their fury. Perhaps some fell into the other flames of the dragonmouth, the reds, the yellows, the burning whites. She hopes so.

As for the rest, they have found her and the remains of her Phoenix Prey even here. The Uroboros has begun, and the Wyrmshod Cadre have brought it with them.

Presently she comes aware of something charnel behind her and turns.

Gemmored and Gel stand there. Both are splashed with fresh death. Their weapons also. What skin of Gel's not wound in his jihad swaddlings is the same colour, as if splashed from within. The archive's bract-thin doors are pulled shut. The Wyrmshod Cadre have abandoned any attempt to enter, though Phariane can still hear their hoofbeats circling the rotunda.

"It's time," says Gemmored.

"For what?" says Phariane.

"The last convocation," says Gel.

"The last convocation has already began," says Phariane.

"Then finish it," says Gel.

Phariane looks at Gemmored. He nods.

There's a snap behind her. Sharp and spidery. She spins. The window behind her, the window she's just looked out from, is an image of a long-haired and sweeping-robed woman holding a star aloft on her palm. A piece of green glass, beside the robe, has cracked.

So has the piece next to it.

Then other snaps come, a venomous hail of snaps rushing from window to window. Crack after crack crevices the latticework of glass.

Phariane looks out again. The Wyrmshod Cadre have unfurled their whips, their barbed whips, from the bazubands on their forearms. They've started to lash the windows as they once lashed the dragonreme as it fled Leviathan.

As the hail goes on, Phariane threads her way through the pedestaled vases to the centre of the rotunda. Gemmored and Gel follow. In a circle of space she kneels on the tessellate floor, sits, pulls her legs crossed. "There are questions I have no answer for," she says softly.

Gel and Gemmored tower over her, like still, solemn golems.

"Why this archive is raised off the ground on pillars, why we found it deserted..."

One of the windows cracked by the Wyrmshod Cadre riders is struck again by one of the teeth barbed whips. Glass shatters this time. Fragments spill onto the floor. The hail goes on. The barbs strike the windows more fiercely. Phariane's head drops. She cups her hands behind her head, palms over her ears. Her lacerated arm still glistens with blood and splinters of vase crystal.

Gemmored looks down at her. His wounded neck scalds - a needle of burn drawn across his corded throat by the sweep of Gel's labrys. It echoes other wounds. The poisoned dagger thrown from the crowd in Dragonkeep's amphitheatre. His own sword piercing him in the chamber in Leviathan with the arcane maggot-faced creature. But these wounds, and the many before them, are nothing more than far, petering balefires.

His gemstone eye still haunts him with glimpses of secrets and promises.

Blood and darkness and fear.

Blood and darkness and fear.

Blood and darkness and fear and something more.

Phariane rocks on the tiled archive floor.

Gel looks down at her. But he hears Bloodbane. The screams of the dead. The ax's slaying crescents have let epochs of blood, gathered countless souls. Now they have tasted Gemmored's. A snick of the swordsman's essence, pulled free with the ribbon of blood sliced from his throat. Gel can hear it, loves it, the voice of the snick, tainted as it is, mingling with the fragment of Gel's own essence held with all the rest. He can feel Bloodbane's growing thirst for the rest of Gemmored's song.

Barbs still lash the archive windows. Brittle thunder. Spidery, staccato, circling thunder.

Phariane stops rocking. She looks up at Gel.

"You asked me one question I can answer," she says. All three of them repeat the words. "Why have we come here to find a way to postpone a battle that always comes and that is always won?"

Phariane prepares to give the answer. The last answer to the last question of the last convocation of the last archivist of her Shadow Cycle. A cold panic calls to her but she knows it can never reach her. Phariane is dead. Even the sweetness of harpsong - for so long within her - even that is gone. She again imagines her sister, Sstheness, her entire body covered in scars, curled up in the darkness of the heart of Leviathan, shivering with ecstasy, shivering with dread, febrile with anticipation.

And she decides there is one more thing to do after she answers Gel's question.

She holds out her hand to him. "Give me your ax," she says. Gel frowns. She holds out her other hand to Gemmored. "Give me your sword." Gemmored looks at Doom, then back at Phariane.

"How old is your ax?" she says.

"Perhaps as old as my realm," says Gel, "old as Gnomon."

"Perhaps older," says Phariane. Almost a sneer. "There are mentions of such weapons in my archive. Bloodbane may have been one of the tools which sculpted Gnomon's dragon into Gnomon's Dragonkeep at the end of a previous Shadow Cycle."

"Or slitting Gnomon's Leviathan," Gemmored adds. Almost a sneer but for the depth of his voice.

"Your sword may be the same," says Phariane. "Even gods may

use tools."

Gel spits a breath. "Hardly a noble destiny."

Phariane's hands still reach out to ax and sword. At Gel's last word she curls them into fists. She stands and starts to weave back through the vases to the rotunda's assailed windows. As she passes the first pedestal she pauses and picks up its vase. It still has the words that formed from its original stippled design. Words Phariane has travelled worlds to find. She weighs the slim crystal piece in her hand, then lets it drop.

Even the sound of its shattering is delicate.

"Destiny? Phariane turns back to Gel. "The harper was right, what he said to you. Destiny is as fragile as these." Then she carries on to the windows.

As she comes near, her footsteps crunch. The stained glass is riddled with cracks and pocked with holes. Whistlings of wind strain through the gaps. She searches out one particular hole. A lower part of the lattice piece is still in the lead. Long. Jagged. Like a dagger. Like a kris. But without a handle. She reaches for it, takes hold with her bare hand. The window depicts a swarm of skeletons, bones disfigured with lichen, clambering up an endless tower. The glass is pigmented yellow. Now a new colour stains it.

Phariane works the shard back and forth. She brings her other hand to the work. The edges of the glass sink into both palms, fingers. There's no hint of wince in her face.

The shard comes free. A piece of the tower. One of the skeletons clings to it. She weaves her way back to the centre of the rotunda, blood trailing her. She pulls at her tunic and cuts and tears a strip, which she winds around the base of the shard.

She sits again between Gel and Gemmored, and lifts the glass to her forehead. As she runs it across her head she starts to speak.

"Why have we come here to find a way to postpone a battle that always comes and that is always won?"

A shaved lock of her auburn hair, streaked with its fear grey, falls to her lap.

"Because it's *not* the battle that always comes and that has always been won."

Another lock of hair.

"Each Uroboros is different."

She tilts her head, takes another handful of hair, brings the shard up to it.

"Each has always been won, though each may have been lost."

"What will happen," asks Gemmored, "if the battle is lost?"

"The Shadow - " The glass shard bites into Phariane's scalp as she cuts. Blood wells. No wince, but she pauses. "If the battle is lost the Shadow will not be thrown back. Or my realm will not pass through to begin again. The Wheel will stop."

"And then?" asks Gel.

"Then the tide of Shadow will wash over the universe, realm by realm, until everything is Shadow." Hanks of hair lie around Phariane, some streaked by white, some with blood. Her head is butchered with cuts. Blood runs down her face. "Then, when there is nothing but Shadow, the Shadow will become something else."

"What?" asks Gel.

"Darkness," she answers.

Gemmored and Gel tower over her without speaking. The Wyrmshod Cadre's barbed siege batters on.

"How do we go back?" says Gemmored finally.

"We may not be able to," says Phariane.

Gel turns his head to the brittle thunder circling the windows. "Because of them?"

Phariane shakes her head. "The way back is the same as the way here. Through fire. The fire of the dragon of Dragonkeep calls back those who rapture to other realms. There's a burning here. A kind of distant roar of heat under the skin." She jabs the glass shard at her chest. "After a time it grows. Those who pass through the dragonflame become flame themselves. If they don't return they're consumed by it." Phariane jabs at her chest again. "But I feel no burning." She darts looks at Gel and Gemmored. "Do you?" Neither answers.

"So it may already be too late," says Gel.

"The Uroboros may already be lost," says Gemmored.

Gel hisses at Phariane. "Perhaps by bringing us here you caused it to be lost. Perhaps the two of us could've given Dragonkeep victory - isn't that why the Phoenix came for us?"

Phariane stares back at Gel. Perhaps he's right. Perhaps she is the one tainted by the visit of the Nightmare Cadre - the one chosen for betrayal. "Perhaps," she says. "There may still be the chance of victory. We may still be able to go back. But victory isn't a simple matter."

"War is rarely simple," says Gemmored.

"But finally," says Gel, "if Dragonkeep overcomes Leviathan the Shadow is defeated. It will be simple," he smiles, "if we kill every one of the enemy."

Phariane shakes her head. "The Uroboros may not be won in that way. Do you think all the archivists through all the generations through all the cycles have searched only for a way to postpone the battle?" She shakes her head again, more slowly. Her eyes squeeze against the trickles of blood running down her brow. Her words begin to slur. "There are hints, glimpses in the annals, the myths, of past cycles... Hooded phrases, clouded references... It may be that a single death in the Uroboros decides the outcome... or the sparing of a life... or some other, smaller act... Even a look... Even a word..."

"A word?" Gel laughs - wavering, mewing, incredulous laughter, echoing among the crystal archive. Then he stops. "So simply the act of returning to Dragonkeep may turn back the Shadow."

"Or be the cause of the Shadow's triumph," says Gemmored.

Gel looks at him. "So you wish to stay here?"

Gemmored gives back the look. "No."

Gel's grin stretches back into being and his gaunt head gives a slight bow. "Where you go, I follow."

They both look down at Phariane.

She tells them what to do in weak shuffling words. Then she starts to murmur.

Gemmored and Gel lift her to her feet and drag her toward the rotunda doors. They take a straight path, ignoring the pedestals in their way. Vases tumble and burst into glittering splashes on the floor.

Phariane dully pulls the doors back. They open easily onto the vast limestone pavement and the ripping wind and the paean and whipcracks of the Wyrmshod Cadre. She still murmurs. Gel and Gemmored lower her onto her knees on the rotunda ramp and stand before her, ax and sword ready.

One by one, the cadre comes to a stop before the ramp. Throat by throat their paean dies. Their black horses jerk and stamp, necks tossing wilfully. Then the first cadreman snarls and claws deep into his mount's mane and urges it up the ramp. Before he dies, entrails flailing, three more start up.

Three Wyrmshod Cadre horses, sinewy slicks, are barely able to fit abreast. Balance jostles, they lose pace and power within a stride. Bloodbane and Doom meet them and deal with them easily. But the swarming has begun. Four or more horses charge at a time, barging and biting to get at the ramp. Some slew off before getting near the top, breaking legs or crushing their riders. Those that reach Gemmored and Gel die. The ramp shakes. Battle-yells and squeals of agony go up. Riders and mounts fall from the sides of the ramp at first but soon a low charnel mound forms of horses and riders. One tattooed and bazubanded arm juts nervelessly, the tattoo unwinding.

Gel skips onto the precarious corpse-cairn and sweeps his labrys through the bodies, letting blood stream down the ramp, turning it slick. But still the cadre come.

Behind it all, Phariane continues murmuring - louder now - clearer - "fire is fury, shadow hatred," she intones, over and over.

A barbed whipcord spits up and coils around Gel's arm, biting into his jehad swaddling. A moment later another wraps around his neck. He finds himself yanked off the charnel mound and pulled ferociously down the ramp, skidding and rolling, Bloodbane still fast in his grip. Another whip coils around Bloodbane itself. The riders urge their horses to speed and Gel is dragged across the brutal karst, his labrys crescents now and then grazing and coruscating on the limestone.

The rest of the cadre continue charging the rotunda. Several thunder up the ramp. Gemmored climbs onto the corpse-cairn. Here there's no chance of taking steps to enhance the power of his sword strokes, but Gemmored's shoulders are like ramparts. They turn and the first rider's head leaves his body. The second rider's mount rears before the mound and Doom sinks into its breast. It falls back, screaming, taking its rider with it. Gemmored turns away to resist the pull on his sword as it comes free of the horse. As it does he swings it wide one-handed. The motion is both attack and ward. The third rider and mount pull back a moment before lunging again.

Nearly all the rest of the cadre have begun staring into the sky before the rider dies, and the one after, both falling to raking cleaving cuts.

"Fire is fury," murmurs Phariane, "shadow hatred..."

She looks up too.

Phariane realizes that she is not dead. Not quite. She is ice. And ice burns as deeply as fire in its own way. But fire is the gateway. Fire has brought her and Gel and Gemmored here and only fire can take them back. She has summoned the fire.

Even the Wyrmshodcadremen dragging Gel forget him and look up.

The sleek frenzy of each of their horses halts in its tracks. They shrill. Furious nostrils gape. Heads toss. Hooves rear.

They all look up at the fire darkening the limestone and listen to the thunder.

This is true thunder. Not the paltry thunder of countless barbs lashing stained glass. Not the petty thunder of wyrmshod hooves on an archive ramp. If thunder were song. If thunder were legend. If thunder were death. If thunder were the sky, this would be thunder.

The revered sails which loft Dragonkeep's dragonremes are no more than slivers of this thunder - slivers of dragon. In Phariane's realm Dragonkeep is all that remains of them. A fossilised ember of glory. But here, in the realm of turbulent winds and bleak skies and clouds like bruised omens, dragons still live in all their fury and sunrise and corona and starlight. Vast as aurorae. Fire and shadow.

The Wyrmshod Cadre and Gemmored and even Gel look up at what Phariane has summoned, and feel the universe turning.

Chapter Seventy-Seven

Harnak of Aftermath waits in darkness.

When first he came to this realm, from the dim dense-with-vermillion-twilight Aftermath, she knew the difference between night and shadow. No more. Harnak knows nothing. Even pain is uncertain.

Even evil.

He remembers the talk on the voyage to Leviathan with Gel and Gemmored and Zantalliz and, of course, Phariane...

Evil is what casts shadow and what it casts shadow upon - without the two there is no shadow - evil is therefore both without and within - is the casting force 'light'? or something else? - is it truth?

Harnak finds it hard to remember who spoke which words...

Here, under the archive, in the utter dark of the deepest of the seed-chambers, she once could draw some peace. No more.

Blood and pain.

The scars on his back shift. He feels them in the darkness. And there is no tow-headed Dream-ward to fetch him light this time. "There are no scorpions in Dragonkeep?" Harnak whispers. 'Oh yes,' the Dream-ward had nodded, setting down his lantern, 'and all in this chamber. But all of them sleep.' Harnak stares blindly upward. There are scorpions again in Dragonkeep. She can hear them among the other sounds drifting down through the storied amphorae: stone groaning, breaking; shouts; cries; howls - and things her dull imagination struggles to fasten on, things he has no names for and so names them *scorpions*.

She thinks they may have entered the archive. But there's no certainty in the dark. Blood and pain flow within him as ever, but now she can no longer feel where one ends and the other begins. All his life, she now realizes, his scars have woven him together. Now even they are unravelling. He feels himself ghosting into his true form: wiry, taut, the hair sandy, the skin tawny... She feels herself fluxing into her true form: young but not youthful, high breasts, lean but not thin... Then wafting back again. There is no truth for him, her, it. No trust. No faith.

The *scorpions* are in the chamber just above, now.

He, she, it stands up amongst the amphorae, among life in abeyance. Death awaiting death.

Uroboros

Phariane and Gemmored and Gel drift onto the causey in Dragonkeep's dragonmouth. They lie as dead on the gneiss. They have tumbled through fire to return - from the blaze of dragonmouth to the blaze of dragonmouth, an infinity of inferno. But here, in Phariane's own realm, the fire is all but gone.

There are no more jabbing or serene ethereal stelae, no soaring sheaths of yellow and red and white silk languidly stretching or jetting high into the air. Even the blue flame is gone.

Only mocking featherings of flame remain, spattering the causey.

Phariane and Gel and finally Gemmored start to stir. Awareness quickens on coldly numb faces.

The thunder of the dragonmouth is gone with the fire. No roar like molten havoc. No roar like volcanoes breathing. The immense vaulted cavern echoes with the silence.

Phariane and Gel and Gemmored stand. Footing is precarious. Gel, despite his battering on the limestone karst, despite one jehad-swaddled arm hanging uselessly, is dully but instinctively sure in his balance - but Phariane and Gemmored sway. The causey is warped, but not by heat. There are cracks in the stone. Not in the way of a limestone pavement. These are shallower, more liquid. More like the crazes in Doom's watering. The causey winds and buckles its way back to the dragonthroat. All three turn to face it.

For the first time they see the only other living being in the dragonmouth - Gemmored's Dream-ward. The same dark hair, sallow skin, cheeks no longer quite so full. She has waited for his return as she has waited for him before. As she has waited ever since Gemmored pulled her from the Shadow and gave her new purpose. Phariane and Gel move past her without a glance. Gemmored stops before her. She looks up at him, her expression still uncertain, still waiting.

Gemmored holds Doom in one hand. The other is free. He brings it up to the Dream-ward's cheek. Then lowers it to her throat. He closes it. The fingers reach all the way around her slender neck. He lifts her into the air. She makes no effort to struggle. Gemmored's vein-raked arm holds her out over the edge of the causey, over the plunging barren cavern. The splinter of dark at the heart of his gemstone eye quivers.

Gel and Phariane clamber over the distorted tongue of gneiss toward the dragonthroat. Gel is quicker, more agile. His damaged arm dangles misshapenly like something shattered, but Bloodbane is an aid to balance. Phariane needs to tuck the shard of stained glass brought from the other realm into her belt. Her wounds have clotted and her strength is returning, but by the time she reaches the end of the dragonthroat, Gel has already disappeared into the city.

She looks out. The vista is changed.

Dolomite flags erupted and broken, basalt paving ripped apart. The floor and sides and roof of Dragonkeep have twined. Avenues, streets, wynds, loggias, gardens and tells curve up and even suspend overhead. Parts of the purple porphyry roof are wrenched down to the ground. The gemstone ribcage, once part of the city's sky, glints. Malachite and topaz and lapis-lazuli cobbles. In what is now the sky, the roof, there are rents. Something glints through these too. Stars.

Looking out from the dragonthroat before this twining, but for the buildings, the forest at the dragon's tail might've been made out at the far end of its length. No more. The dragon curves now.

The twisting of the two wyrms has also twisted their light. The if-light-were-decay gloom of Leviathan has mingled with the cleaner brightness of Dragonkeep to produce a kind of bloodshot twilight.

Somewhere the wolves are howling.

Phariane moves into the city.

The Uroboros still goes on, but there is a sense of *wake*. Battle shambles on. The denizens of the locked wyrms wander about and fall into skirmishes. Only Dragonkeep's Blade-ward and Leviathan's Death'shead Cadre fight with real purpose.

Arches are misshapen and cracked as the causey in the dragonmouth. Granite, jasper, azurite, all stone is unnaturally soft now.

Not only the wyrms are merged. Shadow and fire have become entangled in patches of writhing flicker. Phariane pauses and extends her hand into one of these. She finds it impossible to decide if the pain is burning or freezing. Even heat and cold have entwined.

The city's great amphitheatre is broken apart and angled severely, part way up what is now Dragonkeep's side. But the archive is virtually stabbing out. Phariane climbs a cliff of shattered jabs of dolomite flag to reach the bluestone entrance.

Inside, breathing hard, she crouches on what had been one of the walls of the atrium. It slopes, now more floor than wall. Ahead of her and above her is the now useless stairway leading to the archive's mezzanine and traceried cloisters. To her left, part way up what is still a wall, is the brazen door leading to the ovary chambers and the silvered cavern. She slides herself down toward it. Books and scrolls and tablets scree her way. She can hear them murmur. The Nightmare Cadre infect disarrayed pages, whisper in tablet grooves. Long rills of Shadow, some flecked with flame, stain everywhere.

Squirming and levering herself against skewed surfaces, she reaches the brazen door. She lunges and grasps its handle. She turns it. Now a trap door, it swings downward, its weight crashing against the stone behind it. One hinge rips free. It hangs down into darkness by the other.

The bronze caracol inside still cleaves deep into the dark, but is now virtually horizontal rather than vertical. Phariane carefully climbs onto it, hooking legs around the winding metal, scraping and tugging herself on top. Her way is painstaking, picking her way by hands and feet over the sharp spiralling edges of the steps. Faltering, steadying, carrying on.

As she works her way along, she glances down at the ovary chambers. She can make out the smashed remains of the seed amphorae - jagged hints of wreckage in the dark. The destruction is more savage than might have been caused solely by the tilting of the archive. Yet when she reaches the third chamber the wreckage seems different - not so complete. There is the suggestion of smoothness here and there in the dark jumble of shapes lying below her - as if some of the precious jars remain intact. And there are other shapes. Still shapes. Dead. Phariane clambers on. There is glimmer ahead.

Beyond what had been the floor of the third chamber she emerges into the silvered cavern. Everything the same but changed. The walls are still incised with deep mysterious glyphs laid bare by the glimmering shed. But now the glyphs curl above and below her rather than around her. Ahead of her she sees the bowl that once contained the pool of dragon blood. Once in the middle of the cavern floor, but now a new glyph carved in what is now not ground but wall. The thread of glittering silver still emerges from its centre, still sheds the cavern's light. Still uncontaminated by Shadow. But it no longer arcs back into the bowl. It trickles weakly into nothingness before it can reach the new ground.

Phariane steadies her balance and stares about. She has come here time after time but she seeks something which she had left here, after her return from Leviathan. She finds it. It hangs from almost the end of the spiral stairway. Ethereal in the silvered glow. Neither metal nor leather, not scaled or cut into breeks and jerkins as the armour of dragonreme Sword-Mariners. Phariane's cataphract of otherworldly mail - formed of nictitating dragon membrane.

She reaches it finally. She steadies herself on the stairway and carefully eases off her belt and tunic and breeks and boots. She wavers now and then: her wounds have closed, but her body is stiff with fatigue. Tunic and breeks and boots drop. She lifts the mail, sheer and sheened with cyan. She pulls it on, leg by leg, cool, smooth. She strokes it over her body, foot to neck.

Suddenly the horizontal stairway jerks beneath her, but Phariane compensates. She looks up into the dark. Leviathan and Dragonkeep are still twisting. The archive has shifted another fraction.

Phariane's eyes become thoughtful. She moves her lips against the fingertips of one hand, then lowers the hand to her thigh. A finger traces a long triangle on the sheer mail. She pinches the edge of the shape between the finger and her thumb, and plucks. And the mail, proof against forged whetted steel, peels away. She lays the longest edge of the triangle on the bridge of her nose, just below her eyes, and ties it behind her head, yashmaking her face.

Then she reaches down to her other thigh. This time she traces and peels away a long ribbon of mail. This she wraps around the torn fingers and palm of her other hand. Then she picks up the stained glass shard that tore that hand, takes if from the place she has lodged it while she changed.

She looks up again. Stares. And makes to clamber back the way she came.

Her movements are surer now. The cataphract of otherworldly mail allows her more freedom and at the same time holds her weary body more tightly. Nevertheless, with only one hand entirely free, the return journey is slower.

The silvern glimmer of the cavern fades behind her. Darkness is left. The bloodshot light of Dragonkeep appears ahead.

Phariane's mail bandaged hand, still clutching the shard, emerges into the sideways atrium first. Then her head. The wall housing the brazen door has now twisted enough to be more floor than wall. She looks up at two pairs of boots, at two plastrons over chests, and above these, two skulls. The skull beneath the skin, the steel beneath the skull. They are Death'shead Cadre. Their eye-sockets glow fiercely like insane coals.

One of them has his sickle-bladed sword raised over his helm.

Even as it sweeps down at Phariane, the archive shifts again. More violently this time. The sword wielder, caught between the impetus of his stroke and the jolt to his footing on the wall turned floor, pitches forward. The stroke slices down past the hanging brazen door, through the dark nothingness of the ovary chambers below - and the cadreman follows it. The second cadreman staggers.

Phariane swings and mauls herself clear of the trap door and hurls herself onto the survivor. The floor-once-the-wall of the archive now slopes downward, and the two roll. On and on. The first cloister, now jutting up rather than out, stops them.

The Death'sheadcadreman pulls away, staggers to his feet, draws back his sickle-sword. The cut bites stone. Phariane manages to scale and roll over the balcony-turned bulkhead. The cadreman follows.

Phariane's strength is fragile. Between the first and second cloister she's already slowing. Between the second and third the cadreman almost catches her.

Strands of flame, entangled with the rills of Shadow spattered about, light the pursuit.

Between the third and forth cloister, Phariane turns and faces the cadreman. His eye sockets blaze. He grips his sickle-sword two handed. She crouches. Spots of blood speckle her sheer mail on her arm - her wounds have opened. She holds out her shard dagger. On its smeared surface the skeleton still clings to the tower. Then a scraping sound comes from above.

Between the third and forth cloister juts the mezzanine. In the skewed architecture of the tilted archive, the mezzanine is almost overhead. The table of convocation balances against the edge of the mezzanine. Phariane and the Death'sheadcadreman look up at it - watch it rock above them. Back. Forth. Phariane is the first to break the tableau. She lunges with her dagger-shard. But the movement is caught by the cadreman. He sweeps his sword up. The sickle-blade slices across Phariane's yashmak of otherworldly mail. It fails to cut into the membranous armour or the face beneath. It slides away. But Phariane still reels and falls.

She sprawls on her back. The cadreman lifts his sword over his skull helm. Between them lies the cadreman's thin juddering shadow. Phariane turns the shard in her hand, grips it tightly. She rolls and stabs it into the shadow. Splinters of stained glass jump away. The Death'sheadcadreman coils in agony.

Stillness. Then the cadreman, still bent, takes a step.

Phariane stabs the shadow again. The shard shatters. The cadreman stops again, tremblingly rigid. Then he takes another step.

Phariane climbs to her feet and staggers to the next cloister bulkhead. More slowly than ever she scales it, crawls along one of the pillars of the now horizontal colonnade. Then a hand fastens on her calf.

She and the cadreman drop from the colonnade and roll along the wall-turned-floor of the fourth level. They roll across doors to the various quarters of the Phoenix Prey, until reaching the door to Rorn's chamber. Rorn. The captured Phoenix Prey. The recovered Phoenix Prey. The broken Phoenix Prey.

As Phariane's shoulders press against his door it swings down beneath her. She almost falls. The Death'sheadcadreman, on top of her, holds the sickle-blade of his sword in both hands. Only honed on one side, he forces the cutting edge down across her throat.

Her otherworldly-mailed palm, shored by the other, resists the edge. The yashmak heaves with her breath.

The cadreman bears down, but the blaze in his skull sockets fading.

Time stretches.

The blade quivers closer. Closer still, but nevertheless she struggles not to arch her back away – not to let her head lower into the chamber she hangs over. Something stirs down there. Bubbles. Something without a voice calls.

Time aches.

The sickle blade no longer moves. The breath from behind the skull is ragged and ponderous now.

Time halts.

The insane coals deep in the sockets of the skull helm are dead.

Phariane levers and squirms her way free of the corpse. She still avoids glancing down into Rorn's chamber.

Climbing down from the archive she walks on through Dragonkeep. The way is not easy.

Buildings, ramps, archways are shaped from the rock of the dragon. They travel upward and even overhead with the twisting. But the cropfields formerly on the sky-wyrm's flanks are soil, and as the ground has tilted and risen this has subsided, carpeting and clogging much of the new ground.

And through rents in what is now the roof, more stars.

The spasmodic battle continues among the rubble.

Yet no one challenges or even notices Phariane.

Finally, after passing through the sloping remains of an orchard, tree limbs hacked away for weapons, she sees her destination. Or at least the gateway to it.

Toward the tail the dragon narrows. The forest that grows there is not so distorted as other parts of Dragonkeep. The boles still reach high. The green canopies splay out. She enters the shade which even now resists the bloodshot taint of the rest of the city's light. The ground is still soft and mossy. And even now there is the sound of wolves.

She moves closer to these. Not just howls. Snarls. Snaps.

A shape, tuniced in lamellar, rushes and stumbles through the trees. Other shapes, lower, more flowing, follow. The Corsair is practically in front of Phariane when the first wolves bring him down, laughing and cursing. Their snarls swarm down onto his body and turn liquid. The first wolves are hoar-greys. Now several blacks, sleeker but more suited for the dragonremes, arrive. One or two of the hoar-greys are already turning away, golden irises and pricks of pupil. The Corsair is still dying. Still laughing as Phariane walks past.

More shapes flit through the trees and dimness. More wolf shapes sinew after them. Only wolves. There are no Wolf-ward now. There is no need for them. The wolves move as swiftly as ever, but their movements seem more natural now - not so aloof from time. The end of the world is their time.

As Phariane makes her way through the forest, eruptions of snarl break out now and then. Some are near, but most are distant, deep in the trees. Nothing crosses her way.

Once the end of the forest was the end of Dragonkeep. Now at the end of the forest the trees end but the dimness continues, though its bloodshot taint returns. Phariane looks back once then steps through into Leviathan.

Her journey is as her last journey through the sea-wyrm, but different. Though the Uroboros has softened the sky-wyrm's stone body, the distortion has still cracked and fissured and fragmented the city. In the battle Dragonkeepers have used fragments of stone and gems dislodged from the purple porphyry roof in home-fashioned slings. Leviathan too is twisted. And despite their flexibility, the labyrinths of Leviathan have also ripped and torn, creating new labyrinths, new passageways in which the battle can be fought.

It still goes on.

The same spasms of struggling and killing as in Dragonkeep, perhaps more claustral, more squalid, more pinched. Still no one challenges Phariane. Yet somehow she begins to lose her way. Just as Dragonkeep's gems have been wrung from roof to ground, so the skulls paving Leviathan's floor are sometimes now above. As with the gems they sometimes fall. One drops onto Phariane's shoulder and lunges at her neck before sliding off her mail. Its jaw continues to snap as she walks away. And even now there are echoes. Even more echoes. She can still hear wolves.

Once, in the bloodshot dimness, through what may be a rent in the labyrinth above her, she wonders if she glimpses yet more stars.

She eventually emerges into a wider space, vast enough to be in Dragonkeep. But the kind of cold here could never be found in the sky-wyrm, or even the rest of the sea-wyrm. The chamber stretches into the distance, and throughout that length, hanging from the vaulting ceiling, are the same fleshy stalactites that strew the labyrinths. Except these are longer. And from them hang bare bodies. Men. Women. Children. Dead. Living. Moaning. And because Leviathan is twisted, some of the stalactites are now stalagmites, flaccid tendrils which still entwine bodies. Moaning.

Once the intestine of the giant wyrm, then the feeding gallery of Leviathan, now it provides the nearest thing to a battlefield. In the garden of living corpses there is space for Leviathane and Dragonkeeper, for Death'shead Cadre and Corsairs and Dragonkeep's hawk-helmed Blade-ward to clash in numbers. There is a staccato wash of steel. Though even here there is a weariness about the fury - a feeling of ending.

And in the distant midst of the bloody turmoil Phariane sees two figures.

Gel.

Gemmored.

Even as she sees them they see each other.

Gel's face is almost black, infused with so much blood from slaying. More gaunt then ever. His cheeks are pits. The twin heads of his labrys flush, almost glow crimson. There is no weariness about Bloodbane's arcs. Gemmored's sword is equally tireless, equally crimsoned. The face he turns toward Gel is dead as ice, but also gaunt - as if anger were bones... Gel's breaks into a pure, contented grin, as razored as his ax.

Phariane turns away as the two of them come toward each other.

She leaves the feeding chamber and returns to the labyrinths.

She walks softly, listening to the echoes, until she finds one particular echo. Not the snapping of skulls, or the shouts and screams and moans. Faint, very faint now, but still she finds it. Ghostly monstrous, like an oceanic murmur of gossamer. This is not so much a sound as a pulse. She follows it deep into twisted Leviathan, past and sometimes through the varices, cysts, tumours that form the sea-wyrm's chambers, along old gravewaxed passages and newly torn gateways. Always following the echo.

Until she finds its source. Its heart. A glistening black barrier. A kind of growth. Some kind of goitre. Swollen. Stony. A knot. She recognizes it. Whimpering comes from inside.

In the bloodshot gloom the thread-fine cleft running down the knot is scarcely visible. Unlike many of the blood-sutured entries into other chambers, this has not been rent open. Phariane approaches it slowly. Then she glimpses something at her feet.

A slim, undulated piece of metal ending in a finely carved handle.

Her kris.

She eases onto her haunches and reaches out her otherworldly-mail-wrapped hand. As her fingers near it the blade starts to move, to sidewind away from her. She stops. The blade goes still. She reaches out her other hand, hesitantly, and the kris starts away again. She stops. The kris goes still. For a time Phariane looks at it in the dimness. Then she stands.

She takes the last few steps to the knot. She pulls away the otherworldly mail yashmak and lets it float to the floor. Then she lets something breathed pass from her lips to the cleft, and the needle-thin seal thickens, softens, distends, and she slides inside.

The darkness encysted inside is different as she knew it would be. Transpicuous.

On the cold stone floor something is curled around itself, shivering, all skin and scar. Her sister. Sstheness unwinds from the foetal. She lifts her head. From somewhere beneath dark hair matted and stringed with slime her eyes see Phariane. Her whimpering tears and bursts into shrieks, and her long sigil-thorns leap up.

Phariane feels the fingerstalls clawing over her brutally-shaven head, plunging down her forehead. Then the transpicuous dark is gone. The dark which replaces it is red. If darkness were blood... And it burns.

Phariane staggers back. Falls. Jars on the slick stone. She feels Sstheness' sigil-thorns flailing over her mail, feels the clawing come to life when it rakes the bare skin on Phariane's thighs where the patches of mail have been stripped away.

But pain is something Phariane only remembers.

She reaches through the gouging storm and fastens on one of Sstheness' hands. With the touch Sstheness' shrieks fade instantly back to whimpers. Phariane feels her sister's body collapse onto her, hardly moving. She fumbles along Sstheness' hand until she reaches the sigil-thorns. She grips one. Tight.

The thorn is as sharp, point and edges, as the glass shard had been, but Phariane's palm is mailed. She levers. The thorn gives, slowly at first, then breaks. Sstheness squirms a moment, like the dream of a shudder.

Phariane turns her sister carefully, gently, laying her on her side on the slick hard stone. She lies herself beside her, behind her, and takes hold of another sigil-thorn.

Then the next.

One by one.

Sometimes the finger breaks before the sigil-thorn. The sound is different. Phariane can tell the difference. The bone snaps cleanly, a neat sound. But the sigil-thorns are stubborn, break grudgingly, resentfully, fibre by fibre, like something rotted.

Sometimes Phariane grasps the thorn with her bare hand - not through error but through indifference. Pain is only another, sharper, kind of darkness.

After the tenth, final sigil-thorn is broken, Phariane eases Sstheness against her, cradles her. She no longer even whimpers. She still shivers.

They wait.

They wait.

Though the heart-knot's cleft is sealed up now, even through the thick stony walls, Phariane can hear echoes. Even if only the echoes of echoes. She can still hear the wolves.

Phariane can feel the darkness beyond her own blindness changing. Contracting. This heart-chamber, the core tumour of

Leviathan, is shrinking - crushing itself in death. Crushing its dark into nothingness.

Sstheness is still shivering. So softly. The vibration little more than a purr. The tremble passes from Sstheness' skin through Phariane's sheer otherworldly mail into her skin.

And Phariane finds the thing she has come back from the realm of karst and stained glass to find.

She waits.

She cradles her sister in blood and darkness and fear.

And waits.

Listening to the dim cool cadence of wolves.

Appendix

Storm of Shadow: the Tarot of Sword-&-Sorcery

"But in the end the subject-matter of popular fiction has an inertia... The interstellar drive 'says' only itself. The only emotional charge the sword carries is its swordness. These stock units overbear the metaphors you try to make with them, so that when for instance Gene Wolfe speaks of swords and torture ... he only speaks of swords and torture and how you can become King by eating the brains of your predecessor (which not only dooms you to repeat his barbarism, but is also only what sword-and-sorcery has been advocating since Robert E. Howard)."

M.John Harrison, 'The Profession of Science Fiction'
Foundation Journal # 46, 1989.

"Artists must constantly reject and then rediscover the past in their search for a vocabulary that is both private and universal;"

Michael Moorcock, 'Wizardry and Wild Romance'.

To write sword-&-sorcery in the twenty-first century, it seemed to me, required a redefinition of the form. 'The Shadow Cycles' is my attempt at that redefinition – in effect, the formulation and deployment of a tarot. In this instance the tarot is defined as a set of elements or 'motifs' essential to a genre's identity. Those motifs are 'set down' or 'played' in a narrative. Any genre will change over time, new versions of the tarot will develop, but in order to understand what makes sword-&-sorcery I focused on the form's beginnings. 'Storm of Shadow' is an analysis of these beginnings, but also of its potential.

The tarot I've constructed identifies thirteen sword-&-sorcery motifs, actual or potential essentials of the form.

The tarot analogy goes much further than this in 'The Shadow Cycles'.

But that's not exactly another story, rather one buried deep inside this tale.

Defining the Past

Since the early 1980s up until the beginning of the twenty-first century, the genre or sub-genre known as Sword-and-Sorcery, but for some few scattered stories in magazines, has been moribund. The Tolkien-derived high fantasy novel has, on the other hand, flourished and mutated into six, eight, ten volume series which usually average four-figure page counts. Even though such terms as high fantasy, heroic fantasy, and sword-&-sorcery are sometimes used interchangeably, sword-&-sorcery has come to be viewed as an inferior, cruder form: rougher in style, more limited structurally, stunted in terms of character development even morally questionable (rather than ambiguous). It's 'founder' Robert E. Howard's entry in 'A Reader's Guide to Fantasy' includes the comment: "Others associate him exclusively with blood-and-thunder barbarian tales, sword-and-sorcery in its worst sense." Many of the modern small press magazines which solicit 'fantasy' fiction in various forms specifically note in their market requirements, "No S&S".

"The term is usually attributed to Fritz Leiber, who is said to have coined it in 1960, but the sub-genre to which it refers is much older than that, having been variously called science fantasy, weird fantasy, fantastic romance, and more recently, and perhaps more usefully, heroic fantasy.

"Leiber was one of the members of the Hyborian League, a fan group founded in 1956 to preserve the memory of the pulp writer Robert E. Howard; many professional writers belonged to it; the group's fanzine was Amra. All the members seemed to agree that Howard founded the sword-and-sorcery genre with his 'Conan' stories in Weird Tales: swashbuckling, romantic fantasies, beginning with 'The Phoenix on the Sword' (1932), set in Earth's imaginary past, and featuring a mighty swordsman, violently amorous, who often confronted various supernatural forces of evil. ...

"Mainstream literature, too, had a long tradition of picaresque adventures in imaginary worlds, though usually more demure (and literate), and sometimes less energetic, than Howard's. The usually quoted high points of this tradition up to the time of Howard are the somewhat etiolated medieval fantasies of William Morris, the stylish though mannered romances of Lord Dunsany (often set in a sort of 'Faerie', the rather more swaggering and rambustious adventures of E.R.Eddison, and the elegant, ironic and elaborate 'Poictesme' series of James Branch Cabell. All of these influenced various of the Weird Tales sword-and-sorcery writers ... C.L.Moore was probably the finest of this group, with her 'Jirel of Jory' and her 'Northwest Smith' stories. But there is no denying the colour and vigour of Howard's work. The essential new element which Howard brought to the genre was the emphasis on brutal, heroic ambition in the hero, who is seen (unlike Cabell's heroes for example) quite without irony, as simply admirable....

"Tolkien's long, richly imagined work is as important to modern sword and sorcery as Howard's; the two writers together, in fact, represent the two ends of the genre's spectrum: Howard all amoral vigour, Tolkien all deeply moral clarity of imagination ...

"Michael Moorcock is one of the few English writers to work in the genre, and though his sword and sorcery has been dismissed, not least by himself, as hackwork, and while he certainly wrote too much too fast, his fantasy generally and his 'Elric' books in particular imported a welcome breadth to the genre; good and evil in Moorcock's books are never easy to define ...

"Sword-and-sorcery readers appear to welcome long and sometimes seemingly endless series... It can be said that most of these (Jakes' and Wagner's being perhaps the best) are routine, and that at their worst they are execrable. The genre has, perhaps, too narrow a range of interests, and the constant recurrence of the same themes is likely to make all but the most fanatic enthusiast tire quickly."

from Peter Nicholls, 'The Encyclopaedia of Science Fiction',1981.

This entry is excerpted at some length because, besides serving as a broad introduction, it throws up some of the vague thinking, if not carelessness, surrounding scholarship in this area. Sword-&-sorcery is referred to sometimes as a genre, sometimes a sub-genre. Sometimes sword and sorcery, sometimes sword-and-sorcery is the name given.

To assert that Robert E. Howard created sword-&-sorcery (another variation and my chosen usage - the ampersand has an appropriately arcane, sigil-like appeal!) is a solid assertion. Both Nicholls and Mike Chinn in his introduction to the 'Swords Against the Millennium' anthology cite Burroughs' Martian tales, though both undermine the case by admitting the lack of magic in the stories. But to claim that sword-&-sorcery began with the Conan stories is debatable. Lin Carter, in his essay 'The First Barbarian', makes a far stronger case for Howard's Kull stories, which pre-date the Conan series:

"it is only in retrospect that we think of the August 1929 Weird Tales as sort of milestone, since it contained the first real sword-and-sorcery story ever published. Had it not been for Kull, the issue would have been quite unimportant ... In the first place, Howard welded together three different kinds of story into one. He took the Clark Ashton Smith sort of yarn laid in fabulous, glimmering dawn kingdoms of magic and sorcery, and the Lovecraftian horror tale of prehuman, eldritch evil, and grafted them onto the swashbuckling heroica of Harold Lamb and Rafael Sabatini and the Talbot Mundy of Tros of Samothrace fame. 'The Shadow Kingdom' serves up an equal share of the kind of thrills and fun we expect from each of these very different kinds of fiction. The seams are invisible; the welding is perfect; the three kinds of story merge together flawlessly."

from 'The First Barbarian', published in 'Savage Sword of Conan' # 3, 1974.

Fred Blosser's article, 'Of Buccaneers and Barachan Pirates', published in 'Savage Sword of Conan' # 17, 1977, echoes Carter's list of Howard influences, and adds Robert W. Chambers, James Fenimore Cooper and Robert Louis Stevenson.

Rob Weinberg throws doubt even on this assertion in a responding letter to the magazine where Carter's article appeared, published in issue # 5. Nevertheless, the essay makes the point that Howard, as Tolkien posits for the 'Beowulf' poet before him, stands on the shoulders of older writers to create his tarot or 'Ur-text'. (What I refer to as an Ur-text is not necessarily a single novel or story or collection of stories, though it may be - the Ur-text is a body of work which is seen as in some way original or different from the storytelling forms previously existing and creates a template or tarot for other writers to follow.)

In fact 'Beowulf' can easily be seen as proto-sword-&-sorcery. In a letter quoted in Don Herron's own article in 'The Barbaric Triumph', Howard states that the first "Nordic folk-tale I ever read was Beowulf." And Howard's 'The Valley of the Worm' references Beowulf.

The violence of Beowulf could hardly more strongly echo Howard's treatment:

"A breach in the giant / flesh-frame showed then, shoulder-muscles / sprang apart, there was a snapping of tendons, / bone-locks burst. To Beowulf the glory of this fight was granted; ... The tarn was troubled; a terrible wave-thrash / brimmed it, bubbling; black-mingled, / the warm wound-blood welled upwards."

from 'Beowulf', Penguin edition. 1977.

The swashbuckling element (most blatantly present in the Conan stories of all Howard's series) actually adulterates the horrific and fabulous elements and makes Howard's fiction marketable as popular fiction, just as the 'Beowulf' poet added a Christian gloss to his source material to make it acceptable to his audience.

To return to the encyclopedia quotation, to describe Howard as admiring the brutality of his protagonists at one point and later to describe his writing as 'amoral' is problematic. Howard in fact, in his fiction and non-fiction writing, displayed a strong moral code:

"[My grandfather] wandered over into western New Mexico and worked a silver mine not far from the Arizona line. And in passing, I would remark on his habit of loaning money. The business was informal to a point incomprehensible to the modern business man. Frequently no notes were given, no security put up. A cowman's word was his bond. And in dealing with such men, my grandfather never lost a cent. It was different when the country began filling up with smart gentlemen from more sophisticated sections."

from 'The Wandering Years' in 'The Last Celt' (ed. Glenn Lord).

"The Cimmerian glared about, embarrassed at the roar of mocking laughter that greeted this remark. He saw no particular humor in it, and was too new to civilisation to understand its discourtesies. Civilised men are more discourteous than savages because they know they can be impolite without having their skulls split, as a general thing."
from 'The Tower of the Elephant'.

Dale Rippke, in his article 'Why everything you know about Conan is probably wrong', (www.REHUPA.com), makes some interesting points about Conan's amorality, related to wildness (phasis) versus civilisation. But he overstresses the point. Howard himself, in 'The Black Stranger', describes Conan as having a cultural code in that he "lived according to the code of his people, which was barbaric and bloody, but at least upheld its own peculiar standards of honor." And Clark, Miller, and de Camp in 'An Informal Biography of Conan the Cimmerian', reprinted in 'The Blade of Conan', refer to: "Conan's barbaric, paradoxical code of honor". Beginning with Conan, sword-&-sorcery protagonists have often shared this.

To describe Howard as admiring brutality is simplistic. Darrell Schweitzer, in his (albeit now practically disowned) essay 'Conan's World and Robert E. Howard', notes:

"He sympathised with the primitive and savage himself. Personal freedom was his one driving obsession (as he admitted in letters), and he saw civilisation as unbearably restrictive. He overlooked, of course, the fact that real barbarians are more bound by tribal taboos, customs, and a sheer lack of opportunity than any civilised man. His romanticised version of the barbarian was strong, noble, uninhibited, and free - "

Howard's characters are all, to some extent, informed by the romantic primitivism concept - it imbues those characters with a code which may be brutal but not amoral: "The thought of drawing his sword on a woman, even without intent of injury, was extremely repugnant to him." ('Red Nails'.)

The sword-&-sorcery entry in the Clute/Grant 'Encyclopaedia of Fantasy' comments: "Where epic fantasy celebrates heroic virtue, sword and sorcery prefers a moderate virtue, allied with good sense and a capacity to compromise."

The concept of 'the savage beneath the civilised' is a recurrent Howardian idea. In his only Conan novel, 'The Hour of the Dragon', Conan loses his throne and 'reverts' to a more savage persona. The element is particularly present in the Kull stories. The idea is often echoed in Howard imitators, such as Schifino. "Lupus Lupolius, slayer and lover of great repute, felt the veneer of civilisation peel from him," ('Bloodgold', Fantasy Tales # 4)

A Tale of Two Ur-Texts

When sword-&-sorcery, or fantasy, is discussed, it is telling just how often Robert E. Howard and J.R.R. Tolkien's names are yoked together (Moorcock does this several times in 'Wizardry and Wild Romance' - de Camp also in 'Literary Swordsmen and Sorcerers'. So does Paul C. Allen in his article 'Of Swords & Sorcery' in 'Fantasy Crossroads' # 13. It should also be noted that Allen differentiates between 'swords and sorcery' and 'epic/epoch fantasy'). In the sixties, when the form had a resurgence, they formed two traditions, or two 'Ur-texts' from which other writers drew.

In this sense Tolkien's 'The Lord of the Rings' and other fantasies, and Howard's sword-&-sorcery output were not genre works, but the Ur-texts of the genres which followed them. This is not necessarily a healthy process. History has shown that once a genre is recognized as such it begins to decay. Michael Moorcock in 'Wizardry and Wild Romance', continuously rails against the 'small industry' of Howard and Tolkien imitators. It may be possible to reverse the concept and cite Cervantes' Don Quixote, for example, as an anti-Ur-text - one which put an end to a genre for generations after its publication. In order to rescue sword-&-sorcery, or any genre, from the possibly inevitable process of perpetually weakening sequels and formulaic distorting echoes of an Ur-text, it may be necessary to create a new Ur-text. Steffen H. Hantke comments:

"The formulaic consistency of [John] Carpenter's narrative is not so much an indication of creative exhaustion, of a simple lack of ideas, or the economic limitations of budget and distribution. Rather, it is the result of a narrative strategy that systematically runs through a finite number of possible combinations of story and character, generated by a limited number of basic units of narrative, in order to exhaust its own economy. In discussing de Sade's pornography, Roland Barthes has called narratives like this combinatories"
    from 'The Function of the Sublime in Contemporary Horror', in 'Foundation' # 71.

An important clue to how such a new Ur-text may be achieved comes in a 1936 paper written by Tolkien:

"In 1936, the Oxford scholar and teacher J.R.R.Tolkien published an epoch-making paper entitled 'Beowulf: The Monsters and the Critics', which took for granted the poem's integrity and distinction as a work of art and proceeded to show in what this integrity and distinction inhered. Tolkien assumed that the poet had felt his way through the inherited material - the fabulous elements and the traditional accounts of an heroic past - and by a combination of creative intuition and conscious structuring had arrived at a unity of effect and a balanced order. He assumed, in other words, that the Beowulf poet was an imaginative writer rather than some kind of back-formation derived from nineteenth-century folklore and philology."
    from introduction to 'Beowulf' translated by Seamus Heaney,
Faber & Faber, 1999.

Tolkien describes the anonymous poet as someone who 'built on' a background of folklore to create the poem (using the metaphor of a tower) - the writer took from what had gone before and used it, rather than allowing it to use him (perhaps Harrison's brain eating image has resonance here?). Ironically, as a prototypical sword-&-sorcery text 'Beowulf is certainly closer to the Howardian Ur-text than the Tolkien Ur-text. For one thing, 'Beowulf' does not rely on character development:

"In fact, to speak of nature as an inert stage upon which the human drama is played out is to undervalue nature and overvalue human motive in a characteristic modern way."
    from Alexander's introduction to his translation of 'Beowulf', Penguin.

Moorcock in 'Wizardry' conflates two terms when referring to Fritz Leiber's Fafhrd and Gray Mouser stories: "these are unquestionably the most mature and skilful stories to be written consciously as generic epic fantasy or 'sword-and-sorcery'". In fact if epic suggests anything it suggests scale - 'The Lord of the Rings' is over one thousand pages in length, as are the majority of the Tolkien-style stories/series that have followed in its wake since the sixties. Elizabeth Drake/Nonny Morgan, offers a helpful refinement of the taxonomy in her definition of 'high fantasy':

"High Fantasy is the catch-all term for medieval-esque fantasy that doesn't make it as epic or heroic fantasy/sword-and-sorcery, but contains magic at some level. Sometimes it is used as a label for light reading,"
    from http://www.emdrake.com/for-writers/articles/subgenres-demystified/

This allows for stories containing some of the sensibilities of epic fantasy, such as lyricism and romanticism to exist in the short story form.
    Most of the Fafhrd and Gray Mouser stories are short stories. Most of Howard's work consisted of short stories, fantasy or not, for the pulp magazine industry of the twenties and thirties. Sword-&-sorcery began as inherently a short story form. Epic fantasy, virtually of necessity, exists in highly developed milieux:

"Meantime, Professor Tolkien is working on another project that violates all normal publishing sense. Despite the fact that even serious books shouldn't have too many pages of notes and references, Tolkien

finished his work of fiction with over a hundred pages of appendices -
and the world developed there has been so fascinating that readers
have insisted he give them still more."
from 'A Report on J.R.R. Tolkien' by Lester Del Rey, 'Worlds of
Fantasy' magazine # 1, 1968

The above article was written at the time when the epic fantasy boom
was beginning. Because of the length of such stories not only milieux,
but also character is open to more naturalistic development. As
fantasy writers have continued to write in the Tolkien vein, this aspect
of the form has evolved. Characters have become more
psychologically complex - in fact one of the most common criticisms
of Tolkien targets the lack of character development:

"Sad that an academic and rather emotionally stilted experiment
should become the model for a literary sub-genre..."
from Mike Chinn, introduction to 'Swords Against the
Millennium', 2000.

The template for the modern epic/heroic/high fantasy story comes
through Tolkien. None of these three terms, however, is an
appropriate alternative label for the form of sword-&-sorcery as I
intend to define it. The next order of business is to add precision to the
label.

'Epic', as a title, signals not only size of the fantasy in both
wordage and content ("The action of epics take place on a grand
scale" - Oxford Dictionary of Literary Terms), but also variety in
narrative. ("'Epic' in this sense means essentially narrative, defying
the Aristotelian unities" – 'Fontana Dictionary of Modern Thought':
Epic Theatre; "the term 'epic' is generally given to some form of
heroic narrative wherein tragedy, comedy, lyric, dirge, and idyll are
skilfully blended" – 'Book of the Epic'.).

However, the denotations and connotations of 'epic' can mislead
when applied to sword-&-sorcery. Variety is not a required element -
in fact it potentially detracts from the focus, the intensity, which is a
requirement of the form.

While scale can be present in sword-&-sorcery, it can be present in terms other than the rise and fall of civilisations. It may be epic in the power of the forces involved. It may well be epic in timescale, but in implying great swathes of time, often related to the forces mentioned above, such as Howard's Ymir in 'The Frost Giant's Daughter' or Yag-Kosha in 'The Tower of the Elephant', or Xaltotun in 'The Hour of the Dragon' ("The Cimmerian involuntarily shivered; he sensed something incredibly ancient, incredibly evil."). Such condensing offers an alternative to developing a canvas that gives the reader too detailed an impression of that timescale. Development is anathema to the effect that sword-&-sorcery should aim, in my definition, to achieve.

Time is often characterized in Howard's fiction as vertical - as an abyss:

"He stopped short, staring, for suddenly, like the silent swinging wide of a mystic door, misty, unfathomed reaches opened in the recesses of his consciousness and for an instant he seemed to gaze back through the vastness that spanned life and life; seeing through the vague and ghostly fogs dim shapes reliving dead centuries ... Kull drew a hand across his brow, shaken; these sudden glimpses into the abysses of memory always startled him."
from 'The Shadow Kingdom'.

The term 'heroic fantasy' is, like 'epic fantasy', more appropriate for the Tolkien-derived form. Like 'epic' there are many denotations and connotations to hero - a hybrid of god and human, one who performs brave actions, one who exhibits nobility in the sense of high moral qualities, one possessing superhuman strength or abilities. The term shares many of these definitions with 'epic', in fact the two are closely linked. The actions of the protagonists in 'The Lord of the Rings' and the novels which have appeared in its wake certainly fit into all the above categories (bar the first, which is a little prescriptive - though some protagonists of the form qualify). Frodo's actions are certainly heroic, in the second and third senses, and his human (?) vulnerability adds to the sense of his heroism. Also, the ring bestows superhuman power (invisibility) to him.

However what has become the overriding moral denotation and

connotation makes the term even more misleading than 'epic' for sword-&-sorcery. The protagonists of the form almost invariably fit into the superhuman category (Conan, Kull, Elric, Kane, The Voidal, etc.), but their morality can often be problematic, often paying lip service to amorality. Many writers continue to conflate 'heroic fantasy' and 'sword-&-sorcery', though Clute in 'The Encyclopaedia of Fantasy' (under 'Heroic Fantasy') comments that there may be "a useful distinction" between the two.

I've chosen the term 'high/epic fantasy' for the Tolkien-derived form because it connotes many of the elements listed above, but also because the term seems to me to suggest the perception of superiority the form assumes over sword-&-sorcery. The term 'low fantasy' was used without further clarification in the review column of 'Comics International' # 173, July '04. This was a review of the 2004 Dark Horse adaptation of Howard's Conan stories, issue # 3. It may reference the form's position in the fantasy hierarchy mentioned just supra, but might possibly reference another usage which refers to fantasy where the supernatural element plays a low-key role. In his 'Foundation' # 103 article, Gary Matters contributes another, slightly different, definition of high and low fantasy: low equals story occurring in a world, "almost identical" to ours; high fantasy equals a story occurring in a separate secondary world - usually a romanticised version of mediaeval Europe. This is slightly different to low fantasy as fiction incorporating very little magic, and high fantasy as fiction incorporating a large volume of magical event. Though there are similarities. In any case, I will not be using this name.

Sword-&-sorcery, as 'Ur-texted' by Howard will be my chosen term. 'Sword' implies violence (though not necessarily physical violence) tied with the element of the numinous - this is the aesthetic core of the form, the 'major arcana' of my tarot.

High/Epic Fantasy Versus Sword-&-Sorcery

de Camp makes no particular differentiation between 'high/epic fantasy' and 'sword-&-sorcery' in the introductions to his four sixties anthologies – a vagueness perpetuated by Chinn. de Camp cites

William Morris as the father of 'heroic fantasy'. Tracing its influences back to the Iliad, the Odyssey, myth and folklore, he sees Morris as conflating the gothic novel and Walter Scott's adventure/history novel:

"In the 1880s, William Morris created the modern genre of heroic fantasy by combining the antiquarian romanticism of Scott and his imitators with the supernaturalism of Walpole and his imitators. Morris wrote a number of novels laid in an imaginary medieval world. Most of these stories strike a modern reader as rather dull. Nevertheless, some of Morris' techniques, such as his artful use of archaic language, have passed into general use in the genre."
    from 'The Spell of Seven'.

This quotation implies that de Camp recognizes that there are certain writers at certain times who produce 'Ur-texts', imitated by other writers, thus creating genres. (For example, Horace Walpole's 'Castle of Otranto' may be claimed as the Ur-text of the gothic novel.) He also points out that influences of technique as well as plot tropes and setting pass down from these texts.

Ur-texts, then, are copied and the forms they in some way innovate 'degrade' just as analog copies of sound recordings degrade as copy follows copy. This could be viewed as a metatextual version of the concept of 'thinning' as found in 'The Encyclopedia of Fantasy', where each age is seen as 'lesser' or 'less rich' in some way than the previous. This seems an inevitable process of genre. (Universal's 'Frankenstein' in 1931 may be said to be a cinematic Ur-text that created a genre which terminated with 'Abbott and Costello meet Frankenstein' in 1948.) Harrison, in one of his Viriconium stories, 'The Pastel City' writes of the eponymous city, "What had begun well in fire and blood and triumph lost its spirit." This might equally apply to sword-&-sorcery as a form.

During the 1960s both the Howard-based sword-&-sorcery Ur-text (though created in the 30s) and the Tolkien-based high fantasy Ur-text (though created in the 50s) were both drawn upon by many writers (and the phrase 'drawn upon', palimpsest-like, is not used without thought).

Michael Moorcock writes about the Chivalric Romance genre:

"Deriving from the Romances of Arthur, Charlemagne and the Cid, owing something to Greek and Roman epics, something to fable and a little to history, borrowing language and manners from the metrical epics, from Ariosto, from Aucassin et Nicolette, the decadent Chivalric Romances had superficial resemblances to the originals but lacked their beauty of language and their genuine tragic elements."
from 'Wizardry and Wild Romance'.

And there are obvious parallels which strengthen the idea of a historical process of Ur-text followed by genre.

Tolkien's and Howard's bodies of work formed, if not two traditions, at least the upper and lower castes of imaginary-world fantasy literature. Even the champions of the sword-&-sorcery form saw its virtues and purposes as modest.

de Camp, set, or at least re-enforced this perspective in the introductions to his anthologies:

"The purpose of these stories is neither to teach the problems of the steel industry, nor to expose the defects in our foreign-aid program, nor yet to air the problems of the housewife. It is to entertain. These stories combine the color, gore, and action of the costume novel with the atavistic terrors and delights of the fairy tale. They furnish the purest fun to be found in fiction today."
from 'Swords & Sorcery'.

de Camp touches on the darker elements of the form here, but the main focus of his commendation is clearly escapism. He compounds the idea of sword-&-sorcery as a trivial form in his introduction to the anthology 'Warlocks & Warriors', by referring to it as 'swordplay-and-sorcery'.

This is the perception which has dominated, virtually unchallenged until the present. Mike Chinn accepts and approves the same paradigm:

"When Peter Coleborn of Alchemy Press told me he wanted to

publish an anthology of Heroic Fantasy short stories (or Sword & Sorcery, or Thud'n'Blunder - whichever you prefer)...

"...I've always loved tales of sword-wielding barbarians taking on all comers, stealing the king's crown out from under his nose, killing the (always) evil wizard and getting the girl, to boot. They appeal to the kid in me, I guess."

from Mike Chinn, introduction to 'Swords Against the Millennium'.

Despite Chinn's toeing of the de Camp line, his introduction points out one of the elements which differentiate sword-&-sorcery from high/epic fantasy - the barbarian. Traditionally the 'sword' of sword-&-sorcery, almost always the protagonist, he (or she) represented, originally, in the Howardian Ur-text, an anarchic energy that nevertheless presents the moral (or at least less immoral) force of the sword-&-sorcery story, pitted against the malign 'sorcery'. This energy, or power, of the protagonist, echoes through the genre:

"His brow was low and broad, his eyes a volcanic blue that smouldered as if with some inner fire ... and his velvet garments could not conceal the hard, dangerous lines of his limbs."

from 'The Hour of the Dragon'.

and

"'There is a vital power about you greater than the craft and cunning of my allies.'"

from 'The Hour of the Dragon'.

Howardian protagonists often create an overpowering effect on the characters they encounter - especially Conan. His effect on Balthus in 'Beyond the Black River' particularly comes to mind.

Not just in characterizations, but also in terms of elements such as mood, milieu and plot, both Howardian and Tolkien Ur-texts spawned readily identifiable storytelling templates.

In order to analyse these, I've first set down an 'impressionistic' table of oppositions which for me epitomise the key differences in the forms:

High/Epic Fantasy - Sword-&-Sorcery

Apollonian - Dionysian
Melancholy - Despair/Fatalism
Elegance - Simplicity
Medieval - Dark Age
Medieval Arthur - Celtic Arthur
Knights - Barbarians
Good vs. Evil - A Storm of Darknesses
Folk Music - Heavy Metal
Progressive Rock - Punk
Pastels - Darker/Richer colours
Variety/Variation - Focus/Intensity

The table illustrates the core dichotomy. The oppositions may refer to tone, structure, milieu, character types, style, or a number of these.

It's tempting to see the differences as finally coming down to nothing more or less than the personalities of the two authors, but nevertheless the differences are concrete.

Apollonian -Dionysian

The Apollonian - Dionysian opposition I take from Nietzsche's 'The Birth of Tragedy' where he creates his own set of oppositional concepts to illustrate the artistic process. I find these highly useful in delineating my own definitions of high/epic fantasy and sword-&-sorcery. The Apollonian side, embodying reason, technique, tradition, control, logical clarity relates to the Tolkien Ur-text - while the Dionysian side, embodying un-reason (passion), unpredictability, imagination, subjectivity, obscurity seems to me to fit the Howardian Ur-text. (Obscurity in the sense of the withholding of information is the bedrock of much gothic fiction. H.P.Lovecraft in his essay 'Supernatural Horror in Literature' states: "The oldest and strongest emotion of mankind is fear, and the strongest kind of fear is fear of the unknown.")

This aspect of the Tolkien-Howard duality is readily illustrated by the writers' use of language. Tolkien's Apollonian world is painstakingly worked out even to language. One of his reasons (note the word) for creating 'The Lord of the Rings', he maintained, as mentioned above, was to exemplify certain aesthetic linguistic preferences. As an example of this, Tom Shippey, in the Radio Three essay, 'The Ring Goes Ever On', cites Tolkien's use of the neologism 'Estemnet'. This is the country of the Riders of Rohan. Shippey recounts:

"And you ask yourself, what is an Emneth? And you start looking up answers to that - and you find it's a village in Norfolk - Emneth. It's also a word derived from Old English: 'Even Meadow'. And what it is is the English word for steppe or prairie. You notice in English we don't have a word for steppe or prairie, because we haven't got any! But, Tolkien knew quite well the English had emigrated; they'd come to this country. Many of their cousins turned the other way; they went to Russia, they became Goths, they ended up as Lombards. If they had survived, what would they have been like, he asked himself. And the answer is The Riders of the Mark, living on the Emneth."

The linguistic side of Howard's world-building is something which has been criticised:

"I must admit my imagination was rather weak when it came to naming this character, who seemed to leap full-grown into my mind. Many kings in the Pictish chronicles have Gaelic names, yet in order to be consistent with my fictionalised version of the Pictish race, their great king should have a name more in keeping with their non-Aryan antiquity. But I named him Bran for another favourite historical character of mine: the Gaul Brennus, who sacked Rome. The Mak Morn comes from the famous Irish hero, Gol Mac Morn. I changed the spelling of the Mac, to give it a non-Gaelic appearance, since the Gaelic alphabet contains no k, c being always given the k sound. So while Bran Mac Morn is Gaelic for 'The Raven, Son of Morn,' Bran

Mak Morn has no Gaelic significance, but has a meaning of its own, purely Pictish and ancient, with roots in the dim mazes of antiquity; the similarity in sound to the Gaelic term is simply a coincidence!"
from 'Worms of the Earth', introduction.

Tolkien's Apollonian world is consistent down to language, but REH's eclectic and even contradictory word choices are Dionysian. Even so, it's clear that both Tolkien and Howard, in their different ways, both took extreme care in the naming of characters.

Melancholy – Despair/Fatalism

Melancholy, a sense of longing, dominates 'The Lord of the Rings'. A sense of passing is found on many levels - the passing of the age of the elvish world; the mourning of the Ents for the long-lost Ent-wives, the passing of the ring from Bilbo to Frodo:

"'Well here we are, just the four of us that started out together,' said Merry. 'We have left all the rest behind, one after another. It seems almost like a dream that has slowly faded.'
'Not to me, ' said Frodo. 'To me it feels more like falling asleep again.'"

Yet this sense of passing has a concomitant sense of renewal. The Shire is renewed. The age of men is coming into being:

"There, peeping among the cloud-wrack above a dark tor high up in the mountains, Sam saw a white star twinkle for a while. The beauty of it smote his heart, as he looked up out of the forsaken land, and hope returned to him. For like a shaft, clear and cold, the thought pierced him that in the end the Shadow was only a small and passing thing: there was light and high beauty for ever beyond its reach."

Howard's characters typically stalk milieux which do not just exhibit a Lovecraftian disinterestedness but are actively inimical. There is no sense of optimism, except in the tonally suspect endings of many of his Conan stories - the end of 'Red Nails' being a particularly jarring upbeat appendix to a fiercely bleak story. Virtually the last sentence of 'Rogues in the House' is an exception, fatalistically tempering the protagonist's success:

"There's many a highway I want to travel before I walk the road Nabonidus walked this night."

Melancholy operates within a sense of time - of things lost, the hope to regain in some form. But despair, the lack of hope, does not. Fred Blosser, in his review of Robert Weinberg's 'The Annotated Guide to Robert E. Howard's Sword & Sorcery' concurs particularly on: "the intensity of REH's 'undercurrent of moody despair'" ('Savage Sword of Conan' # 18). Howard pushes this even further. There is a fatalism in his characters rather than melancholy:

"'What of your own gods? I have never heard you call on them.'
'Their chief is Crom. He dwells on a great mountain. What use to call on him? Little he cares if men live or die. Better to be silent than to call his attention to you; he will send you dooms, not fortune! He is grim and loveless, but at birth he breathes power to strive and slay into a man's soul. What else shall men ask of the gods?'"
from 'Queen of the Black Coast'.

Not only is the light not beyond harm in s&s, but the difference between light and shadow is sometimes difficult to define clearly. Rosemary Jackson comments:

"The moral and religious allegories, parables and fables informing the stories of Kingsley and Tolkien move away from the unsettling implications which are found at the centre of the purely 'fantastic' ... expelling their desire and frequently displacing it into religious longing and nostalgia."
from 'Fantasy: the Literature of Subversion'.

Elegance - Simplicity

The elegance/simplicity opposition obviously applies to prose style. From Tolkien on, high/epic fantasy has tended to employ a softer, more lyrical style - if not lyrical, the characteristic style has tended toward a more graceful, accomplished, less brash, sometimes consciously literary angle of attack. Tolkien was a philologist. Albeit the novel employs a variety of styles, both in narrative and dialogue, it is this elegant impression of the book, and the genre it initiated, that dominates.

The next three oppositions are all related.

Medieval – Dark Age
Medieval Arthur – Dark Age Arthur
Knights - Barbarians

There is often a medieval sensibility to high fantasy, as Drake's definition points out. The protagonists adhere to codes, if not ideals, of behaviour which are more closely related to modern values. Their motivations, often to restore order or/and civilisation or/and spiritual health , are more understandable. The medieval Arthur was such a protagonist, however the Celtic or British Arthur, found in early poems and stories (such as 'Culhwch and Olwen' from 'The Mabinogion'), was different:

"And what of Arthur himself? His nature is unmistakable: he is the folk hero, a beneficent giant, who with his men rids the land of other giants, of witches and monsters; he undertakes journeys to the Otherworld to rescue prisoners and carry off treasures; he is rude, savage, heroic and protective."

from 'The Mabinogion', introduction.

This is more of a barbaric than a knightly figure, more a protagonist of sword-&-sorcery than high/epic fantasy, closer to Howard's "brawny, brawling, belligerent adventurers" as de Camp describes them in 'Literary Swordsmen and Sorcerers', than to Tolkien's Aragorn (although Boromir seems to straddle the two stools).

Also, protagonists in high/epic fantasy tend to be royalty or heirs to royalty, as is Aragorn. Though Kull and Conan become kings, neither is comfortable with the role - in fact Kull's discomfort is a theme running through the King Kull stories.

Good Versus Evil – A Storm of Darknesses

Chinn is correct, insofar as the Howardian Ur-text presents a tentative good versus evil dynamic, even if the good is only good in relation to the evil. However Don Herron, in his 'Conan versus Conantics' essay, points out that there is no simplistic good versus evil in the original Howard Conans. The idea of religion and prayer in the de Camp/Carter additions is similar to the Christian additions in 'Beowulf'. David C. Smith, in his 'SwordandSorcery.org' interview states a preference for, "No manichean good versus evil bullshit." Even in the beginnings of the form, the protagonist usually possesses a degree of darkness (if only implicitly) which is foreign to the protagonists of high fantasy. (Albeit Frodo is tempted by the power of the ring, this dark influence comes from outside - later sword-&-sorcery protagonists such as Moorcock's Elric or Wagner's Kane have a dark side as part of their internal being. (Though both these characters have some tentative form of moral code, without which the tragic potential of the form would be lost. Wagner writes that: "Kane was never needlessly cruel." in his story 'Miserycorde'.) Rosemary Jackson makes a comment which touches on both these matters:

"Because of the progressive internalisation of the demonic, the easy polarization of good and evil which had operated in times of supernaturalism and magic ceased to be effective."
    from 'Fantasy: the Literature of Subversion'.

High/epic fantasy may be structured around good versus evil, but sword-&-sorcery has always been potentially just 'versus' - a more chaotic conflict – a storm of shadow. Good versus Evil is usually clearly drawn in high/epic fantasy. Although there are characters in 'The Lord of the Rings' who have crossed from one state to the other, such as Saruman, and others who display aspects of both, such as

Theoden and, again, Boromir, there is no doubt which actions fall into which category and which characters also. Motivation is again the key. To assert that high/epic fantasy characters tend to act from 'high' motives and that sword-&-sorcery characters tend to act to survive is an oversimplification. For me Ur-text sword-&-sorcery protagonists are motivated more by power: survival is a reaction to encountering inimical forces typically as a result of attempts to kill or steal. Both actions tend to be driven by a desire to obtain power in some form. (Howard's characters' motivations are also often complicated by the presence of a deathwish motif, expanded upon below.) Howard wrote in a letter, discussing the depression, the rise of fascism and Soviet government: "There is no question of right or wrong, but simply of necessity and survival." Nevertheless his characters, and moreso some of the characters of later sword-&-sorcery writers, sometimes perform motivationally ambivalent or even ambiguous deeds. Wayne Booth, in his 'The Rhetoric of Fiction', differentiates between ambiguity and complexity with 'clarity'. As high/epic fantasy has developed, characterization has become more naturalistically complex – but I view sword-&-sorcery, as potentially more suited to ambiguity

Hence my term, 'Storm of Darknesses'. I believe that Howard laid the groundwork for a type of fantasy far psychically richer and darker than that achieved by either the Howardian or Tolkien Ur-texts.

The next three oppositions are also related.

Folk Music – Heavy Metal
Progressive Rock – Punk
Pastels – Darker/Richer Colours

These relate first and foremost to the texture, the 'feel' of the two forms. Folk music has a gentle, often melancholic image, often deals with romance, is linked with tradition. Heavy metal is a harsher, more transgressive form of music, often thematically much darker.

The progressive rock - punk opposition is similar. Progressive rock being long, involved, cerebral (speaking in generalities) - punk being short, visceral stabs of sound. In fact this particular opposition points strongly to a crucial difference between high/epic fantasy and sword-

&-sorcery, that of story length. One way that 'The Hour of the Dragon' sustains its length is by interweaving scenes where Conan is absent, or panoramic sequences. These do not advance plot but set atmosphere and foreshadow. These both help sustain tension, the latter also providing a choral effect to the action. (Howard also often goes away from Conan in the short stories, but this has more the effect of emphasising Conan's 'outsiderness' and consequently 'otherness'.)

Yet despite a meta-carapace of plot, 'The Hour of the Dragon' is picaresque in structure. Episodes have an arbitrary feel to them, perhaps largely due to the number of episodes necessary for novel length. The number of supernatural encounters in the novel, and epic fantasy in general, results in a dimming of the numinous effect - a desensitising. (This littering of numinous moments in a sense potentially turns any fantasy novel into its own genre - via repetition.) The encounters seem arbitrary, for example the ghouls in the forest and later Akivasha's appearance.

Short stories facilitate what I call a numinous envelope - a single encounter with the supernatural which has the more impact because of its isolation. Many of Howard's sword-&-sorcery stories use this method (the tower of 'The Tower of the Elephant', the labyrinth city of 'Red Nails', the jungle settings of most Solomon Kane stories, Kull's Valusia in a sense in its entirety, all of Howard's strange lost cities). Virtually all of C.L.Moore's Jirel of Jory stories employ this device.

'Beowulf', my proto-sword-&-sorcery tale, has a feel of several interlinked short stories rather than a novel or epic. Tolkien, in his 'Beowulf: The Monsters and the Critics', admits that it: "may turn out to be no epic at all".

Fantasy is a highly visual form, either in the style of writing or content, and usually the paperback covers of fantasy novels or collections reflected this in the 1960s and 70s. I find that the trend since then has been toward blander visuals. Boulton's introduction to Burke's 'Philosophical Enquiry into the Origin of our Ideas of the Sublime and Beautiful', a work fundamental to the development of the gothic novel fantasy, quotes one of Burke's precursors, Addison:

"To him [Addison] sight is the principal source of material for the imagination:

'We cannot indeed have a single Image in the Fancy that did not make its first Entrance through the Sight;'"

from 'Philosophical Enquiry into the Origin of our Ideas of the Sublime and Beautiful' by Edmund Burke.

Moorcock makes the same connection:

"Epic fantasy can offer a world of metaphor in which to explore the rich, hidden territories deep within us. And this, of course, is why epic romances, romantic poetry, grotesques, fascinated painters and illustrators for centuries, just as fabulous and mythological subjects have always inspired them, as representations of this inner world. The romance's prime concern is not with character or narrative but with the evocation of strong, powerful images; ... In some cases the writer and illustrator have been combined in one person (Blake, Rossetti, Wyndham Lewis, Peake). Even if we exclude all the children's writers (Ruskin/Doyle, Carroll/Tenniel, Nesbit/Millar, Baum/Neill) who have had long associations with particular illustrators, there are a good few adult writers of fantasy who have enjoyed similar relationships - Dunsany and Sime, Cabell and Pape, Burroughs and St John, Howard and Frazetta."

from 'Wizardry and Wild Romance'.

The last pairing is particularly significant for sword-&-sorcery. Frank Frazetta's association with Howard's work began with a series of cover paintings for Lancer Book's 60s reprintings of Howard's (and others') Conan stories. Descriptions of Frazetta's art tellingly mirror the traits of Howard's writing:

"Perspectives are manipulated and slewed for dramatic effect, exaggeration is mercilessly used ... His painting is alive, intensely vibrant, even when the figures are in repose. It is perhaps this quality of life, of energy, which most signally sets Frazetta's work apart ... Anything that has movement captures his attention - his great cats,

reptiles, horses, animals of all kinds [Howard's imagery is heavily doused in animal metaphor], and of course his fiercely battling male figures of Vikings, stonemen, primitives of one kind or another; the writhing roots and branches of trees, the ebb and flow and swirl of water - nothing in the typical Frazetta painting is really still. His work is all sinuosity and movement."
from 'The Fantastic Art of Frank Frazetta', volume one, introduction by Betty Ballantine.

"First, and most importantly, life. And next, life's closest brother, death. These two subjects dominate Frazetta's work ... Power is generally regarded as an abstract element. Not, however, in a Frazetta painting. When Frazetta paints power, not only is it solidly and vividly delineated in every line of his larger-than-life figures, it ceases to be a mere element and becomes an omni-present integrated force"
from 'Frank Frazetta', vol 2, introduction by Betty Ballantine.

Energy and power are vital components in Howard's sword-&-sorcery Ur-text.
Emphasis is often placed on Frazetta's use of colour:

"One responds at once to the breathtaking excitement of his reds, the subtle, deliberately mono-toned backgrounds, the strong blacks and sombre greens."
from 'Frank Frazetta', volume two.

Bright colours are acceptable for sword-&-sorcery, perhaps, as long as they are deep or rich. (As in the Celtic mythology art-books of Jim Fitzpatrick.) One of my first memories of sword-&-sorcery as a visual phenomenon is the vivid Steranko cover of the 1970 de Camp anthology 'Warlocks and Warriors'. de Camp's anthologies before this, 'Swords & Sorcery' and 'The Spell of Seven' and 'The Fantastic Swordsmen' boast lacklustre images.
My pastel analogy to high/epic fantasy represents its 'paler' though more subtle, emotional charge. (It might also be pointed out that the word 'pastel' refers in one sense to a light, poetic prose work.) Others have also noticed/acknowledged this colour connection:

"1/6/04, Lokke Heiss wrote:

I don't see this book [The Lord of the Rings] as kitsch, as least as I understand the word.

Me neither, Lokke. I said I thought the movies are kitsch: that is, imitative (of not only their source literature but all the fantasy art that JRRT and his imitators sparked off), vulgar (see the carmelized[sic]ending of ROTK, minus the anguish of the Scouring of the Shire) and sentimental (that stupid little boat drifting off into a cotton candy sunset -- bad calendar art -- and lots of long, long, long eye-brimmingshots supposed to express emotion."

from Suzy Charnas, International Association for the Fantastic in the Arts electronic discussion list, 9 Jan 2004.

Black and white illustration also played an appropriate part in representing sword-&-sorcery in its formative stages. When Howard was creating the form in the 1930s it found print in the pulp magazines of the time which were characterized by garish covers and (just as importantly) poorly reproduced black and white interior illustrations. The garish covers were by and large too one-dimensional or tame to engender intensity, but the quality of the interior illustrations, the necessity to work in broad blacks and to favour shadowy chiaroscuroed depictions, not only allowed intensity but left space in the readers' imaginations. The use of vivid foregrounds and ambiguous backgrounds in visual sword-&-sorcery allows both intensity and subtlety to co-exist and hints at a way for written sword-&-sorcery to provide the same combination. (Many of Howard's stories, particularly 'Worms of the Earth', take place largely underground or in a similar milieu, exploiting a chthonic sensibility, both physical and psychical, often touched on in sword-&-sorcery. It might be argued that the balrog and shelob sequences in 'The Lord of the Rings' – cited by some critics as the most effective parts of the book – are closer to sword-&-sorcery than high fantasy. The chthonic's restriction of knowledge heightens the sense of unknowingness – i.e. not knowing what lies at the top of the stairs, within the cave, in the darkness.)

Variety/Variation – Focus/Intensity

The final oppositional pair relates to a crucial structural difference between high fantasy and sword-&-sorcery - length.

High/epic fantasy is predominantly a long form – 'The Lord of the Rings' is a novel split into three volumes. The trilogy was often the preferred structure for Tolkien imitators in the 60s and 70s, giving way to even larger forms through the 80s onwards: four, five, ten book narratives. (Often received unkindly by critics: "I wince in sympathetic pain to see Clute single-handedly tackle multi-volume fantasy extrusion-product." from Bruce Sterling's review of 'Scores: Reviews 1993-2003' in 'Foundation' # 90.) Howardian sword-&-sorcery, conversely, had its genesis in the short story. Howard wrote two fantasy novels, however his main fiction output was in the form of short stories for the pulp magazine market of his time.

From this structural difference, many of the other differences between the two forms come, almost of necessity. Here it may help to differentiate between two terms: the sublime and the numinous. Both refer to a sense of wonder, often spiritual, occasioned by an encounter with some form of otherness. However the numinous was maintained by the German theologist Rudolph Otto in 'The Idea of the Holy' to refer to a much more powerful effect. This presents an opportunity to characterize high/epic fantasy as almost necessarily a combination of Burke's beautiful and sublime due to its length of story, whereas the short sword-&-sorcery form can give itself over entirely to a higher intensity thereby serving the numinous effect. Howard's intensity is partly attributable to focus, a vividness - whether the moment is diegetically intense, physically or emotionally, or not. Some of the most often-used Howardian adjectives are 'rough-hewn', 'taut', 'muscular', 'driving', and 'headlong' - while these are characteristic, Howard's style and structuring could encompass very different characteristics at times - but even when his writing is pedestrian or no more than functional, focus remains in some shape or form - the short story length itself aids this.

'The Lord of the Rings' has the space to deploy a large cast of characters and the scope (not by any means fully exploited by

Tolkien) to develop those characters. Milieu, also has a scope for development in the novel length fantasy. The most pointed example of this 'epic' approach can be found in a 1977 interview with fantasy writer Lin Carter in 'Fantastic' magazine. Here he talks to Darrell Schweitzer about a project which was never realized:

"CARTER: And if I want to have a monologue in the middle of a scene on the astrological system of this world for the space of forty thousand words I will simply do it ... The major cast of characters at the current state of the plotting is three thousand and, I think, eleven. Three thousand eleven.

FANTASTIC: How many of these are-?

CARTER: These are major characters.

FANTASTIC: Three thousand major characters? How long is this to be? Are you writing the Encyclopaedia Britannica of fantasy?

CARTER: The novel will cover the period of a thousand years.

FANTASTIC: Isn't this sort of a series of mini-novels?

CARTER: It is a series of everything, including biographical sketches, historical monographs, novels, folklore, legends, and myth. It is the mythological history of an imaginary world, and of one major empire of that world it follows the life of every emperor and empress and so on...

FANTASTIC: This is in Khymyrium?

CARTER: Yes. It's not just a novel: It's a world."

from 'Fantastic' vol.26 no.1.

Tolkien's 'The Silmarilion' is a tumour of unnecessary development of the Lord of the Rings milieu - however fascinating such development can be, however necessary such development is over a long work, such a various structure lacks the 'focus' that a short story, again almost of necessity, must have. A single plot line, usually a single protagonist, restricted or stylised characterization and/or development.

The tightness of the short fictional form, its focused nature, is for me intimately linked with the sword-&-sorcery form.

So, is 'The Shadow Cycles', with its novel length, sword-&-sorcery? Does it play the tarot? Can it play the tarot? And if it can and does, despite its length, does this make it not a novel but something else?

Deathwish and Madness

There is a sense of deathwish to be found in Howard's writing. Sometimes it might be disguised as courage or recklessness or fury:

"'Liars,' panted Conan. 'Dogs! Knaves! Cowards! Oh, Crom, if I could but stand - but crawl to the river with my sword in my teeth.'"

and

"Conan laughed raspingly. 'Come in and try!' he challenged. 'But for my treacherous legs I'd hew you out of that chariot like a woodman hewing a tree. But you'll never take me alive, damn you!"
    from 'The Hour of the Dragon'.

Another aspect of deathwish can be found in 'Queen of the Black Coast'. Here Howard puts a desire for death (again thinly disguised) into the mouth and character of Belit, a kind of female version of Conan, making it almost sexual in nature:

"'There is life beyond death, I know, and I know this, too, Conan of Cimmeria' - she rose lithely to her knees and caught him in a pantherish embrace – 'my love is stronger than any death!' ... 'Were I still in death and you fighting for life, I would come back from the abyss to aid you - aye, whether my spirit floated with the purple sails on the crystal sea of paradise, or writhed in the molten flames of Hell!'"

and

"And she danced, like the spin of a desert whirlwind, like the leaping of a quenchless flame, like the urge of creation and the urge of death. Her white feet spurned the bloodstained deck and dying men forgot death as they gazed frozen at her."

from 'Queen of the Black Coast'.

Particularly in his verse deathwish can be found. Howard wrote much verse. There is even a King Kull story told in verse, 'The King and the Oak', in the verse collection 'Always Comes Evening'. His stylistic and thematic characteristics are often more pronounced in this form, where his personality and beliefs (which provide the thematic underpinning for Howardian sword-&-sorcery) come through much more directly at times. For example 'Black Chant Imperial', from 'Always Comes Evening', concentrates Howard's characteristic rhythmic powers and violent imagery. Though his verse often manifests his deathwish in a depressive, enervated form. Poems such as 'The Tempter' or 'Song at Midnight', or 'An Outworn Story' in Fantasy Tales # 17:

"The dim days come when in men's breast
The heart is shrivelled and dark and cold.
The grey clouds cling like a shroud unrolled
And men, to the brown and bitter mold,
Turn to silence and utter rest
From an out-worn story madly told."

The mention of madness is telling. This is another motif which energises Howard's work at times and often yokes with the energised as opposed as the enervated side of the deathwish motif under the guise of berserker fury:

"The bat-people were taking to the air. No longer would they face this strange madman who in his insanity was more terrible than they. ... He threw back his head to shriek his hate at the fiends above him ... And Kane's last vestige of reason snapped"
from 'Wings in the Night'.

Kane goes insane and at the end of the story he chillingly prays! This is tremendously gothic. The story includes an authorial paean to the Aryan Barbarian. Stephen Trout, in his article in 'The Barbaric Triumph', 'Heritage of Steel: Howard and the Frontier Myth', remarks on this story. He also makes a tacit connection between violence and the numinous.

Other instances of this conflation can be found:

"Up them he went and, as he climbed, that blind fury which is mankind's last defence against diabolism and all the hostile forces of the universe, surged in him, and he forgot his fear."
from 'The Pool of the Black One'.

Loss of reason is often a defence against the numinous for a Howard protagonist - at the same time as becoming one with it.

'The Garden of Fear' is another example of conflating madness and deathwish, this time in the form of hatred. At other times the madness/deathwish relationship is causal - deathwish leading to (berserker) madness. Here 'hatred' controls, even rationalizes, madness.

This multivalenced conflation is a characteristic aspect of the violence embedded in Howard's storytelling.

Related is the Howardian and consequently sword-&-sorcery element of the conflation of otherness and power. These combine in Conan the character:

"Severius was again aware ... of something alien about the king. The great frame under the mail mesh was too hard and supple for a civilized man; the elemental fire of the primitive burned in those smoldering eyes."
from 'The Hour of the Dragon'.

Tarot of Sword-&-Sorcery

All of which, metaphorically eating Robert E. Howard's brains, standing on his shoulders, scaling the tower of his Ur-text, have allowed me to try to formulate a new Ur-text, or tarot, of my own:

Major Arcana = Violence and the Numinous

This means that stories containing a conflation of these two elements, even if the traditional motifs of the form are absent, is potentially sword-&-sorcery.

Motifs:

1. Sword-&-sorcery is intense. All else is subjugated to this effect.

2. Sword-&-sorcery is potentially amoral.

3. Sword-&-sorcery is the combination of violence and the numinous: a double-helix of violences which entwine around intensity.

4. Sword-&-sorcery eschews explicit development of milieu or character or concept.

5. Sword-&-sorcery is naturally a short story form.

6. Sword-&-sorcery contains an element of deathwish in its sensibility.

7. Sword-&-sorcery has a Chthonic sensibility.

8. Sword-&-sorcery has a potential element of tragedy in its sensibility.

9. Sword-&-sorcery combines explicit and implicit horror.

10. The sword-&-sorcery protagonist is a loner - a figure apart or other.

11. Sword-&-sorcery addresses the irrational through the very fact of its connection with the numinous effect.

12. Sword-&-sorcery is about power.

13. Sword-&-sorcery is highly 'visual' (either through the presence or the absence of the visual).

...If not something new then I hope 'The Shadow Cycles' is at least a new version of the Howardian tarot that redefines the combination of blood and darkness and fear at the heart of sword-&-sorcery.

Select Bibliography

Alexander. M. (trans.) Beowulf, Harmondsworth: Penguin Classics, 1977 (rpt.)

Baldick, C. Concise Oxford Dictionary of Literary Terms, Oxford: Oxford University Press, 1996

Booth, W.C. The Rhetoric of Fiction, London: The University of Chicago Press, 1983 (second edition) Bullock, Stallybrass, Trombley (eds.) Fontana Dictionary of Modern Thought (new and revised edition), London: Fontana Paperback, 1988

Burke, E. (ed. Boulton) A Philosophical Enquiry into the Origin of Our Ideas of the Sublime and Beautiful, London: Routledge and Kegan Paul, 1958

Chinn, M. (ed.) Swords Against the Millennium, Birmingham: Alchemy Press/Saladoth Productions, 2000

de Camp, L.S. (ed.) The Blade of Conanm New York: Ace, 1979

de Camp, L.S. Literary Swordsman and Sorcerers , Sauk City, Wisconsin: Arkham House, 1976

de Camp, L.S. (ed.) The Spell of Seven, New York: Pyramid Books, 1965

de Camp, L.S. (ed.) Swords & Sorcery, New York: Pyramid Books, 1963

Guerber, H.A. The Book of the Epic, London: Harrap & Co. Ltd., MCMX1X

Harrison, M.J. Virconium, London: Millenium, 2000

Heaney, S. (trans.) Beowulf, London: Faber & Faber, 1999

Herron, D. (ed.) The Barbaric Triumph, Wildside Press, 2004

Howard, R.E. Always Comes Evening, San Francisco: Underwood - Miller, 1977

Howard, R.E. The Black Stranger, Lincoln: University of Nebraska Press, 2005

Howard, R.E. The Hour of the Dragon, New York: G.P.Putnam, 1977

Howard, R.E. Kull, Rhode Island: Donald M. Grant, 1985

Howard, R.E. The Pool of the Black One, Rhode Island: Donald M. Grant, 1986

Howard, R.E. Queen of the Black Coast, Rhode Island: Donald M. Grant, 1978

Howard, R.E. Red Nails, Rhode Island: Donald M. Grant, 1975

Howard, R.E. Rogues in the House, Rhode Island: Donald M. Grant, 1976

Howard, R.E., Campbell, R. Solomon Kane, New York: Baen, 1995

Howard, R.E. Tower of the Elephant, Rhode Island: Donald M. Grant, 1975

Howard, R.E. Worms of the Earth, Rhode Island: Donald M. Grant, 1974

Jackson, R. Fantasy: The Literature of Subversion, London: Routledge, 1995 (rpt.)

Jones, G. and Jones, T. (trans.) The Mabinogion, London: Dent, 1977 (rpt.)

Lord, G. (ed.) The Last Celt, New York: Berkley Windhover, 1977

Lovecraft, H.P. Dagon and Other Macabre Tales, Sauk City: Arkham House Publishers, Inc., 1965

Moorcock, M. Wizardry and Wild Romance, London: VGSF, 1988

Nicholls, P. (ed.) The Encyclopedia of Science Fiction, London: Granada Publishing Ltd., 1981

Searles, Meacham, Franklin (ed.) A Reader's Guide to Fantasy, New York: Avon books, 1982

Schweitzer, D. Conan's World and Robert E. Howard, San Bernardino: Borgo Press, 1978

Tolkien, J.R.R. Beowulf: The Monsters and the Critics, London: Oxford University Press, 1936

Tolkien, J.R.R. The Lord of the Rings, London: George Allen & Unwin Ltd., 1978

Wagner, K.E. The Book of Kane, Rhode Island: Donald M. Grant, 1985

Philip Emery

OTHER WORKS BY PHILIP EMERY

"Swords at Night," Pioneer magazine no.5, 1972 (fiction)
"The Terminal Strain," Spoke magazine no.16, 1977 (fiction)
"Twilight Shifts'" 'By....And Others' anthology, 1980 (fiction)
"Fourth Incarnation," Comic Strip in Fourth Incarnation magazine no.1, 1980
"The Fading Earth," Fourth Incarnation magazine no.1, 1980 (poetry)
"Ragnorok," Fourth Incarnation magazine no.1, 1980, (poetry
"Rejection Slip," 'Syde Lines' anthology no.1, 1991 (poetry)
"Letter to the Times," Phancy magazine no.1, 1982, (poetry)
"Definition of a Cynic," 'Syde Lines' anthology no.2, 1982 (poetry)
"A Memory," Phancy magazine no.2, 1982 (poetry)
"Stars," Phancy magazine no.2, 1982 (poetry)
"fresh from dreamgames," 'Poems by Strangers' anthology no.2, 1984 (poetry)
"Definition of a Cynic," Bloodrake magazine no.7, 1984 (poetry)
"Dogs of the Insane," Bloodrake magazine no.7, 1984 (poetry)
"Shadrezzar," Fantasy Tales no.15, 1986 (poetry)
"Prison World," Comic Strip in Hardware magazine no.9, 1987
"The Ancient People," New Moon Quarterly magazine no.3, 1987 (poetry)
"Dreamgames," Dream magazine no.18, 1988 (fiction)
"Sighings," Weird Tales magazine, Fall 1989, (poetry)
"Astral Kill," Comic Strip in Enigma magazine no.1, 1990
"Hellsblood," Comic Strip in Enigma magazine no.1, 1990
"Twilight Shifts," Chills magazine no.5, 1991 (fiction)
"The Withering," Peeping Tom magazine no.4, 1991 (fiction)
"The Spell Merchant," Scheherazade magazine no.2, 1991 (fiction)
"Everyday Life In..." Cassandra newsletter June '91 (nonfiction)
"Kalborbriac," Mystique magazine no.4, 1992 (fiction)
"Exodus Over Mara," Nightfall magazine no.4, 1992 (fiction)
"Rejection Slip," People to People magazine no.17, 1992 (poetry)
"Definition 101," Envoi magazine no.103, 1992 (poetry)
"Shards of Sun," Envoi magazine no.103, 1992, (poetry)
"Evergreen," Envoi magazine no.103, 1992 (poetry)
"Scripting Comics," Cassandra newsletter Nov' 1992 (nonfiction)
"Demonstale," Scheherazade magazine no.7, 1993 (fiction)
"British Association Science Festival '93," Mindsparks magazine no.3, 1993 (nonfiction)

"Notes on a Ringbound Lap-Top," Haiku Quarterly magazine no.10, 1994 (poetry)

"The Feasters," Dark Horizons magazine no.35, 1994, (poetry)

"Quest for the Wind of Eternity," Wonderdisk Digital anthology no.7, 1995 (fiction)

"Distance Learning Creative Writing: A Pilot Project," Writing in Education magazine no.5, 1995 (nonfiction)

"MA'ed in Britain," Writers' Forum magazine Spring '96 (nonfiction)

"Cerberus," Scheherazade magazine no.13, 1996, (fiction)

"Definition of a Cynic," (reprint) All Creatures Weird & Wonderful anthology, 1997 (poetry)

"Exodus Over Mara" (reprint) Dark Planet online magazine, 20/8/97 – (fiction)

"Ludchurch," Pendragon magazine vol xxvi no.3, 1997 (poetry)

"50 Things the How-to Books Don't Tell You About Writing A Novel," Lexicon magazine vol 3 no.1, 1998 (nonfiction)

"50 Things the How-to Books Don't Tell You About Writing A Novel," Lexicon magazine vol 3 no.2, 1998 (nonfiction)

"Journal," Star*Line magazine no.21.1, Jan-Feb 1998 (poetry)

"Weird Villanelle," Star*Line magazine no.21.2, Mar-Apr 1998 (poetry)

"Elvensong," Exodus online magazine, December '98 (poetry)

"Feasters," Exodus online magazine, December '98 (poetry)

"Prophecies," Exodus online magazine, December '98 (poetry)

"Virtual Grafix," radio play produced by Minute Radio Drama, 1999

"Castles, And What They Are Not," Core Material anthology, July '99 (poetry)

"Adaptation as a Teaching Tool," Sheffield Hallam University 1999 Creative Writing Conference published proceedings (nonfiction)

"20 Things the How-to Books Don't Tell You About Writing A Novel," Canadian National Post, June 12, 1999 (nonfiction)

"Vicious Circle," Gothic.Net online magazine, August '99 (fiction)

"Chronojourn" published as "Through the Woods," The Zone magazine no.8, Autumn '99 (fiction)

"Keyboards," Krax magazine no.37, '00 (poetry)

"Barley Bree and Autumn," Magazine of Speculative Poerty, vol 4 no.4, Autumn '00 (poetry)

"Barley Bree and Autumn," 2001 Rhysling anthology (poetry)

"Blade," Kimota magazine, no.15, Autumn '01 (fiction)

"Parallel-0-Gram," Raw Edge magazine no.13 Autumn-Winter '01 (prose poem)

"Nightdweller," Abyss & Apex online magazine no.3, May-June '03 (fiction)

"Two Thieves of Kem," Scheherazade magazine no.26, '04 (fiction)

"id," Premonitions magazine no.1, '04 (fiction)

"Negotiating Difference: issues of accreditation," Writing in Education magazine no.34, 2004 (nonfiction)

"Dramatext - Offering Subjectivities," Writing in Education magazine no.35, 2005 (nonfiction)

"Prophecies," The Dark Tower anthology volume # 1, 2006 (poetry)

"The Last Scream of Carnage," Flashing Swords e-anthology 2006 (fiction)

"ID," BBC Radio 7, 28\2\07, 11\8\07, 2\9\08, 16\6\09, 5\1\10, 13\7\10, 2\3\11 (fiction)

"La quete pour le vent d'Eternite," (translation of "The Quest for the Wind of Eternity") Faeries magazine no.24, 2007 (fiction)

"The Birth of Merlin," Pendragon magazine vol xxxv no.1, 2007 (poetry)

"The Last of All Enchantments," Scheherazade magazine no.30, 2008 (fiction)

"The Last Scream of Carnage," The Return of the Sword anthology - 1st Edition 2008 (fiction)

"The Last Scream of Carnage," Return of the Sword anthology - 2nd Edition 2008 (fiction)

"Jettison," In the Telling anthology, 2009 (poetry)

"Coffee Graduands," Envoi magazine no.154, 2009 (poetry)

"Put to Bed," Envoi magazine no.154, 2009 (poetry)

"The Lane," Envoi magazine no.154, 2009 (poetry)

"Celtic Influences in the Works of Robert E. Howard," The Dark Man journal vol.5 no.1, 2010 (nonfiction)

"Streetwise," Electric Spec online magazine vol.5 no.2, May 2010 (fiction)

"Oxlow," Inside Out poetry collection 2010 (poetry)

"Fifteen Breaths," Demons anthology 2010 (fiction)

"Parallel-0-Gram," Space Squid magazine no.9, Fall 2010 (fiction)

"Identity Crisis," Thegoodearreview.com/ November '10 (monologue)

"Blasphemer," Damnation Books - Eternal Press 2010 (novelette)

"Assessment Reports as Exploded Haiku," New Writing International Journal for the Practice and Theory of Creative Writing vol.8 no.1, March 2011 (nonfiction)

Other Works by Philip Emery from Immanion Press

"Necromantra"

"Jem looked out over the Hundred-Towns - over the smoggy terraces, pitheads, manufactories, slaughterhouses, workhouses, shardrucks, the black swellings of other slag heaps. Over the furry points of streetlamp light. Over the ruddy patchwork of furnaces toiling to power countless engines, all night, all day, every night, every day. Over the thousands upon thousands of chimneys. Town after town, all grouted into one with grime."

In the Hundred, the working folk are kept in order by the masters to administrate the various mills, pits and manufactories. Strict records of kept in town halls, every death certified despite a crushing mortality. However, the old grim uncertainties face a new threat with the arrival of the necromancers -- dark-skinned pilgrims, who, by the chant of a strange mantra are able to raise the recently dead, thus throwing the immaculate records of the town walls into chaos.

In retaliation, the masters appoint a number of rectifiers to each town. Reviled and feared by most of the Hundred, their job is to 're-decease' the 'discrepancies' as the risen are labelled.

Jem Nadin is a rectifier. One night he witnesses a resurrection in a cemetery. Caught up in a compulsion, he cannot explain, he goes against orders and attempts there and then to catch the necromancer performing the chant. She escapes, and Jem is left in total confusion.

Meanwhile, in another part of the Hundred, a soldier calling himself Hawbind returns to his native town. He is haunted by a ghost, a spirit of a comrade killed in battle, in a war being fought overseas. It is like a phantom wound, slowly killing him.

The lives of rectifier, necromancer and soldier entwine in a series of nightmarish adventures, culminating in an encounter with the 'Necrocomb', a pocket of supernatural darkness underneath the deepest pit of the filthy conurbation, where the fate of every one of the Hundred-Towns is decided.

About the Author

Philip Emery lives just outside Newcastle-under-Lyme, on the outskirts of the Potteries (which gives added meaning to the term 'potted biography'). He works as a freelance writer\lecturer, teaching creative writing for various universities, colleges, and educational organisations, and was an associate lecturer with Keele University for over twenty years. Stories, verse, plays and articles have been printed, broadcast and performed in the UK, USA, Canada and Europe since the seventies. (But there's still that screenplay languishing at the bottom of that digital drawer…)

He began to write at an early age, a few years later asked for a typewriter for a Christmas present, and the rest is alternate history. In this particular reality, the only useful skill he's cultivated and maintained is the ability to touch-type.

He stopped collecting his rejection letters in the nineties when they became much more boring – he still treasures the rejection from a well-known American editor which read, "Not well enough written or plotted to be of interest to anyone."

He dislikes writing about himself, at least directly, even in third-person.

His one remaining ambition is to see his pseudo-Jacobean sci-fi martial arts black comedy stage play in production. His other one remaining ambition is to write an opera libretto.